The Garden Key

a novel

ANGELA DOLBEAR

Published by

CLOUD PILLAR PUBLISHING

www.AngelaDolbear.com
Nashville, TN, U.S.A.

THE GARDEN KEY
By Angela Dolbear

www.AngelaDolbear.com

Published by Cloud Pillar Publishing, Nashville, TN, U.S.A.
info@angeladolbear.com

Lyrics for "Stupid" and "Autumn Leaves" by Angela Hembree Dolbear © 2004 De La Bear Music Group. Lyrics printed by permission. All rights reserved.
Scripture quotations are taken from the New American Standard Bible®, Copyright © 1960, 1962, 1963, 1968, 1971, 1972, 1973, 1975, 1977, 1995 by The Lockman Foundation. Used by permission. www.Lockman.org
ISBN-13: 978-0-615-31477-8
ISBN-10:   0-615-31477-5

Library of Congress Control Number: 2009908527

Printed in the United States of America

Cover art by Donna Mibus
www.donnamibus.com
Art printed by permission.

Very special thanks to...

Geoff & Catherine Dolbear
For all your amazing support

Richard & Marie Hembree
For your continuous encouragement to write

Carrie Robinson
For all your help in time of need

and

Tim Douglas Dolbear
For all your love in its many forms
I love you, my beloved, my best friend

"'...not by might, nor by power, but by My Spirit,'
says the LORD of hosts."

A garden locked

is my sister,

my bride,

a rock garden locked,

a spring sealed up."

Song of Solomon,
Twelfth verse of the fourth
chapter

Chapter One

I'm not looking over there again. I'm not. I wish I had not seen him walk in. Now I'm all distracted. I'm supposed to be in a state of worship, but instead, I'm fighting with lust. I feel like standing up and saying, "Hi, my name is Madeleine, and I'm a lust-o-holic."

Oh Lord, please help me to stop lusting over this guy. In the name of Jesus, I pray, Amen.

"Maddy!" Maggie, my roommate, and partner in crime, hisses through clenched teeth. "Madeleine!" She jams the offering basket into my elbow, snagging the sleeve of my new crocheted cardigan. I quickly untangle the black thread and pass the basket to the woman sitting next to me.

LUST, you say? Yes, lust. In church, no less. How can this be? A fine, upstanding Christian young lady about to start her last year of college at a fine, upstanding Christian university struggles with one of the most basic and primal aspects of the human condition.

I just can't seem to get him out of my head. I do okay for a little while, then something will happen, some situation will come up, and then let the daydreams begin. This whole elaborate scene starts playing in my head like some cheesy chick flick…what I'm wearing, more importantly, what he's wearing, which is usually a black t-shirt that fits snuggly across his broad shoulders, paired with faded worn-in Levi's 501's jeans that look as if they were tailor-made for him. And I even write elaborate dialogue in these daydreams. He usually says something witty that makes me laugh, which is strange, since, well, I've never even spoken to him.

"So, yawl get much out of the message today?" Maggie asks, as we cross the crowded church parking lot toward my car.

"Yeah, it was pretty good," I mumble.

"Uh-huh. I saw you eye-ballin' him. I can't believe you still have a thing for that guy." Maggie says into the mirror while she expertly outlines and paints her matte blood-red lips.

She double-checks her artistry in the mirror that was clipped onto the passenger's side visor, which she installed in my car during our freshman year. "Hon, I don't know why you just don't go up to him and just say 'hi.'"

"Oh, I don't know. Maybe because I lack the sexual fortitude that others around me exude." *Yikes.* I didn't mean to sound as biting as it came out, but we've had this discussion too many times in the past for it not to irritate me.

"And just what is that supposed to mean?" She feigns a hurt look.

"Oh, come on, Mag. You know I can't. I'd probably trip, fall, or both, and a long dribble of unintelligible gibberish would ooze from my mouth."

I make a quick left turn out of the church parking lot and into traffic. Maggie shrugs and goes back to her make-up application, digging in her purse for various tubes and compacts.

"He's just a guy," she says into the mirror while blotting her chin with a powder puff.

With her Dallas drawl, she makes it sound so simple. Like he's just some *gah* and not my mysterious Adonis. Adonis. A pagan god for my pagan thoughts.

"Just walk up to him and introduce yourself, and let him do the rest," she states and zips up her make-up bag. "Let him do all the talking. Just smile, look him in the eyes, and touch your hair a lot. Guys love that."

I stifle an outburst of laughter at the mental image of myself doing something like that with my extreme lack of feminine smoothness.

Of course, Maggie would think talking to guys is simple. Guys always look up when Maggie saunters into a room. I don't know whether it's her big platinum blonde hair styled very closely to the classic Marilyn Monroe style or her delicate cheekbones, dark brown exotic eyes, and porcelain skin, all of which she inherited from her half-Japanese mother. Or maybe it's just the plain fact that she seems to put "it" out there, and guys take notice.

Maggie describes herself as hip-heavy, "a gal built for comfort and not speed," she once told me. She has three inches and a good fifteen pounds on me and my five-foot, two-inch petite frame. But she wears it so well that it seems like there's always some guy checking her out wherever we go.

"Hon, it's not that hard. Guys only want one thing. And if they think there's even the teeniest chance they might get it, well, then you've got 'em hooked."

"Oh, nice advice. From a pastor's daughter."

Maggie shoots me a look that would harm, followed by a quick icy pageant smile/tilted-head combo.

"Besides, I'm not sure those kinds of tactics would work on a guy like him."

"Not coming from the Queen of Darkness, they won't," she quips.

I return her icy pageant smile, which quickly morphs into a squinty-eyed sneer.

"Maddy, if you are serious about gettin' this guy, you are gonna have to stop dressin' like you raid the closets of Addams Family on a daily basis. And honestly, did you buy stock in black eyeliner or somethin'?"

"Have you been conspiring with my mother?"

"Look, I'm just sayin'. Hon, you need to put your curves to work for you. Shoot, if I had your thirty-four-D's and itty-bitty waist, I'd make sure they were prominently displayed instead of hidin' 'em under some big ol' sweater like you always do. Guys are more attracted to girls with those 'personality traits,' if you know what I mean." Maggie gives me a wicked smile.

"Well, that may be true, but I'm not going to change just to attract some guy. Been there. Done that."

"Even for Mr. Mysterious, with the cute butt?"

"How do you know what his posterior looks like?" I glance at her.

"Oh, Hon, Maggie the Cat knows all when it comes to the opposite sex." A knowing grin slides across her face. "Besides, don't play innocent with me. I know your eyes have strayed on more than one occasion. I bet you could even tell me what those little measurement numbers are on the leather tag on the back of his jeans."

I try not to blush. She's right. I do know. After three years of rooming with her at Biola University in La Mirada, California, she knows me all too well.

I haven't always been this way. I was never really into the whole boy crazy thing. They just weren't my fixation. Not that my world didn't flip upside down for a short period of time whenever a member of the opposite sex would show any inkling of interest in me, especially if he was remotely appealing and moderately attractive. But my world just didn't revolve around guys like Maggie's world does. That is, until about a year ago.

Oh Lord, please help me to stop this lust nonsense. He's just a guy. A guy I've never even met. In Jesus' name, I ask, Amen.

As I finish my silent prayer, I back my car into the driveway of my mother and stepfather's mini-estate in the swanky part of Chino Hills.

"Anybody home?" my voice echoes off the marble floors and twenty-foot-high glass windows in the foyer. No answer. *Thank You, Jesus!* My mother isn't home yet. Maggie and I run upstairs to my room to retrieve the stuff we packed to take to school. Maggie drove in from Texas and stayed the weekend with me so she could get back to her school-time job at the Victoria's Secret in the Brea Mall before school starts next week and to keep me company, which I'm grateful for.

I don't mind being home alone most of the time. I enjoy the peace and quiet and the time to think and dream (yeah, mostly about *him*, I'll confess) without my mother interrupting me with her constant barrage of criticism and general acrimony.

My mother and my stepfather, Dr. Bill, cosmetic surgeon extraordinaire, spend most of the summer traveling through Europe. Usually, they return to the States for a brief stay at the Simpson House in Santa Barbara, California, where my mother recovers in peace and luxury from her latest procedures. Dr. Bill would undoubtedly not only perform these procedures but also stay there with her to oversee her recovery.

This summer, they plan to come home directly from Europe. My mother said she had a little more "shopping" to do there, and then they would be home, which I'm guessing is code for the fact that she had minor procedures done this time and doesn't need the extended recovery time in Santa Barbara. It's always fun to see my mother after one of her "vacations" to guess what has been lifted, augmented, and/or completely reconstructed. Someday, I think I will pass her on the street and totally not recognize her.

We load up the backseat and trunk of my Toyota Corolla with Maggie's dorm room stuff she stored at my house for the summer, as well as the boxes filled with my own dorm life essentials. I carefully place my cherished two-cup coffee maker on the floor behind my seat. We manage to pack up my car and get back on the road before Dr. Frankenstein and his bride return home.

As we drive out of my parents' cul-de-sac, my mind slips into autopilot and instantly starts replaying everything I saw about him in church today. All his movements. The way he walks, the way he runs his hand through the front of his wavy black hair when his head is down and he is reading his Bible. How the back of his long hair fans out across his broad, muscular shoulders...*ugh! Stop thinking this junk already! Oh Lord, help me...*

Okay, lust isn't the only thing that is wrong with me, but it seems to be the sin of the day or year, at least. So what else can I tell you that is wrong with me? Let's see, first off, I'm not your average everyday church girl. I don't have a tapestry cover for my Bible. I'm not what you would characterize as sweet or nice (but I'm working on it). I even tried the "Christian Girl" character on for size for a little while, but it didn't fit. I felt like I was living a lie all the time.

I don't wear white lacy stuff, pastel colors, or stylish matching outfits like Maggie. I think she and I are polar opposites when it comes to fashion. I don't want to get into judging or stereotyping other people because I don't like it when people do that to me, but God made me different.

I wear black—all black, all the time. I love my new Doc Marten nine-lace-hole black patent leather boots, which Maggie and my mother both detest. I like things that are gothic, edgy, and a little quirky. I like my long, coarse, mousey brown hair dyed black, much to the dismay of my bleached-blonde mother. And I like tall, black-haired, beefy-built musicians with eyes the color of light green jade—well, one in particular.

He shops at the music and video store where I work and goes to the same church as me (which I think is peculiarly awesome). He always comes into the store alone. Come to think of it, whenever I see him in the store or at church, he's alone.

I deduced he is a musician since he always buys two packs of GHS Boomers electric guitar strings—eleven gauge, not the nines the wannabes usually buy. He typically wears a black T-shirt, either plain or with a logo from the latest grunge band. Oh, and Levi's. If he ever gets a new pair, that will be a sad day. I know, I know. I shouldn't be talking or thinking like this. I definitely need help.

So, does a person ever stop being an objectified figment of the imagination and just become a person? It stinks that I have built this guy up in my mind so much. I think if I ever actually speak to him, I will suddenly be stricken mute or I will completely pass out, and it will probably be on a day that I'm wearing a skirt that will slide up to display a regrettably placed hole in my opaque black tights.

As we turn onto the main outlet street, Maggie and I pull up next to a mini truck with two high school-aged-looking guys inside in the second left turn lane on Chino Hills Parkway. They instantly start pointing at us and hooting like a couple of deranged owls. When the traffic light turns green, I burn rubber turning left onto Highway 142 and ignore the infantile cat calls coming from the truck.

"Did you at least get his name this summer?" Maggie asks, craning her neck to smile back at the boys.

"I told you, I haven't spoken to him yet."

"I know *that*. There are other ways to find stuff out, you know."

"Like what?" I dare to ask.

"Like, does he ever pay with a credit card or a check? Checks are the best because most of the time you can get the guy's address and phone number." She has picked up a remarkable number of guys working at Victoria's Secret. Go figure.

"No, I don't know," I say. "I've never helped him check out at the cash register."

"Maddy! Why not? That's the perfect opportunity to start a conversation. I bet you purposely let someone else help him, don't you? So you don't have to talk to him."

I feel my lips tighten. I can't speak because what she said is true.

"Yeah, I thought so. You are so hopeless," she hisses, rolling her eyes.

Sometimes I think if I looked more like Maggie or my mother, I would possess the courage to go up and talk to him. It brings to mind a topic of conversion I've had with my mother, once or twice, maybe three or four times now. It usually begins with her addressing me by my full name, which is never good.

"Madeleine Marie Winger, why do you constantly dress like you are in mourning? There are other colors besides black, more *attractive* colors." Sometimes she adds under her breath, which she thinks I can't hear, "you certainly didn't get your fashion sense from me."

Thank God! Most of my mother's skin-tight clothing could be found in the closet of any trend-conscious fifteen-year-old girl. I think she hoped that when I gave my life to Jesus when I was nineteen, I would start dressing "better," maybe more like her. *Gag.*

"You know, you are not in high school anymore, Madeleine. If you want to attract a nice college boy, you need to start acting and dressing like the college student you are," my mother adamantly informed me.

My mind quickly flashed to visions of pleated plaid skirts and corduroy jackets with contrasting elbow patches. Weird, and definitely not me.

"Mom, I'm not going to college just to find a husband, okay? My goal in life is not to get hitched to some guy just because he looks good on paper."

Instantly, I wince at my own remarks, wishing I had not said them. I know. I should be more respectful of my mother, and not give into my sarcastic fleshly tendencies. I'm working on it. One more topic for prayer.

But man, my mother. Doting wife for fifteen years of esteemed plastic surgeon, Dr. Bill Cutter.

When she first started dating Dr. Bill, I *so* wanted to call him "Mr. Bill," after the little clay-mation character on my favorite old episodes of *Saturday Night Live*. I was six years old and wished I could have a Mr. Sluggo of my own to deliver me from my mother's new man. I could just hear Dr. Bill exclaiming "Ohhhh noooo," as my Mr. Sluggo pummeled him into a shapeless heap of clay. Yes!

But my mother insisted I address him properly, since doctors deserve respect. That's when I knew. Her persistent defense of him meant that Dr. Bill was here to stay. He was a doctor and she was going to marry him. He would be her new "Wallet," in that he would be able to support her comfortably *and* perform her upkeep at the same time. How convenient.

But Dr. Bill turned out to be a good guy. He treats us both really well, and he's good for my mother. Much better than my real father, I would venture to guess.

How she ever ended up with my birth father, a part-time musician and full-time off-shore oil rig worker, is beyond me. She skirts the issue whenever I bring it up. She seems miles away from her old life now.

I slow my car as we near the notoriously dangerous S-curves of Highway 142, also known on our local news as Carbon Canyon Road, since sections of the canyon tend to burn up every year during the fire season in early Fall.

Maggie stares out the window at the passing hills covered with the dry brown brush of August and the groves of old Eucalyptus trees. With a heavy sigh, she studies her long French-manicured fingernails. She's quiet, and seems consumed by her thoughts. Her rare moments of silence usually mean she's frustrated with me.

"Look, I hate that I'm totally infatuated with a guy I've never met," I try to clear the air. "I don't know anything about him or his character. I really don't want to have these intense feelings for him. Besides, I'm not even sure I want a boyfriend right now. I've got enough stuff to think about. Like, what am I going to do after graduation? *Agh!* Why can't I stop daydreaming about him? This sucks."

"I know sweetie," Maggie consoles me. "But I think I know what's really going on in that dyed-black head of yours. You're scared."

"Ding, ding, ding! Tell the lady what's she's won, Bob!"

"What's there to be so afraid of? Of meeting some guy you've had a crush on since Noah went into the ark? You might really hit it off with him. Or not. Maddy, you'll never know unless you *at least* talk to him. Come on, what've you got to lose?"

"A lot." I glance stone-faced at her.

Maggie likes to fish for some juicy (gory, more like) details of stuff I did in my life before I asked Christ into my heart. Most of the time I don't like to talk about my B.C. days, unless it's for a good reason.

I pull into the alleyway next to the parking lot of Alpha Chi, the all-female dormitory at Biola where we live. Our room is on First Odd, the ground floor hall of rooms on one side of the building. We start unloading our stuff into our room through the emergency exit door, which is left open only during moving days for easy access to the subterranean floor of the dormitory.

The old building smell is strong after being closed up all summer, but the scent is familiar, and not totally unpleasant.

We're about to begin our senior year, class of 1998. My last year of college. Holy mackerel.

Chapter Two

"Oh my gosh! Hiyeeee! M & M are back, everyone!" Bethany proclaims loudly, her sarcastic greeting reverberating off the hallway walls. Her forced plastic smile reminds me of the overly friendly realtor woman who sold the mini-mansion to my mother and Dr. Bill when I was a little kid.

Bethany Hendricks is the self-proclaimed mega-Christian of our floor. Maggie and I have had the unfortunate pleasure of living in the assigned dorm room right next to her since we all first came to Biola in our freshman year.

She is a local girl from South Orange County. Her father pastors an affluent mega church in the area. I have only met her parents a couple of of times because I keep my distance when I know they are making one of their short visits to the campus.

After I met them for the first time, I overheard Bethany's mother voice her astonishment that such a fine school would admit people like me, and that the school should be concerned that people like me will hurt its reputation. I guess she didn't realize how unsound proof the walls of our dorm rooms are. Or she didn't care.

In the past three years we have shared the wall dividing our dorm rooms, I have mentally concocted over a hundred ways to thicken and soundproof this cinder block wall, primarily so I wouldn't be able to hear every word Bethany gushes about Chad, the Super-Boyfriend.

Bethany gives Maggie and me the once over, only slightly shading her disapproval. I try to keep things civil with Bethany by ignoring her comments, but Maggie gives it right back to her. And then some.

"Magdalena Morris, are you still working in that den of sin?" Bethany asks. I see Maggie bristle. She hates being called by her whole first name, because it's how her stepmother always refers to her. Who does Bethany think she is anyway?

"I sure am. Why? Are ya'll lookin' for somethin' special? I can set you up with a bra from our new line of extreme push-up bras that'll surely speed up Chad's marriage proposal, alright! You're about a thirty-six B, right? I just bought one, so you could try on mine to see if you like it."

"Uh, no thanks," Bethany says with very apparent condemnation.

"Well, okay. Ya'll let me know if you change your mind," a fiendish smile spreads across Maggie's face. "Hey Bethany, check out what I bought when I was back home this summer."

Maggie carefully unrolls a long tube of thick glossy paper she is holding to reveal a black-and-white picture of a shirtless, totally ripped, gorgeous, dark-haired cowboy. He kind of reminded me of a certain someone…

"'Save a horse…ride a cowboy.' Hmmm. Cute." Bethany grimaces.

"You can hang it in your dorm room for a while if you'd like, Maddy,, and I won't mind." Maggie gives her a wide-eyed grin. I try not to bust out laughing.

"I don't think so. It's not appropriate décor for young Christian women to display in their dorm room."

"Really? Well, okay, suit yourself. I think this guy could brighten up any old dorm room, don't you? Besides, he looks just like this guy Maddy has a huge crush on." Maggie winks at me.

"Oh really?" Bethany turns her wrath--I mean attention--toward me.

"No, not really. Maggie is just kidding around." I shoot Maggie an I'm-gonna-kill-you-later look. The last thing I want is for Bethany to start cross-examining me on this subject. Especially this subject.

"Oh." Bethany looks me up and down. "Madeleine, I totally love your outfit. It's so, so black. Is it new?" She smoothed out her new-looking J.Crew khaki skorts, like they are the exemplary attire for all Christian co-eds. As if! I wouldn't be caught dead in anything like that.

Oh Lord, please guard my tongue and keep me from saying something completely acidic. In Your name I pray, Amen.

"How was your summer, Bethany?" I grin innocently at her, purposely changing the subject.

Last semester, I finally discovered a sure-fire way to side-step Bethany's self-righteous remarks. First, I totally ignore what she said, and then second, I make her the topic of the conversation. It works every time.

"Totally fab! Chad and I spent a whole month traveling with his parents through Europe. It was absolutely fabulous!"

"Oh, did ya'll go there on a mission trip or something? Maybe to teach the women of Serbia the appropriate way to dress while livin' under political oppression?" Maggie says with another crazy wide-eyed grin.

Bethany's expression looks as if she is considering the question, like maybe she should take up this cause, but then frowns, and gives Maggie and me a sickeningly sweet smile accompanied with a condescending head tilt, which Maggie promptly returns.

Maggie loves to antagonize Bethany. She says she just gives back to Bethany what she dishes out. But I suspect the main reason Maggie gets so much pleasure out of provoking her is because Bethany reminds Maggie of her stepmother. I think it's sad and kind of mean, and Maggie shouldn't do it, but she never misses a beat when it comes to putting Bethany in her place.

"Hey guys! Welcome back! How was your summer?" Suzette, Bethany's roommate, walks up, her thick wavy waist-length sandy brown hair swaying behind.

I thought Suzette was cool from the first time I met her. I never feel her judging me. Her parents don't judge me either. They are loving and genuine people, just like their daughter, but unfortunately they don't make it out to California very often. They live in Woodinville, Washington, a suburb northeast of Seattle.

Suzette's ex-hippie parents were saved near the end of the Jesus Movement in the 70's. They did some missions work in India for a few years before settling in Woodinville to raise their growing family and to open a plant nursery near their home. Suzette and her other four younger siblings were home-schooled for most of her life. She and Bethany make an odd pairing. But then, so do Maggie and me.

"How goes the man search?" Maggie is always probing her. Suzette shakes her head sadly and then looks down at her new Birkenstock sandals.

As laid back as Suzette seems, her main goal in life is to get her "M-R-S degree," code for those girls who are totally matrimonially minded.

Last semester, during a finals study break, she confided to me that she often cries herself to sleep at night, begging God to bring her a husband. She told me it bothers her deeply that she has only one more year of college left and has not yet found the future pastor to whom she would become a pastor's wife and potentially give birth to and raise four to six children with said pastor. Not nearly enough time, she said, to cultivate the lifelong marriage they would surely share.

I bit my tongue about the "lifelong" part and tried to console her with the fact that she is able to totally focus on school and doesn't have to worry about making time for some boyfriend. But I think my words fell on deaf ears.

I suspect Bethany rubs Suzette's face in the fact that she has what Suzette wants, a long-term relationship with the strong likelihood of marriage. But I'm sure Bethany does it in a subtle, spirit-filled way. Yeah, right.

"Suzette doesn't need the distractions of a boyfriend, do you, Suz?" Bethany answers Maggie's question for Suzette.

"I wouldn't mind—" Suzette tries to answer.

"She is going into the mission field, isn't that right, Suz?" Suzette's dejected look breaks my heart.

Okay, sometimes I just really want to smack Bethany. Well, somebody should do it! She can be such an insensitive wench sometimes.

"Really, Suzi? That's great! Where would you like to go?" I ask, trying to dissipate my anger and make Suzette feel better.

"I, I don't know. I'm still praying about it, I guess," Suzette mumbles as she turns and quickly walks down the hall toward the restroom, her long hair swinging wildly behind her.

Maggie and I stare daggers at Bethany. If looks could harm...

Chapter Three

By the time I make the long hike from the campus bookstore to my dorm room, it feels like my back pack straps have worn trenches into my shoulders, matching the troughs long since dug from my bra straps.

I had to buy eleven books for one of my upper division Communication major classes. Eleven. For one class. They're all paperback books, but still. I drop my backpack with a thud on the floor next to my desk. Vile country music fills my ears.

Uh oh. Maggie is lying on her bed with her arm strewn across her face. I know this posture. It usually means some massive drama has transpired in my absence. Something in the universe has gone terribly awry while I was at the campus bookstore.

"You okay?" I dare to ask.

"Kill me now! I'm gonna be writin' papers this semester 'til my fingers are worn to the bone!" Maggie flings her arm down to her side.

Phew, just a case of "Syllabus Shock." It usually strikes every semester after the first week of classes. You'd think we would get used to hearing about all the projects and papers we will be required to complete over the semester, but it's still an overwhelming amount of information to receive in one week.

"Anyone call?" I ask while stacking my new books on the shelf above my desk.

"Hmmm…yes. Adonis called for you. He wants you to meet him in the Garden of Eden at midnight. Oh, and he said don't wear anything black. Unless, of course, it's a black lace push-up bra with matching black panties!" Maggie gives me another one of her infamous evil smiles.

"Ha, ha. You're sooo funny. I'm astounded by your rapier wit." I hate it when she teases me about him.

"Hey, do you have to work tonight?" Maggie asks, ignoring my sarcasm. "I've been jonesin' for some Del Taco."

Del Taco is classic Southern California Mexican fast food, ideal for college students on a budget. The menu is very similar to Taco Bell's but a little more like real Mexican food. We reserve trips to In-N-Out Burger, the ultimate in SoCal eats, for special occasions. Not that In-N-Out is expensive; it's just special. They make the best burgers ever, especially if you order your Double Double "Animal Style," which means extra everything. *Mmmm.*

"I'm off tonight, but I should go pick-up my paycheck," I tell her.

"Great! It's a date. My treat. Let's blow this joint." Maggie jumps off her bed and begins fixing her face in her vanity table mirror, while I grab my keys and purse.

After a quick bite to eat, we get back in my car and travel the streets to the Whittier Music Plus. The store is not crowded, but then it usually isn't, not like the Music Plus in Chino, where I transferred from when I started going to Biola. That store seemed to be constantly bustling with customers.

The store's glass front and sides gleam in the streetlights and bright signs from the surrounding buildings. As we walk in, Maggie and I are warmly greeted by my co-workers on duty.

"Hey Maddy, I thought you were off tonight?" our resident metal-head Jaime says. He always seems to know my schedule.

"I am. Just picking up my check."

"Cool. You ladies got plans tonight? I'm off at ten."

"Oh, gee Jaime...we've really got to get back to school. Early class in the morning." I grab Maggie by the arm with a squeeze.

She has already slipped into her "Marilyn" posture for Jaime, complete with her long bright red index fingernail hanging on her lower lip, as she bats her long mascara-encrusted eyelashes at him. I try to pull her toward the backroom door. But as I turn, I stop dead in my tracks. *No, no, no! Not with Maggie here! Oh, Lord, please help!*

There he is. *My crush.* Across the store, standing in the "M" section of the rock CD bins. His head is down and his hair is covering his face as he searches through the discs, but I know it's him. I'd know that lovely mane of black wavy hair anywhere. I turn away quickly. Maybe Maggie won't notice. Play it cool. Yeah right!

Good. Maggie is still flirting with Jaime, with her chest thrust forward. I focus on the front door. *Keep your eyes straight ahead...don't look over there.* I pull her toward the front door and quickly wave to my co-workers as we escape out the front door.

"That was quick. I didn't even see you go into the backroom...Hey! Wait a minute!" Maggie steps back from my car and slams the passenger door closed.

Maggie stands with her hands on her hips and a disgusted look on her face. In plain view through the plate glass windows, you can see him inside the store standing in the aisle between the rows of CD bins.

"Maggie, please! Let's go!" I beg her.

"Not a chance, Sugarpants! It's fate, or kismet, or whatever. It's a divine appointment."

"Please, Maggie, no! Get in the car! Let's go! I look completely awful right now!" I say, hoping to appeal to her deep-seated sense of vanity so she will let us go.

"Madeleine, darlin', this is your golden opportunity."

"Come on, Maggie! I'll let you dress me and do my make-up for a day...a whole week! Can we please just go?"

I look Maggie straight in the eye. I feel like I'm going to be sick from the waves of panic crashing down on me. Maggie considers my outfit and appearance consisting of an oversized faded black t-shirt, old black jeans, ailing black Converse Chuck Taylor high-tops, my long hair scraped back in a ponytail, and not a hint of make-up on my pale face. She looks back at the window, and then back at me. With a heavy sigh, she opens the car door and climbs inside.

"Alright, but this is the last time. If we see him at church on Sunday, you *will* go up and talk to him. Or else I will!"

"Hey Maddy, you forgot your check," Jaime calls as he walks toward my car. He is grinning like the Cheshire Cat in Alice of Wonderland. He kind of looks like it, too.

"Oh, thanks, Jaime. I guess I have a lot on my mind." He hands the envelope to Maggie through the open window, and leans down on the car door. His long, bleached blond hair falls forward and brushes the top of the open window. I have visions of him and Maggie wearing rubber gloves and sharing a bottle of peroxide.

"You ladies got any plans Saturday night? My band's playing at the Whiskey in Hollywood." He reaches into the inside pocket of his standard-issue black Music Plus vest and pulls out two tickets. He hands the tickets to Maggie.

"Well, bless your heart, aren't you sweet! Madeleine and I would love to come see your little band play." Maggie is such a bad liar, and I don't think Jaime picks up on her Southern sarcasm, either.

I look up at the store window just in time to see a guy with sandy brown shoulder-length curly hair walk up to my Adonis and say something to him that makes him laugh. Oh, be still my beating heart. What a sweet smile!

"Hey Jaime, do you know that guy in the store there?" Maggie asks, as she notices me starring at him.

"Which one?" Jaime seems a little dejected.

"The tall one, with the dark hair."

"No, not really. But I know his band practices at the same rehearsal room building in La Habra, as my band does. I've seen him there a couple of times. I think he's a guitar player. I've only heard his band play a little. They suck." Jaime says that about all other hard rock bands except his.

"Okay, thanks, Jaime. We've really got to run. I'll see you later." I turn the key in the ignition and release the parking brake.

"Okay. Hey, I'll see you tomorrow. You close, right?" He backs away from my car and walks back toward the store, waving and smiling.

I give a quick wave and pull out into traffic. So, I wonder who that was with him tonight. Like I said, I've never seen him with anyone before.

"See how much information you can get if you only ask?" Maggie looks pleased with herself. "Now you know where his band practices."

"Yeah," I mumble. I'm still reeling from the close encounter.

Okay. So I will admit it. I'm a little scared to meet this guy. Maybe more than a little scared. Scared for a lot of reasons.

"So, now we need to come up with a plan." Maggie looks intently ahead.

"Like what? I just happen to show up at some rehearsal studio when I'm not even in a band?"

Maggie gets a devious look in her eye. "I know! You could–"

"No way! I'm not going to use Jaime."

"Hon, why not? You know he has a major crush on you?"

"Maggie, that is so wrong."

"Oh, come on. It's not like he wouldn't do it to you."

"That doesn't matter. I don't do things like that." I shoot Maggie a serious look. "Besides, if it's meant to happen that I'm supposed to meet this guy, then it will happen."

"What if you miss that opportunity? Like what if it was supposed to 'happen' tonight?"

"It's not time yet, Maggie."

"How do *you* know?"

"I just know."

"Hon, don't you think it's already some kinda providence that this guy goes to the same church as you way out in Chino Hills, and shops in the music store where you work, way out here in Whittier?"

"Yeah, maybe, but I'm not ready for it, okay? So please just drop it, okay?"

"Ready for what? You talk like you're gonna marry this guy!"

Maggie is really starting to irritate me. *Breathe in, breathe out.* "Look, if I do meet him, I'm not ready for any of the potential outcomes, okay?" I try to keep my voice calm. "If I meet him, and he rejects me, I will be devastated."

"Oh, hon, he won't," Maggie tries to reassure me.

"And if I meet him, and we hit it off, and we start dating, I'm afraid of what could happen, you know, being alone with him."

"He is a big strappin' guy, but he doesn't seem the rapist type to me." I'm not sure if Maggie is serious or if she's trying to make a joke.

"Maggie. It's not *him* I'm worried about."

Chapter Four

At first I thought I was just dreaming. More like a nightmare, actually. But the ringing persists as I wake up. I crawl out of my soft, warm bed and answer the phone.

"Hello...?"

"Is Maggie there?" A distinctive Texan accent asks.

"She's asleep. Who's calling?" I am not a happy camper.

"Were ya'll sleeping? Oh, I'm sorry, darlin'. I forget about the time difference. I was just gettin' ready for work, and I thought I'd give Maggie a quick call. Is she there?"

"Hold on." I sigh deeply.

"Who is it?" Maggie asks me as she sits up in bed. I shrug and hold the receiver out to her.

She climbs out of bed to get the phone, which resides on the floor in the middle of the two sides of our room. I hand her the receiver with my best "it's 3 A.M." look of sleepy disdain and stagger back to my bed.

"Hello?...Hi baby, how ya'll doin'?" Maggie uses her best bedroom voice. "Yeah, I miss you, too...I've been thinkin' about you, too."

Oh puke! I pull my pillow over my head to try to drown out Maggie's cooing. She gets the message, picks up the phone and carries it out into the hallway, and closes our door.

I wonder which guy this is in Maggie's menagerie of men. Chris? Jeff? Chad? Yes, Bethany's Chad, you remember, the Super-Boyfriend?

He and Maggie went out a few times during our freshman year. He still calls her once in a while, which I think is strange. Whenever I answer the phone when he calls, he always gives some lame excuse why he's calling. Usually he says something about a class they have together, since they are both Sociology majors. Like I care. I don't think Bethany knows about Chad's calls. If she does, she never mentions it. Come to think of it, Maggie never mentions it either. It seems like it would be something Maggie would love to throw in Bethany's face, but she hasn't yet.

"Maddy!" Maggie whispers as she taps softly on the door. "Open the door. It's locked." I peel back the covers and stagger to the door to open it.

"So, who was that?" I ask since I am awake now, and I know Maggie will keep me awake to recount the whole conversation.

"Bodacious Bart!" She smiles widely and closes her eyes.

"The cowboy guy from Dallas you told me about? Is he the one you said carries around a picture of his truck in his wallet? Is he the guy who also takes his Wrangler jeans to the cleaners to get starched creases put in them?"

"Mmmm…that's the one. He is such a gentleman. He called to ask if I wanted him to ship my clothes to me that I left in the hamper at his house. He already washed them for me. Isn't that sweet?"

"*Maaaggiiie!* I thought you said you were a good girl over summer break."

"Well, I was, mostly. There was just this one little indiscretion the night before I left. He looked so good and was so sweet. And he told me he loved me, and I couldn't resist."

I shake my head and climb back into my bed, and pull my covers up. Maggie climbs into her own bed. I don't say anything.

I don't need to. I know Maggie knows it's wrong. My silence on the matter speaks volumes to her. She silently rolls over to face the wall.

Who am I to judge? It's not like I've never been down that road myself. I've lived the life that Maggie is living. I've done the things she is doing. I clearly remember feeling what she must feel every time one of these guys is finished having his way with her, and then thinks he can come around for more whenever he wants, with one phone call full of sweet talk. I don't think I'll ever forget that gut-grinding feeling that messes with your head until you feel like you might go insane.

The summer before I started attending Biola, I got an information packet in the mail about university life and a short biography card written by my future roommate. I thought it was some cruel joke that someone was playing on me to pair me up with a pastor's daughter—a pastor's daughter from Texas, no less. Maggie and I couldn't have come from more different regional backgrounds. But now I know it was the hand of God working. We have a lot more in common than I ever would have imagined.

I'm a couple of years older than most of the other girls, and I have experienced a lot more than most of them, especially with the opposite sex—a lot more experience—as has Maggie. Maggie and I also have our step-parent woes in common, only her step-mother has been in her life since she was two years old.

According to Maggie, Betina Johnson Morris, "Tini" to all her who know and love her (if that's at all possible, Maggie would add), is a petite, crafty, sly, sneaky, bossy, imposing (plus a few more of Maggie's colorful descriptions I've forgotten) and a sanctimonious demon-woman from the seventh layer of Hell.

She had been attending Maggie's father's small parish in Plano for many years when Maggie's mother died. Tini was convinced it was her duty to slither her way in and ensnare the recently widowed and ruggedly good-looking Pastor Eddie

Morris, only ten months after Maggie's mother's death from breast cancer.

Tini successfully spun her web and snared the handsome young preacher, persuading him that he needed to remarry immediately because a man in his position needed an appropriate wife to care for him. The fact that he had some baggage in the form of a two-year-old "mixed-breed" little girl would be her cross she would have to bear, and she reminds everyone around her on a regular basis, including Maggie.

I think Maggie is still very bitter about the situation. Sometimes, I wonder if she feels betrayed by her father for marrying such a horrible woman. I wonder if she is seeking the love and acceptance, she feels she didn't get at home every time she sleeps with one of her guys. Or maybe she's just plain rebellious.

Either way, I know from experience how much she is hurting herself. Maybe I should change my major to Psychology? *Yeah, right.* I have enough trouble keeping my own head on straight half the time, much less being able to help others with theirs.

I was first alerted to Maggie's "extracurricular activities" a couple of weeks after the beginning of our freshman year. Late at night, I would hear soft tapping on Maggie's window, followed by the sound of her window slowly sliding up and Maggie carefully sliding out. Nobody ever noticed that Maggie didn't keep a screen on her window. She wouldn't come back until the wee hours of the morning.

I knew what she was up to but didn't know what to do. Sneaking out in the middle of the night was definitely against the school code of ethics. But I couldn't report her. That would be like telling on myself, since I felt like I was just as guilty of the same things that Maggie was doing, only I performed most of my acts of debauchery in my pre-Biola days. All I felt I could do was pray for her. So I pray a lot. Daily. Sometimes, hourly.

The Bible story of the Samaritan man in chapter ten of the gospel of Luke really speaks to me when I read it. Not that Maggie is some severely wounded soul lying on the side of the road in a near-death state. Well, maybe she is, spiritually speaking. I don't know. All I know is if the shoe were on the other foot, I would want someone to have compassion on me.

Maggie doesn't need a sermon on purity. Having grown up in the church, she has heard it all before. She knows all the Scriptures about keeping oneself pure.

But when her crying jags start, and they always do after a series of her male escapades, I just wrap my arms around her, smooth her hair, and hand her clean tissues as she huddles on the floor next to her bed, hugging her knees to her chest until the pain subsides enough for her to get up and get back to normal everyday life. That is until the next guy calls.

Chapter Five

"EWWWW! That is the most disgusting thing I have seen!"
"It's *so* hairy!"
"And veiny! Like some deformed hot dog!"
"That is SO disgusting!
"Do they all look like that?"
"I would never touch IT!"

With a quick, curious glance at each other, Maggie pushes aside her word processor, and I flip upside down the third of the eleven books I'm reading for one class. We dart next door to Suzette and Bethany's room, the origin of all these peculiar outbursts we hear.

We stop just inside the doorway of their room where a group of girls are all huddled around a Psychology book, open to a page with a black and white photograph of a penis. Maggie turns her head toward me and rolls her eyes.

"How pathetic!" she hisses to me under her breath. I give Maggie a half smile.

Honestly, I'm jealous of these girls. Jealous of their innocence. I wish I didn't possess the memories I do of all the things I've done in the past. Sometimes, I feel like I have no business living among and breathing in the same air as these pure and innocent young women.

During our freshman year, at Bethany's persistent prodding, Maggie, Suzette, and I attended a purity conference for women at a local church called "A Garden Enclosed." I didn't want to go. I don't fit in with stuff like that, and I didn't need any help feeling more condemned for my past experiences than I already did. But Maggie wanted to go, so I couldn't say no.

On the way there, Maggie claimed she wanted to go because it would be good people-watching, and we could see who broke down in tears the most. Then she confessed that her father had made her attendance at the conference mandatory. Maggie's father, as kind and compassionate as he is, is not a man to be disobeyed.

I learned some valuable stuff at the conference, especially Scripture references I could certainly use today in dealing with my thoughts about my crush. I also renewed my resolve to stay pure until marriage.

However, Maggie didn't seem to get anything out of it. She trashed all the information sheets we received, as well as the little gold key that each of us received.

We were supposed to keep the keys as a symbol of our stand for purity, to remember that each of us is a "garden enclosed." A woman is to remain locked up until her wedding night, upon which she gives the little gold key to her husband.

I keep my key in my underwear drawer, so I see it daily. It helps me remember to clean up my mind when my daydreams about my Adonis start getting too frequent. Maggie tossed her key in the small trash can on the side of our desks. But I fished it out when she left the room and hid it under some books in the bottom drawer of my desk. She will want it back someday. Someday soon, I hope.

"Maddy, have you ever seen anything so hideous?" asks Janelle, who lives two rooms down the hall from us. *Yes, more times than I care to remember, unfortunately,* I think to myself.

"Janelle, aren't you a nursing major?" I ask. Okay, I'm getting too good at this avoiding-the-truth thing.

"Yeah, but I don't have to look at penises all day...or is it 'peni'?"

"Ya'll better get used to it!" Maggie says as she walks further into the room. "'Cause you know, all ya'll are gonna have to do more than just touch IT on your weddin' night," Maggie says, and all the girls stare at her, some with looks of wide-eyed shock and some with looks of incredulous horror.

"I think if it was my husband's, I wouldn't be disgusted by it at all. It would be part of him, so I would be okay with it," Suzette says. She is so sweetly pure. Oh, to be that innocent again.

"I can't believe this school would allow a textbook with nudity in it. It's like, pornographic!" Bethany says with a hiss, always the spoilsport. "Suzette, why are you even taking Psychology? Don't you think it's immoral and hedonistic?"

"Bethany, it's not pornography. And no, Psychology is not immoral. It's the study of human behavior. You should know that," Suzette says.

Hmm...this is new. I've never seen Suzette stand up to her overbearing roommate before.

"Well, Chad said we shouldn't be required to take Psychology, and he and his parents are going to appeal the requirement. Besides, it's not like you're going to need it in the mission field."

"Bethany, give it a rest, will you?" Suzette turns and storms out of the room.

I slip out of the room after Suzette and catch up with her in the bathroom. "Hey, what's up?" I ask her.

"I'm just so sick of hearing about her stupid boyfriend!" Suzette wraps her arms around herself and her forehead wrinkles.

"You and me both. I begged Maggie to swap sides of the room with me this year, but she flat out refused."

"Everything is 'Chad says this' or 'Chad thinks that's immoral.' Chad, Chad, Chad! I'm so tired of it!" Her eyes begin to well up with tears. "I've always been happy for her since she first started dating him, but Maddy, sometimes I think she talks about him so much just to rub it in my face that she has a serious boyfriend and I don't. Especially this year," she says, wiping her eyes.

I get that feeling, too, but I think it's better not to tell her. "Maybe we need to get you some good earplugs or a pair of those big fancy headphones that block out sound," I say, trying to cheer her up.

Suzette laughs, but tears are spilling from the corners of her eyes. "Mostly, I'm tired of being single. Maddy, I pray every day for God to bring me to my future husband."

"I know. Waiting is really hard sometimes." I hand her a tissue from the box on the bathroom counter.

"It's all I want. Does it seem weird to just want to be a wife and mother?" Suzette asks.

"Not if it's the desire of your heart. Besides, who's to say what's weird and what's not? Oh, wait, that would be *Chad's* job, wouldn't it?" I say. Suzette laughs again.

"And I'm not sure about going into the mission field, either. It just seems too scary to me."

"Hey, maybe we should start a club for people who don't know what they want to do after graduation." I give Suzette a big hug. "You and I can be charter members!"

"Thanks, Maddy." Suzette sniffs into my shoulder and hugs me back. After a few moments, Suzette pulls away and wipes her eyes. "Wanna go to Juice Stop? I can't go back in there right now."

"Sure, let me get my keys and ask Maggie if she wants anything."

I run back to our room and grab my stuff. Maggie is still in Bethany and Suzette's room, so I decide to skip asking her. Suzette and I quickly sneak out to the parking lot.

"You oughta know!" Suzette sings loudly along with the stereo, the wind from the rolled-down window whipping her long hair all around. "Oh, I love this song! Bethany won't let me play this CD in our room." Suzette cranks up the volume on my car stereo.

"I know. Alanis Morisette is pretty much the only non-country musician Maggie likes. One time, she was blasting this CD in our room, lip-syncing and dancing around to it, when Bethany walked in and started lecturing us on the inappropriateness of the lyrical content."

"Oh, no way! Did she really? I bet Maggie was not pleased!"

"She was a little miffed. And I think my evil sarcasm is rubbing off on her. She told Bethany, 'oh, ya'll are so right! We shouldn't listen to a young woman singin' her heart out about how the guy she loved with her whole bein' used her and then dumped her like a truck full of cow manure!'"

Suzette laughs at my Maggie impersonation. "What did Bethany say?"

"Not much. It's just something about it still not being appropriate. Then Maggie said, 'Wait 'til it happens to you with your precious little Chad, then we'll see what you say.' Then Bethany said that would never happen to her, and she turned and left our room."

"Yikes! What did you do?" Suzette looks at me with amazement.

"I didn't get involved. I just turned my stereo down and went back to studying."

"Do you think those two will ever actually get in a fight?"

"I don't think so. Maggie told me she doesn't like the stuff Bethany says, but she understands why she is the way she is."

"Wow, that's surprising."

"Maggie is used to hyper-righteousness. Her stepmother is an expert in pointing out the unrighteousness of others. Maggie said her stepmother acts like the Great Commission Jesus gave her go into all the world and point out the wrong things people are doing, not just pointing them toward Christ."

"*Ewww.*"

"Yeah, and her stepmother thinks that I'm a less than ideal roommate for her stepdaughter."

"Let me guess, she doesn't like how you dress?"

"Not just that. She doesn't like that my biological parents are divorced."

"Like you have control over that."

"Yeah, and then there's the fact that my mother brazenly flirted with Maggie's father in front of her step-mother at the parent orientation at the beginning of our freshman year."

"Oh my goodness…" Suzette says.

"Yeah, so I make myself scarce whenever she and Maggie's father come for a visit."

"But again, that's not your fault. That totally stinks."

"It does, especially because I really like Maggie's dad. He's always so cool to talk to." I purposely change the subject. "So Bethany is really starting to get on your last nerve, huh?"

"Maddy, can you keep an extreme secret? I mean, you can't even tell Maggie."

"Am I sure I want to hear this? Is it a matter of national security?"

"Seriously…"

"Wait, let me guess, Bethany and her Super-Boyfriend are doing *it.*"

"Well, I don't know for sure…"

"*No way!* I was just kidding!" I can't believe I guessed it.

"Last night, she came home about an hour and a half late from her date with you-know-who, which is so not like her. And I saw brownish-red marks, like hickies, on the side of her breast when she was getting dressed this morning."

"Ewww! Hickies! That's so junior high. I bet they were listening to Journey or something."

"Maddy, what do I do? Should I confront her?"

"Suz, I seriously doubt Bethany and Chad are having sex. I bet they were just making out."

"How can you tell?"

"Well, Chad is still calling her, isn't he?"

"Yeah, like a hundred times a day."

"Well, there you go. They're not having sex."

"What do you mean? I don't get it." Suzette looks puzzled.

"Look, when the hunter conquers his prey, then the hunt is over. Isn't it? Time to move on to a different unconquered prey, maybe taller, blonder, easier to obtain."

Suzette still looks confused. "But I can't see Chad breaking up with her, even if they are having sex. They're practically engaged," she says.

"I hope not, but he's a guy, isn't he? They are all basically wired the same, aren't they? Bethany and Chad shouldn't be messing around with making out, either. That's like playing with matches in a dynamite factory."

"Maddy, how do you know all this about guys?"

"Experience is a cruel teacher, sometimes." *Sometimes?* Actually, every time.

"You've seriously gone through stuff like this?"

"Yes. Many times."

Suzette looks like she's trying to hide her look of shock. She doesn't know much about my past.

"I speak from experience when I tell you it's really important to do what God says, specifically in the relationship-with-guys department." I have to pause for a moment to let the high-speed mental montage of regrettable guys I've been with, finish playing in my mind. "Because the alternative to obedience is really unpleasant, and always, one hundred percent of the time, ends up hurting like hell."

Thankfully, the line at Juice Stop is short. I guess it would be at eight p.m. on a weeknight. I try not to laugh out loud at the hilarious banter I hear from the group of guys in line right behind me.

"Dude, do ya think you could suck less at practice tonight? You could seriously use some lessons or something," one guy says.

"*Aww* dude, weak! So do you! Your vocals sound like a monkey screaming 'cause his hand's caught in that grinder thing," the other guy retorts.

"Dude, time is not just a magazine. Drummers are supposed to be able to keep a steady beat, or is this news to you?"

"Funny. Isn't the lead vocalist supposed to stay in pitch? Dude, your pitch is all over the place, just like a, like a knuckleball! Maybe someday you'll become an actual singer instead of just a vocalist."

"Dudes, relax! You guys sound like an old married couple," another guy with a smooth, deep voice says. "After you get your drinks, you guys need to say you're sorry and chill-out. We're like a family, remember?"

"Aww shucks, Pete's right. I love you man!" One of the guys says to the other guy he has been teasing.

"No, I love *you*, man!"

"You guys are so strange." The deep voiced guy says, laughing.

"We can't all be rip-and-shred guitar gods, full of the wisdom of the ages and the nobleness of the ancients like you, Saint Peter."

I hear the last guy with a smooth voice laugh as the other guy pushes him into me.

"I'm so sorry!" The deep-voiced guy says.

I turn around and start to say it's okay, but I can't get the words out. I am looking up into the greenest eyes I have ever seen. I can't breathe. My mouth is dry. I literally think my heart has stopped beating. It's him. It's him. *OH MY LORD!* It's him!

"Hey, don't you work at the Music Plus in Whittier?" His voice is so low and lyrically sounding to me. He is smiling at me, his eyes shining like brilliantly polished jade stones.

OH GOD...OH GOD...OH GOD! My stomach is turning continuous summersaults.

"Hey, can you get me a discount?" One of the other guys interrupts.

"Quiet, Ted," he says, keeping his eyes locked with mine.

"Excuuuse me!" Ted feigns insult.

"I, uh, work..." is all I can manage to sputter out. I can feel the blood draining from my face, and my palms are getting sweaty. My knees feel like they are going to give out at any moment. I need to look away, anywhere else but his eyes.

"Maddy, here's your smoothie. Your favorite, chocolate and banana. My treat, girlfriend!" Suzette hands me a large Styrofoam cup. I take it and murmur my thanks. She is staring at me. I'm sure I look as stunned as I feel.

"I, uh, we've got to go. Bye..." I pull Suzette by the arm toward the door.

"Cool, maybe I'll see you at the Plus," he calls after me with a big smile.

"Uh...yeah...sure..." I continue my beeline for the door with Suzette in tow. *Argh!* I'm such an idiot!

"Wooohoo! Peter! Dude! She's hot, man!" Ted says, even though we are clearly still within earshot.

"And she likes you, dude!" The other guy says, playfully punching Peter in the arm.

"Just order your drinks," Peter says as we pass through the doorway of the building.

I burn rubber out of the parking lot. *Breathe. Breathe.*

"Maddy, are you okay? Who was that guy back there? He's gorgeous!" Suzette says as she happily slurps her smoothie.

I try to restore my racing heart to a more normal rate and breathing pattern, as opposed to that of a rabbit that has just escaped from a chasing fox. My hands are shaking on the steering wheel.

Peter. *His name is Peter!*

Maggie will be royally disappointed that she missed this, but honestly, I'm thankful she wasn't here.

Chapter Six

I leave Suzette in her room and tell her I will explain more later. I have to go see what's up with Maggie because I notice signs of distress.

Our door is closed, and I can hear a slow George Strait song seeping through it. I am only able to identify which one of the many male country artists this crooner is due to my years as a product manager at Music Plus. Occupational hazard, I guess.

The door is locked, and Maggie is inside. *Uh oh.* This usually means some catastrophe has happened in the universe, and Maggie is unhappy. I slowly turn my key to unlock the door and open it. Papers and open books are strewn across Maggie's bed. She is slumped over, sitting on the floor next to her bed. A pile of wadded tissues has collected around her feet. Her face is buried in her hands.

"Sweetie, what's wrong?" I drop my stuff on my desk and go to kneel on the floor next to her.

"My Grandma Dora's in the hospital." Her eyes are red and swollen and wet with fresh tears.

"Oh, Mag, I'm so sorry. What happened?"

"She had a heart attack earlier this evening." Maggie sniffs and wipes her eyes.

"How is she doing now?"

"Okay, I guess. My daddy said they're gonna keep her in the hospital overnight for observation but that she is doin' well, especially for an eighty-seven-year-old woman."

"That sounds promising." I hand her another tissue.

"Yeah, Daddy said she's already complainin' about the food and she's demandin' that she be let into the hospital kitchen to show the chefs the proper way to cook-up rice puddin'."

"That sounds like your Grandma Dora. Are you doing okay?"

"Maddy, I think God is punishin' me."

"What makes you think that?"

"Cause right before Daddy called me with the news, I was on the phone with…with someone."

"I don't follow." Not exactly, but I'm pretty sure I know what she is about to say.

"I was mindin' my own business, workin' on one of my umpteen papers due this week, and the phone rings. I wasn't gonna answer it. I was just gonna let it ring. Then I thought it might be you, so I answered it."

"And?"

"It was Bryce."

"Bryce? You mean the guy you were seeing last year? The very minor league baseball player?"

"Yeah."

Oh gag. "Why is he calling you?"

"Well, he was bein' real sweet, and he started askin' how I was, and what was I doin', and what I was wearin'…"

"Okay, thanks. That's enough. I get it. I thought you told him to get lost last year?"

"Well, I found him again. Actually, I've gone out with him a couple of times this year. He's real sweet. He's changed a lot since last year."

I want to scream at her for being so ignorant. This guy, Bryce, is such a creep. One time last year, Maggie talked me into going with her to meet him and his friends at a small pub on the

Newport Beach boardwalk. She said there was a cool new band playing that night, which she thought I would really like.

When we got there, there was no band. Of course. Just a bar full of sports guys and a few surfers, and this guy Bryce and his jock friends. While Maggie was at the jukebox, he leaned in close to me, leering at my chest.

"So tell me, would M and M's melt in my hands?" he slurred, his sour, pungent beer breath almost making me retch.

I wasn't entirely clear on his meaning at first, so I dared to ask him to elaborate. I was hoping he wasn't asking me what I thought he was asking me.

He slipped his arm around my waist and leaned in closer. "My tasty little gothic princess, would you like to join Maggie in making a Bryce sandwich?" he whispered loudly in my ear.

Oh puke, I thought. It was all I could do to keep from slugging him in the gut. I gave him my best evil sneer and got up to join Maggie at the jukebox to share his repulsive request with her and to inform her that my car and I were leaving immediately.

"Maggie, how many times have you been out with this guy since school started this year?"

"Oh, just a couple of times."

I start roughly calculating out the changes I've seen in her attitude and when they occurred. "Like every two weeks?"

"Yeah, I guess so."

"You know he's just using you?"

"Well, I'm usin' him, too." She tries to look indignant.

I sigh, and get up and sit on the edge of my bed, facing Maggie. "I really don't think God gave your grandma a heart attack because you were having phone sex, or whatever, with this guy. But maybe it is a sign or a message, you know? I hate to see you keep doing this to yourself."

Maggie doesn't say anything. She just looks at me with her jaw set in her stubborn way. Then she quickly picks up the pile of tissues, throws them in the trash, and goes back to her school work without saying a word to me.

My head and my heart feel like they're filled with lead bricks. I just don't know what else to do or say to her. But I need to get back to studying, too, so I begin to ask for help.

Oh Lord, please, please help. Help me not to be so angry and frustrated with her. I love Maggie like a sister, but I don't know if I have the strength or patience to stand by and watch her hurt herself and continue to be used like a piece of meat by these swine-like guys. I don't know. I need Your help so desperately.

A still, small voice says in me: *Beloved, remember the Samaritan?*

Yes. Thank You.

I reach over and grab the Bible off the table next to my bed, and open it to Luke 10, and read verses 30-37 to refresh my mind:

> *Jesus replied and said, "A man was going down from*
> *Jerusalem to Jericho, and fell among robbers, and they stripped him and beat him, and went away leaving him half dead. And by chance a priest was going down on that road, and when he saw him, he passed by on the other side. Likewise a Levite also, when he came to the place and saw him, passed by on the other side. But a Samaritan, who was on a journey, came upon him; and when he saw him, he felt compassion, and came to him and bandaged up his wounds, pouring oil and wine on them; and he put him on his own beast, and brought him to an inn and took care of him. On the next day he took out two denarii and gave them to the innkeeper and said, 'Take care of him; and*
> *whatever more you spend, when I return I will repay you.'*
> *Which of these three do you think proved to be a neighbor to the man who fell into the robbers' hands?"*
> *And he said, "The one who showed mercy toward him." Then Jesus said to him, "Go and do the same."*

Instantly, my mind and heart feel refreshed.

Ah, thank You and praise You, Lord. Please be with Maggie, and please help me to maintain an attitude of mercy. Oh, and please comfort and heal Grandma Dora, too. I ask this in Your name, Lord. Amen.

I sit and contemplate the parallel, how Maggie is like the man who fell among robbers and the men she sleeps with are like these robbers who strip her, and symbolically beat her and leave her for dead, and how she, too, is in need of mercy. And the phrase, "Go and do the same," keeps echoing in my mind. This portion of Scripture is applicable on so many different levels. I can barely wrap my mind around it.

A soft knock at our door pulls me out of my thoughts. "Hey guys, how's it going?" Suzette looks at Maggie and then looks to me.

"Fine, come in." I pat my bed for Suzette to come in and sit down.

"Good! I have been dying next door. Maddy, you've got to tell me who that gorgeous guy was!"

"What guy?" Maggie looks up from her word processor.

"Maddy and I bumped into this guy at Juice Stop; well, actually, he literally bumped into her! Maggie, he was so cute--" Suzette gushes.

"Wait, let me guess, tall, muscular build, shoulder-length black hair?"

"Yeah, how do you know?" Suzette looks surprised.

Maggie turns to me. "What happened? Did you finally meet him? It figures it would happen when I'm not there." She turns to Suzette. "Madeleine has had a major crush on that guy for like, forever."

"Really?" Suzette looks at me with total surprise written all over her face.

"Every time we see him at church or at her work, she freezes up like some sort of gothic statue and then bolts for the door." Maggie makes no effort to mask the edge in her voice.

"We didn't get to talk to him much," I say, trying to look and sound casual. "He was with some other guys."

"So what? Just as I thought." Maggie says with a huff. "Madeleine Winger, you are hopeless!"

Suzette and I exchange looks. "What do you expect? A marriage proposal? We were at Juice Stop. I was totally caught off guard," I say in my own defense.

Maggie rolls her eyes at me.

"I did get his name, though." I feel my cheeks start to get hot.

"Finally! And?" Maggie asks.

"His name is Peter." I try not to turn twelve shades of red, but I feel the heat in my face.

His name is Peter. Oh sigh.

Maggie looks at me for a moment, and her face softens.

"Okay ladies, tell me everything that happened, and I do mean everything!" Maggie flings herself on the end of my bed next to Suzette.

Suzette and I recount the events of the evening to Maggie, who is listening intently, like we were relaying the events of a crime scene.

"So we need a plan," Maggie says when we have finished our tale.

"Uh, no thanks, Maggie. I don't need any schemes."

"Maddy, it doesn't hurt to have a plan," Suzette says. I never thought Suzette would agree with Maggie on "man" issues. "Say, he comes into your work one night. If you have some ideas ready of what you might ask or say, maybe you won't get so nervous around him. Remember, 'without a plan, there's no attack, without attack, there's no victory!'" Suzette quotes lines from one of our favorite John Cusack movies, *One Crazy Summer*, making me laugh and shake off the tension Maggie brought on me.

"Okay, okay. I will make a list of pertinent questions to keep in my vest pocket at work in case he comes into the store," I say in surrender. "Like he would ever talk to me again. I acted like a total freak tonight."

"No, you were fine. Just shy and maybe a little mysterious. I bet he is intrigued." Suzette is so caring to try to console me.

"Ms. Winger, I am self-appointin' myself to be your fashion consultant. From now on, I will choose all your outfits for work and church, and you can *not* argue with me." Maggie jumps off my bed and starts rifling through my closet.

"Go for it, Maddy! He seems like a nice guy," Suzette says.

"Okay, Maggie the Cat," I say, completely conceding. "But no visible cleavage or short skirts. Or pastels!"

"Well that doesn't leave me much to work with, now does it?" Maggie asks, with her pencil-thin, perfectly arched eyebrows raised at me.

"Just be yourself, Maddy. He will definitely fall for you." Suzette says. She is so good-natured. I silently ask God to give her a really great guy who will treat her right.

"Oh, and hon, I will also be advisin' you on your hair and make-up. We will definitely rethink the heavy black eyeliner look."

Just then the phone rings. Maggie rushes to get it. "Hi baby," she coos into the phone, as she takes it out into the hall and closes our door behind her.

I turn to Suzette, and sigh deeply. "I'm really glad you were there with me tonight. I know if Maggie was there, she would have totally embarrassed me, or worse."

"Oh me, too! I didn't know you had a serious crush on someone."

"It's not something I'm proud of, believe me. Actually I've been fighting my feelings on the situation for a long time."

"Not to sound like Bethany, but are you sure he's a believer? I mean, he did seem to have a certain air of peace about him."

"That's the thing. After I started noticing him at my work, I happened to look over one section of seats in church one Sunday morning, and there he was, with his head bowed and his eyes closed tight. It was one of the most beautiful sights I've ever seen. That's when I knew I was in trouble. There's more to my attraction to him than just how he looks."

"That's so amazing!"

"Yeah, but sometimes I feel like such an idiot, because I think about him so much. And when I do see him in real life, I just get so flustered and panicky."

"Well, maybe since you've spoken to him now and he has spoken to you, you won't feel so nervous the next time you see him."

"That would take a miracle. I just wish I could stop thinking about him so much. I've given this whole thing over to God so many times, but in my mind and my heart, I can't seem to let go of it."

Maggie saunters back into the room and places the phone on the floor where we keep it. She goes to her lingerie drawer and starts sifting through it, considering various lacy pieces.

"What's up?" I ask casually, but I know what she is doing. She is getting ready to go out.

"Nothin' much. I'm just goin' out for a little while."

"Oh," I say. I can feel Suzette staring at me. I return her gaze with a weak smile.

"Well, ladies, I better get back to my homework. I'll talk to you later," Suzette says, trying to act casual as she gets up and heads for the door.

"Thanks for the smoothie, Suzette," I say.

"Thank you for the memorable evening. I'm glad I got to meet your future husband!" She gives me a big, cheerful grin.

"Yeah, right! As if!" I say, trying not to blush. Again.

"Hey, you know, the cowboy in this poster kinda looks like him," Suzette laughs and gently closes the door behind her.

I sit down at my desk and pray for extreme discipline so that I can stop daydreaming and start studying.

"I'm off. Don't wait up," Maggie checks her Pepto-Bismol pink sweater and lipstick in the mirror one last time and pushes her breasts higher up in her push-up bra.

"Maggie, please be safe, okay?"

"I will, Mother," she says, rolling her eyes. "Don't study too hard." She dramatically blows me a kiss and closes the door.

Oh Lord, please help...help Maggie, and help me. I so need Your help. And thank You for Suzette. In Jesus' name I pray, Amen.

Chapter Seven

"Hey Maddy, what's up? You're closing tonight, right?" Jaime asks, reaffirming his extensive knowledge of my work schedule.

"Hi Jaime," I say in my mad rush for the backroom to clock in. Miss Maggie's House of Glamour almost makes me late for work.

"Hi Leah, how's it going?" I'm so glad she is working the closing shift with me tonight.

I love working with Leah. She is the Senior Product Manager for our store, and she is laid-back, artsy, and funny, which makes her a real pleasure to work with.

She is in her mid-thirties, and reminds me a lot of the actress Dyan Cannon, with her bright smile and beautiful long blonde curly hair. Also, she is a widow.

She used to be a painter, but when her husband passed away five years ago in a motorcycle accident, she stopped painting and decided to get a job outside her home. The settlement from the drunk driver who hit and killed her husband made it so she could live modestly and not need to work, but she told me that the Lord led her to work here at the Plus to minister to us, youngsters. I'm certainly grateful for her and benefit greatly from her obedience to her calling.

She is the only other follower of Christ besides me who works in the store. I love that I get to fellowship with her while we work. I just love talking with her. She makes me feel so comfortable. She is probably the most honest, trustworthy, and wise person I have ever met.

"Madeleine, your guy was in here last night," she says, a small smile playing at the corners of her mouth. Leah knows all about my crush since she has prayed with me on the subject many times—just about every time he came into the store, I would guess.

"Oh, really?" I try to sound nonchalant.

"And he asked for you. By name." She tries to hide her little grin.

"Yeah, right." I grab the top fifty selling CD inventory sheets. We split the stack of pages in half and headed out on the sales floor.

"Honest and truly! I would never joke about such a thing," she says.

I stop and stare at her. "Seriously? He was here, and he asked for me?" My heart starts pounding hard in my chest.

"He asked…let me get this right, if 'the cute petite girl with long black hair was working, I think her name is Maddy.' And you, my dear, are the only staff person here who fits that description."

"Seriously, Leah. Don't joke about this," I say breathlessly.

"I'm quite serious. He seems very nice. Polite, good manners. And he bought a Kate Bush CD."

"No way!" Kate Bush is a British singer/songwriter, sort of obscure in the States, and is one of my all-time favorite recording artists. My mind is spinning.

"Yes way!" Leah laughs.

"Stop teasing!"

"I'm not teasing you in the least." She tries to dim her bright smile. I think she is enjoying this.

"Which one? Which CD?"

"The more mainstream one, with a picture on the cover of Kate and two dogs."

"*Hounds of Love.* Excellent choice." I start imagining him kicking back, listening to Kate.

"He asked me if I was familiar with the CD."

"What did you say?"

"I said to him, 'the young lady you had inquired about, Madeleine, is our resident Kate Bush expert, and she will be working tomorrow evening. You should stop by then, and ask her.'"

"You didn't!" I almost drop my inventory clipboard. My heart is really hammering now, like a Scottish drum corps.

"I most certainly did." She says and nonchalantly continues counting CD's.

"What did he say?"

"He smiled, and said he might just do that. Then he thanked me for my help and left."

Now I know I'm turning at least twenty shades of red. I certainly don't need the extreme amount of blush Maggie applied to my cheeks today. I'm so glad I wiped off some of it on my drive to work.

He asked for me. He actually came into the store and asked for me. *For me!* And by name. Oh my Lord, he knows my name! I feel like I'm going to explode and maybe vomit at the same time. *Okay, breathe.*

"You okay, Maddy? You look a little red?" Leah teases me.

"Oh, uh, Maggie did my make-up today. She's was a little heavy-handed with the blush," I say, trying to play down my feeling of internal combustion. "Leah, what if he really does come in tonight? What do I say to him? I bumped into to him at Juice Stop the night before last, and I acted like such a bumbling idiot."

"I'm sure you were fine, or else, he wouldn't have asked about you, now would he?" She smiles optimistically at me.

"You have a good point."

"Just be yourself, Maddy. You can never go wrong with honesty. They will find out who you really are eventually. Besides, you are a Godly, compassionate, intelligent, and funny young woman. Don't deny him the pleasure of meeting the real you."

"Oh, thanks, Leah. You are so very kind." Her compliments reassure me a little. "It's just that I get so nervous around him. I've never been like this with any other guy. Usually, I'm like, 'whatever.' But not this time."

"You *really* like this guy, don't you?"

"I'm trying not to, really I am. And it's not just because he's so gourgeous. It's too weird. I don't even know him, but I feel this really strong pull to him. What if when I finally meet him, he turns out to be some kind of a freak?"

"Then you two will get along perfectly." She smiles at me and gives me a big hug. "Hey, Maggie did a nice job on your make-up. I thought you looked a little different when you came in, a little softer, maybe."

"Maggie said she was going to throw all my black eyeliner in the big dumpster behind our dorm building."

"Well, you look very nice. I like your outfit, too. It compliments your figure."

"Thank you, and my self-esteem thanks you, too."

"That's why I'm here."

I really am grateful to Maggie for her hand in my greatly improved physical appearance. I noticed a couple of guys looking at me when I was walking from my car to the store. And Jaime keeps staring at me from the video counter. *Ugh*, he saw me looking in his direction, and now he's wandering over to the audio section of the store, where I'm now repricing the CDs that are on sale this week.

"So hows your roommate?" he asks, standing way too close to me.

"Maggie? She's fine."

"You look hot tonight." He blatantly looks me up and down. *Ewww.* "Uh, thanks."

"Hey, I looked for you guys at my show at the Whiskey the other night, but I didn't see you."

"Sorry…um…we were probably writing papers, or something."

"It's okay. I don't think Maggie's my type anyway."

"Oh, yeah…probably not…" My eyes jump to the front door every time someone walks in the store.

"Cause, uh, I think you're more my type."

Huh? What is he talking about? *Double ewww!* I've seen some of the licentious girls Jaime has hanging on his arm when he comes in on his days off. I refrain from using the modern vernacular "skank," to describe his female companions, since it's not very nice even if it is a more accurate description. *Okay, got to try to be gracious.*

"Jaime, that's, um, nice, but I'm kinda interested in someone else right now."

"Yeah, that's what I thought since you and your roommate were asking about that one dude the other night. I wasn't sure if it was you or her that wanted him. But I figured it was you since your roommate was coming on to me."

I just smile at Jaime and continue pricing CDs. Jaime's an okay guy, but he's not the brightest crayon in the box. Too much drug use, I guess.

"I could set you up with him if you want. His band practices––"

"No, no. It's okay. Thanks anyway." *Ugh.* Can you imagine how badly that would go? A line is forming at the video counter, so Jaime returns to his assigned area of the store.

Oh Lord, please help me to stop daydreaming about him, Peter (Yikes! I know his name!), and focus on doing a good job tonight. In Jesus' name I pray, Amen.

It's almost 8:30 P.M., and I've been doing tolerably well so far. I've helped Leah change the end-caps, put up a display, and helped a bunch of customers find the music they were looking for. It's good to stay busy. My mind has only strayed a few times.

But it's only one more hour and a half until closing time, and I'm starting to wonder if he is coming in tonight at all.

Stop thinking about him! Ugh!

He's probably busy, like with band practice or whatever. Or he forgot. Or maybe—he's on a date. *Oh, stop it!*

I exhale sharply and nearly drop the price gun on the sales floor as I try in vain to reload it with an unraveling roll of sticky fluorescent orange sale tags.

"Uh, hi, you're Madeleine, right?" A velvety, low male voice asks.

I paste on a smile and lay the price gun on top of the CD bin. I look up into one luminous green eye, since a thick wavy lock of black hair covers the other eye. He quickly brushes it aside and smiles at me. He has the brightest, greenest eyes I've ever seen.

Suddenly my throat tightens. B*reathe, breathe!* My stomach starts doing flip-flops. *Oh Lord, oh Lord, oh Lord…*

"Uh yes, that's me." *Brilliant response.*

"Hi, I'm Peter. Remember, I bumped into you, quite literally actually, at the Juice Stop the other night?"

I smile and nod. *As if I could ever forget!*

"I was in here last night, and the lady who was at the counter told me you were working tonight."

"Oh yeah, hi." *Another brilliant response. Idiot!* "Leah told me she told you."

"I hope that's okay."

"Yeah, totally fine." I try to swallow the panic that is constricting my throat.

"When I ran into you the other night, I didn't get a chance to talk to you."

"Um, yeah, sorry, we had to get back to school." *Think freak! How about more intelligent answers? The list of questions…what are some of them? Think!*

"Oh, where do you go to school?" he asks. He's much better at this than I am.

"Um, Biola University."

"Oh, cool. I have some friends that went there. I hear it's a great school."

"Yeah, I like it a lot." *Think…think…think!* I glance over at Leah, who discretely winks at me. "So, um, Leah said you had a question about a Kate Bush CD."

"Oh, yeah. I was wondering which of her CDs to get. A producer friend of mine recommended her music. I bought *Hounds of Love.*"

"Good choice. What do you think of it?" *There you go…relax, be cool…*

"It's unusual, but I really like it. I like her voice and all the unique instrumentation on the album. It's a lot different than what I usually listen to, which is mostly hard rock."

"Yeah, Kate is an acquired taste, but I just love her. I think my favorite CD of hers is *The Dreaming*. It's so strange, I love it. It drives my roommate crazy, though. She doesn't get it."

"Hmmm, I'll have to pick that one up, too. So what else do you recommend?" I've never before had a guy look me in the eye—and not at my chest—when he's talking to me. It's a little unnerving, but I like it.

He smiles at me with his perfectly straight white teeth behind his lovely full lips. He looks to be in his mid to late twenties, but speaks and carries himself like a guy who is mature beyond his years. His skin is deeply tanned, making his brilliant green eyes that much brighter. *Sigh.*

"Are you in the market for some more unusual music, or something more mainstream?" I ask, trying to shake the dazed enamored feeling that consumes me.

"What are some of your favorites?" He is smiling at me. It's almost paralyzing.

"Hmm...let me think. Perhaps something with a Latin flavor?" I say with my best over-the-top sales girl voice. "Here's the latest release from Los Tigres Del Norte." It's on the top of the stack of CD's I'm pricing. He laughs. *Yes!*

"Hmm, it looks interesting, but I'm a little intimidated by their costumes. My band could never pull off matching spandex cowboy suits," he says.

Such a quick sense of humor! I'm severely swooning inside. "Well, okay then," I say, smiling back at him, trying to remain calm. "Hmm...how about Soundgarden's *Superunknown*? It's one of my favorites."

"Got it. Love it. Great songs. And Chris Cornell is an awesome singer."

"Sarah McLachlan's *Fumbling Toward Ecstasy*?"

"Have it also. Love her songwriting." He has a Sarah CD in his possession. I'm really falling now.

"Well, let's see...Oh, I know. Dean Martin's Greatest Hits."

"Seriously?" He chuckles.

"Talk about great singers. He was one of the best. You'll start craving Italian food after listening to it for a while, though."

"Mmm, nothing wrong with that. What does the roommate think about this CD?"

"She hates it."

"Then I'll take." As I hand him the CD with my slightly shaking hands, I notice his strong hands, the shiny calluses on the fingertips of his left hand, his thick ropey forearms, the way his T-shirt stretches across his muscular chest...*STOP it!* I quickly look down at the other CDs, as if I'm checking their alphabetization.

He takes a deep breath, runs his free hand through the front of his hair, and then shoves his hand in the front pocket of his jeans. He clears his throat and looks at me a little awkwardly.

"Maddy?" he asks. *My name never sounded so beautiful.* "I was wondering if you'd like to go with me for coffee sometime."

"Sure." I squeak. *YES! YES! YES! A thousand times, yes! Okay, be cool...*

"How about Saturday night?"

"I'm working until 6 P.M., but I'm free after that." *I could quit my job, quit school, so I would be free sooner...*

"Great, I'll pick you up here?"

"Yes." And I nod since I can't actually get any additional coherent words out. My head is spinning. My internal organs feel like they are doing an Olympic gymnastics floor exercise.

"Can I have your number just in case, you know, I muster up the courage to get that Latin CD? Well then, I'll be able to call you to hold it for me," he jokes. He smiles and exhales deeply.

"Yeah, sure," I say, trying in vain to stifle my very girly giggle at his joke.

I try not to be conscious of my backside as he follows me over to the audio counter. This skirt has always been a little clingy on me. No wonder Maggie picked it.

He pays for the CD, and we exchange phone numbers. He is smiling at me the whole time. *Sigh.*

"I've got to get going. I'll get a major ribbing from the guys if I'm late to practice. I'll see you Saturday."

"Yeah, see you Saturday." I watch him walk out the door, and climb into a black late model SUV. Through the glass windows on the side of the audio counter, I can see he is opening the CD he just bought, and he puts it in his CD player.

After a few moments, he laughs. He waves to me before he turns to back out of the parking space. I wave back, feeling a little dopey for watching him. I'm a little light-headed, too. I look over at Leah across the sales floor. She is beaming at me.

How awesome is this? Not only did I meet and talk to him, my huge crush, but we are going out on a date. An actual real live date! This ought to finally silence Maggie's criticism of my slowness with this guy.

Leah slides up next to me. "I take it by your glowing countenance that things went well?"

"He's so nice. I feel like I'm floating on cloud nine. He asked me out. We're going out. Together. Saturday night!" I can almost not contain my giddiness.

"Oh, I'm so happy for you, sweetie!" Leah gives me a big hug. She would have made such a good mom.

Lord, I'm so grateful for her. Thank You. And thank You for my date with Peter. Please help me to not make a fool of myself or do something totally embarrassing Saturday night. Thank You. Thank You so much.

Chapter Eight

"The Freedom of Information Act was a..." *I wonder how it's physically possible for a guy to have such vibrantly green eyes like his...ugh! Stop thinking about him! Focus, focus.* I hold down the delete key to start fresh and stare blankly at my laptop screen. "Journalists around the globe would unite in unanimous agreement that the Freedom of..." *I wonder if my new burgundy lace blouse would be okay to wear Saturday night...*

"Hey Maddy, are you busy?" Suzette pops her head in the doorway.

"Come in, please! Save me from the throws of horrendously dull paper writing. I'm trying to compose an insightful and compelling twenty-page paper on the constitutionality of the Freedom of Information Act. But, I'm not sure it's humanly possible."

"Yikes! Good luck with that." Suzette sits down on my bed. "Where's Maggie? I thought she has a lot of papers to write, too?"

"Who knows. Probably out with some guy. I've hardly seen her in the past few days."

"Won't she lose her scholarship if her grades drop?"

"Don't know. The big question is, will she graduate. Her dad will *kill* her if she doesn't, in a pastor-like sort of way, of course."

"At least you get some peace and quiet when she's gone. Bethany is constantly on the phone. Sometimes I think I want to rip our phone right out of the wall."

"Does Chad call a lot?"

"Mostly it's Bethany calling Chad, and talking to him for hours and hours."

"Yuck."

"You said it. It makes it so hard to study sometimes."

"Well, even with Maggie gone, I still can't concentrate on my schoolwork." A wide smile spreads across my face, and I can't contain the little girly giggle that escapes from me.

Suzette's eyes light up. "Spill it, Maddy!" She knows me so well.

"Oh, there's not much to tell, just that at work tonight, I got asked out on date." I try to sound nonchalant.

"With the hunky Juice Stop guy?"

"Yes! Can you believe it?" The excitement makes me giggle again.

"That is so awesome! Why didn't you tell me?"

"I kinda wanted Maggie to hear it first."

"When did he ask you? What happened? Details!" She grabs one of the pillows from my bed and hugs it to her chest.

I relay the whole stunning event to Suzette, wishing Maggie was here, too. I'm starting to miss her.

"That's so cool! God is so good! I'm so happy for you." Suzette says at the conclusion of my story.

"Thanks. I still can't believe I actually talked to him, let alone the fact that he asked me out. I'm stunned. I just hope I don't act like a stuttering idiot on our date."

"You are going to have a great time. Think positive."

"He's such a nice guy. I'm trying not to fall too hard for him and to keep a level head about the whole thing."

"That must be tough."

"I'm trying, but I don't think I'm succeeding very well. Ever since I got home from work, my imagination has been on overload. I shudder to think if I ran any red lights on the drive home. Me dating is a menace to society!" I say. Suzette joins me in a big laugh.

"I'm sure you were fine."

"Yeah, no victims of love yet," I say, and we both laugh. "I keep telling myself it's no big deal. Yeah right!"

I still can't believe I'm going on a date with him, my Adonis, Peter. *Sigh.* I better calm down or else a huge zit is bound to erupt on my forehead, or the end of my nose, before Saturday night.

Suddenly, there's a sound that can only be described as banshee-like shrieks of hysteria coming from down the hall. They are progressively growing louder.

"Omigosh you guys!" Janelle pops her head in my doorway. "Bethany just got engaged!"

Oh, creeping crud. A wave of sadness washes over Suzette's face. Her posture looks like her whole body has caved inward.

"You okay?" I ask her. "You can stay in here if you want."

"I knew this was coming sooner or later." She heaves a heavy sigh. "I'd so love to stay in here tonight, but I'd better get back to my room and put on my happy face, and go congratulate the bride-to-be." I hug Suzette tightly. She's such a trooper.

"Come on over if you need a break from Wedding Land."

"Thanks." Suzette stops at the doorway. "Maddy, I'm really happy for you, and your date with your juicy Juice Stop guy. Peter, right? Really, I am. I have a good gut feeling about you two. Way more than I do about Bethany and Chad."

I know what she means. There's always been something not right about Chad. Kind of lecher-like. Just the way he looks at girls is disgusting. I ran into him out on the track one warm evening last spring while I was walking with Suzette. He blatantly looked me up and down, like he's never seen a girl in a tank top and shorts before.

And whenever he calls Maggie, it's always late at night, like after midnight, which I know is way past Bethany's bedtime. I know Chad and Maggie are both sociology majors, so his calls are probably not about anything they couldn't discuss in their classes, instead of during a late night phone call.

Now wait a minute…*Oh no.* No. No. No! I've never really given this whole situation much mental attention before. Maggie is such a chronic flirt with every male she comes across, I figured she was just playing with Chad. But oh good grief, Maggie is actually sleeping with him. With Chad. The Super-boyfriend. *Ewww. Double and triple yuck-o-rama.*

Why would she do that? And why didn't Maggie tell me? Maybe she was too embarrassed. Why would she want to sleep with Chad? He's such a letch. And a weasel. And now Bethany is engaged to him. Oh, poor girl. I'm not exactly the biggest Bethany fan, but man, I feel sorry for her. But like Suzette, I figure the nice thing to do is amble next door with forced enthusiasm and offer my condolences—I mean congratulations.

When I poke my head in their doorway, Bethany has her left hand extended out for everyone to get a good look at her engagement ring, a highly prized adornment amongst most of these girls. She is absolutely beaming. I've never seen her so happy. She has no idea her beloved fiancé has been unfaithful with my roommate, one of her least favorite people on campus.

This whole situation is starting to make my brain hurt, worse than writing my twenty-page paper does. This is not the kind of information I want to have freedom to roam around inside my head, that's for sure. I wish Maggie was home. I would love to give her the third degree regarding this matter. And to see her reaction to their engagement.

"Madeleine! I'm going to be Mrs. Chadwick Robert Hensley."

"Congratulations Bethany, that's so cool." I'm such a bad liar. "Have you guys set a date yet?"

"Not yet. We are thinking in the spring after graduation."

"Oh, that'll be nice," I say flatly, my forced enthusiasm waning drastically.

"I need to get your address, so I can mail you a wedding invitation. Oh, and I need Maggie's address too!"

"Oh, that's so nice of you." I try not to cringe with my head so full of unpleasant information. I watch Suzette to make sure she is surviving this travesty.

"Well, you two have been here through our whole courtship," Bethany beams. "I've just got to have M & M at my wedding!"

I can only imagine what a train wreck this wedding will be, especially if Maggie attends, and she probably will show-up dressed to kill, flaunting her best skin tight dress with a plunging neckline just to make Chad squirm like the rabid weasel he is. But poor Bethany. Man, this is not good.

"Okay, I'll get our addresses to you," I say, desperately wanting to escape this room as quickly as possible. "Well, um, I better get back to my homework. My papers aren't going to write themselves. Congrats again."

I glance over at Suzette again before I turn to leave. She is sitting on Bethany's bed, next to a big stack of new bridal magazines. Her eyes are glazed with tears, but she is smiling brightly at Bethany.

Oh Lord, please help her through all this. She is such a kind-hearted person. Please cover her with Your grace, and give her a heaving extra helping of patience. Please help her remember Jeremiah 29:11, especially the part about how You have a good plan for her, to give her a future and a hope. And please help Bethany with…oh Lord, I'm not sure what to pray here. And though this is really hard for me to ask, please work in Chad, too. Please help. And please help Maggie. Please, please, please help Maggie. In Jesus' name I pray, Amen.

Chapter Nine

This has got to be the slowest Saturday of my entire life. Even with the major concert ticket sale taking up most of this morning, the day is still crawling along. And to top it off, Jaime is working the audio counter with me. His constant staring and flirting is starting to get on my nerves.

But I'm grateful that the Jimmy Buffet fans are entertaining. I mean, who gets drunk at 10 A.M. and goes to buy tickets for a concert? At least they don't care where their seats are, so there is no twenty minute search through the Ticketmaster computer looking for better seats with the seating chart for the venue, which in this case is the Irvine Meadows Amphitheater.

I wonder who the designated driver is for these two guys I'm helping right now, because neither one of them looks nor smells anywhere close to sober enough to drive.

"Whoa yeah! Just put us on the lawn! Hey, wanna come with us?" One of the inebriated guys asks me.

"Uh, no thanks." I have images of a vast sea of Hawaiian shirts, spilled alcohol everywhere and pools of vomit.

"Your loss, dudette!" They drop wads of cash on the counter, which I straighten out and try not to gag, since all the bills are beyond moist. Note to self: wash hands after this transaction. I read off the tickets to them, and then they scribble their initials on the back, as mandated by Ticketmaster policy and procedures.

"Dude! We're there! Woohoo! *Margaritaville* here we come!" They barely high five each other, and stagger out the door still whooping in celebration.

Sometimes I wonder how I can possibly be of use to God in this job, given the state of some of the customers. Then He brings me situations that help me understand why I'm here.

"You look really cute today," Jaime says, as he saunters up way too close behind me.

"Uh, thanks." *Ewww.*

"You got a hot date tonight or something?"

I can feel his breath in my hair. He needs a mint. Badly. *Okay, be nice. You can deal with him without being mean or rude.* "Something like that." I say, stepping away from him.

"Who's the guy? Not that freaky black-haired guitar player dude?"

"That's the one."

"What's he gonna do, take you out for some grub, and then back to his place to show you his 'guitar collection?'"

Okay, so here's where I really want to make some snide remark about how that must be Jaime's trademark move with girls, but something inside me tells me to take the higher road. "No, we're just going for coffee. And there will be no going back to his place."

"Oh yeah, at least not tonight. You don't want to give it up too fast, right?"

"No. I won't be 'giving it up' at all. I don't do stuff like that anymore."

"Oh, that's right. I forgot you're a good little church girl. Well, that hasn't stopped some of the girls I've been with in the past, like you're roommate."

WHAT? "What do you mean?" I ask through gritted teeth.

"Easy, I'm just, ya know, using her as an example."

"Please don't."

"I'm just saying, like the song says, '*Good girls don't, but I do!*'"
He sings badly. "Well, I really don't."

"That's a shame." Jaime gives me what I think may be his attempt at bedroom eyes. *Ewwwwww! Disgusting! As if!*

"No, the shame would be to give in, and 'give it up,' as you so eloquently put it."

"I bet Super-Stud, or whatever his name is, doesn't feel that way."

"I bet he does." *I really hope he does.*

"What's the big deal? It's just a little push-push, the horizontal mambo, knockin' boots. It's just sex."

"My days of being used like some piece of meat are over. Besides, I don't purposely do things that would grieve my Savior, or do anything that would hurt my relationship with Him."

"Hey man, that's cool. Whatever." Jaime backs away from me, rolling his eyes.

Leah comes out of the back room holding a stack of inventory pages on a clip board. "Is Jaime bothering you? I could have him pull some over stock."

"No, he's okay. I don't think he will be talking to me much anymore."

Leah looks a little puzzled, and then smiles big at me. "Good girl. I've been praying for him lately. He's been asking me questions about God."

"Seriously?"

"Yes, so if you and Maggie could remember him in your prayers that would be great."

"I will, especially since my prayer for him to stop flirting with me and to leave me alone was just answered." I say, and Leah laughs.

"Here, this will help pass the time until your big date," she says, smiling at me. "And I could really use your extensive musical knowledge in this category." She hands me a clip-board with the Classical CD inventory sheets attached to it.

I'm the only staff person in the store with any inkling of knowledge about classical music, thanks to Dr. Bill. My mother has an intense disliking of classical music, so on select Sunday afternoons, Dr. Bill would take me instead of her to the Dorothy Chandler Pavilion to hear the Los Angeles Philharmonic perform his favorite pieces of music. He would do his best to try to explain what we were going to hear and who the composer was. I was only nine or ten, but I really loved it.

"Thanks! I need something else to focus on, other than the clock," I say as I take the clipboard from her. So I dig into the product inventory, as I reminisce on the fun I used to have going on my musical dates with Dr. Bill.

But the inventory only distracts me for a little while. Slowly my thoughts of the present sneak into my mind. When is six o'clock going to come? I feel like I'm going to get carpal tunnel from twisting my wrist so often to read my watch.

Truthfully, I'm a little apprehensive about this date. Okay, mega anxiety has set in. I keep replaying in my mind the night he asked me out, to make sure I heard him right, and that he really *did* ask me out. I'm such a dork!

At five-thirty, Zelda on the closing shift comes up to relieve me of my audio and Ticketmaster duties.

"Hi Maddy! Leah sent me up here a little early, so you would have enough time to count out your drawers and be able to get out of here on time." She nudges me twice in the side and smiles at me slyly, as she twirls a long piece of her bright purple hair with her fingers and pops her gum.

"Thanks." Leah is so sweet. I'm not the only one she is so considerate with. She treats the whole crew so well.

"Sooo, is he picking you up here? I've seen him in here a couple times. I think he is so fine! My friend Gracie and I saw his band play on the Sunset Strip a couple weeks ago. She has a huge crush on the drummer. I think his name is Caleb. She met him at the Guitar Center in West Covina a couple weeks ago when she was picking out a new strap for her electric guitar. That's when he gave her tickets to their show. I'm not really a hard rock fan, but the songs were pretty good, and he is a really good guitar player. Are they a Christian band? The lyrics sounded like it. It was cool anyway."

"Zelly, by any chance did you stop at Starbucks on your way to work?"

"Yes, I did...why do you ask? Am I talking too fast again? I think the guy with the black spiked hair likes me. He was *very* generous with the double shots of espresso I ordered. Anyway, I hope you two have a great time tonight!"

"Yeah, me too." We finish logging out the computers, and I quickly pick up my cash drawers and head across the store to the back room to count them out. As I walk by the front door, I noticed a black SUV pull into the parking lot. It's him! He's early! My heart starts beating double time, and my palms are starting to sweat. I quicken my pace and I almost run Jaime over in my rush to get to the backroom.

"Whoa! Where's the fire?" he asks, smirking at me.

"Sorry." I mumble as I dodge him and rush to the backroom.

My mouth is so dry. Judging by my racing pulse, you'd think this is my first date ever. I try to slow my breathing and steady my shaking hands. *Oh Lord, please help me calm down, and be normal.*

I finally finish closing everything out with five minutes to spare. I look out the security window and notice Jaime is talking to him. *Oh no!* The conversation seems amicable, Peter (I love it that I actually know his name now!) doesn't look mad or anything. Jaime is pointing to the "P" section of the Rock CD bins. Good, they must be talking about music. Man, does Peter look good tonight! He's not wearing anything different than what he normally wears, but he just looks so gorgeous. I can't believe this guy is here to take *me* out.

Leah approaches them, and Jaime returns to the audio counter. *Thank you Leah, and thank You Lord.* Peter is smiling (*sigh*), and so is Leah. I wonder what they are talking about. I run to the bathroom to make one last inspection of my appearance. And to say a quick prayer.

Chapter Ten

"Hey there, you look beautiful," Peter smiles and looks directly into my eyes. I could get used to this. "You're hair looks really nice."

I try not to appear too astonished at his compliment. Since Maggie and her glamour guidance are missing in action right now, I had to do my own hair, make-up and outfit selection. I guess I did okay. "Thanks, so do you." I say. And he does. Believe me.

"You two have a good time tonight." Leah smiles at us.

"Thanks Leah, we will." He opens the front door of the store for me. He also opens the car door for me, too. He's such a gentleman.

When Peter starts the engine, Kate Bush starts to play from the CD player. Not just any Kate CD, but my favorite. I'm *so* in love right now. I think I'm in big trouble. BIG trouble.

"Oh, '*Night of the Swallow*,' one of my favorite Kate songs. So you picked up *The Dreaming*. Nice." I say, trying not to gush.

"You said it was your favorite." Peter says with a sweet smile.

I swear I'm going to melt right here and now. "Um, so how do you like it?"

"It's cool, very different. I like the song about Houdini."

He really listened to the whole CD, since *Houdini* is the next to last song on the album.

"I love that one, too. I love the idea that before every magic trick, Houdini's wife would pass him the key to the locks on the chains that bound him, through her kiss."

"Yeah, that's a really original topic for a song."

I look over at Peter, and I want to pinch myself. I can't believe I'm actually sitting here, in his car, and we are actually having a real conversation, and not one of my made up daydreams.

"Um, this is a nice truck." *That's all you can think to say? Think!*

"Thanks. I've always owned Toyotas. The 4-Runner works great for me because I can haul all my gear to gigs, and it's protected inside the back."

"That's cool. I have a Toyota, too. A black Corolla."

"With the Peter Murphy and Concrete Blonde stickers and the Biola University bumper sticker?" he asks.

"Yeah, that's me."

"I noticed it in the parking lot. I thought it might be your car."

"I've had that car since my junior year of high school. My stepdad was none too pleased when I put the stickers on it. I'd take them off, but they help me find my car in parking lots, ya know? Especially at church."

"Leah told me you go to Calvary Chapel Chino Hills. I go there, too. Which service do you go to?"

"Second service always. I'm not a morning person."

"Me too. On both accounts. I'm bummed I've never seen you there."

"My roommate Maggie and I are usually late. And she usually wants to leave when the closing worship song starts."

"Maybe we can sit together sometime if your roommate doesn't mind."

Yes! Yes! Yes! "I would like that. I've been sitting by myself lately because Maggie hasn't come with me in a couple of weeks."

"Why?" He looks genuinely concerned.

"I don't know. I haven't really spoken to her in a while. She gets in really late, and she's usually gone by the time I get back to our room from my morning classes. I don't even know if she is going to her classes."

"That doesn't sound good. Skipping church and skipping school. So I take it you don't see her on the weekends, either."

"No, mostly because I've been spending the last few weekends house-sitting at my mom's house in Chino Hills while she and my stepdad are in Europe, so I don't know what Maggie does on the weekends. Sometimes I call her to see how she's doing, but she's never there."

"That's a bummer." He pauses, as if he's contemplating the situation. "So I take it then, the girl you were with at Juice Stop is not your roommate?"

"No, that's Suzette. She's lived in the dorm room next to mine since our freshman year."

"What year are you in now?" he asks.

"Senior. My last year. Actually, it's kinda scary. Graduation day is getting closer and closer, and I still have no idea what I want to do." *Blah, blah, blah...I'm sure he finds this information riveting.*

"I'm sure you'll find your way. God's got a plan for you."

"True, so true."

Yes! I love that he is talking about God. Um, um, um...so what do I say next? I don't want to whine anymore about my fear of the future. Ask him about his schooling. Oh, good idea.

"So, do you go to school?"

"I went to the Musicians' Institute in Hollywood a few years ago. That was enough school for me. I admire you for doing the whole four-year thing."

"Thanks, but the Musician Institute sounds far more intriguing. How was it?"

"I learned a lot, mostly stuff about the music business. I wish I had learned more about songwriting. I guess that's why I've been listening to great songwriters from a lot of different styles of music lately."

"Learning your craft by immersion?"

"Something like that."

"I know people at Biola who have learned languages that way, so it must work."

"I'll let you know if it works for songwriting." He smiles at me. "Okay, so tell me more about Madeleine." He grins at me as he drives.

"Like what?" I return his grin.

"Uh, what's your favorite movie?"

"Just about anything with John Cusack in it."

"Including *Better Off Dead*?"

"'*It has raisins in it…you like raisins.*'" He laughs at my imitation of the nutty mom character in the movie.

"Oh no way! I love that movie. Ok, ok, what about *One Crazy Summer*?"

"Oh totally! It's the sequel that completes the hilarious tale of teenage angst."

"The mock Godzilla scene is p

"Yes! I love the overzealous Boy Scout dad. *Without a plan, there's no attack, without an attack, there's no victory'*…or something like that. Suzette and I quote that all the time."

"I love that character, too! I like when he's teaching a group of kids about first aid, and he tells them that in the event of an emergency they should be prepared to jam someone's eye back in the socket with a stick or something. That makes me laugh every time." His easy laughter and stunning smile are intoxicating. "So what about Monty Python?"

"'*What, you mean the curtains?…but Father I don't want it!*'" I loosely quote in my best British accent. Now I really have him laughing.

"*Holy Grail*, one of my favorites! I've never met a woman with the same taste in movies as me." He smiles and looks over at me.

All I can do is smile back at him and revel in the moment. Things are going really well. I'm way beyond smitten with this guy. I'm still stunned that I'm actually on a date (that's going awesomely) with the guy I've had a crush on for so long.

"Okay, what else?" Peter glances at me.

"About me?"

"Yeah."

"Um, I don't like nuts in my ice cream."

Not that I'm trying to be obscure, but that's all I can think of at the moment.

"Not even in Rocky Road or on banana splits?"

"Nope."

"Hmm, I don't know about that; it just seems un-American," he teases.

"See, it's a texture thing. Ice cream is all smooth and creamy, and then you're left with this crunchy, kind of gunky stuff in your teeth. It's all wrong. Texture is so important when it comes to food, especially ice cream."

"I see your point. But how do chunks of chocolate fair in your texture edict?"

"Oh well, chocolate. Chocolate is a whole other story. Chocolate provides excellent flavor and texture in a good way, and then it just melts in your mouth."

"Oh, I see. So then I'm guessing you are okay with Ben and Jerry's *Cherries Garcia*. Am I right?"

"You are so right. I could eat a whole pint all by myself and gladly endure the brain freeze headache and ice cream overdose stomachache afterward."

"I love that ice cream. The chunks of dark chocolate in it are so awesome."

"Oh, dark chocolate. Mmmm…my favorite." Peter and dark chocolate, what an almost divine combination.

"It rocks," Peter smiles.

"But other kinds of chocolate are okay, too." I add.

"Yeah, we wouldn't want to be too exclusive."

"Definitely."

He is smiling so brightly. I can't help but beam myself. I hope he's feeling even a fraction of the excitement that I feel right now.

We pull into the parking lot of the coffeehouse and park. *"Brewed of Vipers*...I love it! Very clever name for a coffeehouse. Our coffeehouse on campus at Biola is called *Common Grounds." Like he really cares! Ugh.*

"That's funny. I like the play on words. Josiah, the owner of this place, told me he always joked with his friends when he was in Bible college that if he were to ever open a coffeehouse, he would call it 'Brewed of Vipers,' because he likes that part in Matthew where Jesus is chastising the people who put more emphasis on religious rules than righteousness."

Peter circles the crowded shopping center parking lot, looking for a place to park. I like how he stops to let pedestrians in the parking lot pass in front of his vehicle. He has such good manners. I usually speed through, nearly running people over because they're in my way. And I'm the one with the Christian bumper stickers. I'm feeling more than a little convicted now.

He finally finds a parking space and pulls in. I unclick my seat belt and start to open the door.

"Stay here. Let me get that," Peter motions to the door.

He comes around and opens the car door for me and holds out his hand to help me out of his SUV. I take his hand which engulfs mine. His hand is rough and warm. Nice.

He grips my hand firmly as I climb down out of his truck. I'm so glad he has running boards. Getting out of a 4-Runner gracefully in a slightly above-the-knee pencil skirt would have been a very tricky maneuver without them.

He presses the lock and closes the door for me. I resist the urge to take his hand again as we walk the short distance to the coffeehouse. I don't want to scare him off by being too forward. It's funny, I remember a time when I would consider whether or not I was going to sleep with a guy on a first date, and now here I am contemplating if holding his hand is too much. I like it, though. It's definitely a nice change.

Peter looks down at me and smiles. He shoves his hands into the front pocket of his jeans. I wonder if he is thinking the same thing.

"My friend's band is doing an acoustic set here, tonight," he breaks the slightly awkward moment.

"Oh, good. I love live music."

"Really? Well then maybe you would like to see my band play sometime."

"I'd like that." *I really would!* I also like that he has invited me somewhere in the future. Yes!

He opens the door to the coffeehouse for me. I've never been out with a guy who is such a perfect gentleman. Never. I know he's older than any of the other guys I've gone out with before, but still. I don't think age would refine any of those guys in the manners department. *Oh Lord, please help me not to ruin things with this guy. He seems really great.*

"Cephas! How goes thee?" asks the guy behind the counter. He and Peter clasp hands in a high handshake and then a quick back-slapping hug.

His head is shaved, and his face is framed with thick dark brown brows and a dark brown goatee that reaches to the middle of his chest and is bound with elastics at about one-inch intervals. He also has a large silver ring through the septum of his nose, and both arms are completely sleeved in brightly colored tattoos.

He is a good six inches shorter than Peter, but he seems to have a personality that fills more space around him than his physical stature.

"Awesome, man, awesome," Peter grins. "Josiah, meet Madeleine. Madeleine, this is Josiah, the owner of this fine establishment."

"Ah, the fair maiden, Madeleine. Welcome to our humble house of java."

He shakes my hand gently; his large almond-shaped eyes gleaming with friendly warmth. His jovial countenance gives him a youthfulness that seems to defy his age, which I'm guessing is somewhere around the early to mid-thirties.

"Thank you," I say softly.

I feel my shyness kick it up a notch, as I notice a couple tables of people looking at us, at me, mostly. At least they all look friendly for the most part. I get the feeling Peter comes here a lot, and knows most of these people.

And I don't blame him. I would come here a lot, too. The shop has a large floor to ceiling glass wall on one side. The other walls are painted a deep blood red, and are covered with folk art with sacred themes, and the book shelves are filled with books of various shapes and sizes. I spy many copies of various translations of the Bible. There is a small stage in the corner, with many brightly colored hand-painted wooden tables and chairs set around it, and throughout the rest of the shop.

The heady aroma of freshly brewed coffee is so soothing. The self-titled Jars of Clay album is playing, one of my all-time favorite CDs. I love it here. I feel myself begin to relax a little. I had no idea this place was so close to my work.

"Madeleine goes to Biola," Peter tells Josiah. By Josiah's slight nod, I get the feeling Josiah already knows this about me.

"Excellent, I went to Biola, too, some years ago. Actually, I studied at Talbot Seminary, until God called me to open this place." Josiah looks me in the eyes as he speaks. I'm so loving this. "What can I get you two this evening?"

We order two iced coffees and a couple blueberry scones (which Peter pays for—consistently a gentleman), and we head toward an empty table by the front of the stage. Peter greets a few people on the way, and introduces me to them. He pulls out a chair for me at the table.

"So does Josiah always call you 'Cephas'?"

"Usually. The first time he called me that, I was like, 'dude, my name is Peter.' And he said 'that's what I said, Cephas.' Then I just looked at him like he was nuts. And then he started laughing, and explained to me that 'Cephas' is the Greek translation of 'Peter' and which actually means 'stone' and that is what Jesus changed Simon Peter's name to. I probably should have known that, but I didn't."

"I like it. I think you should consider changing it legally."

"You think so? It sort of sounds like the name of a guy who would play in a folk group, or a beatnik experimental jazz trio."

"It does, doesn't it? But he would only go by the one name. No last name. Just 'Cephas,' and he would add like a finger snap after he says it." I wave my arm and snap.

"But of course. Every time he says his name."

"Well, yeah. I think you should go for it," I smirk at him.

"Hmm, somehow I just don't think I could make that seem authentic."

"No?"

"No, probably not. It just wouldn't feel, I don't know, natural," he feigns deep consideration. "I don't think I could pull off the required beret and goatee that go with the name and finger snap."

"Oh well then, definitely not."

I can't help but smile broadly at him. I've never been able to joke around with a guy so easily as this. I'm so loving it.

"Seriously though, my friend's band is playing at seven if you would like to stay and hear them. They are an acoustic trio," he returns my smile.

"Only if they are an acoustic beatnik experimental jazz trio, who wear berets, and snap their fingers after they tell you their single-name monikers." *Oh no! I can't turn the sarcasm off.* I shake my head a little as if to reset my mind. "I would love to stay and see your friend's band. What's their music like?"

"Just acoustic guitar, upright bass, and a cocktail drum kit, like they used in the forties and fifties. They have a rockabilly sound, only acoustical. If you can imagine Brian Setzer or the Stray Cats. It's a great sound. They do a great version of 'Stray Cat Strut.' They're a really tight band."

"Sounds good already."

"I played with them a couple of times because they wanted to add another guitar player. They wanted me to play electric guitar, so I brought my 1959 Guild Bluesbird." His green eyes glimmer as he talks about his guitar. "I would've brought a Gretsch with me like the guitars Brian Setzer plays; that would've been sweet, but since I don't have one, I didn't. Those guitars are way out of my budget range."

I love that his face totally lights up when talks about music. His passion makes me swoon a little more. "Why did you stop playing with them?"

"My playing style is not right for their sound. I'm more of a straightforward rock player. I think you have that kind of rockabilly style in your blood, or else it just doesn't sound right. It needs to be genuine. And not to mention, I definitely don't look or dress the part. So, I gratefully declined their offer to play with them. It was a lot of fun, though. They're great guys."

"I'm excited to see them. They sound interesting. I really love live music of any kind." *Didn't I already say that earlier?* I'm such a goof.

"Oh really? You really like music, eh? Well, I know a guy who's in this hard rock band that I think you would like..." He is smiling at me so sweetly. *Oh, sigh.*

Then his face goes serious as if he caught himself flirting with me. I liked his little flirtatious comment and wish I could tell him so.

"Hmmm, so you're actively recruiting groupies, are you?" I try to give him a stern, serious look, which is really difficult to do when pure joy is bubbling up from your soul.

For a moment, he looks mortified, and then he breaks into a big grin. "You're quick. I'm going to need that coffee to keep up with your wit. I like that."

Our eyes lock together. I hope I'm not really turning the variety of shades of pink and red that I feel I am, like the swatch book from an interior decorator. Peter quickly looks away. Could he be feeling the spark of a connection with me that I'm feeling with him?

"So what are you majoring in?" he clears his throat.

"Communication, with a Journalism emphasis."

"So you'd like to do something in the journalism field?"

"Not really. But it seemed like the direction God was steering me. I think it's an ambiguous enough major that I could use in any job. And I'm learning a lot about writing, which I really love."

"That sounds like a good plan. You have to do what you love. I think that's really important. Me, I'm not much of a wordsmith. I always struggle with writing lyrics. Good lyrics, that is."

"You could do it. It just takes practice."

"Thanks for your vote of confidence," he smiles at me. "So, what kinds of stuff have you written?"

"I've published a few articles in *The Chimes*, our school newspaper, but I'm not much of a journalist. I'd rather be writing fiction. I'm much more proficient with the imagination than reality. I love writing short stories. I've been doing it since I was a little kid."

I feel like I'm rambling, but I'm encouraged by his rapt attention to what I'm saying. I'm so not used to this with guys.

"I'd love to read some of your stories," he says, leaning in, resting his cheek on his hand.

"Only if I get to hear some of your music," I shoot back at him.

"It's a deal," he is smiling at me again.

Josiah brings our order over to our table, even though I spot a waitress straightening the coffee condiments table. He gives Peter a gentle slap on the back as he leaves.

"So I take it you two are buddies?"

"Josiah has been sort of a mentor for me for almost a year now. Ever since I came in here to fill in on guitar for a friend, the guy whose band is playing tonight. I brought a girl with me that night who was dressed in a very short skirt and a way too low-cut top. Not what you would call a nice church-going gal, I guess. And it was pretty evident by the way she spoke and acted and, of course, dressed. You know, not leaving much to the imagination."

"Yes, I know the kind. My roommate Maggie is one of those girls who thinks modesty is the name of a feminine protection product."

He lets out a loud, short laugh. *Yes!* "Anyway, after the gig that night, I talked with Josiah for a while until the girl I brought got really annoyed and made no bones about showing me how displeased she was with having to participate in a discussion that she was not the center of. So I had to break-off my conversation with Josiah to take her home."

"Did you actually stop the car when you dropped her off, or did you just slow down and then push her out?" I ask, hoping he gets that I'm kidding.

"I may have done a kind of rolling stop with a subtle shove for good measure." He gets it. *Yes!*

"Nice. She's lucky," I stifle a girly giggle. "So, what were you and Josiah talking about?" I'm so nosy.

"We were having an awesome time of fellowship. He was telling me everything I needed to hear. He was talking about not being lukewarm in our relationship with Christ, and how damaging it is to let any kind of compromise creep into our lives."

"That's awesome."

Can you imagine such great guys talking about such a great topic? I wish I had been there and not this other girl.

"Yeah, I really needed to hear everything he was saying. I was the Compromise King at the time, as you can tell by the kind of girls I was dating. I was really mixed up. I was not really going to church that much, just once in a while when I would start to feel too guilty about all the stuff I was doing." .

"Yikes," I'm so loving this deep, honest conversation.

I can so relate, but I can't bring myself to admit it to him. It feels so surreal that this beautiful man, whom I've had a crush on for so long, is pouring his heart out to me. I love his genuineness, sincerity, and humility. His telling me all this on our first date is awesome and rare. I think I'm really falling hard for this guy.

"So Josiah invited me to a men's accountability group he has here on Tuesday nights. It's so great. I've learned so much. Then I started coming in on other days to hang out with him and fellowship. Then I asked him if he would mentor me to help me from straying away from God, and he wholeheartedly agreed. So he's been discipling me ever since."

"That is really great. Are any of these guys in here in your accountability group?" I look around.

"Yes, the ones I introduced you to when we first walked in. They know about you and how this is our first time going out."

"Seriously? No wonder I felt so nervous when we walked in."

"All the guys were praying for me."

"Really?" I try to shake off my self-conscious feeling. "You're blessed to have friends like that."

"Yeah, they're a great group of guys. Especially Josiah. He's always there for me. I can call him anytime, which is great when I'm struggling with something, like whether it's okay to ask out a cute girl I bumped into at Juice Stop one night."

He is smiling at me, but now there is something additional in his eyes: a deepness and an extra warmth.

I hope it doesn't show on my face that I feel like all my internal organs are doing consecutive cartwheels. Lord have mercy. I really like this guy. And I think he likes me, too. *Sigh.*

His friend's band takes the stage and begins to play. Peter reaches over and puts his hand on mine.

"Is this okay?"

All I can do is smile at him and nod since my insides feel like they may burst open with joy at any moment. I can feel the rough calluses on his hand, which are wonderful and warm.

This has got to be one of the best nights of my life.

Thank You, Lord, thank You so much.

Chapter Eleven

As I drive home, various parts of my date with Peter this evening play in my head like my own personal favorite movie. I've never had such an excellent time with a guy. Never.

I had grown accustomed to devising new and innovative ways to fend off unwanted advances from whatever guy I was on a date with for the evening. I even toyed with the idea of getting some martial arts training just so I could really give some guy a good karate chop, but I finally decided it would be better just to stop dating altogether for an undetermined length of time.

And then I saw Peter. I thought, unless this guy asks me out, which will probably never actually happen in real life, I would remain single until further divine notice. But he did ask me out!

I think I'm going to have to ask Dr. Bill to surgically remove the smile from my face so I don't look as deliriously happy as I feel.

I pull into the driveway at my mother's house. There are lights on. They must be back from Europe. I sit in my car for a few moments to try to regroup and return to my normal sarcastic, cynical self. Yeah, right!

"Hello?" I close the humongous glass and wood front door behind me.

"In here, Maddy." I head toward the kitchen, the origin of Dr. Bill's voice.

"Hi sweetie," Dr. Bill gives me a warm hug. I hug him back, trying not to be stiff. "You look radiant. You must have had a good evening." Bill says, trying to be fatherly. God bless him for trying.

"Thanks, I did." Quick change of subject: "How was Europe?"

"It was a little on the warm side, but nice. We had a good time. Your mother swears she won't go back, but you know how she is. Give her some time, and we'll be booking a trip to Paris or Milan."

"Yeah, probably."

Even after all these years, I still feel a little awkward trying to make conversation with Dr. Bill. It isn't that he's not friendly or personable because he is. He's loving toward my mother, and I know he genuinely cares for her. Even when she insists he performs more procedures for her. I probably couldn't think of a better guy for her.

Dr. Bill is a mild-mannered man. He is tall, slender, and bald except for a section of light brown and gray hair running around the back of his head from ear to ear. He reminds me of an average-looking James Taylor-type guy with wire-rimmed glasses. But my mother prefers average-looking men. She would never be with a man who might steal any attention away from her.

But Dr. Bill has always been good to her, even when she's in one of her monster mother moods when every little thing sets her off, and she turns into a raging mega-beast. He slips out of the room and says, "I'll be in my office."

Her tirades never seem to bother him that much. In fact, they almost seem to amuse him, as if she were a little child having a temper tantrum. I know he was married once before my mother, so I can only imagine the hell maiden his ex-wife must be to make him immune to my mother's bouts of boisterous madness.

Dr. Bill has always been good to me, too. He has no children of his own, so he has always been prone to spoiling me, much to my mother's displeasure. When I think back to some of the bratty stuff I did and said when I was like fifteen and sixteen, all I can do is groan in shame. I was such a cold little sarcastic wench to him, and he was always sweet to me.

Please forgive me, Lord.

My beloved, it's not just My forgiveness you need to seek.

I know.

Dr. Bill continues to sort through the pile of mail covering the gray granite countertop but glances up at me occasionally and smiles. I imagine it must be pretty awkward for him, too, especially since I became a Christian.

"Thanks for keeping an eye on the ol' homestead for us while we were gone." His eyes crinkle as he smiles at me.

"Sure, no problem." I pause to search for the right words to say. "Uh, Doctor—Dad, um, I was just thinking back to when I was a teenager. I mean, I know at twenty-three I'm not exactly a seasoned mature adult, but I mean, when I was younger, what a terrible wretch I was to you and stuff. And, um, I'm sorry. About everything."

He looks at me. I think he is a little stunned. He adjusts his glasses.

"Oh, sweetie, it's okay." He comes over and hugs me. "We all do strange things when we're young. It's part of growing up." His eyes are a little misty. He clears his throat. "You know I love you no matter what, Maddy. And I think of you as my own child."

I smile and hug him back. "I love you too, Dad."

"Bill! Those idiots in customs! BILL!" The shrieking grows louder as she descends the stairs.

"Your mother is a little tired from traveling."

"Yeah, I guess." I brace myself for her usual wrath.

"Bill, look at this bottle of perfume! It's cracked—oh, Madeleine darling, I didn't know you were here."

"I just got in," I say quietly, mostly because I'm in shock.

Lord God in Heaven, please help me not to stare! The texture of my mother's face looks just like a Barbie doll, and her lips are HUGE, like those wax lips you could buy at a candy store. It's amazing she can speak. I try to mask my shock at her appearance.

"Madeleine, you look...pretty. Bill, doesn't she look pretty?" She says, looking me up and down, eyeing me suspiciously.

"Yes, I told her she looks radiant."

"You should dress and do your hair and make-up like this more often. Then maybe you'll catch a young man."

I already have...I hope. "Maybe so."

I'm not even wearing anything much different: a black skirt, a dark wine-colored lace button-up blouse with a black tank top underneath, black tights, and my favorite shoes, black leather T.U.K. Mary Jane Creepers.

Okay, so I curled my hair at the ends with Maggie's hot rollers and put on the blush and lip gloss Maggie gave me. Also, I bought some gray eyeliner and only put a little from the middle of my eyes to the corners, as it said on the back of the package. It's amazing how it made my hazel eyes stand out. But I'm sure most of my makeup has probably worn off by now.

"Come upstairs! I bought some fabulous shoes in Paris." She turns on her heels, and I obediently follow my mother upstairs.

The one thing, just about the only thing my mother and I have in common, is our love for shoes. Of course, we have totally different taste, but she always comes home with the most beautiful shoes.

"How's school going? Did you work tonight?"

"Fine, and I worked the day shift, and then I went out."

"Oh? Where did you go?"

"Just a coffeehouse."

"With people from work?"

"Um, no. With a guy I met at work who also goes to my church." She stops sorting through her Louis Vuitton suitcases, which are sprawled across their California King-size bed, and looks up at me.

"Excuse me, did you say *a guy*?" She has a strange look on her face, part surprise and part disgust. It's hard to tell with all the surgery she's had.

"Yeah." My cheeks flush and get hot. My mind flashes back to the evening, especially the warmth of Peter's hand on mine and the sparkle in his eyes when we said our goodnights at my car at the end of the evening.

"By the look on your face, it looks like you went back to his place afterward." She always has to ruin the moment by saying rude stuff like that.

"Uh, no. It's just for coffee and to hear his friend's band play. I don't spend the night with guys anymore, remember?"

"I know," she huffs at me and rolls her eyes. "Well, what does he do? He does have a job, doesn't he? He's not one of those gothic boys who wears make-up and doesn't even have a car or a proper job, is he? Honestly, Madeleine, I don't know where you got your taste for useless men." She goes back to sorting out her undergarments, seemingly already bored with the conversation.

Actually, I don't know what Peter's day gig is. The subject never came up. I make a mental note to ask him the next time I see him, which is tomorrow morning at church!

Suddenly, I'm exhausted, and I just want to retreat to my bedroom down the hall. Not even my mother's barrage of questions, which I know she doesn't want answers to, can cast a shadow on my joy this evening.

"Um, I better get to bed. I've got a long day tomorrow. G'night. I'm glad you and Bill got home safe."

"Uh-huh. Yes, goodnight," she says to her reflection in the mirror while admiring a pair of very expensive-looking jewel-encrusted chandelier earrings she holds up to her ears. I turn and walk down the long hallway to the other wing of the house, to my sanctuary, my bedroom.

I flop down on my bed and stare up at the canopy of soft black tulle. When I was fourteen, I replaced the white lace fabric my mother bought when I was like ten years old with this awesome black netting to match the black and burgundy velvet patchwork comforter, I begged for Christmas that year.

I try to shake off my mother's comments and seemingly lack of genuine interest in my life. This time it's much easier to do, because of the most wonderful evening I just had. I'm still in awe that I actually went out with my Adonis (I kind of feel like a loser calling him that now, but oh well). And the incredible time we had.

The phone rings as I lay on my bed, thinking back on the night. After a few moments, I hear Dr. Bill call up to me. I get up and open my door.

"Who is it?" I need to have a moment to mentally prepare myself for whoever it is, especially if it's Maggie with her drama.

"A young man named Peter."

Oh. My. Goodness.

"Okay, thanks. I'll get it up here." I shut my door and race to the phone beside my bed. I take a deep breath. And pick up the receiver.

"Hello?" I hear a soft click from Dr. Bill hanging up. He's so sweet. My mother would have listened for a while and even joined the conversation.

"Hey, long time no hear," he says. The sound of his voice soothes me deeply.

"Hey! It's really great to hear your voice," I gush. *Dope! Don't tell him that!*

"Yeah? Cool. I'm glad I called then."

"Me too." *Sooo glad. You have no idea…*

"I just wanted to call to make sure you got home safe, I mean, back to your mother's house." He sounds a bit nervous, but it's cute.

"Yeah, here I am, safe and sound, back at the house plastic surgery built."

"Yeah, I was just concerned. Cuz, ya know, we did have a lot to drink, even if it was just coffee. Still, I hope the caffeine didn't make you drive too fast. I heard a sonic boom shortly after you left, and I thought it might've been you." I can hear the smile in his voice.

"Yeah, that was me, but I made sure there was at least a full car length between me and Dale Earnhardt when I changed lanes in front of him."

"I hope you gave him a nice wave, too."

"Well, of course! I wouldn't want to be rude to *the* NASCAR racing icon."

"True. I'm glad to hear it." He lets out a little nervous laugh, and then clears his throat. "Well, to be honest Miss Madeleine, there's another reason I called you."

Like he needs an excuse to call me. He could just call me up and recite the alphabet, I would be thrilled. "Hmmm…are you calling to inquire about my long-distance carrier?" I ask.

"No, that's not it."

"You're not calling with one of those really long surveys, are you?"

"Hmmm, not today." He says, laughing. *Yes!*

"Well, then you must be calling to offer me prime office rental space in Newport Beach."

"Yes! That's it!"

"I thought so."

"Seriously now Miss Maddy, I wanted to tell you that I had a really good time with you tonight."

"Me too." *Oh sigh.*

I close my eyes tight and put my hand on my chest to keep my heart from pounding right out of it.

"Also, I hope I didn't come on too strong tonight, uh, by being so honest, you know, with all my spiritual stuff." He takes a deep breath. "I've kind of lost touch with the normal proprieties of dating. I was thinking back to some of the stuff I told you tonight, and I feel like I was a little too honest, too forward maybe, with what I was telling you."

"I didn't think you were forward at all. Are you kidding me? I so love that you opened your heart to me. It's so refreshing to be out with someone who speaks with such candor and sincerity," I say, shocking myself.

I wish I could be as truthful and trusting as he was tonight. But in my shyness, I choose not to tell him so.

"Good." I can almost hear him run his hand through the front of his hair as he exhales. "I'm really glad to hear you say that. I feel so out of the loop with this whole dating thing. I'm glad we got the first date out of the way. Now, we can just be ourselves. I mean, not that I wasn't being myself tonight."

"I know what you mean. You are the new man who has cast off the old ways, and put on the new." Where did that come from? I sound so wise and scholarly.

"Yes! Exactly. I guess that's why I feel so inexperienced now with dating and courtship stuff."

"To be honest, I feel that way too." I'm so loving this conversation with him. Why can't I be like this in person?

"Well, I really liked sharing the coffeehouse with you, it's been a special place for me, and I liked having you meet my friends, especially Josiah."

"I like the coffeehouse a lot. Everybody is nice. And Josiah is a great guy."

"Yeah, he's been a true friend. Man, it's been such a blessing to have him in my life, especially when I need a spiritual kick in the pants."

"I know what you mean." I laugh. "Leah, at my work, is kinda like that for me. She's so awesome."

"Yeah, she is. She really cares about you. When I came in the store the other day and asked her about you, she gave me the third degree. I got nervous when she grilled me about my intentions with you."

"No, she didn't! What did she say?" I kick my shoes off and lay back on my pillows.

"She asked me about my band, what kind of music we played, and if I went to church, and why I was asking about you. I kind of felt like I was talking to your mother. But it was all cool."

"What did you tell her?"

"The right answers, I guess, since I got the feeling that it was okay by her that I ask out her dear friend." I can hear the smile in his voice.. "I also told her my band plays Christian hard rock, and that I named my band 'But Vapor.'"

"What? Say again?"

"You know after James 4:14, where it talks about how life is but a vapor, we don't know what life will be like tomorrow, so we shouldn't worry about stuff."

"Seriously?"

"No." He laughs.

"Why not? That's pretty clever."

"I think most people wouldn't get it. Besides, I like what my bass player Andrew came up with, 'Victor's Crown.' It has a double meaning. His dad, Victor, has really bad pain in his back and most of his body. He has had it for most of Andrew's life. The doctors don't know what's wrong with him. But through it all, he stays positive and faithful to God. Every time I go over to his house, he always asks me how I'm doing, and has some really awesome wisdom for me. He's a great guy. So, the band is named after him, and it also ties into the passage in Second Timothy about the victor's crown."

"That's so cool."

"Yeah, I got saved through Andrew and his family. I mean, they were the ones to bring me to church."

"Really? How? When? Details, please."

"Andrew and I have known each other since sixth grade, and I used to spend the night at his house. We would jam and work on music, and then I'd go to church with his family on Sunday morning. It made an impression on me. So, finally, one Sunday morning when I was seventeen, God said, 'It's time, come on,' so I went forward when the altar call was given."

"Mmm, I love that." I close my eyes, envisioning a young Peter, standing at a church altar, surrendering his life to our blessed Lord.

"Yeah. But I fell away for a while after that. Then I would get serious and start reading my Bible and going to church again, and then after a while, I would start slacking off again. I went through these fluctuations until about a year ago, when I was in another slacking off period, but wishing I wasn't."

"That's when you met Josiah, at the coffeehouse."

"Yeah, that's right. You've been taking notes."

"Pseudo-journalist, remember?"

"Oh, that's right." He laughs. "Anyway, meeting Josiah was like a divine appointment. I was so sick of sitting on the fence with God. Everything I was doing, all the partying, the sleeping around, not being able to control my temper around my father. I mean, every time I would get around him, we would have these terrible fights, like almost coming to blows, and I always felt so bad afterward. I know it was hurting my mother, too. All this stuff was shredding my soul to pieces. I needed to make a change for good. Man, I was a mess." He exhales deeply. "That's when I met Josiah, and we started talking, and I started going to Josiah's accountability group. Then, he started doing Bible studies with me. He's been like a brother to me. He's a real Godsend."

My heart is breaking for him. Also, my mind starts calculating. "So, this was about a year ago when you started getting serious with your relationship with God."

"Yeah, pretty much."

"Wow, hmmm…"

"What is it?"

"Well, I have sort of a confession to make. I guess it's my turn to be brutally honest. I feel like such a goof for telling you this! But okay, here it is." I take a deep breath. "About a year ago, I started noticing you. At the Plus, and then in church. Ohmigosh, this is so embarrassing!" I'm so glad blushing doesn't transmit through the phone lines.

"No, it's cool." I can hear the smile in his voice again.

"Well, there's more."

"Go on."

"Okay. Well, every Sunday at church, I would look for you. I mean, really search the crowd for a glimpse of you. And every Sunday, I would secretly pray that I would see you. Oh man, you must think I'm so disturbed!"

"But that's what I like about you, though," still smiling, it sounds like. "So, you used to pray for me?"

"Well, truthfully, I would pray that I would just get to see you. But yeah, I guess that is sort of praying for you, isn't it?"

"Wow, that's amazing." Peter sounds as if he's trying to absorb the situation.

"I really thought God was answering my prayers, 'cause it got to be that I spotted you almost right away, every Sunday, too. But, I guess God had more in mind than just fulfilling the requests of my girlish crush. Maggie used to give me such a hard time for not going up to talk to you."

"I'm so glad you didn't listen to her. *So* glad! I would have been tempted to ask you out, and I was not ready to get into a relationship yet."

A relationship? Woohoo! "Ha! I can't wait to tell this to Maggie."

"I can't wait to tell Josiah. He's gonna think this is so cool. We talked and prayed a lot before I asked you out."

"Really?" I'm melting all over again.

"Yeah, I wanted to make sure I was ready, and that the time

was right."

"So it's been a year since you dated anyone?"

"Yeah, since that one girl I brought to the coffeehouse. Hey, it's kind of ironic that our first date was there, too. The end and beginning in the same place."

"Yeah, that is ironic." *Beginning…mega-cool! Relax. Be calm.* "So what did you tell Leah about why you were asking about me?" I try to sound more matter-of-factly, but I'm pretty sure my question came out sounding kind of flirty.

"I told her I was intrigued by the girl whose car has Goth band stickers on it, alongside a Biola University and a Harvest Crusade bumper sticker."

"How did you know that was my car? I mean, before I told you it was mine?"

"I guessed. Like I mentioned earlier, it seemed to fit you."

No one has ever understood me like this. My head is swimming. I'm speechless.

"Madeleine? Are you there?"

"Uh, yeah. Um, so what did Leah say, you know, when you said that stuff about my car?"

"She said a lot of great stuff about you. That you have a close relationship with Jesus, and still keep your personality, like you still remain the person He made you to be. And how you don't try to warp yourself into what you think people think Christian women should be like. I think that's really cool. I mean *really* cool."

"Oh, thanks." I feel myself blushing deeply. I'm so glad he can't see me. And did he just refer to me as a *woman*? "Well, actually, a couple months after I got saved, I did try to change myself into a more mainstream "Church girl," I guess you could say. But God showed me that was not what He wanted, and how I looked wasn't important. I mean, as long as I didn't dress slutty or anything like that, which I try to be careful with."

"Thanks. We guys really appreciate that. It's hard enough trying to keep my thoughts under control, and then trying to avert my eyes at the same time could cause me to go into some kind of cerebral overload or something."

"So, would smoke start pouring out your ears?"

"Yeah, and other places, too, I'm sure."

"Yikes!" I laugh out loud. The mental picture of that is too much! "I forget how tough it is on guys, visually speaking."

"Yeah, I wish more girls knew how even the slightest fashion indiscretion sets us off down a mental road we don't want to go," he sighs. "Whenever I would play a show in a club, or some place that's not a church, Andrew and I used to pray for God to protect our eyes and keep our thoughts pure."

"Yeah, I've gone clubbing with Maggie a few times and to some bars. I can only imagine the kind of fashion train wrecks you've witnessed."

"You got that right! It's cool though, 'cause more and more, that kind of really revealing dress seems unattractive and distasteful to me, and seems, I don't know…" he pauses.

"Desperate?"

"Yes. Exactly."

"I've tried to explain that to Maggie, but she doesn't get it."

I hear voices in the background on his end of the phone. "Can you hold on for a minute?"

"Yeah, sure." I hear another male voice and then Peter's voice.

"Maddy, I need to go help Andrew move some stuff out of his truck. I promised him I would do it. So, I will meet you tomorrow just before second service in the front of the church. This time, I will be looking for you."

"Excellent. I'll be there." *With bells on, as the saying goes, whatever that means.*

"Awesome! I look forward to it. You have a good night."

"You, too."

"I will. G'night," he says softly.

"Night." I say softly too, and hang up the phone.

Awesome, awesome, awesome!

Peter is such an incredible, out-of-this-world dream guy. Way better than I ever imagined he might be. I really think I've fallen hard for him. I mean, *really* fallen.

My heart feels all soft, full and warm inside, like my thoughts and feelings have smelted into one. I'm like the Wicked Witch from the *Wizard of Oz* when she screeches, "I'm melting! I'm melting!" And I've become this pile of indefinable goo lying in a pool of bliss on my bed. *Oh, sigh.*

Dear Jesus, thank You for tonight. Thank You, thank You, thank You! Thank You that our date went so well. Thank you for the super cool phone conversation, too. How totally awesome is it to be able to talk about You with a guy? Thank You that Peter is such an extraordinary guy. Even if he never wants to go out with me again (but I really hope he does), thank You that I got to meet such a sweet, gentlemanly and most of all, Godly guy who really loves You. And okay, I must admit, real easy on the eyes too, even though You know looks are not a prerequisite in a guy for me.

And Lord, please help me. Please help me be patient with my mother, and please help me to keep a clear head and a pure heart when it comes to Peter. I need You. I need You so much. And please help Maggie. I miss her a lot. Wherever she is tonight, and whatever she is doing, please send her my love, and Your love, too. In Your precious Name I ask these things, Amen.

Chapter Twelve

This morning is the first time in a long time that I not only made it to church on time, but I'm actually early. I woke up almost an hour earlier than I needed to get up. I guess my subconscious is as excited as the rest of me to see Peter today.

I dress carefully, first modestly, and then attractively. Maggie would not be pleased. Then I take my weekend bag and backpack downstairs to pack in my car.

Dr. Bill is reading the paper and sipping coffee on the back patio next to the pool. September mornings are temperate and pleasant in the Inland Empire of Southern California.

"Well, I'm off to church, then to lunch, and then back to school." I leaned down and kissed him on the cheek.

"Be careful driving. And Maddy, have a good time with your new beau." He gives me a knowing smile.

"I will." A wide smile creeps across my face. I feel my cheeks get warm. I'm such a chronic blusher. "I'll give you all the details when I see you and Mom next weekend."

I return Dr. Bill's wave with a quick wave as I open the side gate. I manage to slip out of the house without waking my mother. *Whew!*

I find a parking space one row away from the front area of the church, which is a series of converted industrial buildings. In the next section of parking spaces over, I see Peter getting out of his truck. I sit and take in the lovely site, as if I'm watching my own personal favorite movie.

He has a well-worn-looking gray leather Bible tucked under his arm. Such a sweet sight. As he walks up to the patio in front of the church, he runs his hand through his shoulder-length layers of wavy hair that looks as if it's still a little damp.

I climb out of my car, straighten my skirt, gather my worn Bible, notebook, and purse, and turn to walk to the front of the church. He sees me and smiles. I smile back while trying to mentally stop the rush of blood to my cheeks, as if I could.

"Hey there, long time no see," Peter says. "You look beautiful."

"Thanks. So do you." And he does. I'm stunned all over again by his gorgeous smile.

I sense that Peter wants to go in for a hug but stops himself and gives me an awkward, light pat on the shoulder instead. *Bummer.* I would love a hug from him, but it's probably best we don't. He steps back and opens the church door for me.

"Can I carry your Bible for you?"

Whoa! I thought guys like this went the way of dinosaurs, disco, and legwarmers. "Um, sure."

I hand him my Bible and notebook. I can't help but think of Suzette, who once told me she dreamed of the day when her significant other would carry her Bible for her to their seats in church. Thoughts like this have never even entered my mind, and now it is, happening to me.

We take two seats a couple of rows from the front on the side of the church where the worship band plays.

I never get to church early, so I take this opportunity to look around a little bit. I notice a couple of people staring at Peter and me with disapproving expressions on their faces while they whisper to each other—something I've never quite gotten used to. I don't think I look that strange compared to some of my freaky friends, but my gothic appearance may be a bit much for some people.

"I know how you feel. People used to stare at me, too, especially when my hair was down to my waist like yours is," he whispers. Was Peter reading my mind?

"How did you know that's what I was thinking? You must be psychotic with ESPN," I whisper back.

We both laugh, him harder than me. I'm stunned that he gets my play on words, and I don't have to explain it. And he didn't try to correct me either. Awesome.

"Your hair was that long? It must have looked so awesome!"

I can't even imagine how stunning he must have looked with long, long hair flowing down his broad, muscular back. I shake off a shiver as well as the image of him.

"Yeah, but man, it was so much work to take care of. I feel for you. But I remember walking into a room and noticing people staring at me."

Probably because you looked so gorgeous, I think to myself. "Your hair must have looked really good on you. I love long hair. Why did you cut it?"

"Well, it all started when I went to a music store in the mall one warm Saturday afternoon in May, just to pick up a few packs of strings and some new guitar cables. See, when my hair was that long, I used to wear it pulled back into a ponytail almost all the time, just 'cause it was easier to deal with. When I walked into the store, I noticed all these middle-aged musicians, some with receding hair lines, wearing their long hair in the very similar middle-part-pulled-back-into-a-ponytail style as me. And I thought, man, do I look like that? Not to be mean or anything, but I realized it was definitely time for a style change. I still have the long ponytail they cut-off. It's a trip to think my hair was ever that long."

"I'd like to see your ponytail carnage."

"Really? I used to have it hanging from my rearview mirror. It kinda looked like a trophy from some kind of tribal raid, like I scalped somebody. I took it down though, 'cause this girl I gave a ride home from Bible study one Wednesday night got kinda freaked-out by it."

"Aren't you afraid someone might steal your amputated ponytail and make a voodoo doll with it?" I like making him laugh.

"Well, I've never thought of that, but now that you mention it, I haven't seen it in a while, and I keep experiencing these sharp pains in my leg, like pin pricks, especially when I forget that it's my turn to do the dishes…hmmm…I'm gonna have to check with my roommate." Now it's my turn to laugh.

"I so love that your sense of humor is as twisted as mine is," I try not to giggle. "You pick right up where I'm at, without missing a beat. That's something I've definitely never experienced with a guy before." I feel a bit self-conscious for being so honest, but it also feels good.

"Yeah, me neither," he whispers. "With a girl, I mean."

He smiles at me. My heart swoons. I am lost in his eyes…and all the other love clichés; all of them applicable and true.

"I went out on a blind date with this guy once, who was so far from my type in every way, especially in the sense of humor department, that it's a miracle we belong to the same biological species. I guess that's bound to happen with most blind dates." I'm a little shocked at myself for telling him this story, but he is laughing, and that's all that matters.

"Oh man, blind dates," he shakes his head. "I want to hear this."

"Okay, well, he was this surfer guy who was really into his mini truck. I mean *really* into his truck. It was all he talked about. He had a girl's name for it, Brittany, I think it was."

"I think I knew a guy like that in high school."

"He looked like he had just come from the beach, with stringy sun-bleached blond hair and a stained T-shirt that looked like it was the only thing he could find to wear from behind the seat in his truck. He smelled bad, too. I wanted to tell him that hygiene wasn't just a greeting for a friend, but I figured he wouldn't get it," I wrinkle my nose.

"That's funny, and sadly, I know people I could share that little sentiment with," he says. "Please go on."

"Worst of all, much worse than his wafting pungent body odor, was that he was skinnier than me by about twenty pounds, and only a few inches taller, which is never good, and he had no detectable sense of humor at all."

"What? You went out with a guy with no sense of humor?"

"Yep. And when he came to pick me up, I can tell by the look on his face, which he made no attempt to hide, that I was not at all what he wanted to be seen with in public. I don't know what Maggie told him about me, but it was definitely not the truth."

"What? He's a fool," he smiles at me sweetly.

"Thanks," I will the extra blood in my cheeks to drain. "So, during appetizers at our local Dave and Busters, I made a half-hearted remark about Minnesota only having five minutes of summer and the rest of the year it's winter, since I had recently returned from visiting Dr. Bill's parents in Minneapolis. He looked at me with a blank stare. I silently counted one—two—three—four, and then he said, 'Oh that was a joke.' I knew at that very moment that my date with this intellectual giant was over."

"No way! That's so awesomely awkward," he throws his head back in laughter. "I had a bad blind date once too, but not nearly as bad as yours."

"Gee, thanks," I kid him, and elbowing him lightly in the ribs. "Okay, then, your turn."

"Okay, oh man, this happened several years ago, so I gotta try to remember what happened."

"Take your time, don't hurt yourself," I say slowly.

"Hey missy, I'm not that much older than you," he gives me a wide grin. "I can't believe I'm telling you this, but okay, here goes. The band I was in a couple years before the band I'm in now, was a secular hard rock band that had more of a bar band sound. I didn't much care for the sound or the songs, but it was a good paying gig. The other guys in the band liked the sound mostly because it attracted a lot of girls." Peter drops his voice to a whisper. "The kind of girls that get drunk, dance, and are easy to get with, if you know what I mean. Disgusting, I know."

I nod in agreement, and raise my eyebrows at him.

"Well these types of girls usually traveled in tight-knit pairs, so if you met one, you would usually need to find a date for her friend if you wanted to seal the deal, so to speak. So Andrew had it bad for this one girl he met at a club we just played at, but this chick wouldn't go out with him unless her best friend had someone to go out with, too, especially since she had just broken up with someone."

"I do know the type of girls you are talking about. Go on," I am loving every minute of his story.

"So Andrew set me up with this girl's friend. I was supposed to go to her house, pick her up, and meet him and his date at this bar and grill place, and then we'd go back to his girl's place afterward. Being the shallow rat-bastard I was at the time—I don't know if I can say that in church, but it's the best description of myself at that time—I had to ask what she looked like. Andrew said she was hot, maybe a little older than us, but it was dark in the club, so he couldn't really tell by how much. This was all right by me, since I was only twenty-five then, so an older woman was totally acceptable."

I nod, and hope younger women are okay too, since there is only five years difference between him and me.

"So, I go to pick up this girl for the date. When she answered the door, she looked at me kind of surprised-like, like she didn't know who I was or that I was her date, there to pick her up. But then she was all smiles, looking me up and down. Then she said she must have gotten the day of our date wrong, and she asked if I would wait outside while she changed. About five minutes later she came outside and was ready to go."

"Why did she make you wait outside? That's rude and weird."

"She gave me the excuse that her roommate was sleeping."

"Hmm, okay."

"In the car, I told her we would be meeting Andrew and Wendy, I think her name was, at the bar and grill. Then she said, 'oh uh, Wendy just called before you got there, and said the place was super busy and that we are supposed to meet up with them at a different bar down the road.' At this time, a little red flag goes off in my head, because her story doesn't jive. But, since she was looking at me like I was gonna get some no matter where we went, I didn't put anymore thought into it, and we headed over to the place she mentioned."

"Uh oh." I look at him wide-eyed.

"So, about a half hour into our date and my pager goes off. I noticed it's Andrew's number, and since they hadn't showed up at the place we went, I figured I should find a phone and give him a call. So I excused myself to go make a phone call. I find a pay phone tucked in a hallway near the restrooms." Peter's voice drops to a whisper again. "As I'm digging for change in my pocket, my date walks up and starts coming on to me. Like hardcore. She starts begging me to take her back to her place, and that Andrew and Wendy won't mind, since they'll get to be alone, too. Since my mind wasn't the controlling part of my body at the moment, what she said sounded good to me. So off we went back to her place."

"Double uh-oh!"

"While we were driving, my pager kept going off, like every ten minutes with Andrew's number on the screen, until she reached over, took it out of my hand and turned it off, and gave me a super seductive look. My only thought was, 'Man, this girl really wants me.' Then she said we couldn't go to her place because her roommate was sick with the flu, and we had to go to my house. I thought 'whatever, as long I get lucky.'"

She's the lucky one, I think silently.

"Immediately after we had done the dirty deed, she said she needed to get home right away, so she could take care of her sick roommate. And I, being the dirty pig-dog I was, thought that this is a miraculous phenomenon of some kind, because now I don't have to figure out how to get her out of my bed, and out of my house."

"Dude! That's harsh."

"Yeah, I know. So disgusting. Please don't hate me."

"I don't judge a person's past. Go on," I want to hear the rest of his story.

"When I get back home after dropping her off, Andrew my roommate is there alone, and he immediately starts ripping into me about how it's so not cool that I stood up this girl when I said I would pick her up and take her out, and she is all upset and so is his date and because of me he didn't get any from this girl he took out."

"Oh, poor Andrew."

"Yeah, I know. Anyway, I started to explain to him that I did pick her up and I did take her out, when our phone rings. It's the girl Andrew had just been out with. He listened for a little while, and then looked over at me kept saying, 'oh man…oh man…no way, oh man.'"

"Uh oh…"

"It turns out, the girl who answered the door and who I took out and then back to my house, was my blind-date's mother!"

"Ohhh, no way! That's so awesomely horrific! You took out her mother? Good grief! You're blind date was waaaaay worse than mine, dude! I'd say you win the award on bad blind dates, if there is such an accolade. You should be in the Bad Blind Date Hall of Fame."

"I know, I know." He shakes his head in disbelief and rolls his eyes to the ceiling. "I had forgotten all about that night. What a nightmare. Thanks for reminding me." He smile and rubs his temples.

"You're welcome." I grin at him. "Can you imagine the mother-daughter catfight that ensued when that girl found out her mother went out with you, and then went all the way with you? Oh ,to be a fly on the wall that night in that house!"

"I can't believe a mother would do that to her daughter, can you?"

"Yes," I feel my face fall serious. "Yes, I can."

Peter looks me in the eyes for a long minute. I glance away and hope my mother will never get that bad. I feel him take my hand in his and gently squeeze it.

"I can't believe what a heathen jerk I used to be," he lowers his head and closes his eyes. "Father forgive me," he says softly. Now it's my turn to squeeze his hand.

The worship band takes the stage, and we begin to pray. I secretly add to the prayer my thanksgiving to God for bringing such a cool guy into my life, so unlike the Dave & Buster's date guy. I ask God to save my mother, and to help me be a better example of Christ to her. And I also ask for help to keep my mind focused on the worship and message, and not be distracted by the fact that I'm sitting here, in church, right next to the most extraordinary guy I have ever met.

I'm so grateful for this amazing day. *Praise You and thank You Lord. Thank You so much. I love You.*

Chapter Thirteen

On my long drive back to school through Carbon Canyon, I replay the whole awesome day in my mind—sitting with him at church, laughing about our bad blind date stories, and then our fun and tasty brunch at Flo's Café at the Chino Airport. I'm going to be full from the ham and cheese omelet with biscuits and gravy for the rest of the day. I love all the great conversation, I mean, really great conversation. Peter made me laugh so hard at one point I almost squirted coffee out of my nose!

I feel so much more comfortable with him than I did on our first date, which was only last night. Now that I know Peter personally, he's even "dreamier"—as Marcia Brady would put it—than I could ever fathom he could be in my crush days.

But then my cynical side keeps rearing its ugly head, trying to convince me that there must be something terribly wrong with him. Like he's secretly a cross-dresser (I could learn to live with that), or he cheats on his taxes (again, I wouldn't judge, just pray for him), or he's a visitor from another country and his visa is about to expire and he's looking for a quick marriage to obtain citizenship (I could make that sacrifice). But the cruelest attack of cynicism to conquer, the real kicker, is the one that keeps muttering its evil voice in my ear, "he probably has a girlfriend." That one is tough to stamp out.

Every relationship I've ever had ended with the guy cheating on me, and me catching him in the act. The last time it happened, I asked God to help me deal with it, and He promised me I would never be put to shame again. He gave me Psalm 31, particularly the first part of verse 17 as a promise, "Let me not be put to shame, O LORD, for I call upon You."

The Word of God really helps me see more clearly, and truly comforts me. So *there*, Morose Madeleine, take that. I'm so grateful to God for His promises and that He will fulfill them. So very grateful.

As I drive through the parking lot of our dorm building, I glance down at the ice plant covered slope, and see light coming from the window of our ground floor room. Maggie is home for once.

As of late, I find that I brace myself for whatever drama I'm about to encounter, particularly when I approach our dorm room and I know Maggie is home. But I'm still so elated from spending the day with Peter that it's almost like I kind of don't care. Is this wrong? Maybe it's that I don't worry about it so much anymore because I have experienced a deeper understanding of how awesome God is, and I know my awesome God will take excellent care of Maggie. I know He will.

As I slip on my cardigan, the smell of Peter's cologne on my sweater that I wore in church this morning fills my nostrils. Oh, my heavens, it smells so good. Not to be such a girly cliché, but I swear I'm never going to wash it.

Suddenly, I miss him, I miss him so much. Should I call him? Just to hear his voice? But I don't want to seem desperate. Would he think I was being too forward if I called him? I would just love to hear his voice again tonight. His voice is such a sweet sound to me. *Sigh.* I'm consumed by these thoughts about Peter as I walk in the door of our dorm room.

"Hey ya'll." Maggie looks up from the floor, where she is sitting and painting her toenails. She returns the brush to the bottle of pearly raspberry pink nail polish, and stares at me. "Hey, what's up with you? Why are you all smiley?"

I quickly try to revert to my serious gothic self, but I find it difficult to dampen the bliss that seems to be exuding from every pore of my being.

"Hey Mag, how's it going?" I try to play it cool.

"Not as good as you, apparently. What's going on?"

"Not much. Just got back from my mom's, and church." As I think back on the totally awesome day, I can't stop the smile that tugs at the corners of my mouth.

"Uh huh, and I'm the next Mrs. Troy Aikman."

"My mom and Dr. Bill got back from Europe. My mom had another laser peel, so now her face looks like genuine plastic. Oh, and she must have drained Europe of collagen, because man, her lips are huge." I continue unpacking my weekend bag.

Maggie just stares at me. I love jerking Maggie's chain. She has no idea I had a date with Peter Saturday night. "Oh yeah, I went to Flo's for brunch with a friend. The ham and cheese omelet was extra good today."

"Excuse me, with whom? Did my gothic roomie have a date? I thought you looked different when you came in."

Maggie duck-walks on her heels toward me and sits down on the end of my bed. I've missed her so much.

"So tell me, who is this lucky young man and where did ya'll find him? He's not a Biola boy, is he? Poor guy, I bet he doesn't even come close to measuring up to your Adonis crush-man. What did you say his real name is? Patrick or Philip, or something like that?"

I look at her, waiting for her to stop asking questions.

"Well, come on! Don't keep me in suspense!"

Just then, Suzette knocks and pops her head in the door.

"Maddy! I thought I heard you. I've been waiting for you to come back. So, how was it?" Suzette nearly squeals with excitement as she sits on the other side of my bed, opposite Maggie.

"How was what?" Maggie looks puzzled and irritated.

"Her big date with Peter!"

"Peter? He's not the same guy you have a big ol' crush on, is he?"

"Yes! It's him! Remember they met at Juice Stop? It was so romantic!" Suzette looks from Maggie to me.

"What? When? How did...I thought you only bumped into him. When did it turn into a date? Seriously?" I think this is the first time I've ever seen Maggie completely perplexed. She actually looks stunned.

"After we ran into him and his friends at Juice Stop, well, actually, he bumped into Maddy. Maggie, he is so gorgeous and super nice, too. Anyway, the next night, wait, was it the next night or the night after that? Oh, Maddy, you tell it!" Suzette is almost as giddy as I am.

"As Suzette, said, it all started one fateful night at the local Juice Stop—"

"Oh hon, spare me the dramatics. I want *details*. What happened? Where did ya'll go? Did ya'll, you know, get some?" Maggie gives me a wicked wink.

"Nice, Mag." I give her my best sneer.

"I'm just kiddin' with ya," she fakes like her feelings are hurt.

Yeah right. Maggie would love for me to tell her that I had lost my resolve to stay pure, and that I had gone down *that* road, just like her. Sometimes, it's hard for me to be patient with her. I wish I could just tell it like it is, kind of how Bethany does.

But then again, am I sure I could maintain self-control if I found myself alone with Peter? It's better to remain patient and compassionate, I think. But for the grace of God, go I, as the saying goes. And oh, how I need His grace.

I take a deep breath and began to bring Maggie up to speed on how Peter and I actually met at my work and talked for a little while and he asked me out, and what an awesome time we had at the coffeehouse, and at lunch after church.

"Did he carry your Bible for you in church?" Suzette looks like a little girl asking me this.

"You know, he actually did," I say incredulously, since this apparently well-known act of chivalry was previously lost on me.

"He did not. Guys don't do stuff like that," Maggie snorts.

"He did. He's very much a gentleman," I try not to sound smug. At least, not too smug.

"At least for *now* he is," Maggie snipes.

I shoot her a look for her comment, and then continue gushing about Peter. "He's very sweet, smart, funny, honest, sincere, and I totally love talking with him. And we have so much in common. The coffeehouse he took me to is so amazing. We'll have to go sometime. It's owned by a guy who disciples Peter, named Josiah. He's a cool guy, too."

"Awesome! I love coffeehouses!" I suspect Suzette is holding back her question if Josiah is single or not.

"What does Mr. Wonderful do, I mean for a livin', other than play his little guitar?"

Man, why is Maggie being such a wench? I figured she'd be happy for me, that I finally went out with the guy I've had a crush on for so long.

"He works for his uncle's construction company. They build custom homes."

"That would explain why he's so tan and muscular." Suzette blushes a little.

I can't help but smile at her and feel a tinge of pride that I'm going out with a guy that my friends think is good-looking, for once. The guys I used to date were, well, a little scary looking.

"Well then, I bet he has lots of skills that will come in handy in the future, especially when he builds your dream house of horrors for the two of you to shack up in." Maggie gets up off my bed and sits at her desk.

I'm rarely on the receiving end of Maggie's caustic comments, so I figure something is up with her. But at this point, I am growing a little tired of her negative attitude, so I get up and continue to put my weekend stuff away.

"Well, I better get back to my homework," Suzette says, probably sensing the growing tension in our room. "See you later, guys."

With her back to Maggie, she mouths to tell her more later. I nod and smile at her before she turns to leave.

My resolve to give Maggie the cold shoulder fades as I begin to reminisce on my time with Peter. I pick up my sweater again that I laid across my pillow, hoping the sweet aroma would transfer to it. I know, that's so girly. I hold it up to my nose, close my eyes and inhale deeply. *Mmmm.*

"You must really be in love with this guy." Maggie is looking at me. I feel myself blush with embarrassment.

"I think so."

"Be careful, Maddy."

"I know."

"I don't want to see you get hurt. And don't you go sleepin' with him. If you even suspect for one minute that's all he's got on his mind, you make like a three-legged horse leavin' a glue factory and get away as fast as you can." She pauses and takes a breath. "You're too good to be some guy's piece of meat," her voice cracks.

The painful expression on Maggie's face is more than I can take. As I go to hug her. Tears spill down her cheeks. And mine, too.

"So are you, Mag, so are you," I say into her hair.

I want to grab her by the shoulders and shake her, and tell her to just stop sleeping around, that God is waiting for her to call out to Him, and that I've been praying for her. But I don't. I don't say anything.

I reach over to her desk and pull a couple of tissues out of the pink flowery box and give her one.

"So, when are yawl going out again?" Maggie wipes her eyes, and then her nose.

"Wednesday night, to a Bible study at the coffeehouse." I wipe at my own tear-filled eyes.

"Woo-hoo, that sure sounds like a hot date."

"Actually, it will be. I'm looking forward to it. Peter is such an awesome guy. I really want to do things right this time."

"Good. I really hope you do."

I think she means it. At least I hope she means it.

Chapter Fourteen

The peaceful, fragrant atmosphere of the coffeehouse is so soothing after a long day at work. Actually, it isn't work that I'm wound up about today. I can't get Peter out of my head, and it's not just daydreams about him.

It's the unhealthy obsessive "I wonder if he really likes me" and "why isn't he calling me every minute" madness that has taken up residence in my brain. But Leah's words of wisdom mixed with the enveloping calm of the coffeehouse are easing my anxiety.

"It's great that he's a gentleman, and he's kind and sweet and funny, it really is. I wouldn't expect anyone less for you." Leah looks down into her hot cup of café au lait. "But Maddy, above all things, make sure his heart is sold out for God, that the Lord is his first love. And that he is daily, and I do mean daily, pursuing a deeper relationship with Him."

Peter called and said he had something to take care of before the Wednesday night Bible study at the coffeehouse and that I should meet him there. This gave steam to the maddening train of thoughts that mentally derailed me the rest of the day.

Since Leah's shift ended at the same time as mine, I asked her to follow me there and join in the study. She immediately loved the coffeehouse, even more than I did at first.

"That was my greatest blessing with Tom. He was a man who made it a point to spend time with God every day, in His Word and in prayer. And not just asking for things, but he listened intently, too. He was always like soft clay in the Master Potter's hands."

Leah pushes a stray blonde tendril away from her bright sky-blue eyes, which are shadowed with sadness. Her sterling silver artisan rings flash in the light as she moves her hands.

"You must really miss him a lot," I look down into my steaming mocha coffee mug. "Well, duh, right? Sorry."

"I do, very much. But I know that he is with his Beloved Savior, Whom he loved more than anything in the world, including me, which is how it should be. It still hurts that he is gone. But he told me not to grieve for him for too long," she pauses and takes a deep breath. She caresses the gold ring she wears on a chain around her neck that looks like a man's wedding band.

"After the accident, he was still unconscious when they brought him to the hospital. I was sitting in a chair next to his hospital bed in the intensive care unit, praying so hard for him to survive. Suddenly, I felt his hand tighten in mine, and I opened my eyes to see him looking at me. He smiled a little. His face seemed to be illuminated by a light other than the cold fluorescent hospital lights in the room. He spoke softly but clearly and told me he was going home now, and I was not to grieve for him after one year, and that I should move on with my life because God has work for me to do.

Leah stops and takes a deep breath and a sip of her coffee.

"He said if I grieved longer than that, I would be of no use to the Lord. He made me promise not to grieve for more than one year, so I promised. Then he told me he loved me and turned his face toward the ceiling, closed his eyes, and stopped breathing."

I reach over and put my hands on hers. She gives me a weak smile and squeezes my hands.

"Even with the bustle of nurses and doctors responding to the flat-lining heart monitor and all the tubes and electric paddles, his face looked so peaceful and serene, a slight smile still on his lips, as if he had seen something so beautiful before he left," Leah exhales deeply.

She wipes the corners of her eyes with her napkin. Then she smiles at me with only a hint of sadness left in her eyes. I wipe away my own tears that sting my eyes and take deep breaths to break the choked-up tightness in my throat. Leah has never told me this story before today.

Lord, thank You so much for her. Please bring her a great blessing.

"Maddy, I'm telling you this because I know you like Peter very much, and I get the feeling he is quite fond of you, as well. But sometimes, when emotions run high, we lose our heads. Sweetie, please promise me you will be careful with Peter, especially when you are alone with him. I don't want you two to miss out on any of the great blessings God has for you. I get the feeling He brought you two together for a special purpose."

"Really?" I'm totally astonished.

"Yes, really." Leah smiles at me and squeezes my hand.

"I promise I will be careful. Been there, done that with other guys, and I don't want to mess things up this time. I really don't want my relationship with Peter to end up like the relationships I had with other guys in the past."

The front door opens, and Josiah and Peter walk in. Oh, the sight of him makes my heart pound hard, and then race the hundred-yard dash. I feel a wave of nervousness crash down on me.

I chastise myself for not checking my makeup when we got here to make sure my mascara hadn't done the 10K run under my eyes. Oh well. I guess it's best he starts to know me as I really am.

He gives a quick wave and smiles. He is holding the deepest red rose I have ever seen, so dark it's almost black, and his worn gray leather Bible is tucked under his other arm.

"For you." He hands me the rose and lightly brushes his hand across my shoulder and a short distance down my hair.

"Oh, thank you," I beam at him.

My throat tightens, and my face feels hot. My cheeks have got to be as red as a rose.

"It's stunningly beautiful. I've never seen a rose this beautiful," I manage to say while holding my tears in.

The rose smells heavenly, so sweet and heady. I've never had a guy give me flowers before, much less a perfectly shaped, deep, dark red rose.

"I'm so glad you like it. The lady at the flower shop said it's from Ecuador. It's called a 'Black Beauty.' I thought you would like it. I wanted to get you something special."

"I love it. Thank you so much." I say softly, looking up into his eyes.

I'm trying so hard to fight back the tears because I'm so moved. Peter clears his throat and looks away. Wait, is he choked up, too?

"Hi Leah, I'm glad you came," Peter changes the subject, thankfully. "This is my brother from another mother, Josiah. Josiah, this is Leah."

They shake hands, and their eyes lock. Is it just me, or is Leah blushing a little?

It must be contagious. Hmmm. They would make a nice couple. It might be time to return the favor she did for me!

Josiah smiles and looks away shyly. As he walks around the other side of our tables, he trips on a chair leg and drops his Bible. He turns bright red.

"How's Charm School, Grace?" He jokes about himself as he picks up his Bible and sets it on our table.

Leah laughs loudly. I don't think I've ever heard her laugh out loud like that before tonight. Hmmm…

Josiah clears his throat and asks that we all take hands and pray before we begin the study. I try hard not to be distracted by Peter's warm hand wrapped around mine, covering it. He gives my hand a gentle squeeze when we finish praying.

The study in 1 Peter 1:13-16 is awesome and so applicable for us right now. Josiah is such a gifted teacher.

The words from that passage keep reverberating in my head, particularly the section about preparing our minds for action and not being conformed by our past lusts that were ours in our ignorance but to be holy like Jesus. That one really hit home.

"That was a great study. I needed to hear it." Peter stretches his arms out in front of him, then up behind his head.

I try not to stare at his arms' thick, ropy, tanned muscles. Oh man, he's so beautiful. What was it that we just studied about girding our minds? I have to look away.

But I mentally note the curious absence of tattoos on his lovely arms. How did this hard rock guitar player make it through the early 90s without getting ink? There must be a story there.

"Yeah, I really liked the study too," I actually did retain a lot from the study, even though I would periodically get distracted by little things I noticed about Peter.

When will the day come when I will not feel the compulsion to study and obsess over every little detail about this guy? If I were one of those criminal suspect sketch artists, I could draw his eyes exactly, with the slight variations in the shades of light green and the thick rows of long dark eyelashes most girls would kill to have.

I could sketch from memory his perfectly straight nose that looks like it's never been broken, his strong jaw and classically square chin, and the deep dimples in his cheeks that flawlessly frame his slightly pouty full lips when he smiles.

His ethnic background would stump me. His smooth, slightly olive skin and dark, wavy hair suggest Mediterranean descent, but honestly, it doesn't matter. I suppose I'll find out one day, along with the details of his mysterious family life, but all that will come in due time–at least, I hope so.

I also wonder if the day will ever come when I stop having such intense, overwhelming feelings when I'm near Peter. It's like I'm nervous and shaky deep inside, and my skin would burn if he ever touched more than just my hands. He's just a guy, for heaven's sake.

Someday, maybe if we got married (do I dare to hope?), being close to him wouldn't affect me so strongly because by then I'd be used to him. Or maybe not. Sometimes, I wish he'd do something jerk-like so I wouldn't like him so much. But then again, perhaps that wouldn't change things.

I move my focus off myself (finally) and notice Leah is helping Josiah clear away the plates and coffee mugs left after the study. They are laughing and talking. They look and move so naturally together.

"So, what do you think is going on there?" Peter asks. He notices me watching Josiah and Leah.

"I don't know. Is he single?"

"Yeah. She is, too, I gather?"

"She's a widow. Her husband passed away about five years ago. She hasn't dated anyone since."

"Whoa. That's rough." Peter looks over at Josiah. "I feel like a jerk, that in all the time I've spent with him, I've never asked Josiah about his relationship experiences. That's so cool that you know so much about people."

"Is it? Sometimes, I think I ask too many questions. I wonder if I'm being nosy."

"I think it's because you care."

"Maybe. I try. I used to be so cold and mean to people, and a real, how can I say it politely, a real witch with a capital 'B'!"

"You? No way!"

"Yes, way."

"I don't believe that," he smirks. I love that he is teasing me right now.

"It's true," I say and smile back at him.

"Well, praise God for the changes He makes in all of us, you know? Seriously, I can't believe how I used to be, having such a nasty temper, and then all the girls I used to sleep with, and how far God has brought me from all that junk. Man, He's so awesome," Peter closes his eyes for a moment.

"Yeah, He is." He *really* is.

Peter carries my Bible and notebook to my car as I carry my beautiful rose. I open my car door and gingerly lay the rose on the front passenger seat. Peter hands me my Bible and notebook, which I place carefully next to the rose.

Thank you again for the rose. It is the most beautiful rose I have ever seen." I smile brightly up at him.

He is standing in front of me, his hands shoved deep into the front pockets of his jeans. The parking lot lights illuminate his eyes as he looks at me. He suddenly looks intense.

Oh no! Please no! Don't tell me you don't want to see me anymore! Wait, he just gave you a beautiful rose. Don't be such a dork, Maddy...

"I'm glad you like it and that you came tonight," he pushes his hands deeper into his pockets.

"Me too. I liked the study a lot."

"Yeah, I always learn so much from Josiah. And I will try to remember to start asking him questions about his life instead of just spewing about mine."

"Ask him about Leah. 'Cause you know, I'm gonna give her the third degree about him next time we work together. Then we can compare notes."

"Yeah," he laughs.

"Madeleine," he looks serious again. *Oh God, help me! He wants to stop seeing me; I just know it...*"Would it be all right if I asked you out on a real date, you know, a DATE date, like a dinner and movie kind of date? I feel strange asking this, but I don't want to be too forward or, you know, scare you away."

Dude, you couldn't scare me away if you were brandishing a razor-sharp machete while wearing a hockey mask! And yes! Yes! Yes!

"Yes." I'm so calm, cool, and collected. Yeah right!

"Dinner, Friday night?"

"That sounds great."

"*Phew!* I'm so out of practice with this dating stuff. And it's all new to me now, you know, doing it the right way. Where should I pick you up?"

"I'm off work on Friday, so at Biola."

"Cool. I'll get to see your stomping grounds. Six o'clock, okay?"

"Yeah."

"Great. Then it's a date." He exhales and smiles brightly.

"You know, I'll be expecting a corsage of some kind, like the ones Richie Cunningham gave his dates in the old episodes of *Happy Days*," I smile back at him.

"But of course. Gee, that would be swell." He does a sort of fifties shy guy swagger.

"I'm just kidding." I so love that I can joke around with him, and he gets it.

"Too late. You're already getting one. A super huge flowery one, with lots of fluffy ribbon stuff, either pink or yellow, maybe some of both. I've got florist connections now, you know. Oh, and I'll expect you to wear it all night."

"Only if it's one of those you wear on your wrist."

"Oh, you know it. A big fluffy, flowery wrist corsage. Maybe I'll ask them to add big plastic butterflies, too."

"Nice! I look forward to it."

"Me too." he laughs. "And to the actual date, too. I'll call you tomorrow between work and band practice."

"Okay. Talk to you later." I climb into my car, and he shuts the door for me.

I wave as I drive past him as he walks to his truck, and he waves back. I try not to take a long look at him in my rearview mirror, as is my usual custom.

Gird your mind and be self-controlled. Self-controlled? Good luck with that.

Please help me, Lord. I really need Your help with this. In Jesus's name, I pray, Amen.

Chapter Fifteen

"No, don't put a tank top on underneath your lace blouse!" Maggie corrects me for the millionth time. "Just a silky black bra. You do want to attract this guy, don't you?"

I try not to shoot her a dirty look. As if! *Grrr.* Of all the nights for Maggie to be home. I should never have told her that Peter was taking me out to dinner. Now she is driving me nuts.

When he called last night, Maggie answered the phone and started talking in her breathy Marilyn Monroe voice. At first, I figured she was talking to one of her guys, but then she said his name, and I almost ripped the phone out of her hand.

I apologized to Peter, and he said it was no big deal. He told me he has a tough roommate situation, too, that it's a long story and he would tell me about sometime.

When he includes me in long-term things, it makes me want to dance a jig, and I'm not entirely sure what a "jig" looks like.

Also, I love that he calls me when he says he'll call—no stupid waiting games.

"If you keep this up, an angry mob of men is going to come after you with pitchforks and flaming torches," I tease him during his latest timely phone call. "Ready to burn you at the stake for doing what you said you would do when you said you would do it."

He laughed out loud. "Well, then, I will be sure to stay off the main highways so the mob can't find me."

I check my outfit in Maggie's full-length wall mirror to make sure all my body parts are covered and that I look decent. I hear Suzette yelling, "Man on the floor," a very necessary thing to do in an all-girls dormitory. You wouldn't want to get caught by a guy walking down the hall while you're in your pajamas, or worse, in just your bra and panties. I pop my head out of the doorway to see what guy Suzette has brought down to First Odd, our dormitory floor of Alpha Phi.

She is gabbing away to a tall, dark, and very handsome guy as they walk down the hall toward our room. I say a quick prayer of thanks that I'm fully dressed and ready to go.

Peter looks more beautiful than he ever did in any of my daydreams, dressed in his 501s and a very cool black velvet sport jacket over a new-looking white T-shirt and shined-up black Doc Marten boots. His long, wavy black hair looks meticulously combed.

I still can't believe that this guy, who is as awesome inside (I'm learning) as he looks on the outside, is here to pick me up. *Me.* Crazy, mixed-up, morose Madeleine.

A broad smile sweeps across his face when he spots me. He keeps his lovely green eyes fixed on me all the way down the hall until he reaches our door. Once again, I feel as if I could melt right here and now. I step out in the hallway to watch him walk toward me, as he leaves a wake of gawking girls as he passes by.

"Look who I found in front of Alpha Phi?" Suzette winks at me.

She knew he was coming to pick me up. The original plan was for him to call our room from the phone on the outside of the building, and then I would come up to meet him at the front door.

"Hey there, I hope it's okay I came to your room." He gives me a sort of hesitant, one-armed side hug. For a brief moment, I can feel the warmth of his hand on my upper back through the lace of my blouse. My skin prickles, and I get goosebumps. Oh my, he smells so good. I can't identify his cologne, but it's now my favorite.

"I told him it was okay to come on down to pick you up and that we have an open floor until nine p.m.," Suzette grins at us. "You can have guys in your room as long as you leave your door open," she informs Peter.

"That's a good policy," flashes his killer smile at me.

His unexpected deep male voice permeates our end of the hallway, causing any of my many floor mates who aren't already watching him from their doorways to emerge from their rooms to catch a glimpse of the rare male species present on our floor.

Okay, so I'm trying not to feel prideful that more and more girls are looking out their doorways to gaze upon this gorgeous guy standing in the hall in front of my door who is here to pick me up! This is definitely a first.

"Hi, yawl." Maggie saunters up and leans against the doorway in her best Tennessee Williams southern belle pose. When did she put on lip gloss and pull the scrunchie out of her hair? Is she actually trying to give him her doe eyes? "Madeleine, aren't yawl gonna introduce us?"

NO! Not on your life! "Maggie, this is Peter; Peter, this is my roommate Maggie."

"We've spoken on the phone." He says as he shakes her hand formal and business-like.

Good. He's not buying her act. Not that I think he would, but you never know. Maggie is full-on checking him out, looking him up and down. Peter turns to look at me.

"Are we ready to go?" He must be sensing my growing irritation with my roommate.

"Yes, I just need to get my purse," I push past Maggie and grab my purse and sweater off my bed at lightning speed.

I hear Peter telling Suzette it was nice to see her again. I could learn from his good manners and excellent social skills. I dart back out of the room, almost knocking Maggie over.

"Yawl have a good time tonight. Don't do anything I wouldn't do," Maggie winks at us.

"Don't worry, I won't," I snap back. *Yikes.* I hope that didn't sound as snotty as I think it did. "Uh, thanks for helping me get ready," I say quietly to Maggie as we turn to leave.

As we walk down the hall to the stairs leading up to the lobby, I feel like Peter and I are some sort of walking parade float, with all the girls wishing us a good time as we walk by. I feel like doing a beauty queen touch-pearls-and-wave move, but I don't. I just offer thanks and reassurance that we will have a good time.

"I hope that wasn't too weird for you." My voice echoes off the stairway walls.

"Nah. It was cool to see where you live. Now I can picture it when I talk to you on the phone."

"I would've invited you in, but Maggie was being weird."

"She's definitely a character. And don't worry about her flirting. I'd like to think I'm spoken for."

I almost trip because of the look in his eyes. *Sigh.* "That's right. You are, and don't you forget it!" I poke his arm playfully. I love that I feel comfortable teasing him now.

"Yes, ma'am," he smiles broadly, his eyes catching the lights, making them sparkle. "I tell you, though, that scene back there, and this whole building really would be a dream to the guys in my accountability group."

"How so?"

"The guys are all single, and actively looking not to be. Here are all these nice girls in one place. It's like a high concentration of potential wives."

"You really think so?" I wonder if he includes himself in his assessment of our dorm. "I never thought of it that way. But I know lots of girls who feel the same way about the all-male dormitory on campus."

He holds the door open for me as we step out into the night air. The cool ocean breeze feels good on my skin.

"I didn't get a chance to tell you back at your room how beautiful you look tonight," he smiles at me.

"Thanks." I'm glad it's too dark for him to see my face turning its usual spectrum of reds. "You look really nice, too. Your jacket is really cool."

"Thanks. I thought of you when I saw it in the store, so I had to get it."

He bought new clothes for our date. How cool is that!

As we approach his truck, we walk past a little red BMW sports car with a couple making out in the front seats. There's only one student at Biola that I know of who drives a car like that, only because Maggie has told me all about it.

I don't want to stop and stare, but I can't believe what I am seeing. Bethany and Chad are totally locked at the lips. And ohmigosh, is his hand on her boob? Oh, I wish; I mean, I *really* wish I had not seen this.

"Do you know them?" Peter asks as we approach his truck. He must have noticed my astonished look.

"That was Suzette's roommate, Bethany, and her fiancé Chad. They just got engaged a few weeks ago."

"Interesting place to make out."

"Tell me about it."

"Man, they are playing with fire." Peter shakes his head.

"Yeah, you can say that again." I try not to think about the fact that I know Chad has slept with Maggie and that he may be trying to go down the same road with Bethany.

Peter shakes his head again as he unlocks the car door and opens it for me. He takes my hand to help me up into the front seat. The make-out session we just witnessed quickly fades from my memory at the feel of his warm strong hand. I breathe in the scent of his shampoo and cologne as he reaches across me to get a clear plastic box off the dashboard.

"For you." He opens the box and pulls out a beautiful corsage made of miniature dark red roses and black and burgundy ribbon. I put out my arm, and he slips it on my wrist. I can't help bursting out in laughter. He is so awesome! He actually bought me a corsage. He closes the door and quickly walks over to his side of the truck. I can see he is laughing, too. He opens the door and climbs inside.

"Thank you! It's so beautiful."

His eyes shine brightly. I want to kiss him right now, on his lovely, full lips.

He clears his throat and looks away. "Well, the florist was all out of big plastic butterflies, so I had to rethink the whole design of the corsage."

"Oh darn, what a shame." I try not to giggle.

"Yeah, well, you know, you gotta go with the flow. I hope this one will suffice."

"It's so beautiful and sweet. Thank you."

"You're welcome."

Our eyes are locked for a long moment. It seems like he's thinking about kissing me, too. My mind flashes back to Chad and Bethany locked at the lips in his car. That seems really tacky to me, not to mention against Biola rules and definitely disobeying God, but I would still love for him to lean over and plant a gentle kiss on my lips.

Peter quickly looks away and puts the key in the ignition. Dean Martin's *That's Amore* begins playing from the CD player. I'm busting up again.

"Italian food, okay?" He is laughing, too.

"Great."

This is going to be another awesome night. Thank You, Lord. Thank You so much.

Chapter Sixteen

etween classes and at lunchtime, I like to go to the Eagle's Nest, a sort of on-campus cafe. I prefer to come here to have lunch because it's much quieter and cozier than the school's main cafeteria, which is usually loud and crowded with the jock guys chasing each other around and posting "No Fat Chicks" signs on the soft serve machine. The Eagle's Nest is the perfect place to sit down at one of the many wooden table and chairs in the place, get a bite to eat, read, and pray, in peace.

"Hey Maddy, can I join you?" Suzette stands in front of me with a plate of food and a Diet Coke.

"Of course, have a seat," I move my backpack from the chair.

"Whatcha reading?" Suzette asks, unwrapping her sandwich.

"The worn-out, dog-eared copy of *Passion and Purity* by Elisabeth Eliot, that's been passed around our floor. It's time to re-read it. Last time I read it, I wasn't in a relationship, but now I need all the reinforcement I can get."

"Oh, I love that book! It's one of my mom's favorite books, too."

"I love the excerpts from her journal entries when she was dating her husband before they got married," my mind filling with thoughts of Peter. "Hey, come to think of it, I think this copy belongs to you."

"Take your time with it," she opens her soda. "It's not like I'm gonna need it anytime soon."

"Oh Suz, don't say that. You never know when God will bring a man into your life. Believe me. I know!"

"Yeah, but I'm beginning to sense that marriage is not something God wants for me right now," she takes a bite of her sandwich.

"Really? What gives you that impression?" This is news to me. Frankly, I'm a little stunned.

"I'm not really sure, but I noticed that lately, I haven't been praying for a husband as much. I've been praying more for God to put me where He wants me, you know? Not what I want, but what He wants."

"Any idea what that is yet?"

"No, not really. But yesterday, during my evening shift at the library, I was talking to a student from China. He had just heard a sermon on a passage in the gospel of Matthew, and he got confused. He asked me if I could explain why the word 'vine' is pronounced with a long 'i' sound, yet the word 'vineyard' is pronounced with a short 'i' sound."

"Huh, I've never noticed that. What'd you tell him?"

"All I could think to do was apologize for English being so difficult."

"Um, wait, back it up. Did you say '*he*'?" I smirk at her.

"Yeah, but it wasn't like that. I mean, he was really nice, but all I could think about was how tough it must be for people from other countries to learn English. Some of it just doesn't make sense," she takes a sip of her soda. "I don't know. Maybe there's something to that."

"Well, I'll pray for you. I know God has a really great plan for you. You know what this means, don't you?"

"What?"

"You're in danger of losing your membership in our club for people who have absolutely no idea what they are going to do after they graduate in less than a year."

"Oh yeah? Well, so are you!" She gives me a wide cheesy grin, displaying pieces of bread stuck in her teeth.

"Me? How do you figure?" I feign shock. "I thought I was not just a member but the president!"

"You're going to be married after graduation. And your life will be filled with wifely duties. And you guys will start having children right away. You'll have about twelve kids, I suspect." She can barely get the last words out through all her giggling.

"Hmm. I don't know about that. And you can bite your tongue on the 'twelve kids' idea. The only way I will ever have that many children around me is if I'm hosting a little league softball game in my backyard!"

"Awww, you don't want to have any children?"

"Not if I can help it. Do I seem like the maternal type to you?"

"Sure. Why not? You would be a great mother to Peter's children. I bet they would be really cute!"

"Any children that came from me would be little deviant devilish fiends!"

"What, like the "Addams Family" kids?"

"Worse!"

"But they would be half Peter's, and he's really sweet."

"Yes, he is, but my genetic material would dominate and contaminate his seed and corrupt the little beasties before they are even born," I give her my best spooky evil grin.

"Yikes! Maybe so," she muses. "Seriously though, how are things going with Peter? I haven't seen you around the dorm much lately."

A broad, sweet smile instantly takes over my face. "Things are so great. I guess we have been seeing a lot of each other lately. We've been sort of going on double dates with Leah from my work and Josiah, Peter's friend who owns the coffeehouse. We've been having a blast! Sometimes I just bring my homework and my laptop to the coffeehouse, and Peter will sit with me and read while I do homework. It is so very cool."

"That sounds awesome. What does he read?"

"All kinds of stuff. Josiah gave him a bunch of books. C.S. Lewis, Alan Redpath, you know, great spiritual stuff. Most of the time, though, he reads his Bible. It's such a beautiful sight to behold." I can't help but smile at the thought.

"I bet. He's a great guy. You are really blessed."

"Don't I know it, sister. Don't I know it."

"And he really likes you. I can tell. I mean, *really* likes you."

"Oh, stop." I feel my face get hot.

"Seriously! I can tell by the way he looks at you whenever I see you two together. Are there any more romantic dinner dates?"

"Just a few. We've been trying not to spend too much time alone together. I think we both feel physically attracted to each other. At least I know I do, and I'm pretty sure Peter does too, since he suggested, well, asked really if we could keep the time we spend alone together to a minimum, if at all."

"That's so cool," Suzette takes a sip of her drink.

"Yeah, at first, I didn't like it. I felt like we couldn't really get to know each other, but we've had really great conversations on the phone. And having another couple with us when we go out really takes the pressure off. The physical temptation isn't nearly as strong."

"I know when Bethany started dating Chad, they used to double date with another couple a lot. But lately, I really worry about her engagement to Chad, you know? Something just doesn't seem right there. I get excited talking about you and Peter, though. I really see God's hand on you guys. But every time Bethany starts going on about Chad, I just get this icky and depressed feeling."

I know the feeling, I think. "She must be driving you nuts with all the talk about her wedding."

"Not really. She hasn't really been talking about wedding stuff so much lately. I think she and Chad are fighting because he hasn't been calling her very much, and she seems upset with him."

Uh oh! Big-time, uh oh! "Hmmm, um, maybe the reality of midterms approaching is setting in. I know Maggie and I are totally swamped with papers to write."

"Maybe that's it, I don't know," she pauses. "How's Maggie doing? I don't see her very often. I miss you guys."

"I know; I'm sorry I haven't been around much lately."

"It's okay. I know you are having a great time," she smiles.

"I think Maggie is okay. Although, she never asks me about my dates with Peter. I don't think she wants to hear about it, which is kind of a bummer. I guess we're just growing apart."

"I'm gonna guess it's because she's jealous of you," Suzette takes a big bite of her sandwich.

"Jealous of what? She dates lots of good-looking guys, well, by her standards. I'm usually the one who's home alone, dateless."

"I think she's jealous that you're dating a gorgeous Godly guy and that you guys are staying pure. She said some pretty mean stuff the other day. I don't know if I should share it 'cause I don't want to gossip, but she said she would put money on it that you and Peter would end up 'doin' it' as she put it, really soon. She told me she knows you, and what you've done with guys in the past, and with how much you like Peter, it won't be long before you end up sleeping with him."

What!? That little wench! I thought she was my friend. I'm fuming mad, and I'm sure it must show on my face. I can't say anything; I'm so mad.

"Maddy, please don't be angry with her. I knew I shouldn't have told you. I'm sorry."

"No, Suzette, you're right. It's okay. Maybe Maggie is jealous, but she's also right. I mean about my past, not the part about Peter and I having sex." *Lord, help me not to…* "Maggie and I are a lot alike, except I've learned from my past not to be some guy's piece of meat. With Peter, it's different. It's weird, but I get this constant reminder that he doesn't belong to me, even though we've been going together for almost three months, you know? Like, he belongs to God, and I have no right touching or even thinking of him in any inappropriate ways if you know what I mean."

"That is so cool. I will pray for you guys."

"Thanks, we need it. And Maggie, too, please." *And Bethany, as well.*

"Yes, I will. I so did not want to be the cause of a feud between you guys. You two have always seemed like sisters with different parents. It must be tough for her to see you have a right relationship with a guy like she should be having," Suzette looks thoughtful.

"Yeah, I guess."

"I think you're making her feel convicted. You are being a good example for her. I know you are for me. You are living proof that God gives us good things if we put Him first."

"That's so sweet. Thank you, Suz. Let's hope I can keep it that way. Seriously."

After my last class of the day, I hike across campus back to my room in Alpha Chi. My mind is a psychedelic Tim Burton-esque mix of sweet images of Peter that get chased around by gigantic calendar pages, with big fat red circles around the due dates of all the papers I need to finish, exams I need to study for, and books I have yet to crack open and read.

I wish I could spend my days just basking in the bliss of my awesome relationship with Peter and the absolute pure joy of being obedient to God for once. But I guess my schoolwork is a good distraction. As I get closer to my room, I can hear George Strait singing loudly from our room, and the door is shut.

"Hey," I try not to shout over the music. Maggie is seated at her vanity mirror applying make-up in a pink lacy push-up bra and unbuttoned tight white jeans, which she will need to lay down on the bed in order to zip up. She has giant hot rollers in her freshly bleached hair.

"Hey, chickie. Your man just called. I asked him if yawl want to join Dale and me at the *Cowboy Boogie* tonight, but he said not tonight. Ooowee! That boy sure does have a nice voice on the phone. It's all deep and sweet and kinda dark, like molasses."

"Uh, yeah, thanks, I'll be sure to tell him you said so." *Yeah right!* I can only imagine what other stuff Maggie told Peter. At least now I know I can trust him. He has more integrity in his little finger than any of the guys I've dated in the past could ever wish for.

"So you're going out again tonight?"

"Don't worry Mother, I finished all my homework."

"That's cool. I was just wondering." I sit down on the edge of my bed opposite Maggie. "So, who's Dale?"

"A guy I met at the gas station. He pumped my gas for me, all gentlemanly-like. He said I looked too pretty to get my hands all dirty from the nasty ol' gas pump. He's really sweet. He's one of the bouncers at the *Boogie*. So don't be thinkin' you're the only girl who's datin' a hot buff guy right now."

"Yeah, okay." I watch as Maggie expertly applies her eyeliner and mascara. "So, you know Bethany and Chad got engaged?"

"Yeah. She made a point to come over and show me her ring. Whatever. She can have him." She slams a hot roller onto the dresser.

"Maggie, did you ever..."

"Did I ever what?" she asks while bent over at the waist, brushing her hair out.

"Did you ever sleep with Chad? I mean, he doesn't seem your type, but..."

"He asked me out once. I used to flirt with him like crazy in class 'cause I thought he was one of those goody-two-shoes guys. Turns out I was wrong. That boy knows how to do things good lil' church boys shouldn't know anythin' about. You know, in the bedroom—"

"Yeah, I get the point. Do you think Bethany knows? I mean, about you and Chad?"

"Oh, *hell* no! She already thinks I'm the wicked Jezebel of our floor. No reason she should find out now, right?" She gives me a stern look. "Right?"

"I guess Chad should be the one to fess up to all the stuff he's done."

"Yeah, you guessed right. Like he would ever do that. If he ever told little Miss Straight-Lace about all of his little indiscretions, she would pass out on the spot. That boy gets around, I'll tell you what." Maggie buttons up her tiny pink blouse.

"But don't you think it's severely tragic that she's gonna marry this guy, and she doesn't even know what he's really like?"

"Not my problem." Maggie waves away the cloud of hairspray she just sprayed, and inspects herself in the mirror. She looks like an exotic, countrified part-Asian Marilyn Monroe.

"I'm off." She grabs her purse.

"Be safe, okay?"

"Yes Mother. Have fun talkin' to your hot beau on the phone." She winks at me.

"He's at band practice tonight unless the other guys don't show up again, so I'll be hitting the books all evening."

"Well, whatever. Anyway, don't wait up." Maggie smiles coolly and closes the door behind her. She leaves me to turn off the foul country music oozing from her CD player.

My soul aches for her.

Oh Lord, I don't know what to pray anymore. Please help Maggie. It's so hard to keep watching her do this to herself. I know from my own past, as well as You know, that she's got to be hurting inside. Please, please help her. In Jesus' precious name, I pray, Amen.

Chapter Seventeen

After a couple hours of solid essay writing, the phone rings. The sound of our phone ringing used to irritate and annoy me to no end. It's amazing how that changed when I got in a great relationship. Now I get all hopeful and excited when I hear that little plastic box chime. I rush to pick up the receiver, and clear my throat.

"Hello?" I try to sound awake and alert.

"Maddy?"

"Yes?" I know this voice, but it's not my beloved Peter calling. Bummer.

"Howdy hon, this is Eddie Morris, Maggie's dad. Is my daughter there?" His voice cracks a little. *Uh oh.*

"Hi Pastor Morris. I'm sorry, Maggie is not here right now." I say, cringing.

"Do you know when she'll be back?" I hear the sound of doctors being paged in the background.

"No sir, she didn't say."

"Uh, okay, I will try back in a little while," he sighs heavily into the phone. "If she comes home, would yawl please ask her to call her moth—, uh, my wife, no, uh, her Aunt Caroline. I'm not at home. I'm at the hospital. Maggie's grandma had a very serious heart attack tonight."

"Oh, I'm so sorry, sir. I will tell Maggie as soon as she gets in."

"Thanks. And Maddy, would you and the other girls please pray for my mother, Eudora? The doctors don't think she's goin' to make it through the night." His voice sounds strained.

"Yes, sir. I will. Um, we will."

"Thank you, hon. I hope ya'll are well. I'm sorry I forgot to ask."

"Yes, uh, no problem. Take care. I will give Maggie the message as soon as she gets in."

"Thanks again, darlin'." He sighs and hangs up.

This totally bites! My heart is racing as panic rises in my chest. Dang it, Maggie!

What do I do? *Think, think, think.* I grab the phone book and look up the number for the *Cowboy Boogie.* I know it's a long shot, but I have to try.

"Cowboy Boogie?" A high-pitched female voice with an unidentifiable Southern region accent answers abruptly.

"Um, yes, I'm looking for Dale. I believe he's one of the bouncers there."

"Yeah, you and about fifty other girls," evident annoyance in her voice.

"Is he there by any chance?"

"No, his shift ended about an hour ago."

"Do you know where I could reach him? It's kind of an emergency."

"Hun, you sound like a nice girl. If I were you, I would forget about two-timin' Dale and find yourself a nice boy."

"It's not like that, uh, I'm looking for my friend. She said she was going out with him tonight. There's been an emergency in her family."

"Look, I don't know where he is, or went, or with who, okay?"

"Okay, thanks anyway." There is a loud click on the other end of the line.

What do I do now? If I go down there, they might have left already, especially if his shift has been over for a while.

Then the phone rings again.

"Hello?"

"Hey, Maddy!" *Oh, sigh.* The sound of his voice gives me such sweet, momentary relief.

"Hi Peter, how was band practice?" I try to mask the tightness in my throat from being upset.

"Not good. Only the singer, Luke, and I showed up. What's wrong?"

"Maggie's dad called looking for her 'cause her grandma's in the hospital, she had a really serious heart attack, and I don't know where Maggie is, 'cause she went out with some guy named Dale who works at the Cowboy Boogie, and I don't think she's going to come back tonight and her dad is going to keep calling and he's going to find out that she's been sleeping around and he's going to be so disappointed in Maggie and Maggie is going to be crushed and her grandma whom she adores is going to pass away while she is out with this idiot guy who is just using her…" By this time, I've completely lost it, and my sobs come thick and wet into the phone.

"Okay, Maddy, stay there. I'm coming to pick you up, and we'll find Maggie."

"I already called the Cowboy Boogie. They said Dale's shift was over an hour ago." I wipe my sopping wet eyes and running nose with pink tissues from the box on Maggie's desk.

"Maybe they're still hanging out there," Peter suggests.

"I don't think so. Maggie was planning to stay out all night with him. Knowing her and the kind of guys she dates, they went straight to his place after work."

"I'm not sure what to suggest." Peter sighs heavily.

"Me neither. I guess there's nothing to do."

"Do you want me to come pick you up anyway?"

"I would love that, but I need to stay here in case, by some miracle, Maggie comes back. I don't want to leave her a note saying, 'Call your dad; your grandma is dying in the hospital,'" I massage my temples.

"That probably wouldn't be good."

"Would you mind coming here? We have open floor time for a little while longer. I could really use the company."

"I'll be there as fast as I can."

"Thank you. Please be careful, okay?"

"I will."

I hang up the phone and glance over at the mirror at my reflection. It's amazing how quickly vanity creeps in, even in the midst of tragedy. My eyes are red and swollen, my nose is shiny and red, and my bangs are a mess and sticking up from me holding my forehead in my hand. I run to the bathroom to splash cold water on my face and return quickly in case the phone rings.

About fifteen minutes later, the phone rings.

"I'm here." A familiar, deep, sweet male voice says.

"I'll be right up to let you in." I run down the hall and up the stairs to the lobby.

He looks so beautiful standing there in his black leather motorcycle jacket, with the lights gleaming in his long dark hair falling in wavy layers just below his shoulders. Again, even in the midst of calamity, I'm still struck with wonderment that this awesome guy is my boyfriend. I open the heavy glass door. His face is filled with concern, but he still smiles when he sees me.

"I'm so glad you're here." I take a deep breath to stop the floodgate of tears from bursting open again.

"You know it," he lowers his head to whisper in my ear as he folds me in his arms, holding me tight and smoothing my hair.

I would love to tell you that all I feel is comfort right now, but to be honest, since Peter and I have never really had more than hand-to-hand physical contact, the shock of feeling more than just his hands rushes through me, causing me to tingle and burn all over. I can feel that his arms are firm and strong as he holds me close against his muscular chest. I try not to memorize the feel of the taught muscles of his waist and lower back where my hands rest.

The smell of his leather jacket, slightly damp from the moist evening ocean air, is intoxicating. I breathe in deeply the scent of his T-shirt. He must have changed shirts right before he came over because the clean detergent smell is strong and fresh. How sweet! The things we do for love.

Oh, creeping crud! I just realized I'm not wearing a bra! I forgot to put it back on after I took it off when I settled in to study. In fact, I think it's still hanging on the back of my desk chair.

Thankfully, I'm wearing my chunkiest, thick black cable knit sweater that hangs past my hips, so I hope he can't feel my breasts closely. But my past experience with guys has taught me, though, that he probably can. Hopefully, he's gentlemanly enough to try to ignore my unbound mammary glands.

He moves his hands to my waist and looks at me with a furrowed brow. His face fills with concern for me again.

"I'm really glad you came. Come in." Reality jerks me away from my fleshly thoughts. I need to get back to my room in case the phone rings.

He follows me downstairs. His hands are shoved deep into the pockets of his jacket as we walk down the hall to my room.

"Come in, have a seat." He takes off his jacket and sits in the overstuffed black velvet chair next to my bed.

"Cool chair." He sits back into it and runs his hands over the soft fabric on the arms.

"That's my reading and writing chair. I saw it in one of the swanky furniture stores my mother drags me to when I'm home. My stepdad bought it for me for my birthday."

"So, this is where you live. It's nice," he looks around.

"Thanks, make yourself at home."

He looks around the room some more, taking it all in. He surveys Maggie's side of the room. A pastel pink lace comforter and matching pillows are crumpled at one end of her bed. Clothes and bras are strewn across the rest of her bed. Underwear hangs out of the dresser drawers. A small smirk breaks across his face as he sees her wall coverings, particularly the shirtless cowboy poster.

"Interesting poster."

"Maggie's favorite. She bought it this past summer in Dallas."

"And that must be the biggest map of Texas I have ever seen. It goes well with the big Texas flag hanging next to it. Hmm, I sense a theme here."

"Yeah, I've had the pleasure of gazing upon her stately decor since our freshman year."

"Lucky you. At least they're better than the posters of naked and nearly naked women my roommate hung all over the house. I asked him to take down the ones in the living room and bathroom. I don't think he liked that very much, but come on, we're not sixteen anymore. Besides, I don't want to be looking at that stuff."

Speaking of boobs—my bra! I casually step over to my desk chair and nonchalantly reach for it. But as I grab it, one of the strap snags on the back of the chair so it unfolds and stretches out in plain view. I'm mortified by the vast size of the half-moon wires covered in black silky fabric.

It's not like I've never had guys see my bra before, but it's different now. Different with Peter. I quickly glance over at him, and he looks away, slightly red-faced, and a little smile at the corner of his mouth. I untangle the bra quickly fold it up, and shove it into my dresser drawer.

He turns his attention to my side of the room. He gets up and walks over to the posters hanging on the wall opposite the desk wall unit that divides the room.

"I like your posters. Black-and-white pictures have a different look like there's a texture to them that you can't see in color pictures. And the light looks different," he muses. "I recognize this one, of the couple kissing in Paris."

"They're all Robert Doisneau photographs. He's one of my favorite photographers. My mom and stepdad bought me the poster of the couple kissing with a hotel in the background when they were in Paris a couple of summers ago."

"Yeah, that's where I've seen it before."

"In Paris? Seriously?" I'm not sure if he's kidding me.

"Yeah, when I was little, little kid. I was only four years old. With my mother. She was visiting some friends and family, and she took me with her."

"Lucky! I've never been to Europe, but my mom and Dr. Bill go all the time."

"I haven't been there since then. I was born there. Not in Paris, but in a small hospital in my mother's hometown in the south of France."

"Really? Whoa, so I'm dating a foreigner. *Ooh la, la,* how exotic," I bat my eyelashes at him like a geek. Learning new things about my guy is *très magnifique.*

"Actually, I have dual citizenship because my father is American, but I was born in France."

"So I gather your mother is French, then?"

"Yeah."

"And you don't go back to visit her family?"

"Just that one time. I don't remember that much about the trip, but I do remember staying at my mother's aunt's house, and there was a bunch of ladies of various ages who strongly resembled my mother there, too. And they kept pinching me and cooing at me in French," he grins.

"I bet you were a darling little boy."

"I guess," he smiles. Then his face goes serious. "I remember going to meet my mother's father. He was such an as—I mean, jerk. I remember him speaking harshly to my mother in French. I don't know what he said, but whatever it was made her cry.

She sat on her bed, crying and holding me tight on her lap for a long time, and then we left for the States soon after that."

"What happened?" I feel nosy, but I'm too curious not to ask.

"I don't know. She never told me. I guess she figures I wouldn't remember anything because I was so young." He continues to stare at the black and white photographs. "I don't see her often. She travels a lot." I can only see one side of his face, which looks sad, and then gives way to a little scowl, and his jaw muscles tighten. "This photo of Picasso is hilarious. Tiny baguettes for fingers on a table, that's pretty funny," he says without laughing. His abrupt change of subject seems very deliberate. Subject closed.

I feel hurt that he doesn't want to talk about this obviously painful subject with me. But I sense that now is not the time to pry. Accurately reading body language was a survival technique I learned growing up since my mother's moods would swing more than a public park swing set on a sunny Saturday afternoon. I quickly learned when it was okay to speak and when absolute silence was crucial.

He does a double take at the four long, narrow tapestries I have hanging on the wall along the side of my bed.

"No way! These are from the Haunted Mansion at Disneyland, from the paintings that stretch at the beginning of the ride. They're so cool!"

"It's my favorite ride at Disneyland. Maggie and I used to have annual passes since it's just down the freeway from here. We used to go and just hang out, eat some food, and hop on a few rides."

"Had she been to Disneyland before she came out here to Biola?"

"No, and she loved it. She said the 'Alice in Wonderland' ride was her favorite, because it reminded her of living with me, how it's all crazy and psychedelic. In our freshman year, we went with Suzette and Bethany a couple of times. Suzette is fun, but Bethany really gets on your nerves after a while, mostly because she's so critical of everything and everyone. She got so annoying the last time we went that when Bethany was in the bathroom, Maggie asked Suzette that the next time we go on the Matterhorn ride, if she would do us all a favor and kindly push Bethany off the ride when it got to the fast and high part."

"Yikes!" His eyes are wide.

"Yeah, I'm pretty sure Maggie was kidding, but to avoid any potential random acts of violence, we didn't ask Bethany to come with us anymore."

"Man, I haven't been to Disneyland in years. We'll have to go some time."

"I would like that. Very much." Spend the whole day hanging out with Peter at one of my favorite places on earth? Heck yeah! It would truly be "the happiest place on earth." Then again, Peter could take me to the city dump, and I would enjoy it.

"My mom and Dr. Bill used to take me to Disneyland every year for my birthday. I would always insist we go on the Haunted Mansion ride three or four times while we were there. I was a strange kid."

"What do you mean 'was'?" Peter teases me and flashes me a big smile as I fake a pouty look. "You know that's one of the things I love about you." His words melt me from the inside out.

I love watching him study my room. Usually, I don't like people looking at my stuff, it makes me feel so self-conscious, but this is cool. He moves over to my bookshelf.

"Anne Rice, love her books."

Watching his fingers gently run over the spines of my books conjures up unholy images in my mind. I squeeze my eyes tight to clear my head. "Yeah, she's one of my all-time favorite writers. She's such a great storyteller."

"What's your favorite book by her?"

"Hmm, probably *The Vampire Lestat*. I read it in two days. I really felt like I was there at all the places Lestat went. I want to be able to write like that someday."

"Yeah, I know what you mean about feeling like you're there in New Orleans and all those places in Europe as you read the book." He continues to look through my books. "Hmm, no Stephen King here."

"I tried to read *The Shining*, but it gave me nightmares, so I had to stop."

"I think I've read most of his books. My uncle and I trade off. I like Frank Peretti, too. *The Oath* was really cool, a great parable of the power of the presence of sin."

"*This Present Darkness* is a classic. I think I've read it twice. Although lately, most of my reading time is spent on books for my classes."

"A lot of Madeleine L'Engle books here. I take it she's one of your favorites, too?"

"I love her so much. And she's my namesake."

"Oh really? Her name sounds familiar, but I don't know if I ever read any of her books."

"Did you ever read *A Wrinkle in Time?*"

"Yeah, actually, my fourth-grade teacher read it to us. I remember liking it a lot. She wrote that?"

"It's her most well-known book."

"That's cool; maybe I'll re-read it," he moves over to my CD rack on the next shelf. We have a lot of the same CDs." He looks through and opens a couple of CDs to look at them and then carefully places them back where they were. Whoa, you have Child of the Son CDs, too. They are so good."

"I love their music and lyrics—they are so testimonial. And I love that they are a married couple who writes, records, and performs music together."

"Yeah, that's really cool. What a blessing that must be for them. The guy is an awesome guitar player and producer, too," Peter looks through the rest of my CDs. "So, what's your favorite Peter Murphy song?"

"Hmm, it depends on my mood, but it's either *Marlene Dietrich's Favorite Poem* or *Cut's You Up*. And you?"

"*A Strange Kind of Love.* I love the acoustic guitar in that song."

"You want to listen to some music?"

"No, not right now." He goes back and sits down in the velvet chair.

"Me neither."

"This feels kinda weird," looks around.

"What does?"

"For one, being in an all-girls dorm room is not something I've ever experienced before." He sits forward in the chair and leans on his knees. "But really, being alone with you. I feel almost nervous, but it's nice at the same time."

"Yeah, for me, too." I feel my face slowly grow hot with a rush of blood. "I haven't had a guy in my room in a long time. Of course, it's different this time, different with you." My face feels like it's glowing red.

"I'm just glad I could be here with you in such a rough situation."

"I'm really glad you're here, too. I know Maggie's dad is going to call back any minute, and I'm going to have to tell him she's not back yet. Part of me wants to leave so I don't have to deal with any of it. But I don't think that's the right thing to do. And besides, I prayed and prayed that she would come home soon and not stay out all night, so then I could tell her about her grandma, and she would be here when her dad calls back."

"That's so good of you. I hope Maggie realizes what a great friend she has in you."

"Thanks, that's kind of you to say. But I'm pretty sure Maggie thinks I'm a foolish prude right now. I don't know. We've been through so much. She's like the sister I never had, but whom my mother would've liked better than me," I try to laugh it off.

"Someday, she will realize how hard all this was on you and how much you prayed for her," his big, beautiful green eyes are fixed on me.

"I really hope so. I really, really hope you're right. I would hate to lose her friendship. I feel like we've grown up together, these past three-plus years. We've been through a lot of good times and crazy predicaments. But it seems like we've been growing apart lately. It really sucks. I miss her."

"It's not because of me, is it?" Peter looks concerned.

"Not you specifically. I haven't really dated anyone since Maggie and I have been roommates. Suzette says Maggie's jealous of me. But really, she started pulling away before I met you, like right about the time classes started."

"What happened?"

"She started seeing all these guys again. Guys that I know she knows are bad for her. It's almost like she doesn't care anymore, and she just does whatever she wants. I know she got hot and heavy with some guy in Dallas over the summer. But it seems like she goes out with one guy after another. I wonder if she just gave up trying to be pure. I don't know. I don't know what to pray anymore." I feel my throat tighten, and my eyes start to well up.

Peter gets up and sits down next to me on the bed. He puts his arm around me, and I put my head on his shoulder. And the sobs start coming hard. Ordinarily, I would feel like such an idiot for losing it in front of a guy I like so much, but it feels really good to have someone comforting me for once. I start hiccupping and my nose is doing the 10K run. Peter reaches over and hands me the tissue box from my nightstand. He's so sweet. *Lord, thank You for him.*

I'm jolted away from my prayer of thankfulness by our ringing phone. I take a deep breath, wipe my nose, and get up to answer the phone.

"Howdy Maddy, is Maggie in yet?"

"No sir, she hasn't come back yet." I hear a deep, heavy sigh on the other end of the line, followed by another heavy sigh. I look over at Peter.

"Okay, I'll try back again in a little while."

"I'm sorry, Pastor Morris."

"Oh no, hon, it's not your fault, not at all."

Yeah, well, I feel like it is. I wish I could have done more to keep your daughter, your one and only child, out of trouble. "Well, um, I'll be sure to have Maggie call her aunt as soon as she gets in."

"Okay, thanks darlin'. You're a peach."

"Thanks. G'night."

I hear a gentle click. I cover my face with my hands and start pacing the floor.

"He knows. I know he knows. This totally sucks! I'm going to kill her! Her dad sounds so sad. Not only does he have his dying mother in the hospital to deal with, but now he's got reason to suspect that his daughter is out late on a school night, doing God knows what with some guy. She's going to get in so much trouble." My growing anger stifles my tears.

"Maybe this will be good for her. Maybe this is her wake-up call to get her to stop doing whatever she's doing. Maybe this is the answer to your prayers," Peter suggests.

I stop mid-pace and look over at him. The wisdom of his words smacks a deep truth in me. I know he's right. "What did I do to deserve such a wise and patient guy in my life?" I sit down next to him on my bed.

"God is good." He whispers as he wraps his arms around me and begins to pray. "Heavenly Father, we thank You and praise You for the work You are already doing in Maggie and in all of us. We know You won't let us go until You have completed this work in us. Please keep Maggie safe and bring comfort and strength to her father and grandmother during this time. And thank You so much for bringing my sweet Madeleine and me together, especially during this difficult time. Please give her strength and grace and help in this time of need. I ask all this in Your Son's beautiful name, Amen."

After he finishes praying, he holds me for a minute or so. Then he quickly pulls away and clears his throat. "It's getting late. I should probably go."

"Yeah, I guess. The open floor hours were over a little while ago."

"You're not going to get in trouble, are you?"

"No, Allison, our Residence Assistant, is pretty cool. She must have suspected something is going on 'cause I don't usually spend the evening as a blubbering idiot. And we've had the door open, and she is just across the hall."

"That's cool." He gets up to go. "Call me if you need anything, okay? Promise?"

"I promise. Scout's honor." I hold up two fingers.

"I was never a boy scout, but I'll take that." He smiles brightly at me.

"Come on, I'll walk you up to the lobby." I grab his hand and lead him down the hall and up the stairs.

He gives me a warm hug before he leaves. This time, instead of lusting after the feel of his body, I feel so safe and comforted in his arms. I watch him as he walks to his truck.

I *so* don't want him to leave right now. I want him to stay all night and hold me—just hold me. And there are no lustful feelings attached to this overwhelming desire—just to feel comforted and loved.

Well, how about that? I think I'm changing, or actually, I'm being changed. *Praise God.*

Chapter Eighteen

I shut off my alarm, and roll over and look across the room. With the little bit of morning light coming in through the windows, I can see that nothing in our room has changed since I went to bed the night before.

There is no body curled up under the pastel pink comforter on Maggie's bed. The clothes left on her bed haven't changed shape. Everything is as I expected.

I always wake-up whenever Maggie comes home in the middle of the night, and it takes me forever to get back to sleep. But there was no Maggie slipping in, in the middle of the night to disturb my already fitful and sparse sleep. I knew it was only wishful thinking that she would be in her bed this morning.

I force myself out of bed, turn on the lights, and start my morning routine. I'm so unbelievably tired. I hardly slept because I kept expecting Maggie to come in, and I couldn't calm my mind from what will happen if she doesn't come back before her dad calls.

My eyelids feel like sandpaper. I feel worse this morning than from any hangover I had in my B.C. partying days. I grab my robe, towel and shower caddy and begin to stagger to the bathroom for a shower. Just as I'm about to leave the room, the phone rings. *Oh Lord, please help.*

"Hello?" I try not to sound as groggy as I feel.

"Howdy Maddy. Is my daughter awake yet?" Maggie's dad sounds tired, too.

Okay, here's where I'm *real* tempted to lie. I could say she's not awake yet, but he might ask me to wake her and put her on the phone. Or I could give the excuse that she left early to go to the library, but this is highly unbelievable since "early" is way out of character for her. It's one of the main things we have in common. But I decide the truth is best.

"No, um, sir, she uh, never came home last night." Everything in me cringes, and I feel like throwing up.

Silence. Then, a heavy sigh on the other end of the phone line. "I was afraid of that. Okay, will you please have her call me at home when she does get in?"

"Yes, call you at home?"

"Yes, Eudora went home to be with the Lord in the middle of the night."

"Oh, I'm so sorry."

"Well, she's not sufferin' anymore. Since there was nothin' else that needed doin' at the hospital, we came home to get some rest before we start makin' all the arrangements and callin' everyone."

"I'm so sorry, Pastor Morris, sorry about everything."

"Me too, I'm real disappointed in Maggie. She told me she was past all this foolishness. Well, I don't want to take up any more of your time. I'm sure you've got classes to get to."

"I will have Maggie call you as soon as I see her." I wish my voice wasn't trembling so much.

"Thanks, sweetheart. Ya'll don't pay no mind to any of this, ya hear?"

"Okay." *Yeah right.*

"Thanks, hon." He hangs up.

This totally stinks to high heaven. I feel so sick to my stomach. I know what Peter said about Maggie is true, about how getting caught is her wake-up call, but I still feel like such a traitor. We've always covered for each other in the past. I know telling the truth was the right thing to do, but man, why does it have to hurt so badly?

I grab my bathroom stuff and head for the showers, where I can let my tears flow freely.

As I brush my teeth at the sink, wrapped in my thick bathrobe and my wet hair twisted up in a towel, Bethany comes up to the sink next to me and starts brushing her teeth. She is still in her pajamas, with her disheveled hair pulled back in a matching headband. She looks like she got as much sleep as I did. And I notice her eyes are as swollen and red as mine are.

Our eyes meet in the mirror. I really don't want to say anything. I'm not in the mood to console someone else, especially someone I don't particularly like all that much.

"Morning, Bethany," I mumble through toothpaste.

"Hi, Maddy." She sniffs.

"Are you okay?" I have to ask, right?

"No, not really."

"What's wrong?"

Her face wrinkles up with a fresh set of tears as she spits toothpaste into the sink. "Chad and I broke up last night."

Whoa! I was so totally not expecting that response. "Oh Beth, I'm so sorry." *Liar.* I turn and give her a hug. She sobs into the towel on my head. "Um, maybe you guys are just getting cold feet, you know, like some people do before they get married."

I know it's a stupid thing to say, but I'm caught off guard here, and I can't think of anything else. Besides, secretly, this is good news to me. Chad is such a weasel. I say good riddance to him.

"No, it's not that. We're definitely not getting back together. Not ever."

"Why? How do you know?"

"I just do. Besides, he broke up with me." She wipes the fresh tears rolling down her face. "I can't really talk about it right now."

"Okay. Um, come by my room if you need someone to talk to, okay?"

"Thanks. You're so nice." She gives me a quick hug, then picks up her bathroom caddy and leaves the bathroom.

I feel bad that Bethany is upset about her break-up with Chad, but man, she has no idea how much better off she is not being with that guy, especially not marrying that little weasel.

I hear country music seeping from our room as I push the door open. Maggie is sitting on the floor, leaning against her bed. I almost gag at the smell that fills our room from the greasy fast food breakfast Maggie is eating. She looks pleased with herself, almost smug, as she sits there munching away and tapping her foot to the vile sound. "Hey there," she says between bites.

"Hey. Call your dad," I say without looking at her.

"Why? Did he call?"

Duh. "Yes, twice last night and again this morning."

Out of the corner of my eye, I can see Maggie's face turn ghost white, and she stops chewing. I feel fresh waves of nausea.

"Did you talk to him? What did you tell him?"

I just look at her. I don't say anything. I'm surprised by the anger rising in me.

"Madeleine! What did you tell him?"

"The truth. That you weren't here. Okay? I had to tell him the truth." I finish combing out my wet hair and begin to get dressed. I can't even look at her, but I feel her looking at me. I quickly finish getting ready and grab my backpack.

I turn to her before I leave the room. I take a deep breath so I don't sound enraged. "You need to call your dad. Your Grandma Dora was in the hospital."

I leave the room before she has a chance to say anything. All the way to the gym for chapel, I swallow hard and take deep breaths to stave off more tears.

My mind is so mixed up. I have trouble paying attention to the chapel speaker. I try to pray, but I don't know what to pray. I have the strongest urge to cut out of here and go to try to find Peter. But even if I knew where his job site is today, I know that's not the right thing to do, especially in my current highly emotional state.

The speaker finishes up and asks us all to bow our heads to pray. His words are drowned out in my head by my own prayer for help.

Lord, I know I did the right thing, telling Maggie's dad the truth, didn't I? Why do I feel so terrible?

Then I hear a voice inside me, speaking to me so softly and gently. *Yes, beloved. Sometimes doing the right thing hurts, but I cause all things to work together for good to those who love Me, to those who are called according to My purpose.*

My eyes well up with new tears. But this time, they are tears of comfort and grace, at the sound of this sweet, still, small voice I hear inside me. It's just a few words, but they carry a whole chapter's worth of meaning to me.

I wipe my eyes with my sweater sleeve and walk to class feeling refreshed, reassured, and renewed. I realize that I am living and experiencing the Scripture, "Therefore let us draw near with confidence to the throne of grace, so that we may receive mercy and find grace to help in time of need."

I can't wait to share this with Peter. It's one of his favorite verses in the Bible.

Thank You, Lord. Thank You so much. I love You.

Chapter Nineteen

uzette and I pull into the Del Taco parking lot. The weather has turned cold and damp, so we put on our coats to make the trip to the front door of one of our favorite dining establishments.

The warm air and zesty scent of taco seasoning fills my nostrils as I open the front door of the restaurant. We order our food, and sit at one of the tables with the matching bright orange Formica benches.

"Thanks for coming out to eat with me. I needed to get out of there." Suzette says as she looks down, and pushes the white plastic triangle with her order number on it to the edge of the table.

"You don't need to thank me. I've been trying to avoid Maggie all week, since I was forced to tell her dad the truth about her 'indiscretions,' as she calls them. I'm still so angry with her." I take a deep breath, and let it out slowly. "So how's Bethany doing?"

"She's still really upset. She cries a lot. I feel really bad for her. But secretly, I'm glad she's not with Chad anymore."

"I know the feeling." Boy, do I know the feeling.

"There's just always been something not right about that guy," Suzette looks out the window.

Again, I know the feeling. "Did she tell you why they broke up?"

"Yes." Suzette looks away. "I'm not supposed to tell anyone. I mean, she probably wouldn't mind if you knew. I know she thinks a lot of you." *Really? I would've guessed differently.*

"You don't have to tell me, but judging by the chain of events I've witnessed, I can guess," I try really hard not to sound smug. And relieved.

"Really?" Suzette looks at me.

"Totally."

"What would you guess happened, 'cause that wouldn't be like telling you, right?"

"My guess would be that Chad and Bethany had sex, and now Chad broke up with her because he doesn't want her anymore, for any number of reasons. It could be: a) he's completed his conquest, so now he wants to move on to the next challenge; or b) he doesn't want her anymore because she's defiled and not pure anymore, so she is no longer the ideal wife material for him; or c) all of the above."

"What makes you think all that?" Suzette looks truly astonished.

"Well, let's look at the facts pertaining to the Weasel and all his weasel ways."

"Who's the 'Weasel'?"

"Oh, that's just what I call Chad in my head. No offense to weasels."

"I like it! it fits him." She laughs.

"Thanks, I think so, too." I nod. "Anyway, he used to call Bethany a lot, right? Then, all of a sudden, he isn't calling so much. What changed? There's also the little incident Peter and I witnessed in the parking lot."

"What incident?" Suzette looks very puzzled.

When our order numbers are called, I grab our little white triangles and take them to the counter to get our trays of food. I put Suzette's tray in front of her, and we asked God's blessing on our tacos and burritos.

"What incident?" Suzette repeats herself, staring wide-eyed at me, as I tear open little red packets of hot sauce.

"It was a while back. On the first night, Peter picked me up for dinner at our dorm room. As we were walking through the parking lot to his truck, we passed by Bethany and Chad totally making-out in Chad's car."

"No way!" Suzette looks stunned. "Why didn't you tell me?"

"'Cause I didn't want to gossip. But I guess it doesn't matter now."

"That's so not like them. Are you sure it was them?"

"Well, yeah, Chad's little pricey sports car is pretty recognizable in a parking lot full of early-model student-owned clunkers."

"Did they see you guys?"

"No, they were really into what they were doing."

"Oh my goodness." Suzette still looks shocked. "What did Peter say?"

"He seemed kind of taken aback, and then he said they were playing with fire. But you know, I'm kinda glad we witnessed that because hearing Peter say what he said really helped me suppress the super strong desire I had to make out with him. But for the grace of God, go I, the same place as Chad and Bethany. I try to never forget that."

"That's really smart. And wise, too."

"So am I right about why they broke up?"

Suzette lets out a long, sad sigh. "Yes."

"A, b or c?"

"C, all of the above."

"That is so lame! That little weasel! Did he actually tell Bethany she wasn't pure enough for him?" For some reason, I'm really angry.

"Not in so many words, but she said he told her that he realized that she wasn't the sort of woman he wanted for his wife."

"You're kidding? He didn't really say that to her?"

"He did. Bethany is so upset, mostly at herself. You have to promise not to tell anyone, please! Bethany is already crushed, but I think she thinks no one else knows about her and Chad having sex. And please don't tell Maggie. I have a feeling she would love to rub it in Bethany's face since Bethany has always been very vocal about her disapproval of Maggie's love life."

"Oh, I know she would. But don't worry, I won't tell Maggie or anyone. I'm not really speaking to Maggie right now, anyway. I'm still so angry at her for putting me in the middle of her and her dad. I need to just get over it. I mean, it's not like she did it to me on purpose. I don't know. Maybe I'm just frustrated with her."

"Yeah, but that was a really awkward position she put you in by not coming home that night. I'm surprised it didn't happen sooner."

"No kidding. Peter said maybe this is an answer to my prayers and that getting caught was her wake-up call."

"That sounds so right. He's pretty wise."

"Yeah, he is." I look out the window, surprised by how much I miss him right now.

"Weren't you guys supposed to go out tonight?"

"He asked me to go to *Brewed of Vipers* with him, but I told him I wanted to go out to dinner with you because of everything you're dealing with, Bethany."

"That's so sweet of you. But I don't want you to miss an evening with your man."

"I know, but when I told him why I wanted to spend the evening with you, he thought it was the right thing to do, even though he said he would miss me." I try to suppress the sappy smile that's inching its way across my face.

"Awww, that's cute," Suzette joins me with a sentimental grin.

"Seriously though, I told him everything about Bethany after I ran into her in the bathroom the morning after Chad broke up with her. He gave me the guy's insight about Chad and the possible reasons why he broke up with her. He said he would pray for them."

"That's so awesome of him."

"Yeah, I think so." *Really awesome.* "He also told me that most guys are ruled by their inner caveman, who only wants to conquer and multiply. That is, until Christ comes inside their hearts and minds, cleans up the place, and brings the cavemen out of the dark, craven cave and into the light. And He makes them walk upright, bathe regularly, and stop scratching themselves." I try to contain my laughter.

"That's funny! Did he really say that?" Suzette giggles.

"Yes! Now I have this constant mental picture of guys wearing animal skins and carrying big clubs, and jumping up and down, and scratching themselves in their privates."

"Now that you mention it, that fits Chad perfectly."

"Doesn't it? Only his skin would be a weasel skin." I have to laugh at the mental picture I have of Chad the Weasel Caveman, all hunched over and drooling.

Suzette laughs with me for a moment; then her face gets serious. "So what are you going to do about Maggie?"

"I don't know. I can't avoid her forever. Peter jokingly offered that I could stay with him at his house until things blow over, but as much as I would absolutely love that, we both agreed that was definitely not even a possibility."

"I agree, but that was sweet of him to think of it and to offer it to you."

"Yeah, and he's got his own roommate woes to deal with right now. His roommate, Andrew just had his girlfriend move in with him. And apparently, she likes to walk around the house wearing only her skivvies."

"In front of Peter?"

"Yes!"

"Ewww! That's kind of skanky, don't you think?"

"Well, yeah! I hate it! That fornicating trollop parades around almost naked in front of my man. And Peter said Andrew and his girlfriend are really loud if you know what I mean."

Suzette leans in close to me to whisper. "He can hear them having *sex*? *Double ewww!*"

"And he can't really say anything to Andrew about it, because it's Andrew's dad's house he is renting a room in."

"That's tough. Could he move out and rent a room somewhere else?"

"He said he prayed about it, and his uncle offered to help him buy a house of his own, but he feels that he should stay with Andrew while he is on the spiritual skids. And Andrew is his best friend, so he feels he shouldn't abandon him."

"Oh, so he's a believer. That makes it even tougher."

"Yeah, he is. So Peter can really sympathize with me and my trouble with Maggie. I'm really trying to be forgiving toward her, but then I think she didn't really do anything to me that I need to forgive her for. But I'm still so mad at her."

"But for the grace of God, go—"

"—go I? I know, I know. Believe me, I know. I guess I need to apply that saying to this situation, too."

"Maybe." Suzette looks down at the table.

"No, you are right, I do. I could easily be in Maggie's situation, except my mother wouldn't care if I slept with Peter. She would just lecture me about taking precautions and not getting pregnant unless, of course, he had a really good, high-paying job. But that's another story." I pause for a moment to eradicate images of sleeping with Peter from my mind. I literally shake my head a little, as if my mind was an Etch-A-Sketch. "How are you doing through all this?" I ask Suzette to purposely change the subject.

"I'm okay. All this drama has certainly squelched my desire to be in a relationship, that's for sure. Funny how that happens."

'Really?" I wish I didn't sound so astonished.

"Yeah. Remember when I told you about that Chinese student I helped at the library?"

"Yes."

"Well, I was praying about that a lot because there just seemed to be something about that situation that struck a chord in me. So, I went by the Intercultural Studies office to ask if there was some kind of program for teaching English overseas."

Suzette lights up as she animatedly tells me about this program, she is applying to that involves teaching English overseas as part of the mission field. She is so excited as she describes how great the organization is and what a great opportunity it is to spread the gospel.

"And the best part is that my parents are really excited about it too, and they are raising funds among our family and friends at our church to pay for all my costs!" She is almost glowing with excitement.

"Suz, that is amazing! I'm so excited for you! What a great opportunity," I'm so excited for her.

"Isn't it awesome? I couldn't go if I was tied down with a boyfriend or fiancé, so I'm glad I'm single right now. I'm also glad not to have to deal with guy drama in my life right now, either."

"So true." I can't believe I'm hearing these words coming from Suzette, the former diehard marriage-seeker.

"Not that all guys cause drama; I mean, you and Peter seem to be okay."

"Yes, we are okay. Beyond okay. He's the best thing, besides getting saved, that has ever happened to me." I feel my throat tighten as I realize what I just said is the truth.

"That's so fantastic. Maddy, I'm so happy for you."

"Thanks. Despite all that's going on, I'm pretty happy, and Peter seems to be, too."

"You guys look so right together. And I mean not just because you guys are both rockin' gothic type people. There's just something else between you two."

"Yeah, I think so, too." I miss him a ton right now. We should get back. I've still got a couple of papers to proofread before I can turn them in tomorrow." Okay, I'll admit it. I want to call Peter, too, just to hear his voice.

"Oh, don't remind me. I guess I'll go to the library to study so Bethany can grieve in peace."

We pick up our trays, dump the trash in the big square trash cans, and place the trays on top. As we walk out to my car, the cold moist ocean air gives me the chills, but it feels refreshing.

I feel much better having talked with Suzette about stuff. I feel ready to get back to my dorm room, get over myself, and be the sort of caring and compassionate roommate that Maggie needs and that God originally planned me to be.

Chapter Twenty

"**M**ad, you'll need some earplugs, do you have any? If not, I have an extra set for you." Peter always takes such good care of me.

"Are you guys that loud?"

"We can be, and it's a small rehearsal room."

I study his profile as he drives, his straight nose and strong jaw. I still want to pinch myself sometimes to make sure I'm not dreaming that this awesome guy is my boyfriend. He looks over at me and smiles as if he knows what I'm thinking. Sometimes, I wonder if he does know.

I told Peter I wanted to see his band rehearse before their next big show. I just plain love spending time with him, no matter what he's doing.

"Are you hungry?" he glances over at me.

"Yes. I came right from my last class, so I didn't eat dinner yet."

"See, I knew that. I've got your class schedule down now. Where would you like to eat?"

"Hmmm...how about In-N-Out?" I smile at him. I know it's his favorite.

"Oh, you're speaking my language. A Double-Double sounds so good right now."

"Animal style, of course," I add.

"You know it. That's my girl." He smiles at me again.

I so love the sound of him calling me "his girl. " He turns the corner and heads to the nearest In-N-Out Burger.

Peter and I have been practically inseparable lately. It's like we've become best friends, and I guess we have. I'm at the coffeehouse with him when I'm not in class or at work. We go to church every Sunday together and then hang out all day. And now I'm joining him at his band rehearsal.

Suzette and I haven't been able to hang out much since she is busy with all the applications and preparation to participate in the ministry to teach English overseas after graduation. So, I don't feel so guilty about spending all my free time with Peter.

Maggie has sequestered herself to schoolwork. After her father found out about her "extracurricular" activities, she met with her counselor and professors to work out a plan to help her get somewhat caught up with her assignments. Since she was way behind in her homework, she will work toward at least passing her classes.

It seems as if Maggie has turned a corner in her life. She doesn't say much to me, and I don't push or pry. I just try to be sweet and supportive. She isn't going out at night anymore — thank God, big time. She won't even answer the phone. Sometimes, we eat lunch together, but even then, she is quiet. Peter and I pray for her a lot and for Andrew, his roommate, too.

Peter pulls into the driveway and parks under the giant signature yellow arrow sign. After much playful chastisement on his part, I've learned to wait for him to come around my side of his truck to open the door for me and help me down. He also opens the door of the restaurant for me, too.

I can almost taste the engulfing, mouth-watering scent of grilled onions and French fries. Peter orders two Double-Doubles, animal style, two orders of fries, and two large Diet Cokes. He pays and takes the plastic tent card with our order number on it. We take a seat at a table by a window so we can keep an eye on his truck since his guitars and music gear are stowed in the back. He leans forward and puts his hand on mine. He looks serious behind the hair that falls forward around his face.

"Hey, Mad, I've got a question for you."

He started calling me "Mad" a few weeks ago. He said "Madeleine" is beautiful but formal, and "Maddy" is cute, but that's what all my friends call me, and he wanted a name that only he calls me. And he said it suits me, seeing as I'm a little bit nuts (but in a good way, he says). I like it. I like it a lot.

"Ask away." *Gulp.*

"Would you come to my brother's rehearsal dinner with me and then be my date at his wedding? Before you answer, I must warn you. It probably won't be a very pleasant experience."

"You know I'd love to go anywhere with you, especially a major family event like your brother's wedding. But Peter, I didn't even know you had a brother." I have this sort of weird mixture of sadness and excitement rolling around in my gut.

"I know, I'm sorry. I guess I should've said something before," Peter looks tense. "Matt and I only talk once in a while. But he called me last night, and we talked for a long time."

"I've never heard you mention him or the fact that he's getting married." I'm hurt that I didn't know this about him after all this time we've spent together.

"Family stuff is not something I like to think about, much less talk about," he runs his hand through the front of his hair. "It's hard to explain, at least without going off on my family in a direction that, you know, sheds an unfavorable light on them, shall we say. Uh, my entire family, in general, is not close. Not at all."

"Oh," is all I can think of to say. Peter looks uncomfortable, but he continues to explain.

"It starts with my father. I told you about how he and I don't get along at all. God has dealt with me severely on this subject, about how I need to respect him because he's my father, even when he says cruel asinine things to me. I don't need to agree with him, but I must honor him because he is my father, even though he has made it very clear that he doesn't approve of me, what I do, the choices I've made, and of my general existence, I guess."

"What makes you think that?" I'm saddened that Peter feels this way about his father. What kind of person wouldn't absolutely adore him?

"Well, I used to have no idea why. I thought maybe I barfed or peed on him when I was an infant, and he never forgave me for it." He lets out a tense laugh. "But Matt and I got to talking about our father, and he told me some stuff, stuff from the past that I'm still trying to wrap my head around."

Peter takes his hands off mine and folds his arms across his chest. The center section of his forehead that isn't covered by his hair is deeply furrowed.

"Matt thinks our father holds a grudge against me because, to him, I represent the worst time in his life."

"Really?"

"I was born during the time he and our mother were separated," he squeezes his arms tighter across his chest. "They were separated because he was having an affair with another woman."

"Ohmigosh."

"Matt also said he thinks our father has such a dislike toward me because, for a long time, he suspected I was not his child. He thought I might be the product of an affair our mother might've had while they were separated when she was staying with her family in France. And that's why he treated me so badly when we were growing up."

"Whoa! Oh man…" I'm astonished.

"Matt said this whole family drama started when he got a call from our mother while he was away at boarding school, and it sounded like she had been crying. She told him something happened that made her sad, very sad, and she was going to stay with her family in the south of France for a while."

I nod that I'm following his story, and for him to go on.

"Matt said when he came home during Christmas break, he wanted to send our mother a letter because he missed her. While he was searching through her desk at home for a postage stamp, he found a recent newspaper clipping from a gossip column with a picture of our father smiling and holding a woman who was not our mother."

"Oh, my goodness! Poor kid! He must've been devastated. And you weren't born yet, right?"

"This all happened about eight months before I was born. My mother didn't know she was pregnant with me when she left our father."

"That's horrible! Your poor mother."

"Yeah, no kidding. I had to do some serious praying when Matt told me all this because I really wanted to go by my father's office and rail into him. How does he think he can get away with disapproving of me and the things I do with my life when he's done the things he's done?"

Peter takes a deep breath, and lets it out slowly, and puts his hands back on mine.

"But I didn't," he smiles weakly at me. "Matt said that while our mother was in France, our father called her all the time, begging her to come back to him, especially when he found out she was expecting a child. Matt said that was the only time he'd ever seen our father cry."

I try to process all this information while Peter pauses. I get the distinct feeling this is very hard for him to talk about. "She didn't go back to him, right? Since I remember you told me you were born in France," I'm trying to put the story together in my head.

"Right, she stayed in France. My Aunt Mureille, my mother's sister who raised me, told me once when I was little when she was trying in vain to get me to eat the Brussels sprouts on my dinner plate that I have my mother's stubborn streak."

"I'll keep that in mind," I squeeze his hand. "I wonder why your father didn't fly out to France to see her."

"Yeah, I asked Matt that same question. He told me our mother told our father not to come, and she and her new infant son were being fiercely protected by her aunts and cousins and that they made it very clear that he was not welcome in their house after what he did to her."

"I thought French women were more tolerant about men having mistresses."

"I don't know about that. I think only if the men are discreet about their affairs. He publicly shamed my mother. She fled to France because she found out about my father's affair in the newspaper. And so did all her high society friends. At least, that's what Matt told me. I guess that's what angered her relatives so badly."

"That would totally suck. I mean, being cheated on is bad enough, but then to find out from the newspaper, and all the people you know find out that way as well, man, I would have left the country, too," I shake my head. "I feel bad for your mother, and I can totally see why you don't get along with your father. But your mother eventually went back to him at some point, right?"

"Matt said she came back as soon as she had recovered enough from giving birth to me to make the long flight back to the States." Peter stops and takes a deep breath. "Matt said our father wouldn't let her see him again, meaning Matt unless she came back to him."

"So, Matt didn't see your mom for almost a year?"

"Yeah. He said that even though he was back at boarding school in Boston, he still had to live with the fact that his parents were separated, that his father wouldn't allow him to visit his mother, and that there was a chance he might never see her again—or his new little brother. Pretty tough stuff for a seven-year-old to have to deal with, he told me."

"Holy mackerel, that's so sad." I squeeze Peter's hand. "So how is it that your father blames you for all this? When he's the source of this pain and tragedy."

"I know. Learning about all this has refueled my hatred for him. I've really been struggling with it, praying like crazy and reading Scripture," he closes his eyes and lowers his head. Matt reassured me that our father is not like that anymore. At least he's not as bad as he was. And he no longer doubts that I am indeed his biological offspring."

"I guess he finally did the math."

"Yeah, well, there's that and the fact that I look just like him," Peter leans back in his seat and rubs his eyes. He looks exhausted.

"Did you ask Matt if he knew what happened when you went with your mother to visit her family when you were four, why her father was so mean to her?" I feel kind of like I'm prying, but I really want to know.

"Matt said all he knows is that my mother didn't visit her family for four years before that trip, and it was not by her choice. And our father did not allow her to bring him along with us," Peter frowns. "He said he didn't know any more about it, but whatever happened during that trip caused our mother to remove me from her and my father's house."

"So, was that when you started staying with your aunt and uncle a lot?"

"Yeah, I think so. Most of my earliest memories are living with them." Peter looks down at the table. "Matt said he knows our father absolutely hates our mother's family, and he has nothing to do with them. And the feeling is mutual with my mother's family. My father never allows any of them to visit my mother, not even my Aunt Mureille, the only person in her family who lives in the States. One of the worst fights he and I had was over this issue. He was being so rude to my mother about not allowing her sister to visit. I was nineteen and as big as him, so I stepped in and told him what I thought. It was an ugly scene."

He stops and looks into my eyes. The mixture of anguish and frustration on his face sends a chill through me, and I have to swallow hard, so I don't break down in tears.

"Mad, I hate my father so much and know I'm not supposed to. I hate him in every possible way. I'm really trying not to." He closes his eyes tight and lowers his head.

I lay my hands on top of his and squeeze them gently. I have no words of wisdom to share with him. I don't know what to say. I silently pray that God will bring him peace in this situation.

"Well, I thank God that you are nothing like him." I break the silence.

"Yeah, ain't that the truth?! I couldn't be more different from him. Truly, thank God for that," he exhales deeply. "My father is this big-time CEO corporate guy and has been ever since I can remember. His whole life is about work and his company. It has always come first, way before his family. Whenever he did have some spare time to be a father, it was spent grooming Matt to take his place one day."

"Do you think Matt will end up like him?" I ask, fearing for his brother.

"No, I really don't think so. His personality is totally different, and he's not serious enough. Matt's a prankster, and he likes to have fun. No, he will be a good father." A smile breaks across his face as he seems to be far away in his thoughts for a minute. "One summer when he was home from boarding school, my mother brought me home from my aunt and uncle's house to stay with them, I guess so her family could be together. My father was being a total jerk to me, not saying two words to me, and Matt decided to make me feel better. After dinner one night, he called me into his room and told me to lock the door when I came in."

"How old were you?" I ask, trying to picture the scene.

"I was about ten, almost eleven, I think," he smiles. After I locked his door, he went into the back of his closet, brought out this large shoe box, and put it on his bed. Then he asked me if I liked girls yet."

"Uh oh! I think I know what's in the box."

"Yep. You guessed it. At least a dozen magazines of various names, but all from the same 'literary genre,'" he let out a little embarrassed laugh. "He told me that since I had started puberty, it was time for him to do his big brotherly duty and educate his little brother all about the birds and the bees, so to speak."

"He didn't!"

"He did. He also said he figured no one else was gonna do it, and he didn't want me to start dating girls and be ill-informed."

"How thoughtful of him," I smirk at him.

"Yeah, I think so," he laughs. "Matt spent the rest of the night telling me all about girls, what they like, and what to do with them. He was very thorough, using visual aids from the print material we had lying out before us, and he willingly answered all my questions."

"He totally corrupted your young mind!" I say, half kidding. I despise those girly magazines.

"Yeah, but it wasn't anything I hadn't already seen at friends' houses when they proudly shared the discovery of their dads' secret magazine collection. Actually, Matt clarified a lot of things for me that came in handy much later. Especially the part about how *not* to get a girl pregnant."

"Yeah, but it's not like you needed that information at ten years old." I feel like I sound like a prude.

"True, but Matt's heart was in the right place. It was a true brother-to-brother bonding moment—one of the very few we've ever had. Really, I think it was his way of trying to protect me from our father and his way of showing that he really cared about me."

"That's really great of him, I guess, even if he did increase your exposure to pornography," I grimace at him. "How are things with your father now?"

"Whenever I'm around him, which isn't often, thankfully, I always feel awkward and then angry because when he does finally speak to me, it's never anything good. He's never going to be part of my life."

"I'm so sorry, Peter. Hopefully, things will change someday." My heart wrenches for him all over again.

"Maybe, someday, but for now, I've learned it's better for everyone if I just keep my distance. I wasn't sure I was going to go to Matt's wedding at all, so there wouldn't be a chance of any problems with our father and me, but then Matt asked me to be his best man, so not only do I have to attend the wedding, but now I'm also in it."

"It's so great that he asked you to be his best man, especially since you guys aren't that close," I say, trying to cheer him up.

"Yeah, I was surprised when he called me last night, and then he really shocked me when he asked me to be his best man. Matt works for our father's company, so I know he works a lot, which doesn't leave him much time for anything else. We don't have much of a relationship because we've led such different lives. We've just never spent enough time together to really get to know each other, even as adults."

"Maybe that can change now," I smile. "So, you didn't see him very much when you guys were growing up, right? I know you said he was away in boarding school."

"Yeah, not as much as I would've liked," he frowns. Even when Matt was home from school, my mother would leave me, 'the baby,' with my aunt and uncle while she, my father, and my brother traveled all over the world."

Peter looks down at his hands. He grasps tightly to both sides of the little plastic tent. The shorter pieces of his hair fall forward and mask his expression, but his shoulders and arms look tense.

My heart breaks for him. I so want to get up and go sit next to him and put my arms around him. How could anyone leave this lovely human being behind and not want to spend every waking hour of the day with him?

"I gather you've spent much of your life with your aunt and uncle." *Well, duh.* In my deep empathy for him, I struggle to find the right words to say.

"They pretty much raised me. They're great people. They call me a lot to invite me over and stuff, and they always give me a hard time about not meeting you yet. But I feel like I don't want to impose on them. They've done so much for me."

I want to meet them, too, but I don't tell him so. I understand now that meeting Peter's family will have to happen only when he is ready for it.

When our order number is called, Peter gets up and goes to the counter to get our tray of food. On his way back to our table, he stops at the condiment counter and fills several little white paper containers with ketchup.

"I'll say grace for us?" he stretches out both hands.

I nod and put my hands in his. He bows his head and squeezes my hands tightly, almost to the point of being painful, but I don't mind. I squeeze back. I bow my head and secretly add my own prayer of thanksgiving to his verbal one.

When he finishes praying, we unwrap our burgers and dig into our food.

"It breaks my heart to hear that you have had such a sad upbringing," I look deep into his eyes. "Here I was feeling sorry for myself because my biological father hasn't called me in such a long time."

"No, it's okay. Mad, please don't feel sorry for me. It's all been for the best. Really. My aunt and uncle couldn't have kids of their own, so they always told me how great it was that they got to raise me. And I'm sorry to hear about your father. He's missing out, big time." Peter smiles at me oh so sweetly.

"No biggy. My mom says we are better off without him."

"Do you believe her?"

"Sometimes yes, sometimes no. How about your mother?"

"I guess she thought it was better for me to be with my aunt and uncle because my father is such an, uh, not a nice person, and maybe that's why she left me with them a lot."

"Have you ever asked her directly?"

"No way. One does not ask Mrs. Marcus McManus such direct and personal questions. At least, I don't. She and I never talk about personal stuff. Never have. We just don't have that kind of relationship. I can ask her about her many charity functions and events, or where she went on holiday, or what shopping spree she has gone on lately, but we never talk about personal things." His face is masked from emotion. "She never brings up anything about her 'procedures' either. We are supposed to just assume that her long stay in Switzerland is the reason her eyes look so youthful and well-rested." He laughs a little as if he's trying to lighten the mood.

"Whoa, our moms have much to 'not' talk about together!" I make him laugh, which makes me feel better. His body language tells me that his heavy mood is lifting.

"Yeah, no kidding," he smilws. "Well, Matt's wedding is going to be a big snobbish social event, with like two hundred of our parents' closest friends. Matt was teasing me that I would have to cut my hair since his fiancé was less than pleased to find out her future brother-in-law, who will be the best man at her wedding, has hair down to his waist. He didn't know I had it cut shorter. Now I kinda wish I hadn't," he says with a little rebellious grin.

"Do you think he'd really want you to do something like cutting your hair off just for a wedding?"

The mental picture I'm beginning to formulate of this wedding is not good. I totally can't see myself fitting in at some high-society wedding. I may need my mother's help with this one.

"No, in fact, Matt was disappointed when he heard that I had cut my hair. He said now he'll have to find something else to taunt his fiancé with other than her future super long-haired musician brother-in-law and his saucy gothic girlfriend. I told him to tell her that you and I just got matching neck tattoos."

"That's so awesome! I love it! So, you told him about me?"

"Well, yeah, of course. It was great to talk to him about stuff like that. We normally don't have that much to talk about. He told me all about his future wife. He said, yeah, she's kind of a snob, but he said she hides it well. He's really looking forward to meeting you."

"Seriously?" *Yikes! I can't believe he talked about me with his brother!*

"You're the first serious girlfriend I've ever had. Everybody who knows me is eager to meet you."

"Really?" I say as I try not to explode with joy on the spot. But now there's a whole lot more to be nervous about in meeting all these people. More importantly, the words "serious girlfriend" keep reverberating through my head. I try to contain my girlish giddiness.

"Yeah. Remember, I used to be one of those pig-dogs guys, like the ones you tell me about that use Maggie, and like the guys you've told me about that you dated a long time ago. I would get what I wanted from a girl, and then never call her again. That's why I'm so thankful I didn't meet you until *after* God did some major house-cleaning in me. I'm very grateful for that every day." He looks at me with a sweet smile that totally melts me to the core.

We finish eating, throw all the wrappers and paper French fry trays on the main tray, and Peter carries it to the trash while I put on my coat and grab my purse. He opens the door of his truck for me and hands me my huge cup of Diet Coke when I'm all buckled in, and we head to his band rehearsal. He seems consumed by his thoughts and is silent the whole way there. I am, too.

We pull into the parking lot of the building that houses the rehearsal rooms. He grabs his gear, and I sling my backpack and laptop case over each of my shoulders. Peter stops before we enter the main doors of the building. I can see in the bright parking lot lights that there is a slight scowl on his face.

"Let's pray before we go in." He puts his stuff down on the sidewalk, and I do the same. He takes my hands in his, takes a deep breath, and closes his eyes. I do the same, and I try not to be distracted by the warm, very firm grip of his hands around mine.

"Heavenly Father, thank you for such an awesome evening with my Mad. Please give me strength in dealing with the guys and in being a good friend and brother in Christ to Andrew," Peter sighs heavily. "And please give me direction with the music and the grace to play excellently." Peter's grasp on my hands tightens significantly as he continues. "Please protect Mad and me when we are alone together. Thank You so much for her and for Your perfect timing in bringing us together now at this stage in our lives, for such a time as this. In Jesus' name, I ask these things, Amen."

"Amen," I whisper and hold my breath. I don't want the sob in my throat to escape. I can't begin to tell you how much I love this man. My heart feels like it's burning, and it's definitely not because of anything I ate. And my knees feel weak. I want to tell him how I feel so badly, but I can't.

"I love you, Madeleine," he says as he reaches up and gently wipes the tear that has slid down my cheek. "I know this isn't exactly the most romantic place to tell you this, but I really feel like I needed to tell you."

Oh Lord, these three precious little words have never sounded so beautiful. I keep inhaling, but I can't seem to let any breaths out.

"And I'm so very grateful for you. My life is so crazy right now, with my brother's wedding and all my family stuff," Peter says, tightening his grip on my hands. "Also, the stuff with

Andrew and his girlfriend, them making our house their own personal fornication palace. You are such a gift from God to me, and I love you so much."

"I love you too, Peter." I manage to utter as I finally exhale. I want to tell him that I feel the same about him and that he has been a huge blessing to me, too, but my throat is too tight with a huge sob.

He wipes my tears again, kisses me lightly on the cheek, and folds me in his arms. I want to stay here forever, in his arms, in this parking lot. But he lets go of me, wipes his eyes quickly, and clears his throat.

"We better get inside," he says softly. He reaches down and picks up my backpack and laptop case, swings them over his shoulders, and then picks up his guitar case and gear bag.

Oh Lord, oh my sweet Lord Jesus. Thank You. Thank You. Thank You. I love You.

Chapter Twenty-one

As we walk down the long hallway to Peter's band's rehearsal room, I hear a variety of music seeping out of the different rooms. The stench of smoke and beer with a hint of urine mixed in is a little much and I have to stifle a gag and hold my breath.

Peter unlocks a series of locks and padlocks on the door to their rehearsal room. We are the first ones to arrive. Thankfully, it doesn't contain any of the other pungent aromas, just old building smell.

The walls are covered in egg crates and foam. There is a large oriental rug on the floor that looks as though it may have been beautiful at one time in vibrant hues of reds and rich browns, but now looks as though it has definitely seen better days. An old seven-foot leather sofa that sits against one wall appears fairly innocuous, nothing crawling out of the few tears in the cushions and no mysterious stains. The small battered wooden coffee table in front of the sofa is covered in papers, pens, a couple of music magazines and a Bible.

The bulk of the room is filled with the band's equipment, a full double-bass drum set, various amplifiers, racks of electronic equipment, microphone and guitar stands, and cables running across the floor.

"The couch is clean. We have strict rules about its use—for sitting only," Peter lifts one dark eyebrow.

"Good, I'm glad to hear it." I laugh.

"The band I was in before this one—oh, you don't wanna know what took place on the couch in that rehearsal room. That whole experience was the last straw that made me swear off being in secular bands. Not that these guys are perfect, and neither am I, but they don't do drugs, and most of them lead celibate lives as far as I can tell, except for Andrew, which you know about, and our lead singer since he's married."

"Sounds good," I say as I sit on the couch.

I fire up my laptop to begin working on one of my many papers as Peter sets up his gear and tunes his guitars.

After a while, the other band members start filing in. Peter introduces each of them to me as they come in. I try not to seem too overly nice when I meet Andrew, who ducks his head and gives me a quick wave, then quickly starts setting up his bass rig.

I can see where Andrew and Peter would've gotten into a lot of trouble with the opposite sex. Andrew is almost as tall as Peter and has a similar build. He is also deeply tanned, which sets off his blue eyes and sun-streaked sandy brown corkscrew curls that fall down to his shoulders. Maggie would be all over him if she were here, "like flies on a pie at a picnic," she would probably say.

The guys give each other the usual ribbing as they set everything up, much like the banter I heard back on that night at the Juice Stop when I first met Peter. When they finish setting up, Peter suggests they pray before they start.

"I'll start us," says the lead singer, who I'm pretty sure is named Luke. It's hard to keep straight who is who in the band. "Madeleine, would you like to join us?" he asks me.

I get up and go stand next to Peter, who takes my hand in his. This is so awesome being around these cool, Godly guys. When we finish praying, Peter kisses my hand before letting go of it. I'm so glad he's not one of those guys who is too cool to show affection around his friends. I'm so grateful for him.

I carefully step over all the cords on the floor and make my way back to the couch. When I turn to sit down, I notice a bunch of heads quickly turning away. Peter is smiling at me. Touché! It's his turn to have his friends check out the person he is dating as the girls did to me the first night he came to pick me up at the dorm. I feel my face get hot, but I try to play it off like I didn't notice that I was just majorly being checked-out.

Then the drummer clicks the song off with his sticks, and this huge wall of sound nearly knocks me back on the couch. I reach into my backpack for the earplugs. I can still hear the music perfectly, even with earplugs in my ears. I like it a lot, and not just because I know Peter co-wrote most of the songs.

After a while, the large Diet Coke that Peter bought me at In-N-Out has worked its way through me, and I feel the call of nature. I excuse myself to go to the restroom. I had made a mental note that the restrooms were near the main entrance of the building when we first walked in.

Possessing the tiny bladder that I have, I have developed the habit of scoping out the location of the ladies' room in all the places I go, especially when I know I will be there for an extended length of time.

I prepare myself for the worst public restroom state of uncleanliness, but actually, it's not that bad at all. I guess the ladies' room here doesn't get used as often as the men's room. I can only imagine the giant Petri dish of germ cultures and biological samples present in the men's restroom.

On my way back to the rehearsal room, I notice the door is open a foot or so, and I hear the guys talking. They must be taking a break. Thanks to my beloved black leather Creepers, my footsteps are virtually silent. As I approach the door, what I hear stops me dead in my tracks.

"Hey Pete, you gettin' any yet?" one of the guys asks, laughing.

"Yeah, bro, come on. You can fess up to us. She looks like a goer," another guy says.

Ugh! I begin to fume.

"Yeah, man, she's a little hottie Goth girl. Nice little bod." the first guy says.

"Yeah, dude, she's got a nice pair of, um, eyes," another guy snickers.

"You guys are seriously depraved." I hear Peter's say, with a bit of an edge in it.

Yes, Peter! You tell them!

"Oh, come on, you two have been together for like months now, and you mean to tell me you haven't hit that yet? Dude, I think she's playin' ya."

"Nope." Peter proudly affirms.

Yes! Yes! Tell'em, Peter! I love that my man is open about our resolve to not sleep with each other.

"Ah, dude, the Pete-meister's losing his touch!" another guy chimes in.

"Just give them time. They'll be knockin' boots soon enough. Tigers don't change their stripes, you know." Andrew's voice has a jealous bitterness in it.

"Ooh, Andy! Them's fightin' words, dude!" one of the guys says.

I hear a heavy sigh come from Peter. "Not this time, man, not this time. I know you've seen me slip up in the past, but things are different now. Madeleine's special, and I'm not screwing this up. Literally."

My stomach does a summersault when I hear Peter say this. I know I shouldn't be eavesdropping on their conversation, but my feet feel glued to the floor where I stand.

"That's very cool, bro'. Me and my old lady will pray for you guys," I hear Luke say. "And you know, it'll be good to have another married couple in the group soon."

I hear a small grunt of approval from Peter.

Oh. My. Lord.

"Thanks, bro', I need it." Peter noodles a few notes on his guitar.

I try to enter the room softly and as inconspicuously as possible, but as I enter, the other guitar player (I can't remember his name) starts playing the familiar intro to the hard rock song *Madalaine* from the eighty's hair band, Winger. The whole band kicks into it. Peter is laughing and smiling at me.

"Thanks for the serenade, guys!" I say after they slowly fall out of playing the song after the first chorus.

I try to go back to writing my paper, but I can't seem to focus. I feel bad for listening in on their conversation (just a little bit), but man, nothing tells you more about what your guy is really made of until you hear him stand up to his buddies when they are giving him a hard time about you and him.

The guys play a few more songs, working on specific parts of some songs. They finish rehearsing and start to pack up their gear while continuously rib each other about various things, particularly who messed up which song in rehearsal, and slowly, they all leave.

"How did you like the rehearsal? I hope your ears aren't ringing," Peter looks concerned.

"You guys are so good. And the earplugs were a great help." I smile up at Peter from where I sit on the couch as I pack up my schoolwork, and he puts his gear away. "I especially liked being serenaded with the Winger song. It was one of my dad's favorite songs. He used to play it a little on his guitar whenever I visited him."

"Really? Your dad was a guitar player?"

"Only as a hobby. He used to work on those big offshore oil drilling rigs."

"How did your parents meet?" Peter continues to wind up his cables and clean up the place a little.

"They met on the Redondo Beach pier. My mother was a waitress in a restaurant and bar on the pier that my father used to go into during his time off ashore. They dated for a little while, got married, and shortly thereafter, I was born. They split up just before my sixth birthday. My mom said it was because she was lonely all the time and that she didn't get married to be alone."

"That's sad," he looks tenderly at me.

"Yeah, I guess. But I don't remember her being lonely, though. I remember having several cool babysitters take care of me while my mother got all dolled-up and went out in the evenings. I think that's when she met Dr. Bill, although she won't admit it. I only remember my parents having one fight; really it was just my mom yelling and crying, and then shortly after that, my mother packed up our stuff, and we went to live in this really nice townhouse in Orange County. Dr. Bill was over there almost every night."

"Whoa, that's rough." Peter shakes his head.

"Actually, it wasn't that bad. My father wasn't really there when he was there, you know what I mean? Mostly, he would sit on the couch and drink beer and watch television, until it was time for him to go back to work. Occasionally, he would shut the TV off and play guitar, but those moments were few and far between."

"That must've been hard for you, though, being so young, and not really having your father around."

"It was. Something else you and I have in common, I guess."

"Yeah, unfortunately," he says, sadly.

"But it was good to have Dr. Bill come along. He always brought my mother and me gifts and would sit and talk with my mother for hours. I remember once, he bought me the Barbie Dream House I so longed for, the one I had coveted from the pages of the Sears catalog for years. He sat on the floor the whole evening, putting it together for me. He's really sweet. He wants to meet you. But I'm totally *not* ready for you to meet my mother. She is a piece of work. I must warn you. I love her, but some of the stuff she does and says makes me want to keep my distance."

"I can understand that," he frowns. "We'll get all our family stuff straightened out, all in due time. But for now, I like that it's just you and me," he says with a big smile.

"Yeah, me too," I return his smile.

"The other night, I was reading in Genesis about Abraham and his nephew Lot." Peter closes his guitar case and latches it. "Man, Abe would've been so much better off if he had not taken his nephew with him on the journey to the Promised Land, you know? Sometimes family is more of a burden than a blessing." He stacks his guitar cables in his bag.

"I never thought of that story in that way, but now that you mention it, it makes sense," I remember all the trouble the Israelites had with Lot's descendants.

Peter finishes packing up his gear, and I put my laptop and folders away. Then he locks up and we head out to his truck.

He keeps looking over at me as he drives me back to school with a big, sweet smile on his face. "I bet you were a really cute little girl."

"My mother says I was intense and dramatic and that she regrets naming me after a writer. She named me after Madeleine L'Engle, because she loved her *Wrinkle in Time* books. She said she always thought her name was pretty. Even though I wasn't named after that song you guys played, it still makes me laugh whenever I hear it."

"The guys have been razzing me with that song since you and I started dating. Ted, the rhythm guitar player, seems to think it's hilarious to play it, especially since your last name is Winger. I think some of the guys are jealous 'cause I found someone special." He smiles at me.

All I can do is smile back at him the rest of the way to Biola, since it feels like my entire insides are melting, including all the physical parts necessary for coherent speech.

Oh Lord, thank You for him. Thank You for an awesome evening. Please help Peter sort out the stuff with his dad and help us cope well with Matt's wedding. And please help us to be strong and stay pure. I so need Your help with this. In Jesus's name, I pray, Amen.

Chapter Twenty-two

The following evening after Peter's band practice, we spend our Friday night hanging out with Josiah and Leah at the coffeehouse for a while, who by the way, have become a full-blown item like Peter and me. Josiah even hired a couple of extra people to help out at the coffeehouse, so he could spend less time behind the counter and more time with Leah.

After about an hour or so, Josiah and Leah take off to go to the movies. Peter turns to me and takes my hand and kisses it lightly.

"What would you like to do tonight? Would you like to go to a movie, too?"

"Nah, I'm not really in a movie mood." His touch makes me shiver slightly.

"Me neither. I have an idea."

"What's that?" My mind creates intimate images that it shouldn't.

"I could use your help with some lyric ideas I'm working on. Are you up for that? And I want to read some of your poems and stories, like you promised you would let me read a long, long, long time ago." He gently nudges my arm, smiling brightly.

"Sure, I'd love to help you if I can. And, yes, you can read my stuff."

"Great. So, I guess we should head to my house."

"Sure." This sounds innocent enough, but truthfully, I'm a little nervous. We've never hung out at Peter's house before. But at the same time, I'm eager to see where he lives. I can handle this and be an adult about it, right?

We travel through some residential surface streets of old town Whittier that open to a wide park area, which is surrounded by quaint, impeccably restored vintage homes. He turns down one of the side streets opposite the park and pulls into the driveway of one of the cutest houses I've ever seen.

It's a one-story white house with black trim. The driveway is long and narrow, as the house sits a ways back from the street, so there is plenty of room for all the cars belonging to Peter, Andrew, and Andrew's girlfriend.

A huge willow tree dominates the center of the front yard and looks as if it would shade the entire front yard in daylight. The porch, which stretches across the entire front of the house, has a porch swing off to one side of the front door and a white wrought iron bistro set with a table and two chairs off to the other side.

"This is such a cute house!" I stand in the driveway, taking it all in.

"Isn't it cool? I helped Andrew's dad restore it after he bought it."

"That's awesome." I marvel at how well it's been taken care of.

"Yeah. It's a classic craftsman-style house built in 1923. We updated the electrical system, replaced the pipes with copper piping, and refinished the wood floors throughout the house. We put in French doors out to the deck we built in the backyard. I also helped him replace all the appliances in the kitchen and the fixtures in the bathroom. We kept the original tile in the bathrooms and just replaced the grout. The guest bathroom has one of those cool old claw-foot bathtubs. I had to go under the house and reinforce the foundation, which was a tough job, but all in all, it was a fun project to work on."

"That sounds like a ton of work. Did he hire your uncle's company to remodel it?"

"No, just me. We made a sort of barter agreement. I live here rent-free for doing all the work. It was cool because I worked on the house while I was living here. After it was done, I offered to start paying rent, but Andrew's dad wouldn't take my money. He said he would keep me on retainer to make any repairs that might come up."

"That sounds like a good arrangement."

"Yeah, it works for us. It's another reason I don't want to move out, besides staying alongside Andrew while he's, uh, living in his fallen state, I guess you could say. And I don't want to stick Andrew's dad with having to find a reliable repairman. Also, I love this house. I know it inside and out, and it would hurt my heart to think someone else was working on it. Besides, not paying rent is an added bonus. Come on inside, you gotta see all the cool built-in features."

"I didn't know you were so into houses." I smile at him. I love learning new things about him.

"I've learned a lot working with my uncle. The modern houses he designs and builds for people are awesome, but man, there's nothing like these old houses. They just have so much character and charm."

He opens the front door for me, and I step inside. The front room is cozy, with two overstuffed leather sofas and beautiful area rugs. The dining area off to the left is lined with built-in cabinetry and drawers. What looks to be the original molding surrounds all the doorways and windows.

Andrew and, I presume, his girlfriend are curled up together under a blanket on the larger sofa, and a violent action film is playing on the huge television in the corner of the room.

"Hi," I shyly wave as I stand there, feeling very much like we have interrupted something intimate.

"Hey," Andrew says nonchalantly without looking at me.

"Maddy, you remember Andrew; this is his girlfriend, Bella." Peter introduces us.

"Hi, it's nice to meet you." I give her a quick wave.

"Sooo, this is the infamous Madeleine? It's about time, Peter. I was beginning to think Peter was making you up." Bella says to me and then continues to look Peter up and down.

"Yes, yes. Here I am. In the flesh," I feel more than a bit awkward and slightly irritated.

"I can see that," a sarcastic edge in her voice.

Ugh, she's so charming. Instantly, my inner radar goes off, and I don't like her.

Bella is now overtly looking me over as if I'm not good enough for Peter. The way she said Peter's name gives me the creeps, too, like she has a crush on him or something. I decide it's better to take the high road and that I should probably make an effort to be nice.

"Bella, is it? That's a pretty name." I try to sound sincere.

"It's short for Jezebel."

"Oh." *How fitting.* Her long, straight yellow hair, which resembles my mother's, is tangled and disheveled, and her black eye makeup has run and is smeared under her eyes.

"You look really nice tonight, Peter." Her words are slightly slurred as if she has been drinking, which I'm guessing is the case since Andrew's face shows no recognition of her obvious flirtatious remarks to Peter. He just stares blankly at the television.

"Uh, thanks." Peter quickly turns to me. "Mad, the studio is through here." He guides me out of the room with his hand on my lower back.

We head toward the back of the house, passing two bedrooms on the way. One is messy, with an unmade bed, clothes strewn about, and the infamous girly posters on the walls of women dressed in bikinis and some not dressed at all.

We stop in the next bedroom, and Peter reaches over me and flips on the light switch. I stand in the doorway, looking around. I breathe in deeply his strong scent. He goes to a large old wood desk to get some papers that are sitting on top. His room is neat. There are no clothes on the floor. Everything has a place and is in it. I feel guilty because I'm sure his room is way cleaner than half of my dorm room.

Next to the big desk is his tightly made queen-size bed. I instantly block the thoughts that come rushing in my fleshly mind of how beautiful he must look sleeping in that bed and how it might feel to be lying there next to him.

On the nightstand next to his bed, there is a Bible, a copy of *The Screwtape Letters* by C.S. Lewis, and the strip of photos in a frame that he and I took in one of those cheesy photo booths on our date at the Universal City Walk. My photo strip from that night is also next to my bed.

In the corner of the room, next to the bed, is a beautiful acoustic guitar that looks old but very well cared for. On the other end of the room is a weight bench, with a thick bar going across with huge round weights on each end. There are hand weights on the floor underneath the bench, with more big, heavy-looking metal discs bolted on each end.

He catches my line of sight. "I try to stay in shape. It also helps me lift heavy stuff on job sites."

"Oh." More thoughts to block, images of my lovely shirtless, sweaty man working out.

I stand in the doorway. I love looking around at the place where Peter spends a lot of his time. I just want to stay in here and breathe in the exquisite smell of him. But he gathers all his papers in a worn spiral-bound notebook, and I continue to follow him down the hall.

The master suite of the house has been turned into a music studio. Parts of the walls are covered with textured dark gray foam. The areas that aren't covered are painted a steel gray that matches the rugs. Under the various area rugs are the same gleaming hardwood floors that are throughout the house.

Several guitars and bass guitars sit on stands along one wall. The room seems to be centered on the large black, multi-tiered wood desk, which dominates one whole side and is covered with a computer, speakers, and a mixing board. A black overstuffed couch, smoke-black glass coffee table, and end tables occupy the space opposite the large desk.

Peter turns on some lamps and sets his notebook and papers on the coffee table.

"This is a *really* cool studio. I would never leave this room if I had a room like this in my house." I try in the whole space.

"Yeah, I spend most of my time here when I'm home. It's a good place to pray, read my Bible, and work on music. One of the best things about this room is that it doesn't share a wall with Andrew's room, like my bedroom does."

"Is it that bad?" I sit down on the couch next to Peter and set my backpack and laptop bag down on the floor next to the couch.

"I can hear pretty much everything they do," he grimaces.

"Yikes! And I thought I had it bad because I could hear Bethany talking to her weasel boyfriend on the phone."

"It never used to bother me that much. I mean, what other people do is their business. To be honest, though, I'm jealous of him, in a twisted sort of way," he runs his hand through his hair. "The thing that bugs me the most is that he is in there going all the way with a girl he really doesn't like all that much, and I have to be totally hands-off with the woman I love because I know that is what God requires of me. It drives me nuts sometimes. I've had to come in here to sleep on this couch more than a couple of nights 'cause it got so bad."

"Really?" I say, but my mind is starting to conjure images it shouldn't.

"Some nights, I'll be lying in bed, just about to drift off to sleep when I hear them going at it, and it sets my mind off down a road that I know it shouldn't go."

"What road is that?" I hear myself ask in a flirty tone. *Fool! Why are you asking him this? Stop flirting!*

"You know." He looks at me with one eyebrow raised.

"Know what?" *Shut up Madeleine! You're so sick that you want to hear him say it!*

"Like what it would be like to have you in my bed with me." He leans back into the couch, and folds his arms across his chest, which were resting on his knees. "There. I admit it. I'm a sick, lust-filled pervert who has unholy thoughts about what I want to do with you."

"Well, I'm no better," I confess.

"No way. Girls don't think about stuff like that."

"Oh yes, they do!"

"Then I vote we change the subject and get to work," Peter suggests, giving me a subtle smile.

"I agree." Only because I know it's what we must do. My old nature wants to tap into the growing sexual tension between us and slide over to his side of the couch and…and…I have to stop thinking about it! *Right now.*

He clears his throat and leans forward to reach his notebook on the table. "Okay, here are some lyrics I have been working on for some time. I have a cool chord progression for the song, but I can't seem to make the two come together. Andrew usually helps with this part, but he has been a little preoccupied lately." He opens the notebook, flips the cover and preceding pages back, and hands it to me.

There are five stanzas, with scribble marks intermittent between the words. The lyrics are about finding and living in God's peace. I like it.

"I'm no wordsmith. Like I said, this is usually Andrew's duty. But I feel like God has put this song in my heart. Whenever I play

the chord progression, the idea of His peace comes to my mind,"
Peter explains.

"I like it, but I'm not sure how much help I can be with
putting words to music. Would you mind playing the chords for
me?"

"Not at all." Peter gets up and grabs one of the acoustic
guitars off the stand, then sits on the arm of the couch. He
removes the pick that is set into the strings and checks the
tuning. Then, he begins to play a beautiful, melodic, up-tempo
song. His guitar playing is so awesome that it seems anointed.

"That is so beautiful." I'm stunned. He is so talented.

"Thanks," he grins and lowers his head.

"I'm not sure what to suggest. I'm no songwriter."

"That's okay because I just now had some new ideas. You
must be my muse. I think I need to change some of the chords in
the chorus before I can begin to develop the lyric melody."

"Yeah, you know, that's what I was thinking you should do."
I tease, like I know what he's talking about.

"Yeah? Okay, smart guy. Fire up that computer. I want to see
some of your writing now!"

"Oooh, so demanding! What are you gonna do to me if I say
no?" *What? What is up with me? Why am I flirting with him?*

"See here, young lady. We'll have none of that teasing in this
studio, you hear? It's all work, all the time," he teases with mock
seriousness.

"Okay, okay. Here, I have hard copies." I take a folder out of
my backpack. "Here's a sort of testimonial poem. It's called
'Stupid.'"

I hand him a piece of paper with my poem on it:

> *It'll be over, as soon as it starts*
> *I'll be cleaning up the carnage of my dismembered heart*
> *I've got to be wiser in my short-lived days*
> *I've got to be smarter than in my past mistakes*

I knew better than to embrace his affections,
But knowing didn't change that I still ran in his direction

I feel stupid
Foolishly idiotic, simple, and senseless
Dim-witted, asinine, inane, and dejected
Again
I feel stupid

Here is a place I want to be a long way from
How did I get in this shameful predicament?
I have only my gullible heart to blame
For letting the infatuation beast out of her gilded cage

I knew better than to accept his attention
But knowing didn't take away my nasty obsession

I feel stupid
Foolishly idiotic, simple, and senseless
Dim-witted, asinine, inane, and dejected
Again
I feel stupid

Breaking promises to myself just wounds me inside
I ask for a reason, but I get no reply
Give me strength in my weakness and guard me from lust's
bleakness
Deliver me from my destruction
'Cause I feel stupid

I knew better than to embrace his affections,
But knowing didn't take away my nasty obsession
I feel stupid

"Mad, this is awesome! I love your play on words. It has a powerful meaning. When did you write it?".

"About a year ago, when I thought it might be a good idea for me to quit dating for a while."

"This could easily be put to music and should be. I think you are a natural-born lyricist."

"Really?" I'm awestruck that he likes it so much.

"Seriously. Even the format lends itself to a verse-chorus structure. Do you sing?"

"Who me? No!"

"I mean well enough for songwriting?"

"No."

"I bet you do."

"I bet I don't."

"We'll work on it. I think you have a gift and need to use it."

"Doesn't Luke write lyrics?"

"No, sadly, he doesn't. He doesn't really have an interest in it. Do you have any more like this?"

"Yeah, lots." I sift through the papers and decide on one piece of writing. "Here is one that is kind of based on a true story." I hand him "Autumn Leaves":

> *As magnolias bloomed, she was kissing her groom*
> *Life seemed so sweet and new*
> *But as the sun grew high*
> *She kissed Graceland good-bye*
> *To head for Pacific Heights*
>
> *As the years flew by, his affection ran dry*
> *She slept alone many nights*
> *The cold Bay area wind numbs her within*
> *As she speeds from the horror she's seen*
>
> *Her love, her soul in the arms of another*

Him acting like he has no other
The stained brown spread blanketing
The orange shag carpeting

Like dead leaves fallen to the motel floor
A scene forever carved in her core
In the turning of the seasons
She saw her love's treason
So Autumn leaves
Autumn leaves

The crisp October air is
Whipping through her hair
Streaking her floodgate tears
So it's come to this
He killed their marital bliss
Of ten devotion-filled years

Her love her soul is in the arms of another
Him acting like he had no other
The stained brown spread blanketing
The orange shag carpeting

Like dead leaves fallen to the motel floor
A scene forever carved in her core
By the time she reaches Memphis
She'll have come to her senses
So Autumn leaves
Autumn leaves

"This poem is awesome, too. Really sad. These could totally be lyrics to a song. This is a good story. You said it was true?"

"Mostly true, with a few artistic and geographical embellishments thrown in for good measure."

"Whose story is it?"

"Mine."

"Seriously? Some bonehead idiot cheated on you? When did this happen?" He seems genuinely bent like he might go beat this guy up right now if I asked him to.

"When I was in the last semester of my senior year in high school, I totally fell for this guy who was in the Navy and ran in the same circle of party friends as I did. After some heavy-duty flirting at a couple of parties where his band played, we had one night of sharing poetry, music, and sex. He told me he loved me," I say dramatically.

"Ugghh, of course," he groans and rolls his eyes. "Please continue."

"I waited for him for six months while he did his tour of duty overseas. We were going to move in together when he got back and be engaged, or so his letters promised to me."

It's weird how as I'm telling Peter about this, the old feelings start flooding back.

"While he was gone, I became better friends with his friends because we would all hang out after school and on the weekends. Not good for him because I found out from them that he was back two days sooner than he told me he was going to be, and I found out where he was staying. I walked in on him having sex with some common blonde tart in a trashy motel room." I'm surprised at the residue of anger that is rising in me.

"Oh, Mad," Peter cringes.

"It was all I could do to stop myself from blowing chunks right there on the spot. Then I wanted to kill him. I truly desired to murder him. But then I decided he wouldn't be worth it."

"That's horrible! What an a**! Pardon my French. I can't believe someone would treat you like that." Peter exclaims.

"I know, poor me," I shrug off the old pain that I thought had long since dissipated.

"He was a musician, you said?"

"Guitar player," I smile ruefully.

"Damn guitar players," he smirks. "They're all dogs."

"Not *all* of them," I smile, and think how grateful I am that Peter is so different than other guys.

"Seriously, Mad, I'm sorry that happened to you. It must've been really painful."

"Yeah, but I think everything happens for a reason. I learned not to be so naïve, for one thing. More importantly, the whole situation drove me to my knees, and I was saved not long after."

"How did you get saved? You've never told me your testimony."

"It was dark and stormy night..." I say with dramatic eyes.

"Seriously." Peter reaches over and tickles my side, which makes me jump. We both laugh.

"Okay, okay. The whole situation with that guy was like the last straw for me. But I should start back at the beginning," I take a deep breath, hoping I can get through this without weeping like a willow. "Okay, it all started when I met this one guy at one of my friend's all-Gothic parties. I was seventeen, a junior in high school, and still a virgin, but convinced I needed more life experience, especially if I was going to be a writer."

"No one told you you should wait until you get married to have sex?"

"I probably heard it somewhere, but it was not in the forefront of my mind."

"Bummer," he looks at me despondently.

"Well, he was eighteen, a senior at a neighboring high school, and a musician. Again. I think I see a pattern here," I scowl, and he smiles and raises one eyebrow. "He was a real goth guy, with multiple piercings on various body parts and tattoos to match. My mother was not pleased, but that didn't stop her from flirting with him when he came to pick me up."

"Yikes!"

"Anyway, we hit it off right away, and he said he liked me a lot. He asked me to the 'Anti-prom Party', which is an annual tradition that our school's gothic and punk kids throw every year at somebody's big house in Carbon Canyon, the same night as the conventional prom. It was always loads of fun and became known at our school as an event that was more fun than the actual prom."

"Sounds wild. I always hated all that prom stuff."

"Yeah, it's not really my thing either. But the party was a blast. I used to have so much fun. Too much fun. I barely remember the details of any of the parties due to my heavy consumption of various alcoholic libations. Anyway, I foolishly gave myself to this guy that night at the party. He called me only a couple of times after that, and then I caught him at a friend's party full-on, making out on the couch with some sleazy girl. I was devastated, and that was the end of him."

"That's awful. My poor little Mad." Peter says sincerely.

"I know, so tragic, right? But wait, there's more. A few months after we graduated from high school, I moved out with two of my wild Goth girlfriends when I was eighteen. My mother had been driving me crazy, and I was again convinced I needed more life experience. We all moved into this crappy little apartment on Fullerton Road in Rowland Heights. It was a bit of a commute for me since I was working at the Music Plus in Chino at the time and going to Mt. San Antonio College in Walnut also, but I didn't care. I went to parties and clubs, and I was finally able to stay out all night or as long as I wanted. I was finally free, or so I thought."

"Sounds very much like my late teens and early twenties. Way too much partying," he shakes his head.

"Oh, I know. We threw so many parties in that little apartment! Crazy, raunchy, drunken, explicit parties. I don't know how many times I woke up with a passed-out guy in my bed. *Ewww*, that's so nasty!" I'm sickened by my old self. "I can't believe I'm telling you this."

"Hey, I was doing the same things as you, so you'll get no judgment from me."

"Anyway, I was surprised we never got evicted from that apartment because of all the parties we had until I found out one day from the woman in the apartment complex management office that we were the only tenants who not only paid their rent on time but who actually paid their rent at all on a regular basis."

"Oh man, that's crazy!"

"It was a bizarre time. I was still hurting from the Navy guy, and all the heartbreaking drama that went down with him. He would still call me occasionally, trying to sweet-talk me, especially since I had my own Party Pad. After a while, I was so sick of partying, getting drunk, being heartbroken, and getting used and hurt continuously by idiotic guys. I was sick of my life in general and I wanted a reason for existence. I was really in a bummer state of mind."

"Let me guess, you felt like your soul was full of dead dried-up bones?"

"Yes, exactly! That's exactly it," I marvel at him.

"I remember that feeling well. I hated it."

"I was so miserable and empty. I had to do something, something had to change, 'because I felt like I was going to shrivel up and die." I have to pause as that old feeling of utter despondency momentarily rears its ugly little head. "Then one of my roommates moved out, and I couldn't afford the rent anymore, and Dr. Bill asked me to move back home under the guise that he needed someone to watch the house while they were going to be away all summer on various trips."

"That was really great of him."

"It was. Later, he told me he was really concerned about me because I seemed even more morose and depressed than usual, and he wanted to keep an eye on me. So, I moved back home, took some summer classes, and vowed to get more serious about school. Also, I swore off guys, well, most of them, especially the musicians."

"So, how's that working out for you?" Peter smiles sweetly at me.

"Great, until a few months ago!" I so love teasing him. "Anyway, after a couple of weeks at home, I was still trying to sort through my emptiness when this girl I worked with at the Plus asked me if I wanted to go to this sort of big free concert event at Anaheim Stadium with her and some friends. I had nothing else to do, and I was game to try new things, so I went.

"Nice," a smile spreading across his face.

"It turned out to be a Harvest Crusade. At first, I didn't like it. It wasn't really my scene. But everyone seemed so genuinely nice, even nice to me, this crazy chick all dressed in black with heavy black eyeliner. This preacher man came up and started talking. I don't even remember what he said exactly, something about being forgiven for everything, but when he gave the invitation for people to come forward and ask Jesus Christ into their heart, I felt like God was saying to me, 'Madeleine, I know you have been searching for Me for a long time. Come on. It's time.' I remember that so clearly, what He said to me that night."

My throat tightens, and my eyes mist over. Peter smiles brightly at me and takes my hand in his.

"So, I got up from where I was sitting on the first base side with my friends," I inhale deeply. "And made my way down to the field, tears streaming down my face, to ask Jesus into my heart as my personal Lord and Savior. Instantly, it felt like the heavy dark shroud that had been smothering me was lifted off, and was gone. Totally gone. In an instant," my voice catches in my throat. "And my life has been such an awesome trip ever since."

I blink a few times to release the tears that have pooled in my eyes to slide down my cheeks. Peter's eyes are glistening, too. He scoots closer to me and gently wipes the tears off my face with the back of his fingers. Then he wraps his arms around me and holds me for a while. He starts rubbing my back. He feels so good. So very good.

"I love you, Madeleine," he whispers in my ear.

Before I can say anything, he pulls back some and kisses me. On the lips. So softly, so sweetly.

My head is spinning. He puts his hand on the side of my face, pulling me into him, and he kisses me harder and more passionately. His full lips are so soft and wet on my lips.

My whole body begins to tingle, from my lips to my toes. His other hand moves from my shoulder down my back. I know I should stop this. I should really stop this.

Suddenly he pulls away. "Sorry, sorry, I'm sorry. I got carried away." He quickly slides over on the couch. He leans forward and puts his head in his hand.

"It's okay." I try to reassure him.

"No, it's not okay. I know myself. I know I have to be more careful than that." He runs his hands through his hair and sighs heavily.

"It was just a kiss." I don't want him to feel so bad. He seems really upset.

"That's all it takes! I wish every girl could walk around for one day with a pair of testicles. Then they would understand how hard, uh, how difficult it is to keep a pure mind."

"Hmm, that would be a little weird, but I think I know what you mean. I think it's tougher for you and me, you know, to keep a clear head because we've already had sex, so it's not such a big deal to us to do it," I reason. "We've already rounded the bases before, so to speak, so there isn't as much anticipation and fear of uncharted territory. Do you know what I mean?"

"Yeah, I think that may be part of it, but still, it's no excuse. I prayed with Josiah that I would be a new man with strong self-control. It just stinks that I can't even kiss you without almost losing it."

"I'm sorry." I don't know what else to say.

"No, it's not your fault. You're always so modest, so careful in the way you dress. And believe me, I really appreciate it."

"Yeah, but I was flirting with you earlier this evening, and I shouldn't have done that."

"I can handle a little harmless flirting. It's the physical contact that sets me off. I know that about myself. And it doesn't make it any easier that you are so beautiful. Sometimes, when we're together and I look at you, all I can do is think about what it would be like to kiss you."

"So now you know. Nothing special, right?" I smile and try to make light of the situation.

"On the contrary. I will be thinking about, or trying *not* to think about, that kiss for a long time." He looks so deeply into my eyes it makes my stomach flutter. "I should probably take you back to Biola now before it gets too late."

He clears his throat and gets up from the couch. I get the feeling he is speaking about more than just the time of night.

"Yeah. We should probably call it a night." I start to pack up my stuff.

"Can I keep your poems? I'd like to read these stories, too." He picks up my papers from the coffee table. "I really like your poems a lot, and I expect to read more very soon."

"Yes sir," I say and salute him, and he laughs. "Thanks for playing your song for me. And I, too, expect to hear more in the future."

"Yes, ma'am." We both laugh. The tension in the air is subsiding.

We drive to Biola in almost total silence, except for a little small talk. He carries my laptop case for me to the front door of the dormitory.

"I'll call you later, before bed. We can pray together," he looks softly at me.

"Yeah, that's a great idea. Call me when you get home."

"Okay." He seems like he feels a little awkward, so I go to give him a hug.

"I love you, Peter. Any other guy wouldn't have stopped like you did tonight. You are such an extraordinary guy, and I am so blessed to be with you."

He hugs me tighter. So tight it hurts a little, but I like it.

"Thanks, that means a lot to me." He gives me a quick kiss on the cheek and pulls away. "I love you, too. I'll call you when I get home."

He hands me my laptop bag. I wave to him as he walks to his truck, and he waves back. *Sigh.*

I'm so in love with this guy it physically hurts. I begin to pray as I walk to my room.

Oh God, please help me. Help us. I didn't know he felt as strongly about me physically as I did about him. I guess I will have to be more careful in the future.

Oh, but what a kiss. Lord, honestly, I have never been kissed like that before, so tender and so passionate at the same time. And he is so wondrously rare to pull away from me. So awesome.

I'm so sorry that I thought I could handle being alone with him on my own. I was so foolish. So very foolish. I have to confess, Lord, I know I would have let him go all the way with me tonight. Thank You so much for giving me such a marvelously miraculous man who knew better and restrained himself. Thank You, thank You, thank You. In Jesus's name, I pray, Amen.

Chapter Twenty-three

Ordinarily, I would be super-stressed with the date of final exams looming so closely, but I feel calm and relaxed. I'm also prone to walking around with my head in the clouds whenever I have been in a relationship, and this should be magnified tenfold with a guy as magnificent as Peter. But again, I feel calm, and grounded. Praying my way through every time we are together has got me into the habit of praying throughout the day, about anything and everything, which has blanketed every aspect of my life in peace.

I ponder this awesome thought as I walk down the hall to my dorm room, but I stop and double back as I pass the room next to mine.

Half of the room is the same, with Suzette's brightly colored pillows from Thailand and India, and a new map of the world posted on the wall with little colored thumbtacks on certain places. The other half of the room is empty. Not a poster, or a book, or a sheet on the bed.

Gone are the quaint pastel-tinted black and white pictures of little kids playing, and the framed snapshots of a certain smiling young couple. Gone are the rows of neatly stacked sweaters from the Gap and J.Crew, with matching Keds and espadrilles lined up on the floor in front of the closet. All that's left is the bare cinder block walls, the empty built-in Formica desk unit, and a naked mattress on its metal frame. I stand in the doorway with my mouth hanging open. Suzette looks up from her desk at me.

"Uh, hi Suzette. Is everything okay?" *Idiot! Of course, it isn't!* Suzette gives me a weak smile. I can tell she is on the verge of tears. I step into her room and close the door behind me. I drop my backpack on the floor and rush to give her a hug. She immediately burst into tears. I just hold her for a while, periodically handing her tissues. In the back of my mind, I wonder if there is a Tissue Ministry in God's Kingdom. I feel her take a couple of deep breaths and pull away as she wipes her nose.

"Bethany left." She says between short sobs.

"Yeah, I guess so. When?"

"Her parents came to get all her stuff this morning."

"Why?" I have to ask.

"Oh Maddy, I'm not supposed to say."

"Well, have you talked to Bethany?"

"Just a couple of days ago, before she went to visit her parents for the weekend, but not since."

"Is she okay?" With that, a fresh set of tears erupts from Suzette. "She's not sick, is she?" I ask, starting to feel uneasy.

Back in our sophomore year, a boy had to leave school mid-year because he was diagnosed with an aggressive form of cancer, and he had to start chemotreatments right away. It was really sad. We were all supposed to pray for him, but Maggie and I were too busy with our degenerate social lives to really stop and care. I'm so thankful I'm not caught up in that life anymore.

"No, she's not sick." She wipes her eyes and takes another deep breath.

"It's okay. You don't have to talk about it. But if you get too lonely and you need a place to hang out, don't hesitate to come over, okay?"

"Okay. But I won't be alone here for long. There's a girl moving in here tomorrow from another dormitory, Hart Hall, I think. I guess she's been on a room change waiting list for a while. I'm not sure why she's changing rooms, but it will be good not to be alone."

"Yeah. I hope she's cool."

"Her biography card said she is applying for the same teaching English overseas ministry as me. So, at least we have that in common."

"Oh, that's good."

"Yeah, but I miss Bethany. We've been roommates for three years. We've been through a lot together."

"You could still keep in contact with her, even though she's gone."

"I doubt she will want to or have time to." What could that mean? Now, my inquiring mind is spinning.

"Well, I'm really glad to hear you will have a new room-mate and that you won't be alone in here," I try to comfort her.

"Yeah, it's a blessing, I guess."

"I better get to studying for finals. Come by if you need anything, okay? Even if it's just for a hug, okay?"

"Okay. Thanks, Maddy. You're so sweet." I give her a tight squeeze, pick up my backpack, open the door, and head next door.

I try not to gawk in amazement at Maggie, typing furiously at her computer. Her blonde curls (with about an inch of never-before-seen dark re-growth coming in) are pulled up in a scrunchie. She has a pencil in her mouth and one behind her ear, and she is wearing her glasses.

I haven't seen Maggie wear her glasses since our sophomore year when she lost her contact lens just before Labor Day weekend. We came home a bit intoxicated one night, and she dropped it in the bathroom while trying to take it out. Because it was Friday, she couldn't get a replacement until Tuesday after the holiday.

She is also wearing a very unglamorous oversized sweatshirt over her flannel pajamas. There is a blank spot on the wall where the infamous shirtless cowboy poster used to hang. *Praise God.* Seeing him hanging there on her wall was not a good thing for me since he reminds me so much of Peter. It makes me start to imagine what Peter looks like without a shirt on.

"Hey, chickadee!" She says as she removes the pencil from her mouth.

"Hey, how's it going?"

"Good, really good. Darlin', I think I'm gonna make it! I've only got two more three-page position papers to write, and then I'm all caught up. Hallelujah! I do believe you are witnessin' a bona fide miracle!" I haven't seen this chipper, happy Maggie in a long time. I've missed her.

"That's so great! Don't let me interrupt you."

"Nah, you have perfect timin'. I'm about to print the book review I just finished, and I could use a little break."

I drop my backpack on the floor by my desk and sit down on Maggie's bed. "I just came from visiting Suzette."

"Sad, isn't it? Really sad. Dang, that could've been me, you know?"

"What do you mean?" I'm confused.

"Suzette didn't tell you?"

"Tell me what?"

"Bethany's pregnant."

I feel my jaw drop toward the floor. *"No way!"*

"Yes, way, at least two months."

"Are you sure? I mean, how do you know?"

"My dad became buddies with her dad through some pastors' conferences they both attend regularly. And now, maybe they're both in some kind of pastors' support group for unruly, promiscuous, and wayward daughters, or maybe they'll create one. Anyway, her dad called my dad to ask for guidance and prayer. My dad called me and told me about Bethany only because he wanted me to know that I could've easily been in her situation and that I should thank God that I'm not. So, you better believe I do thank God, even though I was always very careful. Still, I'm grateful it didn't happen to me."

"Yeah, no kidding. Me too. That's crazy. Did she drop out of school?"

"Yep."

"That's odd. Couldn't she finish the rest of the year and graduate before the baby came? Then she'd at least have finished her college education."

"That's what my dad said. He thinks her parents are overreacting. But he said they are totally freaked out and didn't want their unwed pregnant daughter to begin to show while attending a Christian university."

"Given the way Bethany used to act, I guess her parents would be like that as well. I mean, she had to get it from somewhere, right?"

"Yeah, no kiddin'."

"What about Chad? I have to assume he's the father."

"I saw him in class this morning. He was actin' like nothin' happened at all."

"Now I know he is a major weasel!" I say, feeling furious.

"You got that right. If it had been me he knocked up, he would've met with the business end of my Daddy's 1949 Winchester double barrel shotgun, which he only fires on special occasions."

"I could totally see him doing that. Your dad rocks."

"He says the same about you. Oh, I'm not supposed to tell anyone about Bethany, but I figured you should know, on account of you spendin' so much time with your man. I don't want you vanishin' all of sudden too, 'cause you got knocked up."

"No, no chance of that," I try not to sound too proud.

"Still? Good girl." Maggie grins at me.

"Yeah, can you believe it?"

"Yes, I can. I'm so proud of you, Maddy. He's such a hottie. I know it must be hard for you to resist."

"You have no idea. I think the only way we can stay out of trouble is through massive amounts of prayer and Bible study on both our parts."

"Well, keep it up."

"Yeah, please pray for us if you think of it."

"I will. So things are still goin' good with him?"

"Oh, Mag, he's so wonderful. Every time he tells me he loves me, I could just melt on the spot. Normally, I don't fall for that line, but I can tell he really means it."

"Really? Still, watch out. Keep your eyes open."

"I know, but it's not like that. The first time he told me he loved me, we were standing in the parking lot of the building where his band rehearses, and we had just finished praying together."

"If yawl weren't alone together in his truck or his bedroom or some place where he might think he could get some, then I guess you could say he really meant it."

"Yeah, I could tell. I've had guys tell me they loved me before, but nothing like this. Besides, why would he lie? It's not like he's trying to get me into bed. Honestly, if that was really his intention, he would've got it already." I sense the need to honest with Maggie. "Sometimes, it's so hard to keep my hands off of him. And sometimes the only thing that stops me is the fact that I know he would be shocked and appalled if I started, you know, kissing him or touching him or something."

"Oh darlin', I seriously doubt that," both Maggie's dark brows raise. "I've seen the way that boy looks at you. I bet if you started his launch sequence, he wouldn't stop you until yawl saw fireworks together."

"That may be, but I *really* don't want to find out. One time, we were at his house, and we started to make out, and he totally pulled away. If it wasn't for him stopping us, I know I would have ended up sleeping with him. He's absolutely extraordinary."

"Whoa, are yawl sure he's male? I mean, that's unheard of." Maggie looks shocked.

"I know. He's *so* awesome. I'm so blessed. Dating him is like my own personal classic film adaptation I would call 'Miracle on Alpha Chi Row.' I love the way things are between him and me. None of the old relationship worries exist! I never have to constantly worry about when he's going to stop calling me, or if he really likes me, or if I shouldn't sleep with him again so he doesn't think I'm a slut, or if he just using me for sex. There's none of that garbage this time. And the coolest thing, the absolute coolest thing ever, is that we talk about God for hours and hours. It's so completely awesome! I've never had that experience with a guy before."

"That's amazing. I'm happy for you." Maggie's face is strained, like either she doesn't know what I'm talking about or she does and longs to have that experience with a guy, too. I'm hoping for the latter.

"Thanks. I hope the same for you someday."

"Not right now, though. I promised my Daddy and God, that I would remain man-free for a while. I need to focus on school right now. And gettin' my head on straight," she sighs. "Look, I know I've been a witch with a capital 'B' lately. I don't know what's got into me. Wait, yes, I do know—Justin, Chad, Bryce, Dale, well, um, you get the idea. Maddy, I'm tryin' real hard to be good, but it gets so difficult sometimes."

"Don't I know it! You're preaching to the choir, sister."

"Especially when the phone rings in the evenin'. I had to just quit answerin' it all together. I told my Daddy, don't call me in the evenin' 'cause I'm not answerin' that darn phone anymore. It's too much of a temptation. One night, Dale called me, and he started sweet-talkin' me, and askin' me what I was wearin' and so on. I literally had to hang up on him. He was none too pleased but tough. I ain't gonna be his little voodoo doll anymore."

"His what?" I'm not sure I heard Maggie right.

"You know, one of those little dolls you stick things in."

"Oh, oh, I get it. That's funny! I've never heard that before. It's a good analogy. Good for you. That's the way to do it."

"I keep thinkin' about what Grandma Dora used to tell me when she found out I was startin' to date boys."

"What's that?"

"She would take my hand and say, 'Miss Magdalena, remember dear, no farmer is gonna buy the cow he can milk for free.'"

I try not to laugh too hard because I can totally picture Maggie's grandma giving her that little nugget of wisdom. "So true! Awesome words of wisdom to live by."

"I didn't entirely understand what she was trying to tell me until I was a little older, but she was right. I'm so tired of being used."

"Amen to that," I say with conviction.

"I tried to tell myself that I was using them, too, but it still hurt. Every time I feel tempted, I just remind myself of how it feels afterward, how the guy can't get me out of his bed fast enough, and then he never calls me again. And then there's the whole walk of shame."

"Oh, man, that's the worst," I sneer. "When you're driving home, and you look at your trashed-out self in the rear-view mirror, and your hair is all messy, and your makeup is running, and you feel totally dirty and used as if no long hot shower on the planet would make you ever feel clean again. And you tell yourself, never, never, never, again."

"But of course, you do." Maggie adds.

"Not anymore. Maggie, I never want to feel that way again. Now that I have tasted the sweetness of a pure relationship with a guy, I never want to feel used and dirty from sleeping around ever again. Never again."

"I don't either, but sometimes I'm scared I'm not gonna make it. I mean, right now is easy 'cause I have the fear of not graduating starin' me in the face, and that's kept me on the straight and narrow, but that's almost done. So, then, what? Hon, I'm scared. I don't want to let everybody down, like my Daddy, God, you, me, Grandma Dora. And I really like not feelin' shameful and guilty all the time. It's such a nice change."

"Let's make a pact to pray for each other when we are feeling really tempted. And we have to be totally honest with each other about it when the temptations arise." I stop and look around the room. "Oh, I know!"

I spring up from Maggie's bed and go to my desk. I open the bottom drawer and pull out some black satin cording and a pair of scissors. I measure out and cut two long strips of cord. Then I dig out Maggie's little gold key that I hid under a small copy of the New Testament, and I go over to my dresser and get my key out of my underwear drawer, and I string each key on a piece of cording and knot the ends together. I hand Maggie her key necklace and put mine around my neck.

"Where did you get these?" She gets up, comes over, and sits down on my bed.

"Freshman year, at that purity conference, remember?"

"Yes, I remember. And I remember throwin' mine out."

"Well, something told me to fish it from your wastepaper basket and save it for you. It may seem kind of corny, but I think this will help us remember to pray whenever we feel severely tempted."

"Are you seriously gonna wear that?" Maggie looks at me like I'm crazy.

"Yes, I seriously am. I need all the help I can get! Have you *seen* my boyfriend? Do you know how sweet he is to me? Do you have any idea what it does to me every time he smiles at me?" I make big, dramatic faces at her.

She laughs. "Okay, then I'll wear mine, too. Maybe we'll start a new trend."

"I hope so." In more ways than just a fashion statement.

"What are you gonna say if someone asks you what it's for?"

"The truth. That I am a garden enclosed until my wedding night, at which point I will remove the key and give it to my husband because then, and only then, do I belong to him, and he can rightly enter my garden, so to speak."

"Hon, I think you're one taco shy of a combination plate!"

"I know it sounds crazy, but Maggie, I'm totally serious about this."

"Okay, okay. Me too." Maggie puts the black cord around her neck and adjusts the key so that it falls in the center of her chest, right over her heart.

"There, it looks cool! Okay, now promise me you will pray when you feel weak, or when you feel scared you won't make it, or you think you might be tempted to fall into bed with some guy. And promise me you will ask me to pray for you, too, okay?"

"Okay, I promise," she nods. "We should memorize that scripture from the Song of Solomon. My Daddy sent me a list of Scriptures to memorize about purity, and that was on the list." Maggie hands me a sheet of paper off her nightstand that looks like it's a page out of a long, handwritten letter.

"Yes, great idea! I'll print it out on a bunch of index cards, and we can put them everywhere, like on our desks, in our purses, on our bureaus…"

"You know, Maddy, you sure are a nut, but I'm real glad God made you my roommate."

"Thanks, I'm glad you're my roommate, too." I sit down next to her and give her a hug.

"I love you, M." Maggie smiles weakly at me.

"I love you, too '& M.'" I say as she laughs at our old joke from our freshman year about us being M & M's. Then she lets out a choked sob.

"Maddy, I'm so sorry." Maggie cries as I hug her.

"It's okay." I smooth her hair.

"No, it's not. I know I've been difficult to live with, and I know that whole deal with my dad when my Grandma Dora died, must've been a killer for you to deal with. I'm so sorry."

"It's all in the past. Let's move on." I pull away, grab a couple of tissues from the box on my desk, and hand her one.

"I just can't believe what a horse's behind I've been. We used to have so much fun together. Then I was scared we were growin' apart, but then I realized it was just me and that I was being horrible."

"Oh, you weren't that good!" I tease, and she laughs, then wipes her eyes and nose with the tissue.

"Thanks for everything." Maggie sniffs.

"For what?"

"For being such a good friend, for stickin' by me instead of judgin' me, when I full-on deserved it."

"Peter and I prayed for you a lot."

"I don't doubt that. I swear I could feel it sometimes."

"Really? I believe it."

"Yeah. Thanks for havin' faith in me."

"I knew you'd come around. I knew God was not going to let go of you."

"Well, I really appreciate you and your man prayin' for me."

"You're welcome. And I'd appreciate it if you would return the favor and pray for us, and his best friend Andrew, too. We're not giving up on him either."

"Hmmm, what's he look like?"

"Never mind that!" I shoot Maggie a stern frown.

"I'm just kiddin'. Too soon to joke about it?"

"Well, yeah!"

"Okay. And yes, I will include all yawl in my prayers."

"Thanks." I give Maggie another quick hug and throw our used tissues away. Then, we go to our desks to begin a long night of studying for finals.

Oh Lord, thank You, thank You, thank You!! Praise You! Thank You for bringing Maggie around. I'm so grateful. In Jesus' most precious name, Amen.

Chapter Twenty-four

The rush of customers in the coffeehouse has thinned out some. When Leah and I first sat down this evening, the place was packed with people presumably taking a break from their Christmas shopping judging by the abundance of large bags and packages sitting on the floor around most of the tables.

Leah and I relax with a couple of mugs of hot apple cinnamon tea after a long busy shift at Music Plus. This year, I don't seem to mind the hectic pace the holidays bring to working in retail. I'm just glad to be finished with all my papers, and finals are over, and I have a few weeks off from school.

"Did you ever get a hold of him?" Leah sips her tea.

I must not be hiding how uneasy I feel. Leah witnessed my frequent and somewhat frantic attempts to call Peter all day. She told me Josiah was going to meet up with Peter at some point today, so I figured they would probably come here whenever they finished whatever they were doing.

"No. I guess he's busy. When we had coffee with his aunt and uncle last night, they were talking about how his uncle had a meeting with a developer and didn't need Peter today, so I know he's off. I wonder what he's doing."

"Guy stuff, I guess. I know he called Josiah late last night and talked to him for a while."

"Hmm, really?" I'm a little more anxious now about this information.

I hope Peter is okay. I'm trying hard not to be one of those girls who goes totally berserk whenever she can't get in touch with her boyfriend. But it worries me to hear he talked to Josiah for a long time late last night. It must have been after I talked to him on the phone shortly after he dropped me off, which was much too brief because he seemed fine then.

My mother has this new rule that while I'm home for Christmas break, she doesn't like me to be on the phone for long periods of time. I have to keep my calls to Peter short, which I really don't like, but at least I went to sleep at a decent hour last night. If I'm on the phone for more than thirty minutes, she either gets on the line and starts nagging me to get off the phone, or she stands in the doorway of my room and protests loudly.

She also has been nagging me about the fact that she hasn't met Peter yet. But I must confess, I'm a little embarrassed to bring Peter home to meet my mother. Since her latest breast procedure, she has taken to wearing low-cut and super-tight tops with no bra. I don't know what Dr. Bill did to her, but she looks like she is constantly cold, if you know what I mean.

Mainly, I'm afraid she'll start flirting with Peter. I'm not sure how I would handle that. But she and Dr. Bill are leaving for another trip today, so I will have peace and solitude again.

"I'm sure everything is fine," Leah reassures me as she spots the worried look on my face.

"Yeah, you're probably right."

"How are the plans going for his brother's wedding?"

"Good, at least from my perspective. Matt's fiancée decided to move the whole rehearsal dinner, wedding, and reception to a much less swanky hotel in Long Beach by the Queen Mary. I guess Peter's parents were not pleased at all, and there was a big fuss about it, but she has her mind set on it."

"Why did she move everything there?"

"I'm not sure. Peter said Matt told him that his fiancée went to a conference there and fell in love with the place. I guess it's right on the shore of the bay. Anyway, I'm glad about it, not to be selfish or anything. I'm sure it's a much more casual place than the Biltmore in downtown Los Angeles. The venue change seriously cuts down on my nervous factor."

"What do you have to be so nervous about? You'll be fine," Leah smiles at me.

"Mostly about meeting Peter's family. What if they don't like me?"

"You still haven't met his family yet?"

"No, and he hasn't met mine either. I've been too busy with school, and both sets of our parents are always out of town."

"Whatever happens, always remember, it's only the two of you that matter. Don't let any family drama get in the way. The Lord tells us to leave our parents and cleave to our spouses, I mean, um, our boyfriend or girlfriend, for a reason."

"You sound as if you're speaking from experience."

"Let's just say Tom's mother still blames me for his accident. I think in her eyes, a better wife for her son would have insisted he quit riding that foolish motorcycle, and hence, he would still be alive," Leah sips her tea, looking at me over the rim.

"Ouch, that's harsh. Do you still talk to her?"

"Not often. But when I do, it's only by the grace of God that I'm able to be cordial to her."

"I'm not looking forward to meeting Peter's mother. She sounds scary, all proper and high society-like."

"But maybe she's sweet, like her son, who is a doll, and treats my dear friend Maddy very well." She smiles.

"Yes, he does." I can't help but smile widely. I feel pangs of missing him in my chest. "But what if she doesn't think I'm good enough for Peter?"

"She won't, don't worry. And it doesn't matter, anyway. That's for Peter to decide, right? Besides, if she thinks that about you, then she's the one who's not good enough."

"Maybe so. I just don't want to add to the troubles in Peter's life right now. Along with all his family strife over his brother's wedding, his band broke up. He said it's probably for the best, but I know he is seriously bummed about it."

"Oh no, why did they break up?" Leah asks. I get the feeling Leah is trying to sound and look surprised by this information. Odd.

"The lead singer left because Andrew, his bass player and best friend who also writes all the lyrics to the songs, never came to any of the practices anymore. So, they all decided to call it quits."

"That's terrible. Peter seems to really love to play music."

"Yeah, I feel bad for him. But he's already started to look for a new band. Only this time, he is doing it without Andrew, which he's not happy about. Andrew told him he wants to take a break from music for a while. Those two have been playing music together since they were kids."

"That's a shame. Peter must be heartbroken."

"Yeah, and I guess it's put a strain on their home life, too. Peter said he's praying about getting his own place."

"How do you feel about that?" Leah looks at me intently.

"Okay, I guess. A little apprehensive about the possibility of being alone with him more. But I think it would be good for him to get out of that house. There's so much tension there. And I don't like Andrew's girlfriend. She always looks at Peter like she wants to get her hooks into him next. I don't trust her. And it's not because I'm being a jealous girlfriend. Well, okay, maybe a little jealous. If I'm not allowed to lust after him, then no other girl is either!" I scowl, and Leah laughs at me.

I realize that I've finished my second cup of tea, and my tiny bladder reminds me it's time to visit the ladies' room. Leah says she will get us refills while I'm gone.

On my way back to our table, I notice a striking new painting on the wall opposite our table. The painting is completely white but is sculpted by some light clay or thick paint in some areas. As I stand there looking at it, I realize it's a face, like the face of Christ. It's captivating.

"That painting is new, isn't it?" I ask Leah as I sit down in my chair.

"Yes, it is."

"It's amazing, almost haunting. The face looks so full of wisdom and peace, and the eyes look filled with pain and love at the same time. It's stunning."

"Thank you, I'm really glad you like it," a shy smile playing at the corners of her mouth.

"Leah! Is it one of yours?"

"Yes," she says, humbly.

"I didn't know you were painting again. When did you start?"

"A few weeks ago. I was showing Josiah some of my old paintings because he kept asking to see them," she pulls on a long ringlet from the back of her hair. "After he saw them, he strongly encouraged—almost threatened—me to start painting again. He said I have a gift, and I need to use it," she's almost glowing as she smiles.

"I agree with him. That painting is just so...it's really...it's anointed!"

"That's what he said when he saw it. He liked it so much that he asked if he could hang it in the coffeehouse. Of course, I couldn't refuse."

"He's lucky he saw it first 'cause I would've begged you for it."

"And I would've given it to you," she smiles sweetly at me. "Maybe you guys can take turns with it."

"No, it fits here. And I'll get to admire it every time I come in. Plus, more people will see it here than if it hung in my dorm room. It's really special."

"Thank you, Maddy," she squeezes my hand.

The front door of the coffeehouse opens with a swoosh from the blustery December wind, and both our heads snap toward it to see if it's our men entering the shop. I see a familiar guy with a shaved head, followed by an even more familiar, tall, long-haired, handsome guy. They are both laughing and talking.

As they approach us, I notice Peter looks tired. Josiah walks around to Leah and gives her a hug, lifting her hand to kiss it. Peter leans down and wraps his arms around my shoulders tightly. He lets out a long, slow sigh.

"I missed you today," he whispers in my ear. Having his lips close to my ear makes me quiver inside. He kisses my cheek lightly.

"I missed you, too," I put my hands on Peter's arms.

After a moment, Peter unwraps his arms from around me. He pulls an empty chair close to mine, sits down, and puts his arm around my chair. I notice his eyes are bloodshot with dark circles under them, but they still shine brightly with an inner brilliance. He has what looks to be about a day and a half of razor stubble on his face, which looks nice on him.

"Hi, Leah. How are you?" He smiles at her. As tired as he looks physically, he seems to have a peaceful air about him, and he is almost glowing.

"I'm well, and you?" Leah asks casually.

"I'm good, really good, a little tired though. It's been a long day."

"I heard you guys were up late last night," I look at Peter.

"Yeah, I have yet to get some sleep," he smiles at me sweetly.

"Pete, coffee?" Josiah calls from the counter.

"Please! With a double shot." Peter answers him.

"Coming right up. Ladies, can I bring you anything?" We tell him we are fine.

I turn to Peter. "What happened? When I talked to you last night, you were going to bed, and it was like, not even midnight yet." I try not to look as concerned as I feel.

"Well, let's see, after I got off the phone with you, Andrew and I had a little discussion."

"Uh oh. About what?"

"Andrew wants to move into the master bedroom because he and his girlfriend need more room."

"So, he wants to get rid of that beautiful studio you guys have?"

"That's right." The muscles in his jaw tighten.

"Well, maybe you can move the studio into Andrew's old room when they move into the master bedroom."

"That might work, if they didn't need that room for the baby."

"The WHAT?" I ask too loudly. I hope he didn't say what I think he said.

"The baby's room. Andrew's going to be a father. His girlfriend is pregnant."

"Is he sure it's his?" I'm pretty sure that was a rude question, but I'm in total shock.

"Yeah, I guess." Peter seems sad.

"Is that the real reason why he quit the band?"

"I think so. His excuse about taking a break from music is totally not like him. He loves playing music. He's a solid bass player, and he writes killer songs. Anyway, I told him I would look for another place to live, and he said that would be a good idea."

"I'm so sorry, Peter. This sounds like an awful situation," I feel so sad for him.

"Moving out doesn't really bother me; I kind of saw it coming. Josiah said I could stay with him for as long as I needed to. So, I'm renting a room from him for a while. I'm moving my stuff into his house tomorrow."

"That'll be so good for you. How awesome of Josiah to help you like this." This is such good news. Leah is beaming, and we both turn and smile at Josiah, who gives us a quick wave from the counter.

"Yeah, he's a lifesaver. And it will be a good change for me," Peter plays with my hair that is hanging over the back of my chair. "But I'm still really bummed for Andrew that he's giving up music and having a kid with that girl. He's my best friend, and I just want to take him by the shoulders, and give him a good shake, and yell, 'What are you doing?!' He's throwing his life away, and I can't stop him. He's helped me through so much stuff in the past, but I feel like there's nothing I can do to help him in this situation."

"Just be his friend. He's going to need you." I put my hand on his, which is resting on my shoulder, and I give it a little squeeze.

"That's what Josiah said, but I get the feeling Andrew's not really interested in being friends right now. And there's the fact that I won't be around that much to help him. Which leads me to the next reason for my tremendously tired state."

"Wait, wait. Hold on for a minute. What do you mean you won't be around much?" I try to contain my panic. My heart is starting to beat extraordinarily fast.

"I was getting to that. After my little talk with Andrew, I got a call from Luke, my former lead singer. He called to tell me that he passed my number on to a buddy of his who is the manager for a national act that is about to go on tour and needs a lead guitar player right away. He said the guy was familiar with our music and liked my style of playing. Luke said he told the guy that he could call me no matter how late it was.

"About five minutes after I got off the phone with Luke, the phone rang again. It's Dave Kincaid, the manager of Faith Not

Fear. We talked for a little bit, and then he asked me if I was available to come down to audition the following day."

"No way! You're kidding me!" My excitement for him mixes with the dread in the pit of my stomach, forming a sort of noxious stew of emotion.

"Aren't they that band that has that hard rock song with something about being the nails driven into the Savior's hands, right?" Leah looks excited, too.

"That's them. Their music and lyrics are so inspiring. They've had a couple of big songs on the Christian rock charts, and they have a huge following," I tell Leah.

"That's right. We just upped our order of their latest CD for the store. That's great, Peter!" Leah smiles.

"Peter, that's so awesome!" I'm truly excited for him, but the fear in the pit of my stomach is beginning to rise and tightens my throat.

"I drove out to Dave's house in the Valley this morning," Peter continues. I walked around back to the studio like he told me, and there were all the guys from the band, getting ready to rehearse without a lead guitar player. Dave introduced me to the band, and they asked me a few questions. We prayed and then rehearsed."

"Wow! Were they cool guys?" I hear myself ask with an interviewer's fake enthusiastic tone.

"Yeah, super cool. They are very serious about their music and about serving God. They had to fire their last guitar player because he wouldn't stop sleeping with groupies. And he was married. They said they couldn't have that in their ministry, so they had to let him go."

"Bummer for him. How did the audition go?" My voice sounds dry and distant in my ears.

"Really well, I guess, because they asked me to come on tour with them. I have four weeks to learn the songs and rehearse with the band, then we hit the road."

That fear that was in my throat rises to my mouth and leaves a thick, sour taste there.

"Oh, how cool." My voice sounds weak. I feel the blood draining from my face, and I fight the tears rising up, burning my eyes.

Stop it, Madeleine! Stop being selfish! You know this is what Peter has always wanted. Be happy for him.

"I'm so happy for you." I turn and give him a quick hug.

Be cool. Be cool. It was fun while it lasted. Put on your big girl pants. You can deal with this. You can totally let go and lose it when you get home.

I sit back in my chair and try to think about anything else except Peter breaking up with me and leaving me to pursue his dream. I try to think of a viable excuse to get out of here so I can get in my car and go bawl my eyes out in some random parking lot somewhere.

I feel his eyes on me, and I fake a weak smile. I wish the blood would return to my face. I try to return my breathing to a normal pace.

"But that's not all that happened after I got off the phone with you last night," Peter is smiling directly at me.

"Really? It sounds like you had a pretty busy evening and day, as it is." I try to sound cool, calm, and collected, the exact opposite of how I feel inside. I'm starting to feel quite nauseous, so I may have my excuse to leave very soon.

"Yeah, I did have a busy day, but I had to run one more errand when I got back from the audition." He is still smiling at me.

Suddenly, I'm aware of everyone's eyes on me, including the staff and many of the regular customers. Leah is smiling at me, and her eyes are misty. Josiah comes over and puts his hand on Leah's shoulder. Peter gets up from his chair and pushes it aside. He reaches into the front pocket of his jeans, takes a deep breath, and drops down on one knee right in front of me.

OHMYLORDOHMYLORDOHMYLORDOHMYLORD!!!

He puts his hands on my knees and gently turns me toward him. Then he takes my hands in his.

"Mad, I haven't been able to get you out of my head from the first time I saw you. I knew after the first time I talked to you that I wanted to be with you," a soft, watery glaze coming over his sparkling green eyes. "I know it's only been four months, but I feel like I've loved you all my life, and I know God has brought us together. So, Madeleine Marie Winger, I ask you, in front of our dear friends and all these people, will you marry me?"

He opens a small black velvet box and takes out a beautiful white gold ring with filigree designs on the sides that wrap around a brilliant round-cut diamond in the center.

The ring quickly fades from my focus as a torrent of tears clouds my eyes and flows down my cheeks. The floodgates burst open, and a heavy, wet sob escapes my throat. I look into Peter's eyes, which are at my eye level since he is kneeling in front of me. His eyes are glossy with tears, and he has a big, wide smile on his face. I throw my arms around him and bury my face in his neck. He wraps his arms around me and hugs me tight.

"Is that a 'yes'?" he laughs.

"Yes!" I squeak out.

I pull back and try to wipe my eyes. Leah hands Peter a napkin, and he hands it to me. Then he takes my left hand and slides the ring on my shaking ring finger. Then we kiss softly and sweetly on the lips. Everyone claps. Leah and Josiah yell their congratulations.

"I love you, Mad," he whispers.

"I love you too, Peter," I whisper back.

He rises up from his knee, pulls me up to him, and hugs me tightly for a while. Then we sit down at the table as Josiah and Leah bring a tray of sparkling apple cider in champagne glasses they pass out to everyone.

Josiah raises his glass. "To Peter and Madeleine, the Lord bless you and keep you on the road of life that together you will share as one. Cheers!" We all say cheers and clink glasses.

The cider washes down the nausea and acrid taste of fear. Now, all I taste is the sweetness of pure joy. I grab another napkin to dry my eyes and wipe off my running makeup.

"For a minute there, I thought you were going to say no. You seemed kind of upset," Peter squeezes my waist.

"I thought you were going to break up with me," I wipe under my eyes again wishing I had put waterproof mascara on today. "You could tell I was upset?"

"Well, yeah. I know you pretty well by now. And usually, when someone's face goes ghost-white all of a sudden, it's a good indication that something is wrong."

"Oh."

"Mad, how could you think I would break up with you?"

"I guess since you have this exciting opportunity in your life, like the thing you've always wanted, you wouldn't want to be tied down for it."

"No way! I wouldn't sacrifice the most incredible relationship in my life, aside from my relationship with God, because of some career opportunity. You are truly a gift from God to me. I got the full realization of that last night when I was talking with Josiah," he squeezes me again. "My life is at a crossroads right now, and everything I prayed about, which road I should take or which way to go, I saw that you were part of all of it. When I was praying with Josiah, I heard God tell me, 'The two shall become one.' I knew in my spirit exactly what He meant and what I needed to do."

"Oh, Peter," is all I can say breathlessly before my eyes well up again, my nose starts to run, and I have to grab yet another napkin.

"Mad, I got so excited I wanted to drive right over to your mom's house and propose to you right then. But I realized it was three A.M., and I should probably get you a ring and do it up right. Josiah called Leah this morning, and she gave him the address of a good jewelry store."

"You knew?" I turned to Leah.

"All day long, it's been killing me not to tell you! Especially when you were so worried that you couldn't get in touch with Peter. But I knew I couldn't say anything. Josiah told me this morning that Peter was going to propose to you when he asked me if I could recommend a good jewelry store. I gave him the name and address of my favorite store."

"Thank you!" I give her a big hug.

"It's such a beautiful ring. It almost seems like it was made for you," Leah says, holding out my left hand, and smiling brightly at me.

"It's so beautiful." I look up at Peter, who is smiling back at me.

"The lady in the jewelry store told me it's an antique. I looked at all these new rings in the store, but they just didn't seem right for you. They were either too plain or too usual-looking. I wanted to get you a ring that I could see you wearing. The lady at the store asked me a few questions about you and the kind of things you like. Then she went over to another counter and pulled out this ring.

"She said she bought it at an estate sale years ago because she felt the ring was special, but she never felt quite right about wearing it herself, so she decided to sell it in the store. She said it has sat in the store for years without anyone even taking a second glance at it. When I saw it, I knew it was for you. It's so cool that it even fits you."

"I love it. Thank you." I start misting up all over again.

"I thought you would." Peter smiles. "I love you so much, Mad."

"I love you too." He hugs me tightly.

Oh Lord, thank You. You are so amazing. I don't even know what to pray; I'm speechless and full of awe. I praise You and thank You. I love You.

Chapter Twenty-five

eter and I exchange hugs with Leah, Josiah, and other friends in the coffeehouse, who congratulate us on our engagement. I'm overflowing with love and blessings from all these wonderful people, especially from my new fiancé.

Oh, my goodness…I am engaged to him! He's going to be my husband. And I'm going to be his wife. I think it's going to take a while to truly sink in. The beautiful vintage engagement ring shining brilliantly on my left hand is a very real reminder.

As I float back to earth, we all begin to gather the champagne glasses from around the coffeehouse, and Leah and Josiah take them back to the kitchen. Peter and I sit down at our table. He takes my hands in his, and we smile at each other like grinning fools in love. I swear, I would marry him right now. If a judge, priest, or even a ship's captain walked into the coffeehouse, I would nab them to marry us before an order was placed.

"So, listen," Peter says, his face going serious. "I need to know that you're going to be okay with me being gone for a while."

"I'll be okay. I won't like it, but I'll be okay. God will get me through it. I will miss you terribly, but I know my Lord, and He will help me out. I'll have school, work, and Maggie's drama to keep me occupied," I smile at him.

"Good. Oh man, I'm gonna miss you. Dave hasn't given me the schedule yet, but I know the next leg of the tour is at least five months long." Peter frowns.

"That's a long time." I can't even think about how much I will miss him.

"I know. But hey, I was thinking we could set the date for after your graduation, sometime after June, so you don't have to try to plan a wedding while you're in school."

"*Ugh!* I have to wait that long for our wedding night?" *Oops!* I didn't mean to say that out loud. Peter's going to think I'm some sort of a sex-crazed lunatic. Oh well!

Peter laughs. "Well, we could slip off to Vegas tonight." He's kidding, I think.

"Yeah! We could get married at the Elvis Chapel. That would be so awesome!"

"That sounds great. Let's go." He has a mischievous spark in his eye I've never seen before. I like it—a lot.

"Okay, let's go." I challenge him.

"Okay." The spark still gleaming in his eyes.

"My mother will be so upset with me." This fact doesn't deter me all that much. Not at all, actually.

"I'm pretty sure mine will be, too," his mischievous spark dims.

"Hmm, and I think Josiah and Leah should be there."

"Yeah, definitely. And what about your friends from school?"

"Yeah, them too. And uh, I'm supposed to open the store with Leah tomorrow morning. I think she would be upset with me if I ran off and got married without her there and did not show up for work, leaving her a staff person short during the Christmas rush."

"Good point, we probably shouldn't do that," he laughs. "Seriously, Mad, I would love nothing in the world more, short of Jesus returning, than to marry you right now, but we can't do that. It would upset too many people. But mostly, I can't marry you, then turn around, leave, and be away from you for five months. I just couldn't do that."

"I know, and I would be too tempted not to finish school if we got married right now. I would want to come with you on the road and be your own personal groupie." I give him an impish smile.

"That would be nice. I mean, really nice," he smiles. "Not the part about you putting off school, I mean. That wouldn't be good. But having you on the road with me. Yeah, that would be sweeter than sweet."

"Seriously? You would really want me to come on the road with you? I was kidding."

"I would love to share that with you. Maybe after we're married, if everything works out with the band and they keep me on, I'll take you up on that personal groupie thing." He smiles sweetly at me.

"That would so be fun." *That's the understatement of the year!*

"I think you would have a blast. A couple of the other wives tour with the band, too."

"Really?" *Omigosh...I'm going to be Peter's wife!*

"Yeah, after the rehearsal, when they told me I was in, we were all sitting around talking about life in general. I told them I was on my way to buy an engagement ring and then propose to my girlfriend. All the guys were glad to hear it and told me it's a tough life, but some of their wives come on part of the tour with them, making it not so hard."

"It's kinda strange," I say, thinking out loud.

"What is?" he asks.

"To think of myself as your wife. Well, your future wife anyway."

"I already feel like we are part of each other. It will be really cool when it's official," he takes my hand in his and kisses it.

"Yes, it definitely will." We can't stop smiling at each other, and Peter hugs me tightly.

When I get home, I'm so grateful that my mother and Dr. Bill have left on their trip already. Boy, are they going to be shocked when they hear my news. I can see it now, *"Oh, hi, Mom; while you were gone, I got engaged to a guy you've never met, but it's all good."* She is going to totally freak out, but truthfully, I'm not all that concerned. I know that sounds cold, but it's been so nice not having to deal with my mother's madness.

I know her impending mega-beast rant will have little to do with my actual engagement but will be an excuse for her to get super dramatic. She hasn't had much of an opportunity for drama since I became a believer. I'm glad she's been gone so much this year. I cherish independence, as well as peace and quiet.

As I lay in bed, I wonder how on earth I am going to wait until June or possibly later to become Peter's wife. I couldn't care less about the wedding stuff. Well, okay, maybe I care a little. I just really want to be with him. To be joined to him. To be his. The next five months or so are going to be tough. In a way, I'm grateful we will be physically far away from each other. That will definitely help with waiting to make love much easier.

Oh Lord, thank You for Peter. Thank You for giving him wisdom. I ask You to please be with us tonight, tomorrow, and for the days to come. Please teach me what I will need to know to be a good wife. No, a great wife and helpmate, as Your Word says. The kind of mate he deserves. And help him become an awesome husband. Please help me to stay focused on the things you have before me right now, like school and helping Maggie. Again, I thank You for Peter. In Your precious name, Lord Jesus, I pray, Amen.

Chapter Twenty-six

" **W**ell, I'm glad I *finally* get to meet my future son-in-law," my mother snipes as she zips up the back of my dress. "Even if it's for only a *few* minutes."

Peter is coming to pick me up to take me to Long Beach for the weekend where all of his brother's wedding festivities will take place. This will be his first visit to this house. Since we have a very important destination to get to, we can't stay long. A perfect opportunity for Peter to meet my mother. And yeah, I'll admit it, I planned it this way. I don't want there to be any chance of my mother scaring Peter off with her flirting, or worse.

"Mom, please don't start," I say softly. She has been trying to put me on a guilt trip ever since they returned home from their trip to the Cayman Islands.

When they first got home, she noticed my engagement ring right away. She totally freaked out and started shrieking and crying throughout the house that I betrayed her and how could I do this to her, her only daughter. She then declared that she would not pay for my wedding. I told her that was fine. I wanted to tell her that Peter and I would make our joke about the Elvis Chapel in Las Vegas a reality, but I decided not to add insult to injury.

Somehow, I feel kind of disconnected from her, not that I don't care, but her drama seems to have little effect on me anymore. It's a bummer that I will forever have this unpleasant memory of my mother's reaction to my engagement as extreme drama, complete with tears of perceived injustice, instead of her shedding tears of joy and telling me how happy she is for me.

After about an hour of my mother carrying on dramatically, Dr. Bill finally calmed her down. He probably gave her some sort of sedative because I did not hear so much as a peep from her for the rest of the night.

He came into my room later that night and apologized for her, and he promised he would speak to her. He also told me he would be honored to pay for any type of wedding I wanted, regardless of what my mother said. I apologized to him for not bringing Peter around so they could meet him. He said it was okay and that he understood.

I also told him that Peter told me that he feels bad that he didn't think to come to him to ask for my hand in marriage like a proper gentleman would. Dr. Bill seemed really surprised and said he didn't think young people even thought about that kind of stuff anymore. He told me to tell Peter not to worry about it, that he was flattered that he even considered doing it.

He and I actually had a real heart-to-heart conversation. He asked me a lot of questions about Peter, and not just fatherly stuff like how is Peter going to support me, type of stuff. He asked about our relationship and if I was sure this was the guy I should marry.

I was honest and open with him about how God has had His hand on both Peter and me through our relationship and always will, and how He brought Peter and me together at just the right time in our lives. He asked if I would be moving in with Peter soon, and I told him we would not be sharing a bed until our wedding night. He said he was really impressed with our vow of purity.

I hope I'm getting through to him spiritually. I would love to see him and my mom get saved. Peter and I have been really praying for them.

In hindsight, I feel bad that I didn't introduce my mother to Peter before announcing our engagement, and mostly for not trusting God that He would've taken care of any situations that might have come up if I had brought Peter home to meet her. I definitely need more wisdom and maturity in this area of my life.

At least Maggie was happy for me. In fact, she was extraordinarily happy for me. When I called her at her dad's house in Plano where she's staying over Christmas break, I was expecting her to poke fun at me for getting married and make some sort of sarcastic comment about how I sold out and will be getting my "Mrs." degree after all. But she got a little choked up when I told her I was engaged.

"Ya'll better invite me to the weddin'," Maggie sniffled.

"If we have a formal wedding and we don't end up running off to Vegas, then I would love it if you would be my maid of honor," I stifled my own tears of joy.

"Oh, Maddy," a sob caught in her throat. "I would love to be your maid of honor."

"Good, but we may not have a big wedding. My mother was pretty upset with me."

"Oh hon, I would be honored to do it even if yawl do end up at the Elvis Chapel in Vegas. Remember, yawl will need a witness, and I would be more than glad to take on that duty."

"So true. Thanks, Maggie."

"Does this mean I get to throw the bachelorette party?"

"Uh—"

"I'll recruit Suzette to help me hold auditions for the young men that we'll hire to dance for us at the party! This is going to be so much fun!"

"Well, I don't—"

"Hey! I know! Do you think your hunky man would jump out of a giant cake for you if we asked him nicely? I figure he's the one you'd really want to see dancin' half naked, right?"

"Maggie! Thanks, but no thanks. Please, no bachelorette party for me, okay? I don't need to feed my brain with images of half-naked men dancing seductively, *especially* Peter when it's already nearing the overload point."

"Oh, alright. Only a good, clean, fun bridal shower, then."

"Yes, thank you. Thank you very much."

"That doesn't mean the girls and I won't kidnap you and drag you off to the Cowboy Boogie's 'Ladies Only Beefcake Night!'"

"Oh Lord, no, please no!" We both giggled hysterically.

In these last few weeks, before Peter leaves on tour, nothing seems to get to me—not my mother, not any irate customers at work, nothing. I kind of feel like I'm walking around in a dream.

Peter and I have been spending as much time together as possible. I started going to the Faith Not Fear rehearsals with him because the guys said it was not only okay for me to tag along, but I was welcome to join him.

Peter and I get to talk and pray together during the hour-long drive to the rehearsal studio in the Valley and back home, which is wonderful. I usually bring a book to the rehearsal, but I never end up reading it. I watch Peter the whole time. He is so amazing and talented. He plays so passionately it's like he's worshiping God when he plays guitar. It's so awesome. And all the guys in the band really like him. In fact, they all get along very well, like life-long buddies. It's so amazing to watch.

Peter seems happy, and seeing him so full of joy and peace makes me ecstatic. Maybe that's why my mother's little dramatic episode and her barbed comments don't get under my skin.

While we were shopping for stuff for this weekend, she commented that I was ruining my life by getting married. She was appalled that Peter gave me a "used" engagement ring, even if it was an antique. But these comments seem to bounce right off of me. I spend so much of my day in the presence of God that I feel like I'm coated in His grace. I think that's why I'm so impervious to unnecessary drama and negative comments.

"I'm just saying it will be nice to finally meet him. Turn around. Let me look at you," my mother turns me by the shoulders. She holds her perfectly manicured fingertips up to her mouth. "Oh Madeleine, you look so beautiful. Absolutely elegant and beautiful! So grown-up and ladylike."

"Thanks." I can't help but feel awkwardly embarrassed. My mother's adoration and compliments are few and far between.

The day after her episode, I tried to apologize to her and tell her I didn't mean to hurt her feelings, but she just interrupted me and started discussing the wedding plans and how we must use her favorite caterer and florist, and so on and so forth. That's her way of telling me everything is okay between us.

I look at myself in the mirrored closet door in her dressing area. My mother and I spent the whole morning in her favorite salon getting facials, manicures, and pedicures and then getting our hair and makeup done.

The end result is pretty good. I do look nice, but not really like myself. Maybe like a grown-up version of me. My hands don't really look like mine, with the soft pink and white French manicure on my nails instead of my usual deep dark burgundy (I stopped wearing plain black nail polish in the tenth grade) or no polish at all. My hair is parted on the side, curled softly in a sort of forties style, and flows down my back in big, smooth curls. I like the way my makeup turned out. My eyes are done in a soft, smoky, light gray shimmer, and my lipstick is a matte dark red.

My mother picked out my dress. It's an off-the-shoulder, form-fitting black satin dress that hugs my body. I feel like I resemble a petite, dark-haired version of Jessica Rabbit, Roger Rabbit's shapely cartoon wife. And I feel kind of naked and vulnerable without a big sweater to shelter me.

When I first tried the dress on, I told my mother no way, that it was too sexy, but the lady assisting us in the high-end dressing room at Nordstrom's assured me that I looked elegant and not at all like a brazen hussy, as Maggie would put it. At first, I didn't believe the saleslady, figuring she just wanted to make a sale, but this dress was not the most expensive one I was trying on, so I figured she must have been telling me the truth.

My dress fits me perfectly. It hits me just below my knees, and most importantly, my breasts are all covered and not hanging out anywhere, including my cleavage, which is quite a feat. Most dresses in a size eight don't account for an ample bosom, so I'm usually busting out of the neckline (pardon the pun).

As I look at my reflection, I feel like such a woman, but also like I'm playing dress-up. Underneath my dress is a silky black strapless La Perla bustier my mother insisted she buy me to wear under my dress, which actually supports my breasts perfectly and draws my waist in. The super smooth black silk stockings feel so slinky on my legs. A far cry from the drugstore tights I usually wear. And I love the vintage dangling marcasite and diamond earrings and the matching necklace that my mother gave me for this occasion, which also matches my engagement ring beautifully.

But my favorite part of my woman's outfit is the shoes. I'm still totally shocked my mother insisted I wear her black satin Christian Louboutin four-inch pumps with the signature crimson red soles, which she purchased in Paris (for a very large sum of money, I'm sure). They are, by far, my favorite pair of shoes she owns, and she has hundreds of pairs of gorgeous shoes. They are so stunningly beautiful, like fine art for feet. I've never even dared to try them on, and now I am wearing them out of the house to a swanky restaurant on the Queen Mary. I will absolutely die if I spill anything on them. I know they're just shoes, but they're just so exquisite, it would be an awful shame to ruin them, not to mention my mother would be royally upset with me. A thousand times worse than she was about my engagement.

"Oh, Madeleine, you look so beautiful. Your young man is not going to be able to keep his hands off of you!"

"Thanks, Mom, but that's not really what I'm going for."

"I know, I know," she rolls her eyes. "Okay then, he will be very proud to have you by his side."

"I'll take that." I conveniently failed to mention to her that I will be meeting my future in-laws tonight, and my goal is to make a good impression. "I better go get the rest of my stuff together," I teeter down the hall toward my room.

"You have everything for tomorrow to wear to the wedding?" She follows after me.

"Yeah, I think so."

My mother bought me an equally beautiful burgundy velvet dress to wear to the wedding, an additional pair of black silk stockings, and lent me her ruby necklace and earrings, burgundy Chanel velvet platform pumps, and a matching velvet clutch bag.

She follows me into my room and helps me double-check everything. I close up my bags and lay my new long black velvet coat and evening purse on my bed, more purchases from my mother for my weekend in Long Beach with Peter and his family.

"Wow! My goodness! Madeleine, you look so beautiful!" Dr. Bill stands in the doorway of my room.

"Thanks." I feel my cheeks get hot.

"Bill, bring Maddy's bags downstairs."

"Certainly." He grabs the garment bag and overnight suitcase and takes them downstairs to the foyer.

Just then, I see out my bedroom window a familiar black 4-Runner pull up in front of our house.

"He's here." I feel a little nervous. *Oh Lord, please help my mother behave herself, and please help Peter be okay with my appearance.*

I watch Peter get out of his truck. He is wearing a black silk suit, and oh my, he looks so gorgeous. Believe me.

He straightens his tie and smooths his hair, which looks shorter, as he walks up to the front door.

"Oooh, Maddy, he's really handsome!" My mother cranes her neck to look out the window, nudging me over so she can get a better look at him. She quickly turns on her heels and heads down the hall to the stairs.

I hear the doorbell ring, grab my coat and purse off my bed, make one last quick inspection of myself in my dresser mirror, and then head downstairs. I hear Dr. Bill unlock the front door and greet Peter warmly, and they exchange introductions.

"Maddy will be down shortly. Please come in." Dr. Bill's voice fades in the direction of the study.

"Well hello there! It's so nice to finally meet you, Peter! Maddy has told us so much about you! I'm Gwendolyn." I hear my mother's loud voice say, but it sounds innocuous enough. I carefully descend the stairs as quickly as I can in four-inch couture pumps.

I lay my coat and purse on my bags in the hall and head to the study. As I approach the study, I hear my mother still speaking loudly and dramatically about her latest travels. When I enter the doorway, Peter stands up from the couch where my mother was sitting too close to him. He has a look of pleasant surprise and admiration on his face.

"Wow…you look amazing." Peter walks over to me and gives me a gentle hug with a big smile spread across his face.

"She has her mother's figure, doesn't she?" my mother interrupts loudly.

I ignore her comment because I can't take my eyes off Peter. "Thanks. So do you. That suit really suits you."

"Hmmm, you really think so? It's my mother's request through my aunt. I don't think I'm going to make a habit of it." Peter laughs.

"Yes, Peter, you look very handsome," my mother chimes in. "Armani suits are so delicious."

"Thank you, Mrs. Cutter."

"Oh, please call me Gwen." She gets up and walks over to us.

"Well, we'd better get going in case we run into traffic, and we need to check in to the hotel before the rehearsal." Peter starts to walk over to Dr. Bill. "It was really nice to meet you, Dr. Cutter. I promise to take excellent care of Madeleine this weekend." Peter shakes hands with Dr. Bill.

"It was very nice to meet you as well, Peter. Please have Maddy bring you around more often."

"I will." Peter turns to my mother. "Mrs. Cutter, it was very nice to meet you, too." Peter extends his hand to her.

"Oh, call me 'Mom.' We'll be family soon," she says slightly seductively as she hugs him closely. "Oooh, nice muscles," she squeezes his arms and thrusts out her newly renovated and bra-less softball-like boobs.

"Uh, thanks...Mom." Peter says, joking. Dr. Bill tries to stifle a big laugh. I laugh out loud at Peter's little joke. My mother doesn't seem to notice it.

Eww! I hate it when my mother flirts with my boyfriends. And she has never been this bad before Peter. He stands stiffly and looks over at me as she gropes his arms. I subtly give him the I-told-you-so look since he didn't believe me when I told him that my mother would most assuredly flirt with him.

"We'd better get going," I grab Peter's hand and lead him into the foyer. He picks up my bags. I take a quick, deep breath, exhale, clear my mind of evil thoughts, and turn to my mother.

"Thank you so much for everything, Mom." I give her a hug.

"You're so welcome, sweetie. You look so beautiful. Call me if you have questions about doing your hair tomorrow." The hairstylist taught me how to put my hair up in a sort of messy but elegant French twist that is supposed to be really easy and look good even with slept-on curls.

"I will. See you later. And thanks again for everything," I hug Dr. Bill.

"You're welcome, sweetheart. You two have a great time," Dr. Bill smiles. "Peter, please tell your brother congratulations for us."

"Thanks, I will," Peter nods.

I follow Peter out to his truck as he opens the back. He puts my borrowed brown leather Louis Vuitton bags in the back.

"Nice luggage. I think my mother has the exact same set."

"My mother insisted I use her bags. She lectured me on the importance of traveling in style. I just gave in to get her out of my hair."

"That's cool. I'm just teasing ya." He grins at me as he turns the key in the lock so the back window goes up. He looks me up and down with a big smile on his face. "Dang, Mad, you look truly amazing."

"Really, it's not too much or inappropriate?" I feel a little self-conscious, but honestly, loving every minute of his appreciative gaze.

"No, you look really beautiful. And that dress shows me that my cute little betrothed wife has some really nice curves. More than I thought. Not that I think about your curves, or at least I try not to. Nice. Really nice. Gives me a lot to look forward to." He gives me a little knowing grin.

He walks around to the truck's passenger side to open my door for me, still grinning all the way.

I slip on my coat and he takes my hand and helps me up into the seat. "Mmm, nice legs, too." Now I know I'm blushing. He walks over to the driver's side, removes his suit jacket, which he lays in the back seat, and climbs in.

"Thanks. You look pretty gosh darn good yourself. I like your haircut. Not too short. It looks nice."

"Thanks," he smooths the back of his hair down. "The stylist at the photo shoot for the new band promo pictures suggested I go a little shorter, so I let him cut it. He wanted to wax my eyebrows and put this mud stuff on my face, too, but I told him I'm just the guitar player and to give that kind of attention to the lead singer." He turns the key in the ignition, and we wave to my mother and Dr. Bill, then drive off to Long Beach.

"Why not?" I ask, picking up the conversation. "You should have seen the amount of gooping, scrubbing, and plucking I went through this morning."

"It's just not my thing. That stuff looks great on you, though, not that you needed it." He smiles at me.

"You're sweet." I smile back at him.

"You're beautiful and sweet." He takes my hand in his and kisses it. I feel little flutters in my stomach.

Peter looks so handsome in his shirt and tie, although I can tell he is a little uncomfortable with the tie because he keeps tugging at it. His dress shirt is a pale sage green that matches his eyes, which I can see much better now with his hair cut shorter. The layers in the front of his hair frame his angular cheekbones and square jaw perfectly and taper back to fall just above his shoulders in the back.

I still have to periodically pinch myself that this gorgeous guy I have had a crush on for so long turned out to be an awesome man of God and is now my fiancé. He will be my husband in less than a year. My husband. And I will be his wife. Holy mackerel.

Chapter Twenty-seven

We pull up under the carport in front of the West Coast Long Beach Hotel and park behind a long black limousine. The entire walkway in front of the hotel is made up of glossy ceramic red clay tile that leads up to huge glass and brass doors. The doors are framed on both sides with enormous potted queen palm trees.

Peter comes around to my side of the truck, opens the door, and takes my hand to help me down. He reaches into the back and grabs his suit jacket, puts it on, and adjusts his tie. He holds his arm out to me, and I take it. We walk up to the entrance, and the doorman opens the door for us.

I have to adjust my posture to walking in high heels, which feels a little awkward but not totally unpleasant. I still feel like I'm playing grown-up. I feel so womanly, especially on Peter's arm with him so handsomely dressed in a suit.

The hotel lobby has the same glossy clay tile as the outside, which gives the room a rustic and cozy feel. To the left of the front desk is a sitting area with big, overstuffed neutral-colored couches surrounding a lit fireplace. On both sides of the fireplace are floor-to-ceiling two-story glass windows that reveal the spectacular view of the bay. The ocean looks cold and dark even with the January sun shining on it, but it's still magnificently beautiful.

"Madeleine, this is my mother, Chloe McManus. Mother, this is my fiancée, Madeleine." Peter says, jolting my gaze away from the ocean.

I was so taken by the view of the ocean that I hadn't noticed Peter talking to a beautiful, petite, very thin, impeccably dressed woman with the same deeply tanned skin and jade green eyes as Peter. Her dark hair is slicked back into an intricate knot at the nape of her neck, revealing huge diamond cluster earrings. And no noticeable scars. Dr. Bill would be impressed.

"Hallo Madeleine, I'm so pleased to meet you at last." Mrs. McManus says with a heavy French accent. I take her extended, tiny, thin hand, and she squeezes my hand lightly. "Peter has told me so much about you. I am so very pleased he has found such a wonderful young woman to be his wife."

She seems genuinely pleased, and I feel more at ease. The panic that was beginning to rise in my stomach subsides.

"Mrs. McManus, I'm so happy to meet you, too." I feel a little weird meeting my future mother-in-law in the lobby of a hotel, but the meeting was bound to happen sooner or later.

Behind her, there is a hotel luggage cart stacked with the same brown leather luggage as I brought, with the familiar gold "LV" logo. I also notice Peter's posture has become rigid. He doesn't seem like his usual relaxed, fun-loving self. I get the vibe that he is more than a little uncomfortable. I grab his hand, smile at him, and try to comfort him. He smiles back at me and squeezes my hand.

"Have you checked in yet?" Peter asks his mother.

"Yes, but our room is not ready yet. Check-in is not until three o'clock. Your father insisted I meet him here early. Bien sûr, I wait here still, for him and your brother to arrive from their meeting."

Just then, the door opens, and two strikingly handsome men in black suits similar to Peter's suit stride in. The taller, older man with a cell phone to his ear must be Peter's father since Peter bears a striking resemblance to him, with the same sharp masculine features, similar height and build, and the same wavy black hair, only his father's short hair has gray streaks at his temples. He stalks over to the large windows, still barking orders into his tiny phone. I can see that Peter will still be quite attractive when he gets older, not that it matters much to me.

The shorter, smaller-framed man must be Peter's brother since he has more of a heart-shaped face like their mother, but with a square dimpled chin and short, straight dark hair. He has the same cool steel-blue eyes as their father, but Matt's eyes flash with warm personality. A broad smile sweeps across his face as he sees Peter, and his eyes grow wide as he approaches us.

"Hey, hey, little brother! How's it going, bro? Dude! You really chopped your hair off! It looks good, though; you're starting to look like a real rock star!"

"Hey Matt, how's it going?" Peter asks while the guys hug each other tightly and slap each other on the back. It's funny that Matt calls Peter his "little brother" since Peter is about five inches taller than him and much larger in stature.

"I'm great. Ready to get fitted for my ball and chain," Matt winks at Peter, and elbows him in the side. "Speaking of getting hitched, this must be my lovely future, sis.' How very nice to meet you, Mademoiselle Madeleine," Matt speaks in overdone French accent as he takes my hand and kisses it instead of shaking it.

"Alright, Romeo, that's enough." Peter laughs at his brother, and playfully takes my hand away from his brother.

"You done good, lil' brother. She's a beauty." He winks at me and gives me a playful grin. I'm kinda glad I still have my coat on. "My beautiful wife-to-be is off getting her hair done, and should be joining us shortly." I instantly like Matt, he seems really personable and laid back.

"What is going on? Our room is still not ready? What kind of a hotel is this?" Peter's father says as he stalks past us to the front desk and presumably says some stern words to the girl behind the desk, who instantly grabs the phone and dials nervously.

"Hey Pete, what room are you in?" Matt asks.

"We haven't checked in yet."

"Well, snap to it, bro! Pre-rehearsal cocktails are in my suite as soon as you get settled in."

Peter and I walk up to the front desk, stand next to his father, and wait for our turn to be helped. Peter's posture stiffens again, but he seems more tense than uncomfortable.

"Peter," his father gives him a small nod of acknowledgment.

"This is my fiancée, Madeleine," Peter squeezes my hand so tightly and places his other hand on my lower back as if to shield me. "Madeleine, this is my father, Marcus McManus."

Just as he is about to turn to me, his cell phone rings, and he turns away to answer it.

"Good afternoon; how may I help you today?" A friendly, thin blond man named Michael looks up at us from behind the front desk.

"Hi, we're checking in. Two rooms under the McManus wedding party, one under 'Peter' and the other under 'Madeleine Winger,'" Peter tells him.

Michael does some searching on his computer. "Hmm, I have a reservation for one room, a bay view suite on the fifth floor, for two nights, listed as a double occupancy under the name 'Peter and Madeleine McManus.' But I don't see a reservation for a 'Madeleine Winger' in the computer." he says, smiling at us.

Omigosh...I just realized my name will be Madeleine McManus when Peter and I get married. That sounds so awesome!

"Matt must think he's funny. I specifically told him many times not to book us in the same room together," Peter tells me, resembling his father a little more in his growing agitation. He turns back to Michael. "Do you have any more rooms available near that room?"

"No, I'm sorry, sir, there are no available rooms. The hotel is booked up solid all weekend."

"Really? There's nothing available at all?" Peter asks, so Michael checks the computer again and shakes his head.

"I'm sorry, everything is booked."

"Would you happen to have the number for the Hilton across the bay?" Peter asks and then turns to me. "I'll try to book a room there, and you can stay here with everyone else."

Before I can say anything, Michael answers Peter. "I do have the phone number, sir, but I know from calling the hotel for other guests of our guests here that the Hilton is also completely booked this weekend with a convention."

"Do you think any of the girls in the bridal party would be willing to share their room with me?" I ask Peter, secretly hoping he says no. The girls talking to Matt with the freshly done hair don't seem like they'd be very hospitable, especially not to some mad Goth chick in a tight black dress and thousand-dollar shoes.

"No, all the bridesmaids are married and are here with their husbands, most of whom are Matt's groomsmen, except for me, of course," Peter exhales. "Matt told me how excited their friends were that they could all be in the wedding party together, because it meant a party-filled weekend away from their kids." Then Peter turns to Michael. "You're absolutely sure there are no other rooms, or like a broom closet or something?"

"Yes sir, I'm sure," he says, chuckling. "I'm sorry, we are completely booked up."

Peter turns to me. "Mad, it looks like we have to share a room. Is that okay?"

"Yeah, we have no choice, right? It'll be alright." *Oh Lord, please help me be strong...*

"Are you sure?" Peter asks me with much trepidation in his voice.

"Yes. We'll be fine." I smile at him and try not to reveal how nervous, and well honestly, excited I am. I realize this means I get to spend more time with Peter. Since he is leaving in a couple of days for the tour with the band, every second with him is so totally precious to me.

"Okay. We'll take the room." Peter gets his credit card out of his wallet. He seems more than a little aggravated. I put my hand on his arm, and he smiles at me.

"Oh sir, the room has already been paid for, as well as any incidentals or room service charges," Michael smiles.

"Let me guess, Matt thinks that will make me less upset with him," Peter says to me through gritted teeth. He exhales sharply and turns back to the desk. "Thank you so much for all your help."

"You're welcome. I'm sorry I couldn't find you another room." Michael hands Peter a small white envelope.

"It's okay. Thanks anyway." Peter takes the envelope with the card key in it, and we head for the door.

"You! I want to speak to you later!" Peter says, pointing to Matt as we approach him.

"What? Me? I didn't do anything!" Matt fakes an innocent expression and then laughs. "Oh come on, lil' bro, lighten up. Have some fun. It's my wedding, I insist!"

We walk past him and out the door to the truck, where a young guy who looks barely out of high school is waiting with a tall brass luggage cart to help us with our bags.

Our room is beautifully decorated in warm earth tones and sturdy wooden furniture with black wrought iron details. One wall is floor-to-ceiling windows, with a sliding glass door leading out to a balcony overlooking the bay.

A large gift basket sits on the bureau, overflowing with various chocolates, candles, a bottle of wine, massage oils, and colorfully wrapped condoms. A little white card is under a giant bow on the top of the basket.

"What does it say?" Peter asks as he places my bag on the luggage stand.

"It's from Matt, wishing us a 'love-filled weekend,'" I try to hide my smile at Matt's little joke.

"Damn him!" A large vein that I've never seen before is popping out in the middle of Peter's forehead. "Sorry. I'm just really angry at him right now."

"He's just messing with us."

"He knows that you and I are not planning on sleeping together until our wedding night," Peter exhales deeply, the vein receding. "I've told him how important it is to us."

"He doesn't understand. Most people don't." I lay my purse and coat on the bureau next to the gift basket. "My mother thinks it's ridiculous. She told me this morning at the beauty salon that if I didn't 'put out' soon, as she so delicately stated, I would lose you."

"No chance of that," he grins at me with a sweet smile, as he hangs up my garment bag in the closet. "No way, no how." His smile makes me swoon.

"What about the rest of your family? What do your parents think about our unworldly stance against pre-marital sex?" I continue to unpack my things.

"My aunt and uncle just think it's a nice, old-fashioned thing to do. Sometimes, my uncle teases me that he doesn't believe me that we haven't slept together 'cause he knows I'm so in love with you."

Oh sigh.

"But my parents, I don't think they really care," he puts his T-shirts in a drawer. "My father has made it clear that he thinks my 'religious commitment' is foolish, and I don't know what my mother thinks about it or if she even knows. She's never discussed it with me. Her only acknowledgment of anything relating to God in my life happened about six months ago. She thanked me for not fighting with my father anymore, even when he's being an, uh, when he's insulting me. She said she was grateful for my 'change.' That's all she's ever said on the subject."

Peter stops talking, and I notice his jaw is tight and his shoulders look tense. He abruptly walks into the bathroom with a small black bag in his hand. I read his non-verbals loud and clear. End of discussion.

The sliding glass door to the balcony is open, and the ocean breeze fills the room. I walk out onto the balcony and take in the unseasonably warm January sun. The temperate, moist ocean air feels good on my skin. I turn to Peter, but I see a troubled look on his face.

"What's wrong?" I go back inside the room to him.

"Mad, I just realized there's only one bed in this room. One bed."

It's a huge king-size bed, but he's right. I've been so distracted since we first entered the room that I didn't realize it either. There's only one bed in the room. Oh, how the mind reels with sensual images, it shouldn't…

"Oh, hmmm," is all I can say. "I'll sleep on the loveseat."

"I can't let you sleep on the couch for two nights. You take the bed. I'll sleep on the couch."

"Are you going to fit all six feet two inches of your big self on that little loveseat? I don't think so. You take the bed. I will be perfectly fine on the couch," I tell him sternly, and I sit down on the loveseat like a stubborn child.

Peter walks over and sits down next to me. "No way! You're not sleeping on this sofa. Man, it's uncomfortable."

"I know. It's hard as a rock," I wrinkle my nose. "But you're not sleeping on it either. Hey, is this our first argument?"

"I think it's more of a discussion." He smiles at me taking my hand in his, and leans back on the couch.

"What are we going to do then?" We simultaneously look over at the bed. "You know, in some cultures, it's customary for the betrothed couple to sleep together before they are married. I mean, not consummating the marriage, just spending the night together in the same bed," I try to sound like the commentator of some cultural documentary.

"Mad, I don't think it's a good idea for us to sleep in the same bed together. Wait, let me rephrase that. I *know* it's not a good idea for me to sleep in the same bed with you."

"Why? Would you get fresh with me?" I lean into him with an exaggerated, seductive look.

"Hey now, there'll be no teasing, especially while you're wearing that little black dress and looking all beautiful like you do," he grins like a schoolboy.

"You're right. I need to be good." I straighten up.

"We need to get to the rehearsal. We'll think of something. God said He'll always provide a way out, right?"

"Right." He gets up from the couch, and I take his outstretched hand to help me up. He pulls me into himself closely and wraps his arms around my waist.

"I love you, Mad." He looks into my eyes.

"I love you too," I whisper.

He leans down and kisses me lightly on the lips. Oh, his lips feel so soft and inviting. He gently pulls away.

"We have to go," he clears his throat.

"Okay…"

I feel like I'm in a dreamy state, still feeling his arms around me and the sweet moistness of his lips on mine. I grab my coat and purse and float out the door.

Chapter Twenty-eight

I sit under a tall palm tree on one of the cast iron benches that face the bay, while Peter and his family run through the marriage ceremony on the large grassy area outside of the hotel. I can't help but imagine what our wedding will be like. I think I might like to have it here, with the ocean as our background.

I sincerely hope Peter looks happier at our wedding than he does right now, standing in the front next to his brother. He looks rather serious and uncomfortable. He laughs and shakes his head every once in a while, whenever Matt leans over and says something to him. But then Matt's fiancée gives him a dirty look, and Matt returns her grimace with an appeasing grin. Periodically, Peter looks over at me and gives me a small wave, and I wave back. After a short while, his mother notices our discreet exchanges, and rises from the bench she is sitting on near the walkway and comes over and sits next to me.

"May I join you?" she asks politely.

"Of course." I scoot over so she has plenty of room.

"Do you have thoughts of your own wedding?" she asks in her French accent.

"Yes, a few." I try not to blush.

"Ah, yes. It is a special thing to dream of one's wedding day." Her accent makes her words sound so romantic.

"Did you have a big wedding when you married Mr. McManus?" I ask.

"Bien sûr, it was a majestic affair." She looks out over the water. Other than a hint of sadness in her eyes, she shows no emotion on her face. "Madeleine, you must not feel as if you are obligated to have a grand wedding yourself," her gaze remains on the sea.

I'm a little shocked by her candid remark. But my journalism training takes over, as well as my natural curiosity. "Would you have had a smaller wedding if you could do it over again?"

Maybe I'm getting too personal with her. I remember what Peter said about how she doesn't talk about personal things. But I can't help it. And I get the feeling she won't mind my prying question, especially since it's relevant to the topic at hand, which she brought up.

"Oui, bien sûr. But it was not my choice." Good thing I remember from high school French classes that she said, "yes, of course."

"What kind of wedding would you have chosen if you could choose again?"

"An intimate affair at my family's villa in the south of France, in Cavalaire-Sur-Mer, on the beach, where I used to play as a child. There is a beautiful view of the sea. I spent many summers there as a young girl, swimming in the ocean."

"That sounds wonderful." Having never been to Europe myself, I can only imagine how beautiful it must be. My mother did not mince words about her trip to the French Riviera, about how much she disliked it because everyone was only speaking French, and she couldn't get what she wanted when she wanted it.

"It is a wonderful place. But things were different back then." She seems far away in her thoughts.

"How so?" I pry again.

"I was a different girl, and Marcus was a different man. I would have followed him anywhere. I lived only to please him." She shakes her head ever so slightly.

I resist the urge to ask, 'and now?' but I don't say anything. I'm already stunned by the fact that she is sharing personal information with me, and I want to tread carefully.

But she continues without any prompting from me. "But Pierre…pardonne-moi, Peter, he is much different from his father, yes? He was born with a tender spirit. He carries a gentleness in him."

"I love that about him." I pause. "Is that why you had him stay with his aunt a lot when he was growing up?"

I can't believe I dared to ask her this, but I really want to know.

"Oui, c'est vrai…this is true. Mureille, my younger sister, she is the wise one. She married a kind, big-hearted man who also has a gentle soul. I thought it best for Peter to be with—how do you say—a kindred spirit." Chloe looks pained for a moment. "Does he speak of his upbringing much with you?"

"Only a little. He warned me that he doesn't get along with his father, so he feels it's best if tries to stay away."

"Sadly, this is true. He is a very different man from his father. Peter is the only man to ever stand up to Marcus and speak honestly to him. Marcus is not accustomed to people speaking their minds to him, so he does not handle it, shall we say, very well. But he respects Peter for it, in his own way."

Interesting. I make a big mental note to be sure to share this with Peter tonight. To share this whole discussion with him.

"But now is not the time to speak of difficult things but of joyous things, like weddings. You will have the wedding of your choice, yes? Promets-moi? Promise me?" She puts her tiny, thin hand on my arm, her enormous diamond rings blinding in the sunlight.

"I promise," I smile at her.

"Très bon! Come, they have finished." We get up and walk toward the wedding area. Chloe links my arm to hers as we walk. I feel like I have known her for years, maybe because she is so much like Peter. Now I know where he gets his gentle nature. But I know beyond the shadow of a doubt that his tender, gracious spirit comes from God.

After the rehearsal, Peter's mother and father, Matt and his fiancée, and Peter and I all climb into a limousine that takes us on the short trip down Queensway Drive to the Queen Mary. Peter's father severely chastises a poor soul on the other end of his cell phone the entire trip over. Peter looks over at me as if to apologize and holds my hand tightly.

We all walk together through the Queen Mary to Sir Winston's restaurant, where the rehearsal dinner will take place.

I love the old wooden plank decks, and the art deco decoration of the ship. Black and white pictures of famous past passengers line the walls of the hall of the interior deck. I have never been on this ship before. I know my mother and father had one of their early dates on this ship, in a little café on board. I try to imagine them on a date, enjoying each other's company.

"Are you doing okay?" Peter senses my turn to a pensive mood. "You're so quiet."

"Oh yeah, I'm fine. I'm just taking in the sights. This ship is so beautiful."

"Yeah, it's really cool." He smiles at me and squeezes my hand.

We reach the restaurant's entrance, and Peter's father informs the maitre d' that we are here for a rehearsal dinner. The restaurant is very warm and romantic, with its wood-paneled walls and candles softly lighting the white linens on the tables. He leads us to a row of tables arranged along the windows, which frame the beautiful Long Beach shoreline.

One end of the table is occupied by a group of the most generic blond, fair-skinned, and expressionless people I have ever seen. If they were products in a supermarket, they would be plain white packages with a blue stripe across them and labeled in plain black font, "Upper-Class People."

A number of them share Matt's fiancée's facial features, though the group is largely indistinguishable in appearance. Their expressions only change slightly to acknowledge our arrival—mostly just raised eyebrows and stiff smiles. They all have the same expression Matt's fiancée has had on her face since the first time I saw her at the rehearsal—cool politeness with a slight underlying sense of disdain for everyone else. With all his mischievous personality, it makes me wonder what Matt sees in her.

Everyone makes their introductions. The man sitting at the head of the table gets up and rushes to shake Peter's father's hand, who only responds with a quick, cold, condescending grin. The men seem to disregard Peter when they are introduced to him, but the women take private notice of him, holding their gaze on him a bit longer than would be usual.

I could fade into the woodwork, and nobody would notice, which is fine with me. That is until I take off my coat and hand it to Peter before we sit down. I bask in Peter's admiration of my curvy little dress, but I feel additional eyes on me, particularly Peter's brother and father.

Matt looks me up and down and whistles. "Dang, bro! You seriously want me to believe you haven't tapped that booty yet?" Matt says a little too loudly with slurred speech, most likely due to an abundance of pre-dinner cocktails back at the hotel and in the limo.

Those seated closest to our end of the table stop their conversations, glance over at us briefly with no detectable change of expression, and then resume their conversations.

"Dude. Not cool." Peter says in an angry whisper. He gives Matt a serious look, as he pushes my chair in for me as I sit down.

"Maybe tonight, huh? By the way, how do you like your room? You can thank me later." Matt laughs loudly and looks pleased with himself, and takes another big gulp of his amber-colored cocktail.

"It's nice, but it's short one bed." Peter seems to be struggling to maintain a sense of decorum in this conversation.

"Hey, you guys are engaged! Relax and have some fun. What are you going to do? Call the front desk to bring up one of those little rolling cot things?"

I see a light go on in Peter's eyes. "Excuse me for a moment. I need to go make a phone call." He gets up and kisses the top of my head before he leaves.

"Oh, come on, Pete! Madeleine, you'll have to excuse my prude of a brother. He never used to be like this. If you were my bride-to-be, I'd make sure all your needs were taken care of, if you know what I mean." Matt's fiancée pokes him in the side, then glares at me slightly, like it's my fault for making her fiancé say these things.

"That's quite enough, Matthew. I apologize for my son's rather tactless remarks." Mr. McManus finally speaks up from the head of the table. "So, Madeleine, what do you do?" I'm stunned he is speaking to me. I thought he was apologizing to Matt's fiancée.

"I'm a senior at Biola University."

"Hmm, never heard of it. Is it a decent school? What is your major?"

"It's a very good school. I'm majoring in Communication with a journalism emphasis and minoring in Biblical studies. I'm also a Product Manager at the Music Plus in Whittier."

"That sounds like an immense load for a pretty little lady to bear," he says with a faint creepy smile, then takes a drink from his yellowish clear cocktail. His intense, attentive stare makes me uncomfortable, but I refuse to squirm in my seat.

"It is, but I'm used to it," I say with a formal smile without breaking his eye contact.

Just then, Peter returns and sits down. I see his posture take on a protective stance when he notices his father's attention is on me. He straightens his back and puts his arms on the table with his hands closed in fists.

"Well, I'm surprised such an attractive young woman like you doesn't seek the companionship of another educated person, even if it is an education acquired at a local university." Mr. McManus says. "All the McManus men have attended Harvard. Well, that is except for Peter here, who opted to attend a trade school and a pretty useless one at that." I see the muscles in Peter's jaw tighten, but he doesn't say anything.

Peter's heavy sigh gives me the feeling this topic of discussion has come up before, probably many times. He lowers his head, undoubtedly in silent prayer.

What a jerk! I straighten up in my chair and look Mr. McManus in the eye.

"I imagine the training Peter received at the Musicians' Institute was instrumental in helping him hone his God-given talent to obtain the lead guitarist position in one of the top ten-grossing Contemporary Christian music acts on the charts right now," I say evenly, maintaining eye contact with him, but inside, I'm shaking in my lovely couture pumps, remembering what Chloe told me about people not usually standing up to her husband.

But I had to say something. I couldn't just sit there and let my man be insulted, even if it is by his imposing big-time CEO and somewhat pervy father.

I can tell Peter is trying to hide his look of shock and the little smile that is curling his lips. He sits back in his chair and puts his arm around my chair, and he relaxes a bit.

Mr. McManus leers at me and grins slightly. "That may very well be." I notice his line of sight has dropped, and he is blatantly staring at my breasts. *Ewww!* Peter may resemble his father physically, but that is where the similarities end. What a pig!

I casually bring my arms across the front of myself and rest one hand on my neck. Out of the corner of my eye, I notice Chloe watching me. She has a little proud smile playing at the corners of her mouth.

The waiters begin to distribute the first course plates around the table. Peter leans in close to me and drops his arm down from the back of my chair, and I feel his hand come to rest firmly on my waist.

"I am so loving you right now," he whispers in my ear. Then kisses my neck so softly. It makes me shiver and smile. When I open my eyes, I notice Mr. McManus and Matt's fiancée staring at us.

"Attention everyone, how about a toast," Matt's future father-in-law rises from his seat at the opposite end of the table from Peter's father.

Everyone raises their glasses of various beverages, ice tea for Peter and me. "To Jane and Matthew, may they have a long and happy life together. Cheers." *Generic, plain white toast,* I think. But everyone clinks glasses. Matt's fiancée's family finally smile enough to show that they all possess the same straight white huge teeth, similar in size to a horse's incisors.

The rest of the dinner is uneventful. The food is wonderful. I'm not sure what most of it is, but it's delicious and beautifully served on white China in little neat portions, garnished with bright-colored tropical flowers.

Still, it pales in comparison to the juicy charbroiled goodness of an animal-style Double-Double wrapped in paper with the bright red In-N-Out insignia printed on it, especially when it's consumed in the company of my awesome Godly fiancé. *Sigh.*

Chapter Twenty-nine

When we get back to our room after the rehearsal dinner, a single-sized roll-away bed is set up near the king-size bed, all made with fluffy pillows, soft sheets and warm blankets.

"See, the Lord's promises always come through," Peter smiles sweetly as he takes off his suit jacket, tie and dress shirt. He looks so good standing there in a tight white t-shirt and dress pants.

"Yes, I see that. I have to confess though," I sit down on the couch and slip off my unblemished shoes (thank God!), and begin to rub my tired feet, "I was kinda hoping I would get to know what it's like to share a bed with you. I really want to know what it feels like to sleep in your arms." I smile at him shyly.

Peter comes over and sits close to me on the couch and puts his arm around me.

"Mmmm, that sounds nice. But patience, my dear," he rubs my shoulder. "In a few months, it will be our crazy wedding rehearsal dinner. And you can rebuke my father again when he says something rude or insulting." I laugh, and swing my legs over in his lap and he begins to rub my feet. Oh man, does it feel good.

"I know. I just get impatient sometimes." I lean back against the pillow on the arm of the couch and close my eyes.

I can't help but moan, as my tired feet are massaged in his strong hands. I just plain love the feel of his hands on me.

After a while, and much moaning on my part, his hands work up to my ankles, then my calves. I keep my eyes closed. His massaging feels so good, especially since I'm not used to walking around in four-inch heels.

Then I feel his hands run up the silky fabric of my dress on my thighs, to my waist. I open my eyes slightly as he runs his hand around my waist to my back and pulls himself down on me. I close my eyes again.

His moist full lips feel so sensuously good on my neck. I hear myself moan softly. I run my hands over his thick arms, shoulders, and back, and through his hair, holding him close to me. His lips find their way up to mine, and he kisses me hard with parted lips. Our tongues touch and mingle with each other's. My whole body is tingling. The length of his body on mine feels amazing. I'm burning with a delicious fire.

He feels so good. I know we should stop, but I don't want him to stop. I know this is wrong. Stop already, Madeleine! One word from you, and he will stop. But I don't want him to stop. He's going to be my husband anyway, right? Oh man, he feels so good. I love the feel of him more than any--

Suddenly, he stops kissing me, pushes himself off of me and off the couch, and sits down hard on the floor with his back to the couch. He leans forward and puts his head in his hands. He is quiet for what seems like an eternity.

"Peter, are you okay?"

"No." He shakes his head, which is still in his hands. He grits his teeth.

"What's wrong?"

"Madeleine, I want to make love to you so much right now. Every fiber of my being wants to pick you up and lay you down on that bed, strip off all your clothes, and make love to you like no one ever has before." He pauses and sighs heavily. "But I can't. And I won't. Not until our wedding night."

I don't know what to say because I feel the same way. My flesh wants him so bad, too, and if I tell him so, I think that may persuade him to do it. So, I say nothing.

"I shouldn't have such a strong desire, right? Especially the desire to be so disobedient," he lifts his head.

"Probably not," I mumble, not knowing what else to say. I slide down off the couch and sit on the floor next to him.

"You know what made me stop right now? I wish I could say it was an overwhelming spirit-filled conviction to stop, but it wasn't," he groans.

"What was it?"

"It was that little key you always wear around your neck."

"My little garden key? Seriously?"

"The image of it kept showing up in my mind. And then I started thinking about what you told me when I asked you about it. And then those Scriptures from the Song of Solomon you showed me and that I just recently read, since Josiah and I just finished studying that book together. One scripture was about not arousing my love until it pleases, so I was starting to feel convicted because it seemed like I was arousing you when I shouldn't have been."

Goodness, you certainly were...you have no idea, I think.

"And the image of that little key came very sharply into focus in my mind, especially when I started to rationalize that it would be okay for us to make love since we are engaged. That little key reminded me of what you told me about how you are a garden enclosed, locked up, and that you would give that key to your husband on your wedding night because you would then belong to him, and it would be his garden to unlock."

"So true," I whisper, tears stinging the corners of my eyes.

"That's just it. You don't belong to me, Mad, not yet. I have no right entering your garden, so to speak."

"You're right. I know you're right," I say softly.

I think about what he said. "So we pretty much have to keep our hands off of each other, I guess. And making out is probably out of the question." I reluctantly agree. *Bummer.*

"Especially no making out. Mad, I'm just afraid that if we ever get in that situation again, I won't be able to stop myself, and no vision of a little key would stop me either. And that would be something I know I will regret."

Peter drops his head in his hands again and sighs heavily. After a few moments, he wraps his arms around himself and lifts his head. There are tears in his eyes.

I feel so bad for him. I should have asked him to stop kissing me, and maybe then he wouldn't feel so angry with himself. But I couldn't ask him. I wasn't strong enough. But omigosh! The thought hits me like a lightning bolt. No, I was not strong enough to stop us. Neither of us is on our own.

"Hey, you know it *was* the Holy Spirit who gave you the strength to stop us from going all the way. He put the Word and the image of my garden key in your mind and gave you the power to stop," I tell him.

He turns his head to look at me, and a slow smile spreads across his face. I reach over and wipe the tears off his cheeks. *Oh Lord, I love this man…*

"Yeah, that makes sense. The image of that little key and what it means was so strong. As strong as the realization that I would be taking something that didn't belong to me. Something or, more specifically, someone, meaning you, who belongs to Jesus."

We sit there, looking into each other's eyes for a long moment. I feel the urge to hug him, but I don't dare since I can still feel his touch on my skin, and I fear it may be the same for him.

"That's so amazing," I grin, wide-eyed. "I'm very glad He gave the vision to you and not to me."

"Why?" Peter's brows are furrowed.

"Because I had already decided that I was going to let you have your way with me, 'cause that's what I wanted, so that's that. I know I wouldn't have paid attention to His working." I confess.

Peter rests his arms on his bent knees and then rests his chin on his arms. He is silent for a moment. He seems to be mulling over what I just told him.

"We need to stay true to our new hands-off policy then, for both of us, and that goes double for me," he declares. "Oh, Mad, I would love to be constantly touching you and caressing you and kissing you, but I can't. Mad, I just can't. Tonight just proved to me that I'm not strong enough to resist on my own, and I don't want to drag you down with me. I can't give myself permission for even casual physical contact with you. At least not right now."

"I know. You're right. That goes double for me, too." I smile at him. "It's a shame, though. You're a really great kisser. The best."

"Thanks. You're not so bad yourself and your body. Man, I'm going to need some serious prayer to get the feeling of you out of my head."

"*Grrr*, this is so hard." I grit my teeth, grab the pillow off the sofa, and squeeze it tight to my chest.

"I know, but it will be worth it."

"Yeah, I know."

"I have an idea," light returns to his face. "How about we set the date. That way we'll we have a sort of countdown."

"A countdown to lovin'! I like it!" I smile at him.

"Well, not just that, although I will definitely be looking forward to it," he raises one dark eyebrow at me. "I think it will make it easier on both of us when I'm on the road. I know I will miss you a lot, and it will help me to have a definite date to look forward to."

"I am so thankful that you are so wise. That's a great idea, and I know it will help me too, to get through the time you are gone. What's a good date?"

"A few months after you graduate because I don't want you to have to deal with wedding stuff when you have your school work to think about."

"Since I graduate in May, how about July? That should give me plenty of time to get stuff done. Besides, I don't want to wait any longer than July."

"We need a calendar," Peter goes to the desk in the room and pulls the drawer open. He rummages around and comes out with a small business card from a local touristy place with a calendar printed on the back of it. He brings it over, and we sit down on the couch together. We both stare at the month of July.

"How about the tenth?" I suggest.

"The tenth of July sounds great. I'll be home from the tour all summer. The guys don't tour when their kids are out of school, so they can spend time with them and go on vacations with their families."

"That's so cool!" I squeal. "July tenth it is."

"Yeah, July tenth. Less than seven months away. Man, I can hardly wait. Are you sure that will be enough time to plan a wedding?".

"Oh hon, it's goin' to have to be. This girl's not waitin' any longer to be with her man!" I try to do my best Maggie impersonation. He laughs with me.

"Great. Until then, my beloved, you are locked up, a garden enclosed, and I will stay away until you give me the key on the evening of July tenth," he says, his eyes glimmering more than usual.

"Evening? I was thinking we could have a quick sunrise ceremony, maybe serve the coffee cake as our wedding cake, and then send everyone home, so we can make love all day, the rest of the day, and into the night."

"Mmmm, I like the way you think. It would be an unusual ceremony, but I think people would understand." We both laugh. He leans his head on mine. "I love you, Mad. I can't wait to be your husband."

"I love you too, Peter, so much. I am so grateful for your wisdom and strength, especially for the strength you were given tonight. And I'm so looking forward to being your wife. You know what I'm going to do? I'm going to make one of those paper chains that you tear one link off each day until the big day arrives."

"That'll be cool. You can drive Maggie nuts with it."

"Oh yeah! And I'm going to get a bunch of those big bridal magazines and spread them all over our dorm room." We laugh.

"What kind of wedding do you want?" he asks.

"I don't know. I've never really given it much thought. I grew up with a tainted view of the institution of marriage since my parents divorced when I was young. How about you?"

"I really don't have any specific ideas. Nothing too big and fancy. Although, we might have to fight my mother on that."

"Nope. She made me promise her that we would have whatever type of wedding we wanted."

"She really said that?"

"Yep. When we were sitting together on the bench earlier today at the wedding rehearsal. We had a good chat. Your mom is really nice. I like her a lot."

"I'm glad to hear you get along with her."

"Not to change the subject or anything, but I have to ask. Why did you and Josiah study the Song of Solomon together?"

"Things are getting serious with him and Leah, as in I think they will be married before us. Please don't tell Leah, though."

"Oh, how totally cool! I won't tell her, I promise. I'm so excited for her!"

"Because things are getting so serious with them, and since you and I are engaged, Josiah thought we would both benefit from studying that book since it's all about relationships."

"That's so awesome!"

"And, uh, he had some questions about sex." Peter smiles and rubs his forehead.

"What kind of questions about sex?" I smile expectantly at him.

"Guy stuff. Nothing too specific."

"So, he's never had sex before? How old is he?"

"He's thirty-five, and he's still a virgin. He says he's waiting for his wedding night."

"Wow! That's so amazing,"

I'm totally stunned that someone could stay pure for so long. I wish I had resolution like that. How awesome it would be to never have done the things I did. It makes me sad. Very sad.

"What's wrong?" Peter asks, seeing a cloud come over my face.

"I wish I was still a virgin. I wish I could give myself to you on our wedding night, totally untouched, unspoiled, and complete. With no hang-ups or bad memories from past experiences."

"I know. The same goes for me. But just remember, God has restored you. And me. There are lots of verses that talk about it, but check out Ezekiel 36. It's really cool," he says softly.

"What does it say?"

Peter gets up and grabs his Bible out of his bag, and comes to sit down next to me again. He flips a couple of pages and then reads verses 25-28 to me:

"Then will I sprinkle clean water upon you, and you shall be clean from all your uncleanness; and from all your idols will I cleanse you. A new heart will I give you and a new spirit will I put within you, and I will take away the stony heart out of your flesh and give you a heart of flesh.

And I will put my Spirit within you and cause you to walk in My statutes, and you shall heed My ordinances and do them.

And you shall dwell in the land that I gave to your fathers; and you shall be My people, and I will be your God."

"That's so beautiful." I reflect on the words he just read.

"Yeah, it is," he says, closing the Bible and holding it tightly in his hands.

We sit on the couch in silence for a while, with his head leaning on mine. I silently say a prayer of thanksgiving to God for Peter and for this solemn, tender moment. I don't think I've ever loved another human being as much as I love Peter.

Then we get up so I can go into the bathroom and change out of my dress and stockings, which are starting to itch my legs.

"I need to ask you a big favor."

"Anything for you."

"Um, could you help me with the zipper on my dress?" I ask as I turn around. I can't reach it."

"Sure."

His hands feel warm on my back as he unhooks the little hook above the zipper.

"*Oh man!*" he groans as he takes the zipper down past my waist. I forgot that my back is totally bare except for the bustier clasps at my waist. "July tenth, July tenth, July tenth," he chants as he turns away quickly. I can't help but smile.

I grab my PJs and head to the bathroom. When I come out from changing and washing my face, Peter has changed into sweatpants and a black T-shirt and is sitting on the cot, playing guitar.

I'm a little embarrassed. Peter has never seen me like this, in my black flannel pajamas with Jack and Sally from "Nightmare Before Christmas" on them, my face freshly cleansed of all make-up, and my hair pulled up in a high ponytail with a black velvet scrunchie.

"Cute PJ's. You look so adorable, all ready for bed." He is smiling at me with pure sweetness.

"Thanks." I go sit on the bed opposite him. He tries to stifle a big yawn. I'm pretty beat, too, and I yawn as well.

"Pray with me before we go to sleep?" He puts his guitar back into its case.

"Yes, of course." I get up and go stand next to him. He takes my hands in his.

"Father in Heaven, thank You for this day. Thank You and praise You for providing for us, especially for providing a way out of totally sinning against You. Please forgive me and help us be strong and stay pure for the next seven months. Thank You for my dear, sweet Madeleine. I ask these things in Jesus' most precious name, Amen."

"Amen. Thank you."

He kisses me lightly on the forehead and leads me to the bed. He pulls back the covers for me. I climb into bed, and he pulls the covers up on me.

"Sleep well, my beloved." His hand brushes my cheek softly.

"I will, and you too, my July tenth husband." I take his hand and kiss it quickly.

Peter reaches over and shuts off the lamp next to the bed, and the room goes dark, except for the lights from the city skyline across the bay coming in through the glass door and windows.

I watch him walk to the bathroom, and he shuts the door. I can hear him brush his teeth. I love observing all the little intimate things of everyday life that I've never experienced with him before.

When he comes out of the bathroom a few moments later, he is shirtless. He drops his T-shirt on his bag and walks over to the cot. I can see in the softly illuminated room that he has a beautiful body, sculpted almost like one of those huge Greek statues in the Getty Museum in Malibu. I try not to stare at him as he gets into bed.

"G'night, Mad. I love you," he whispers.

"G'night, Peter. I love you, too." I whisper back.

Just a few minutes later, I hear Peter's breathing get slow and deep, and he is sound asleep.

I drift off to sleep, daydreaming about the evening seven months from now, when he will be climbing into bed next to me, and I will feel his body against mine, and we will consummate our marriage with our Heavenly Father's blessing on us, so totally thankful we waited. How cool is that?

Chapter Thirty

I slept so soundly last night, I wasn't sure where I was when I woke up. But a glimpse of the ocean through the balcony railing reminds me that I am in the hotel in Long Beach. I roll over and see that Peter is still sound asleep on the cot. *Sigh.* Never before has the morning given me a reason to smile.

I slowly pull the covers back and quietly get out of bed. I tiptoe over to the big sliding glass door. The ocean glimmers brilliantly in the morning sun. All is quiet down on the lawn where Matt's wedding will take place this evening.

I softly pad over to the bathroom, past my sweet, gorgeous fiancé lying on his back asleep. I close the bathroom door gently. I splash cold water on my face, and pull the scrunchie out of my hair, and smooth down my bangs, all in an attempt to look somewhat presentable after a night of hard sleep.

When I come out of the bathroom, I can't help but stop and take in the awe-inspiring sight of my man sleeping peacefully in the soft white sheets. His black hair is splayed across the pillow and part of his face. The sheet is pulled down to his waist, exposing his naked, tanned, and muscular torso.

Okay, I know I shouldn't be standing here ogling him like this, but it's like finally getting to see something you've wondered what it looked like for so long. I've never seen Peter without a shirt on before, so I can't help but study him. The smooth texture of his skin, the sheer unfamiliar masculinity of him.

A little perversely seductive voice inside my head starts speaking to me. *Go to him, lay with him. He won't put you out of bed. You're his fiancée, and you will be married to him soon, so what's the difference? He said he loves you, right? Imagine how good it would feel to be lying there next to him. You know you want to..."*

Shut up! Shut up! SHUT UP!

Okay, that's it. It's time to end this madness. I am so tired of being ruled by my lust. Tired of my mind being filled with images and feelings that I know are disappointing to my Lord. But most of all, I know it's true what Peter said about us not belonging to each other yet. If I don't belong to him, then he doesn't belong to me either. He is a precious child of God, and I need to think of him that way, and I need to stop taking opportunities to lust over him.

I need a weapon in this battle against these disgusting thoughts. Hmmm...*duh! Of course.* I tiptoe over to my bag and quietly pull out my Bible and notebook. I sit cross-legged near the end of the bed, facing away from Peter, so I can't sneak peeks at this handsome sleeping man. I open my Bible and my notebook in front of me.

I turn to the concordance and begin to look up passages that have to do with purity, the flesh, and self-control, and list them in my notebook: Song of Solomon 2:7, I Peter 1:13-16 and 2:11; Ephesians 5:3 and 6:12; Galatians 5:19, 24 and 6:8; I Corinthians 3:16, 6:18 and 7:1; Romans 7:23, 8:5-9, and 13:14; I Peter 2:11; I Thessalonians 2:12 and 4:1-6, to start with.

I look up each scripture and write it out to eventually memorize it. Yes! I will not be a slave to these thoughts anymore. Peter is a gift from God to me, and I need to treat him as such. I really want God's blessing in our lives, and I really need His help. I want to be an excellent servant of Christ and an excellent helpmate for Peter as well.

After a while, I hear stirring behind me. "Hey, Mad, did you sleep well?" Peter sounds groggy.

I turn my head halfway to speak to him. "Yeah, really well. I didn't know where I was when I woke up."

Peter climbs off the cot and sits down next to me on the edge of the bed. "What cha' studying?" He rubs my back and leans in close to me.

I look at him and a smile spread across my face, and I have to start the freshly studied Scriptures scrolling in my head. He looks so unbelievably captivating, with his disheveled hair and a shadow of a dark beard on his face. The morning sunlight illuminates the brilliant green of his eyes and reflects off the smooth skin of his defined chest and arms.

"Some much-needed Bible study on purity, self-control, and the flesh. Can you do me a huge favor?"

"Anything." He smiles at me with so much love in his eyes that I feel my chest tighten.

"Would you put a shirt on, please? Your beautiful nakedness is beginning to arouse and awaken my love before it pleases." I quote from the Song of Solomon and smile back at him, dramatically averting my eyes to the ceiling.

"Oh, man! Sorry. I wasn't thinking. I'm still half asleep." He quickly gets up, pulls a black t-shirt out of his bag, and slips it over his head. He rubs his face briskly and then runs his hands through his hair.

"Thank you. You're not the only one who has to chant 'July tenth' to yourself to keep your mind on track!" I grin up at him.

There is a knock at the door. Peter goes to answer it.

"Hey, love birds! Rise and shine!" Matt walks in the door with a garment bag draped over his shoulder and then hands it to Peter. He looks over at the cot and then at me sitting on the end of the bed that is only half unmade, with my Bible open and my notebook in my lap, and he shakes his head. "Good morning, Madeleine. You're not doing homework on my wedding day, are you?"

"No, no. I'm out of school right now. Just doing a little personal study."

"Oh." He looks over at Peter, who gives him a big, proud, sleepy smile.

"So, today's the big day, huh? You ready to become a husband?" Peter asks his brother.

"Yeah, it's all good. 'Cause you know, if it doesn't work out, she signed the prenup, so it's no big deal." Matt notices Peter and me looking at him with utter shock. "What? You guys make such a big deal about everything."

"Matt. *Dude.* Don't you love this girl? Don't you want to share your life with her? Maybe have a family with her?"

"Yeah, sure I do. It's just not such a big deal, you know?" He tries to look nonchalant. "Anyway, here is your, uh, tux. Let me know if you need help with any of the accessories. Old Uncle Liam emailed the specifics of how all the stuff should be worn. Well, gotta go. Gotta go, ya know, get ready for a wedding. Talk to you kids later." He turns and leaves as quickly as he came in.

"What do you make of that?" I ask Peter as he hangs the garment bag in the closet. He then comes over and sits down next to me on the bed and stares out at the ocean.

"Truthfully, I think he's scared."

"I hope it's just nerves. I've never heard anyone speak so flippantly about marriage before," I turn to stare at the ocean, too. "Not even my mother."

"Yeah, I would guess he's really nervous and scared. Poor guy. I guess I would be also if I wasn't marrying someone as awesome and sweet and beautiful as you." He puts his hand on mine and kisses me lightly on the cheek. "I'm a really blessed guy."

"Me too." My cheeks get instantly hot, but I don't care. He's got to be used to my chronic blushing by now.

"I guess I should get ready. I have to be downstairs in an hour for pictures." He gets up, grabs his bag and the garment bag, and heads for the bathroom.

I get up, put my Bible and notebook back in my bag, get out my makeup bag, jewelry, shoes, and hair, and then start laying out my dress and undergarments. About a half hour later, Peter opens the bathroom door.

"Promise not to laugh?" he asks from within the bathroom.

"I would never laugh at you."

"Yeah, I'm going to remember you said that." He walks out of the bathroom and stands in the small hallway between the bathroom door and the room's front door.

I'm stunned by what I see. "You look so very, very handsome." And he does. Believe me.

First, his hair is slicked back into a ponytail. Now, normally, I dislike the slicked-back ponytail look, but it looks totally awesome on him. It accentuates his cheekbones, square jaw, and eyes—those beautiful, shining, bright green eyes. *Oh, sigh.*

Next, the black waistcoat tuxedo jacket with silver Celtic buttons on the sleeves and on the front frames his broad shoulders and narrow waist perfectly. Below the jacket is a smooth blue and green plaid kilt, belted with a wide black leather belt with a shiny silver buckle. Around his waist, hanging from a chain in the front is a round silver and animal skin round thing. He has knee socks in the same tartan as his kilt, with garters on the sides, and black leather shoes.

"I kinda feel like I'm dressed for Halloween." He grimaces into the closet door mirror and pulls at his bow tie.

"No way! You look really nice. Quite captivating," I smile a little deviously.

"Thanks," he drops his head, and looks up at me.

"You didn't mention you were wearing a kilt. I didn't even know you were Scottish. Well, McManus. I should've guessed," I feel a little dim-witted.

"Yeah, I'm half Scottish and half French. And I didn't know for sure if the kilt thing was going to happen. Matt was teasing me about it, telling me that Grandfather McManus insisted on it and that he was buying kilts for all the McManus men to wear, and they're really expensive. But Matt said his fiancée was not pleased with the idea because the colors of our family's tartan don't match her color scheme for the wedding. So the story goes."

"Well, you look really good. Mmmm, almost too good." He really does. Believe me.

"Thanks," he lifts one eyebrow and gives me a playful smile. I better get downstairs. I'll be back for you as soon as we finish with the pictures." He comes over to me, kisses me lightly on the cheek, and then leaves.

Okay, Peter is definitely wearing his kilt at our wedding. Grandfather McManus knows what he is talking about!

I spent the next hour showering, doing my hair, applying makeup, getting dressed, and dreaming about my wedding day.

I'm glad my dress for the wedding isn't as form-fitting as the silky black dress I wore last night. But I still look elegant and all womanly, like a grown-up. I guess I should, since I'm getting married soon. On July tenth. Less than seven months away. Yikes!

Chloe insists I sit in the front row next to her at the wedding since I am practically family. Peter's Aunt Mureille and Uncle Gabriel sit next to me.

I watch Peter as he stands uncomfortably next to his brother in front of the large flower-covered arch that frames the beautiful bay. It's another gorgeous sunny day.

The rest of the wedding goes off without incident. The dinner is elegant, and the toasts are eloquent.

Peter's toast to his brother is really kind and thoughtful. I notice many women in the room watching him intently. I feel very proud to be sitting next to him for many reasons. When Matt toasts Peter and me and our wedding in the near future, I notice several female faces fall.

The most memorable part of the evening was slow dancing with Peter. It was wonderful. We had never danced together before, and I loved the feeling of swaying to the music in his arms. As a student at Biola University, technically, I'm not allowed to dance, but I think slow dancing with my fiancé at his brother's wedding is a viable exception to the rules.

As the reception comes to a close, we receive many invitations to various parties in various rooms of guests who attended the wedding, but Peter and I decide to call it a night and head up to our room.

While Peter is in the shower, I quickly undress, undo my up-do hair, and slip into my pajamas. I step out onto the balcony. I gaze at the twinkling lights of Shoreline Drive across the bay and over at the brightly lit up red and black majestic smoke stacks of the Queen Mary. Peter comes out and stands close to me on the balcony. His hair is still damp. He looks tired.

"Did you have fun today?" I ask him.

"Yeah, it was fun because you were there. Honestly though, I've had my fill of family events to last me a while. Did you have a good time?"

"Yes. I liked meeting your family. And I especially liked dancing with you."

"Yeah, that was my favorite part, too." He wraps his arms around me from behind. His warm body feels good since the cool ocean breeze is starting to make me cold. I try to memorize the feel of him, the smell of him.

"I saw you talking with your mother," I say casually.

"Yeah."

"You two were talking for a while."

"She really likes you," he squeezes me lightly. "She told me she's glad that I settled down with such a great woman. She said you're everything my aunt said you were and more."

"Really?" I turn my head to look at his face.

"Really."

"That's really, gosh, that's great," I'm more than a little dumbfounded. But my curiosity prevails.

"Did you talk about stuff, you know, other personal stuff with her?"

"I asked her about our trip to France when I was four years old and what happened with her father." I silently nodded to encourage him to go on. "She seemed shocked when I asked her about it. She was surprised I remembered anything from that trip because I was so young.

I silently nod again and squeeze his hand.

"She told me that her father told her that if she could not remain in France, and had to return to the States, then it would be better to leave me with him and the family than have 'that man' raise me," he stops and exhales. "She told me that her father said Marcus was a despicable man and would destroy her and eventually me and that if we stayed with him in France, he would try to help her bring Matt to France, too."

"So, he wasn't yelling at her. He was giving her advice."

"Yes, though from what I remember, it sure sounded like he was giving my mother a hard time," his voice sounds strained. "She told me that on that trip, she made the decision to ask her sister to raise me so I would be a safe distance from my father's influence. She couldn't stay in France because she promised my father she would come home, and she refused to leave Matt behind. But she couldn't leave me in France with her family either. She said she knew what her father said was true, so the best solution was to ask my Aunt Mereille to raise me. That way, she could still see me whenever she wanted, which wasn't very often." He stops speaking and exhales again.

"I'm so sorry, Peter." I feel terrible for encouraging him to try to improve his relationship with his mother. Maybe I shouldn't have interfered.

"In one sense, I feel better because I understand a lot more now why she did what she did," he sighs. "But then I think it was better when I could just blow the whole situation off and forget about it."

"I'm sorry. I didn't mean to pry and bring up all this bad blood. After talking to your mother yesterday, I just figured you two had just misunderstood each other. " I turn around to face him.

"No, I think it's better that I find out what happened. Now, I don't have such a dark cloud over my past and my relationship with my mother. I don't know. There's still a lot I don't understand." he smooths my hair. "But one thing I do know, my present and the future look pretty gosh darn great." He smiles, but his eyes still look sad.

"Mmm, yeah it does." I am thoroughly enjoying his company. "But I can't believe you will be leaving on tour in two days. I already miss you."

"I know. It's so bittersweet, you know? On one hand, I get to go play music with this awesome band for thousands of people, and then on the other hand, you won't be there to share that experience with me. But they're going to give me a cell phone, so I can call you anytime from just about anywhere and you can call me, too. Mad, I would like to get you a cell phone too, before I leave, if that's alright with you."

"That would be awesome!"

"Promise me you'll remember to turn it off when you're in class, okay? I don't want to get you in trouble with your teachers." he laughs. "They might make you, ya know, stay after class and clean the chalkboard erasers or scrape gum off the desks."

"They don't do that in college, silly!" I gently poke him in the ribs. Oh God, I'm really going to miss him. I feel hot tears well up in my eyes. I stifle a sob.

"Come here." Peter hugs me closely as I weep profusely into his T-shirt. I feel his hands smooth my hair and rub my back.

"I'm going to miss you so much," I mumble.

"I'm going to miss you, too. I've been trying not to think about it."

I pull away and see tears on his cheeks. I reach up and touch them with my finger.

"My father would chastise me for being so weak."

"No way. One of my favorite verses in the Bible is John 11:35, 'Jesus wept.'"

"So true." He smiles and hugs me close.

We stand on the balcony in silence holding each other for a long time. The overwhelming dread of our looming separation keeps any lustful feelings away. The cold, moist ocean wind makes me shiver a little bit.

"I think it's time we go in and hit the hay. I'm exhausted."

I nod in agreement. He leads me by the hand to the sliding glass door, opens it for me, and closes it behind us.

I go into the bathroom to get ready for bed. When I come out, Peter is sitting on the cot with his Bible and my notebook open.

"I hope you don't mind, I'm using your study notes."

"Please! Help yourself." I'm tickled he wants to see my notes.

"I added Romans 15:30-33. Wait until I leave for the road to look it up, okay?"

"Okay." I wish I could remember what these verses say.

He yawns, closes the books, and places them on the nightstand next to the bed. He gets up off the cot, and sits next to me on the side of the bed.

"I'll pray for us before we go to sleep?" his hand out.

"Yes, please." I put my hand in his and close my eyes.

He asks for protection for us, and that God would use the time we are apart to help us grow into the servants He wants us to be. He thanks the Holy Spirit for giving him strength when we were tempted last night.

When he finishes praying, I climb under the covers, and he pulls them up for me and tucks me in. He leans down and kisses me quickly and sweetly on the lips.

"I love you Mad." he brushes his hand against my cheek.

"I love you too, Peter."

He turns off the lamp on the nightstand and climbs into the cot. "I'll stay fully dressed this time."

"Oh, but I was going to take my pajamas off tonight, too." I say, teasing him.

"Oh, man. Please don't!" he laughs.

"Well alright, if you insist."

"Goodnight, Madeleine!" he's still laughing.

I hear him roll over, and his breathing gets slow and deep almost instantly.

Oh, Heavenly Father, thank You. Thank You, and praise You for being so good to me and to us. I thank You in advance for answering Peter's prayer to keep us strong while we are apart and for changing us to be more of what You want of us.

I barely get out the words, "in Jesus's name I pray, Amen," before I fall into a deep sleep.

Chapter Thirty-one

The dreaded day is here. I sit on Josiah's couch and watch Peter as he packs a few last-minute items. We have been inseparable for months, spending all our free time together, and now we will be separated for what seems like an eternity while Peter goes on tour with the band all over the Midwest and southern portions of the United States.

I can't even think about it. *Oh Lord, please help me be strong and not weep uncontrollably like an idiot when it's time for him to leave.*

Peter's aunt and uncle came by this morning to wish him well, so I got to visit with them a little more than I did at Matt's wedding. They are such awesome people. Peter's Aunt Mureille is a stunningly beautiful woman. She looks just like her sister Chloe, with the same heart-shaped face and bright green eyes; only Mureille is not waif-thin, but a more normal weight, and there is more life flashing from her eyes. She is kind but still a little distant, like Chloe. I can't tell if it's a trait of French women or if that's just how their family is.

Peter's Uncle Gabriel is a handsome guy in a rugged sort of way, with bright blue eyes, wavy blond hair with a touch of silver mixed in, and the biggest, benevolent smile. He is easy-going, has a pleasant demeanor, with a quick wit and a generous sense of humor. I can see where much of his personality has rubbed off on Peter. Another of Gabriel's nephews, James, who is interested in the construction business, has stepped in to help him out while Peter is gone.

"James has a long way to go before he will be a comparable replacement for you, but I think he'll get there one day," Uncle Gabriel told Peter when we were all visiting on Josiah's back patio.

"Oh, so you're replacing me now? I go away for a few months, and you're replacing me for good, are you?" Peter teases his uncle.

"Son, you're not coming back to construction. I couldn't let you. You're way too talented of a musician to be swinging a hammer for a living," he declared. "And even if this particular gig doesn't work out, I know it's going to open a lot of doors for you. The only construction I will allow you to do is on your own house. Which reminds me…" Peter gave him a little cut sign and looks over at me.

"What?" I sensed something big.

"Nothing. It's a surprise." Peter kissed my hand.

"Tell me, please? Please don't make me wait for that, too!" I said much too quickly. I try not to blush.

"Okay, you're right. And it is a major decision that affects both of us. There's a piece of property I've always loved in Laguna Beach that has been for sale for a long time. The house on the land needs to be demolished because it's in really bad shape. But the lot is a good size for a single modest home and a yard. It's not big enough for a mansion, so I'm guessing that makes it undesirable for wealthy developers. But it has an awesome view of the ocean. I was thinking, when I get back, we could go look at it, and if you like it, we could buy it, and Uncle and I could build a new house on it."

"Oh, Peter! That sounds so awesome! I love Laguna Beach!" I gave him a huge hug.

"I knew that about you," he hugged me back. "Well then, I'm really glad I told you about it. I thought you'd like the idea."

"Oh, my goodness! I can't wait." I tried to feel the excitement of building a home that we would live in together, but the exhilaration became engulfed by the thought that we were about to be separated for almost half of the next year.

I notice Josiah catch Leah's cue as they sit together on the loveseat in the front room, across from me. He gets up from the couch and Leah grabs her purse off the entry hall table.

"Well, we're off to the grocery store," Josiah tells us. "Gotta go get the ingredients to cook my lady some dinner." He smiles so sweetly at her it makes my heart swell with joy that she has found love again.

"What are you cooking?" Peter asks as I get up from the couch and stand next to him.

"My world-famous carne asada," Josiah smiles proudly as Peter holds his stomach and moans. "Too bad you gotta leave, man, I'm grilling up a big batch."

"Not fair. Now I'm gonna be craving Mexican food the rest of the day."

"I tell you what, make it back safe and in one piece, and I'll cook up another huge batch upon your arrival."

"I'm gonna hold you to that," Peter smiles.

"You got it," Josiah says and then gets serious. "Well, we better get going. Let me pray for you, my brother before we go." Peter nods in agreement silently.

We put our arms around each other. As Josiah asks for wisdom, protection, and God's grace and favor on Peter while he is on the road, torrents of hot tears run down my cheeks. Peter squeezes me tighter and rests his head on mine. I hear light sniffling from Leah's direction. Josiah finishes, and we all agree with a big "Amen." I quickly wipe my face with the sleeves of my sweater.

"Please take care of her," Peter asks Leah as he hugs her tightly.

"You know I will. We'll be praying for you," she smiles with glistening eyes.

"Thanks," Peter pulls away. He seems to be struggling to maintain emotional control.

"Be strong and courageous, my brother," Josiah hugs Peter, and Peter nods.

"Thank you for everything," Peter says quietly.

"You know it. Take care, bro.'" Josiah says as they slap each other on the back.

"You too," Peter wipes his eyes as he pulls away. Then smiles at Josiah. "Be strong, too, my brother. Remember, it's so worth waiting for."

"Pray for me," Josiah grins from ear to ear as he looks at Leah, who immediately blushes bright crimson red. "I need it."

"Yeah, well, if I hear you two have gone off and eloped while I'm gone, I'll understand. Believe me," he wraps his arms around my shoulders from behind me.

We all laugh, and I secretly wish eloping was an option for Peter and me because right now I would take it in a heartbeat. Oh Lord, how I'm going to miss him. We walk outside, wave to Josiah and Leah as they drive down the street, and then silently walk back into the house.

Peter zips up his bags and stacks them all together by the front door. The car is due any minute now that will take him to the rehearsal studio where the band will board the tour bus. I watch him from the couch, with my heart in the pit of my stomach.

Peter wouldn't let me drive him to the studio. He said I would have to make the hour-long drive all the way home from the Valley by myself, and I would probably be pretty upset. That was a good call on his part. I already know I'm going to have to take some time to compose myself after Peter leaves just to be able to make the short drive home.

He comes over and sits down next to me on the couch. He puts his arm around me, and I lean into his chest and breathe in deeply. It will be a long time before I smell this scent again, his scent, my absolute favorite smell in the whole world.

"Have you got everything you need?" I ask him.

"Yeah, I think so."

"Guitar picks?" My feeble attempt to make light of the moment.

"I think so. And I'm pretty sure I could get some if I forgot them."

"Well you never know. Everything is different outside of California."

"That's true. I would just have to send for you to bring me some."

"Yeah, but only if I can fit it into my schedule, 'cause you know, I only have a few months to transform myself into one of those totally wedding-obsessed psycho brides."

"Oh, yeah?" he smiles at me.

"Actually, there isn't a whole lot left to do. When I told my mother we picked a date and place, she was on the phone in a hot second booking the date for our wedding," I tell him. "It's interesting that the tenth was the only date available in July for the place. My mother even ordered the food, and flowers and booked the rooms. I reminded her that you prefer to have your own room."

"What?! You did not."

"I know how shy and private you are." I try to keep a straight face.

"Yeah, right! I'd find your room and break the door down. I would run around the hotel yelling, 'Where's my woman?! It's time to arouse and awaken my love! Where's my garden? I have the key!'" We both laugh hard at that image. "You think I'm kidding, don't you?"

By now, I'm totally cracking up. Then, I hear a car pull up in front of the house and then a super annoying honking noise. Suddenly, I'm not laughing anymore. Peter gets up and grabs his bags. I pick up his guitar case.

"Mad, I can get that," Peter says softly.

"Let me help you." I need something else to focus on, to get my mind off the sudden nausea and light-headedness that is coming on. I follow him outside.

The driver pops the trunk, and Peter puts his suitcase, gig bag, and guitar case inside and closes the trunk. Then he turns to me.

I'm trying to take deep breaths to keep my tears at bay, but it's not working. I feel my forehead tighten and my face wrinkles up with my ugly I'm-about-to-cry-really-hard face.

"Madeleine, please don't cry. You're gonna break my heart because I know my leaving is the cause of your tears," Peter tells me as he cups my face in his hands.

"Hey, that sounds like it could be a line for a cheesy love song." I sniff, wipe my eyes with my sleeve, and try to make light of the moment.

"It probably is. And if it isn't, it will be," he smiles. He wraps me in his arms and holds me tight. "I'm going to miss you so much, my beloved."

"I'm going to miss you, too. Terribly." I'm trying so hard not to totally break down.

Peter pulls back, looks into my eyes for a long moment, and smiles. Then he gently places his left hand on the back of my head and his right hand around my waist pulls me tightly into himself, and kisses me long and slow on the lips.

Suddenly, I don't feel so much like crying anymore.

Suddenly, my whole body feels like it's on fire.

He slowly pulls away. It takes me a moment or two to catch my breath, open my eyes, and stop my head from spinning.

"A little Song of Solomon kiss for you." He grins at me. "I love you, Mad. I'll call you when we get on the road."

Then he turns and gets into the car. He waves out the window as the car pulls away, and I wave back. *I love you too, Peter, so very much.*

I stand in the street for what seems like an eternity and then head back into the house, still stunned. I have never been kissed so passionately before. Never. Holy mackerel.

Chapter Thirty-two

I hadn't planned on getting all dressed-up for our wedding rehearsal and the dinner immediately following. But when I walk out of my room wearing a cap-sleeve black lace blouse paired with a simple black silk skirt, my mother just about loses it.

"MADELEINE MARIE WINGER!" she shrieks. "WHAT on earth are you wearing? Why aren't you wearing a dress? Don't you appreciate anything I do for you? I went to a lot of trouble to plan this evening and make it special for you, and the least you could do is make an effort to dress a little nicer!"

Yikes. Where is Dr. Bill with his magic sedatives when you need him? I just stand there in the hallway outside my room and stare at her. It's been a long time since I've been the victim of one of her tirades.

"I, um, I didn't know what to wear," I refuse to let my shock morph into anger. I won't let her ruin this day for me.

"Come in here. Now!" I leave Suzette and Maggie sitting on my bed, looking quite shocked and uncomfortable, and follow my mother into her room.

She stalks into her walk-in closet, which is more like the size of a small bedroom, and she starts rifling through her dresses. She considers various dresses of different colors and finally decides on a short, black, satiny dress with tiny straps at the top.

"Here! Put this on." She jabs the hanger at me.

"Mom, it's nice, but—"

"Madeleine, I'm in no mood to argue!"

"Okay…" I take the dress and head for my room.

"That looks like a nice dress," Maggie tries to console me as I hand her the hanger.

"Yeah, maybe for her. Maggie, my mother, and I are not the same size. Or style. There's no way I'm going to fit into this dress."

"Maybe, let's just try it, okay?" she is wearing her bright salesgirl smile.

I roll my eyes and start to undress. I dig through a not-yet-sealed box marked "bedroom" to find my strapless bra, slip it on, step into the dress, and zip it up as far as I can.

"Turn around," Maggie slides the zipper up the rest of the way. "There, that was easy. Turn around."

"Oh, Maddy, Peter's going to love it!" Suzette clasps her hands together after giving me tiny claps.

I walk over to my mirrored closet door. I'm shocked by how form-fitting the dress is and the bit of cleavage showing where the dress dips down in the front. But I guess it's not that bad. I'm really surprised that the dress fits at all.

"I don't know…it's not really my style. My cleavage looks like I have a baby's bottom coming out of the bust line of my dress."

"Oh, you do not. Hon, it looks great. A itty bit of cleavage is okay. I've helped a lot of women at the store pay big bucks to try to get what you got goin' on there," Maggie examines me from every angle.

"Really, Maddy, it's not bad at all. It fits with the style of the dress." Suzette reassures me.

"Really, guys? I kinda feel like I look cheap."

"In a Dolce & Gabbana bustier dress? I don't think so, hon," Maggie shakes her head. "You look great. You're rockin' that dress, darlin'! I would honestly tell you if I didn't think so."

"Yeah, Maggie's right. You really look like the wife of a musician now!" Suzette is so sweet.

"Hmm, thanks. I'll take that," I smile shyly. Besides, I can hear my mother yelling at Dr. Bill about something, so I know protesting her dress choice is definitely not a good idea. I open my closet door and find a black and gold lace shawl I bought a long time ago at a garage sale because it reminded me of Stevie Nicks (my secret fashion icon). I drape it across my back and throw one end across the front of me, covering my chest.

"Hey, that works," Suzette grins.

"It looks okay, but hon, you don't need to cover up. You look fine," Maggie pulls the shawl down to just around my shoulders. "Besides, your mother's gonna be madder than a hornet if you cover up that dress."

I know she's right, so I toss the shawl on my purse, figuring I'll cover up when we get to the hotel. I slip on the black kitten-heel Mary Janes I wore to my graduation, brace myself with a quick prayer for patience, and head back to my mother's room to get her approval.

She is packing a series of bags laid out on her bed for our wedding weekend at the hotel. She turns around and almost drops the bag of cosmetics she is holding.

"My goodness, Madeleine. You must have lost weight. I thought I was going to have to squeeze you into one of my dresses. Good thing the fabric is stretchy with some give," she says coolly.

I clamp my back teeth together like a vice grip and press my lips together tightly so I am completely incapable of retorting with something unpleasant.

"But you look lovely, though. That dress fits you perfectly. Wrong shoes though…hmm, try these," she says, handing me a pair of black satin pumps (not the Louboutins, of course) that look as if they've never been worn.

"Thanks, Mom. I guess we better hit the road. We have to check into the bridal suite and drop everything off before the rehearsal dinner."

"Yes, and don't be late. Drive carefully, and try not to wrinkle your wedding dress too much," she gives me a quick hug. I exhale quietly and head down the hall to my room.

"Everything okay?" Maggie asks.

"Yeah, let's go. Quickly. Before she thinks of anything else."

We dodge around the boxes of the last of my stuff that will be moved into the house Peter rented, grab our bags and dresses and head downstairs. I wish all my stuff was already moved there so I wouldn't have to come back here, but I'll have to deal with that after the honeymoon.

"I bet that's the last time you'll have her comin' down on you like that." Maggie checks her lipstick in her compact as we speed down the freeway toward Long Beach.

"How come your mom got so mad at what you were wearing?" Suzette asks. "I thought you looked fine."

"It's a control thing," I change lanes to make my freeway interchange. "She is in control overload, especially about the wedding. For example, I don't even know where the rehearsal dinner is going to be tonight. She planned it all."

"Really?" Suzette looks puzzled.

"Yep. Peter has a map, but he's been there before. It's some kind of country club in Palos Verdes."

"Why there?" Maggie blots her lipstick with a tissue.

"I'm not sure. Maybe she's trying to impress my future in-laws because they live in Rancho Palos Verdes," I try to relax as I drive, forgetting the whole ordeal back at my mother's house. I will be in the arms of betrothed very soon, and that's all that matters.

As we drive, my mind retraces the time when Peter was on the road and how I would have given anything to be holding him, like I will be in a few short miles when we meet up at the hotel.

It had been a hard five months while Peter was gone, but it went by faster than I thought. At first, I thought I wouldn't make it. I spent the first two days after he left curled up on my bed at my mother's house, pining away for him, weeping and hugging his pillow and the t-shirt he changed out of just before he left, both of which I grabbed from his room at Josiah's house. Both smelled so deliciously of him.

"How ya doing, my love?" Peter asked during one of our daily phone calls about a week after he left.

"Not so good today," I sniffled into the phone. I ran my fingers over the hem of his t-shirt, which I was wearing at the time.

"I'm so sorry, Mad, to put you through this." He exhaled deeply. I imagined him running his hand through his gorgeous mane.

"Nothing to apologize about. It's life. It is what it is," I try to sound rational and strong. "I mean, it's not like you're away fighting some war in a foreign land, like there's a danger of your bullet-ridden body returning in a body bag, right? I need to stop being so dramatic or melancholy or whatever."

"True. It's not a physical war, anyway."

"What do you mean?"

"Uh, nothing. Don't worry about it."

"Peter, tell me."

"Mad, it's tougher and much darker than I thought. There are drugs and groupies everywhere. Backstage, at every show. The only safe haven is our tour bus. And that's only because the guys are vigilant about keeping it clean and clear of that stuff. I mean, I've been around that stuff before and it never bothered me. I guess I didn't expect it to be there this time, but it is."

Groupies? Oh Lord, please keep those, those, those "women" away from my Peter. "I will add your protection to my prayer list. Big time."

"Thanks; I really need it. Mad, I miss you so much. And I love you more than I can physically say."

"I miss and love you too, so much," I squeak, trying to maintain my composure so we can get through at least one phone call without me completely coming apart.

After talking to him on the phone for almost an hour, I hung up and suddenly remembered the Bible verse he wrote in my notebook while we were in Long Beach. I grabbed the notebook and my Bible off my desk.

My fingers traced over his writing in my notebook, where he wrote the Scripture reference. It seemed like a lifetime ago we were there together. He also wrote that he loved me deeply. *Sigh.* I looked up the verses and wrote them out in my notebook:

> *"Now I urge you, brethren, by our Lord Jesus Christ and by the love of the Spirit, to strive together with me in your prayers to God for me, that I may be rescued from those who are disobedient in Judea, and that my service for Jerusalem may prove acceptable to the saints; so that I may come to you in joy by the will of God and find refreshing rest in your company.*
> *Now the God of peace be with you all. Amen."*
> -- Romans 15:30-33

These verses brought fresh tears. Peter's inclusion of this passage in my notebook was his way of asking me to pray for him while he was out on the road. And I did, many times a day.

Never before has the Word of God been so real to me. I felt like I was living in those words. They surrounded me and held me up, especially when it got really tough when I missed Peter so much I would physically ache.

A few days after he left, as soon as we were allowed actually, I moved back into the dorm to get ready for the spring semester. Maggie had just got back to school from her home in Plano, so we got to spend a few days together talking, laughing over bridal magazines, praying together, going to the movies, shopping and talking some more. All the great stuff we don't really get to do when classes are in session and academic responsibilities run our lives. I told her to tell me when she was sick of hearing about Peter, but she never did.

While my mother had all the wedding plans covered, Maggie appointed herself to make sure the wedding night and honeymoon were in order.

"Hon, it still freaks me out a little bit to see an engagement ring on your finger," Maggie looked at my hand as I flipped through the racks of lacy bras at Victoria's Secret. Light reflected dazzlingly off the diamonds on my ring.

"I know. I'm still not used to the fact that I'm engaged, either. It's not like it freaks me out, but I just wish we were already married. This waiting thing is horrible."

"I don't know how you do it," Maggie shook her blonde head. "If it were me, I'd tell him to meet me in Las Vegas when their tour went through there, and then I'd drag him off to the nearest justice of the peace. Then we'd spend the evening consummatin' the marriage, and I tell you what."

"Oh, you don't think we still talk about that? But I can't do that because that would leave you without a roommate," I smirk at her across the table of folded underwear.

"You'd do that for lil' ol' me? Oh, bless your heart!" She fake smiled back at me. It's so good to have Maggie back. My Maggie. "What about these?" she held up tiny strips of sheer red cloth.

"What is that?" I squinted at the item in her hand. "That's not something you wear, is it?"

"Hon, it's a thong. Do I need to educate you on the importance of good lingerie? What kinds of things does your man like?"

"I don't know. The subject of his boudoir undergarment preferences never came up."

"Well, you need to find out. Before your weddin' night."

"Don't you think it's a little soon? We still have four months, two weeks, and three days before he comes back." And yes, I did make a paper chain so I knew exactly how many days were left, only I made it for the date of Peter's return instead of our wedding day.

"Hon, it's never too soon to start preparin' to please your man."

"How do you know all this?"

"I used to listen in on a couples' group my Daddy used to hold in the livin' room at our house."

"They talked about lingerie? Really?"

"Well, not exactly, but I was sixteen. I got the point."

"Okay, but how am I supposed to find out what kinds of stuff he likes? Do I just casually slip it into the conversation? Like, ' Hi Peter, I hope the tour is going well, and by the way, what kind of sexy underwear does it for you?' A little awkward, don't you think?"

"Maddy, you need to find out these things about him and stop bein' shy. He's going to be your *husband*. Yawl are gonna be with each other through the good and the bad times. He'll be the one holdin' your hair back as you puke your guts out when you get sick, and since he's got all that lovely long hair, you can do the same for him!" A woman shopping near us frowned at Maggie as she moved to the next table of underwear, which made me spit out the laugh I was trying to hold in.

"Oh, Maggie, you're such a romantic!" I laughed.

"I'm just sayin,' it's time for you to start gettin' used to thinkin' like a wife."

"I know. I know you're right. But I think the topic of lingerie can wait a little bit."

"Okay, but yawl need to start gettin' over your body issues," she raised her pencil-thin eyebrows at me. "Hon, you have got to get used to the idea that you should be comfortable bein' naked in front of your husband."

I knew Maggie was right about this. I've been praying for help with this issue ever since.

"And these big 'ol sweaters," she continued as she pulled on the sleeve of the sweater I was wearing, "have got to go. You need to make your man proud to have you standin' next to him. You need to wear clothes that actually *fit* and are not two sizes too big." She stopped and gently put her hand on my arm. "Besides, Maddy, you got *nothin'* to be ashamed of. Sweetie, your man is gonna drop to his knees praisin' Jesus when he sees you naked!"

"Thanks, Maggie," I blushed. "You truly are my Barnabas when it comes to matrimonial nudity." I hugged her for her encouraging words.

"Well, hon, that's what I'm here for." She hugged me back tightly.

When we pulled away, Maggie's eyes were moist. I squeezed her hands and had to take deep breaths myself.

"Um, I need to go to the Christian bookstore after we finish at the mall," Maggie said quietly.

"Sure, what for?"

"I need to buy a new Bible. I need a new Bible for my new start."

"Okay, but only if you let me buy it for you," I had to breathe deeply again so I wouldn't get more emotional in the middle of Victoria's Secret.

"Only if you let me buy this negligee for you for your honeymoon!" She held up a totally sheer and beautiful short black nightgown with roses embroidered around the top and at the hem.

"Maggie, it's totally see-through!"

"I know, that's the point, darlin'." She smiled smugly at me and headed for the cash register.

After we finished at the mall, I drove us to the Christian bookstore across the street. I parked in a space right in front of the store window. Maggie unbuckled her seat belt, grabbed her purse, climbed out of the car, and stopped dead in her tracks. I followed her line of sight, and instantly, my hand covered my mouth, and I choked on a sob.

"Oohwee, that boy looks mighty fine! Hon, you did good," Maggie put her arm around me as I wept, standing in front of the store window, gazing at a huge "on tour now" poster for the band Faith Not Fear.

"Yeah, he does," I wiped my eyes and nose with one of the two dozen white lacy handkerchiefs Maggie bought me as a joke, but they had come in handy on more than one occasion.

"You must be so proud of him." She smiled at me sweetly.

"Yeah, I am. I know he's happy. But Maggie, I miss him so much. So much…" I stopped before I started to cry again.

"Come on, let's go inside and see if they'll give us one of the display pictures," she grabbed my hand. All I could do was nod "yes."

I got less and less emotional as the weeks went on. I stopped crying whenever I remembered some little thing about Peter or something we did, which was at first hourly, then daily. I thought I was going to have to buy a waterproof prayer journal because I cried every time I would sit down to write my requests. But I asked God to help me to be stronger while Peter was away because I was starting to grieve for his presence. Isn't that weird? I think I needed to put God back in first place and grieve for *His* presence.

And Peter. *Sigh.* It felt like nothing else in the world was going on when I was on the phone with him. The sound of his voice was the most beautiful, soothing, familiar, and inviting sound I've ever heard. I would just melt listening to him tell me how much he missed me and loved me and how much I would like being out on the road with him.

"I saw the band's promo pictures in a bookstore today," I told him over the phone.

"Really? The new pictures are out already? I haven't even seen them yet."

"Yeah, and you look good. *Really* good."

"Thanks," he said softly.

"The girl in the store didn't believe Maggie when she told her that you were my fiancé, and she wouldn't give me one of the promotional pictures. She said they were all spoken for by other girls who worked in the store."

"I'm sure I can get you one if you really want one."

"You know I do! Remember, I'm your number one fan and the only groupie you'll ever need." I hope I didn't sound *too* flirtatious.

"Mmm, I'm looking forward to it." His voice was so low it made me feel warm.

I loved hearing Peter gush about what a great experience it was playing with the guys in the band on stage for all those people, what great times of fellowship he was having with them on the long bus rides between shows, and how much he is learning from them and growing spiritually.

Then there were the calls when I tried to cheer him up after they had a show that didn't go well because it was full of technical problems or the guys were just having an off night. I would make him laugh about all the outlandish wedding stuff I saw in the magazines.

Then there were the phone calls where we prayed through our tears because we missed each other so much when not being together became too unbearable at times.

We always ended our phone calls by counting down the days until our wedding day. Last night, in our next-to-last goodnight phone calls, before we went to sleep, Peter figured out how many hours until we were officially married. So, all day, we have been counting by hours instead of months or days.

During those five months we were apart, the semester marched on at a steady pace. There were always books to read and papers to write, which occupied so much of my time. And there was work. Jaime has completely left me alone ever since the day I showed up with an engagement ring on my finger.

Josiah and Leah announced that they decided to get married in June on the beach at Corona Del Mar. Leah wanted just a simple ceremony right on the beach at sunset. So work became more fun as she and I spent a lot of our break time discussing wedding stuff and talking about our awesome men.

Josiah and Leah were a tremendous comfort to me while Peter was gone. We spent many hours talking and drinking coffee at the coffeehouse. I even brought Maggie along to join us when she was free. She said she had a great time with them.

Finally, at the end of those long five months, Peter came home in mid-May, two days before my graduation. I made arrangements with one of my professors to take my last final early so I could drive out to the Valley and meet the tour bus when it came in. Peter told me he would make plans for a car to drive him home, but I said no way. I was not going to wait another second to see him. He didn't argue with me.

"The bus is coming! It'll be here in a few minutes!" Lydia, the drummer's wife, exclaimed as she waddled toward me. She slipped her cell phone into her purse and gingerly rubbed her enormous protruding belly.

I already knew what she told me, having just talked to Peter on my own mobile phone, but I loved hearing it anyway, and I returned her huge, excited grin.

"When are you due?" I asked her.

"Yesterday! We were praying this little one would wait for his daddy to get home. And he has!"

I secretly prayed that the baby would wait just a little bit longer so she wouldn't have to give birth right in the rehearsal studio parking lot.

Just as I finished my little prayer for her, a massive dark grey bus with black tinted windows pulled into the parking lot. My heart and my stomach jumped into my throat at the same time.

One by one, the guys staggered off the bus and fell into tight embraces with their wives and families. Peter was the last guy to step off the bus. He was holding a single long-stemmed red rose, and a big smile spread across his face.

He threw his arms around my waist, picked me up, and squeezed me so tight I thought my ribs might not take the pressure. But I loved it. I inhaled the aroma of him. He was home. My beloved was home.

He kissed me so sweetly, then put me down and wiped away the tears that had poured down my cheeks.

"For you," he said, handing me the rose. "It's no 'Black Beauty,' but it was the only rose I could find this morning."

"Thank you," I hugged him again, thinking I would never let him go. "It's beautiful."

"You're beautiful. The most beautiful thing I've seen." Tears seeped out the corners of his eyes.

Even though he looked tired and thinner than he did before he left, I've never seen a sight more breathtaking that filled my heart to its fullest as I did him and the love in his eyes. I felt remarkably whole again. The big fissure I had felt inside me after he left filled up and was now gone. I prayed a prayer of gratitude: *Oh Lord, thank You so much for bringing Peter back to me safely. Thank You! Thank You! Thank You!*

Peter held my hand all the way home as he told me about the last leg of the trip home and asked me how my final went this morning.

"So, you're officially finished with college now. How does it feel?"

I had to think about it. It hadn't hit me before he asked. "It feels great. But having you home is the best!" I smiled at him and he kissed my hand.

In the big blur of everything that was going on, I didn't realize until my graduation day that God had answered one of my biggest prayers, which I had been pestering Him with for a long time.

During my graduation ceremony, as I sat in a plastic folding chair completely enveloped in a long black graduation gown, peeking glances over at Peter, who was sitting next to Josiah and Leah (not next to my mother, thank God!), I realized that at some point along the way, I had stopped worrying about the future.

I used to be utterly consumed with the anxiety of not knowing what I was going to do with my life after I graduated from college. What a waste! God had a plan for me all along, as He showed me so many times in His Word, but I was too lacking in faith to take Him at His Word. I wasted so much thought and emotion worrying and being filled with dread and anguish. As I looked over at Peter again, he smiled at me. He is part of God's plan for me to minister to this awesome guy as his helpmate and his wife. God is so great.

Speaking of anxiety, I was a little apprehensive about Peter and I being alone together once he came home, but my fears were quickly put to rest.

We were both totally exhausted all the time. Peter was recovering from the grueling schedule at the end of the tour, and I was dead-tired from all my school work deadlines, an internship at a local magazine, work at the Plus, graduation stuff, and a few wedding tasks (which I actually didn't mind doing). On top of all that, Peter and I were part of Leah and Josiah's wedding, which was so beautiful and romantic.

Also, Peter moved out of Josiah's house just before their wedding. He rented a cute little two-bedroom cottage on some property that belonged to some friends at our church. Since I will be going on tour with Peter at the end of the summer, buying property and building a house will have to wait. Peter said he didn't have peace about it anyway, so we will wait on God.

Peter said he thought of me when he toured the little cottage because one of the bedrooms had a view of the garden with a little waterfall that flowed into a koi fish pond. The room is big enough for both of us to work in, since we will of course be living together after we get married. *Yes!* I can't wait.

I totally love that we aren't even married yet, and he is already in the habit of considering me in all his plans. I was very tempted a few times to move into the house with Peter a few weeks before our wedding day because my mother was driving me totally out of my mind with all her obsessive planning of my wedding. But I didn't, even though I love the little house and feel totally at home there already. We've come this far, keeping our hands off each other. Blowing it in the last few weeks would be a real shame.

As if Peter's move, Leah and Josiah's wedding, and all the other stuff wasn't enough to keep us busy, there were, of course, all the last remaining things to do for our own wedding that my mother couldn't take care of. One of the most difficult things was trying to get Andrew to participate in the wedding as one of Peter's groomsmen.

Peter was convinced that asking Andrew to be one of the groomsmen was something the Lord wanted him to do. So after many unreturned phone calls and then some short phone calls, Andrew told Peter that being in our wedding was not something he could do right now.

But Peter kept in contact with him, calling every week to see how he was doing and usually just leaving a message on his answering machine.

Andrew was really down in the dumps because his pregnant girlfriend left him for her boss, who is the owner of the company she works for. She told Andrew that she hated living in that depressing little house, but after Andrew told her they could move, she confessed the real reason she was leaving him was because she thought he was not good father material, he wouldn't be a good provider, and that he didn't look as good on paper as her wealthy boss who she had been having an affair with for months. Can you say "paternity test" when the baby is born?

So, instead of Andrew, Peter asked Philip, the other guitar player from Faith Not Fear, to be one of his groomsmen, which he gladly accepted.

Philip and Peter became really good friends during the tour. Peter said he was like his "Josiah" on the road. I'm looking forward to hanging out with them when the band goes back out on tour at the end of the summer.

As we exit the freeway, I call Peter and tell him we are almost at the hotel.

"Mmm, I can't wait to see you," the sound of his deep, smooth voice makes me quiver. You and the girls are all checked in, and your rooms are ready."

"Thanks so much."

"You know it." *Sigh.* He's so wonderful.

We pull into the hotel, and Peter and Matt are standing outside talking with some of the guys who work at the hotel. Peter looks so handsome in his soft white button-up shirt and velvet sports jacket, the same jacket he wore on our first "official" date. His hair is blowing softly in the ocean breeze. He's not wearing a tie at our rehearsal dinner. I want him to be comfortable.

Peter comes over and helps me out of the car. He slips his arms around my waist and kisses me quite passionately. He steps back a little and whistles. "Dang girl, you look gorgeous," he raises one eyebrow at me. "July tenth—wait—tomorrow! Tomorrow night," he chants softly.

"Thanks," I chastise myself for forgetting to put on my shawl as I planned. "My mother's dress."

"Yeah, I thought so. You look really good in it, almost too good."

"Thanks," I say, wrapping my shawl around my shoulders and knotting it at chest level.

I introduce Maggie and Suzette to Matt, who seems to relish in his newfound female audience. I wonder where his wife is. He turns up the charm, making both girls laugh several times as we unload my car with our stuff and put all our bags and dresses onto the luggage carts. Peter doesn't seem to notice Matt's exchange with the girls. I think this dress is distracting him because he keeps looking at me and smiling. Thank God we only have one more night of this celibacy stuff. *Thank God!*

We get everything settled in the bridal suite. We carefully hang up our dresses and get ready to head down to the lawn area for the wedding rehearsal. I grab my lace blouse and slip it on over my dress, leaving it unbuttoned. Maggie rolls her eyes at me.

"What? I'll take it off when we get to the dinner, okay? I think this dress is a bit much for a rehearsal, don't you?"

"Uh-huh. Just remember what we talked about. About thinking like a wife and making your man proud to have you as his wife."

"I know…you're right," I say, slipping off my blouse and laying it on my bag.

"I think Maggie's got a point," Suzette agrees. "And I know Peter will appreciate it," she giggles.

"You look good, hon," Maggie smiles at me. "And besides, this is your day, not your mother's. All eyes should be on you, not her."

"Oh, I don't even want to go there," I shake my head and lift my eyes skyward as we walk out the door.

Peter, Matt, Josiah, Philip, Maggie, Suzette, Leah, my parents, and Peter's mother all stand around listening to the wedding coordinator instruct us in a kindergarten teacher's tone of voice on what precisely we are to do tomorrow. It must be an occupational hazard for her. I'm having trouble paying attention because I keep looking at Peter. He keeps looking at me. I wish I could speed up time so that this part is over and the wedding night is here.

"So, why don't you ladies ride with me so the love birds can ride alone together?" Matt offers to Suzette and Maggie as we head out to the parking lot. Again, I wonder where his wife is. I'm about to ask him, but something in my spirit tells me not to.

"That's a good idea," Suzette smiles at Matt, and he smiles at her. "As long as it's okay with you, Maddy."

"Totally fine," I try to read the subtext of what's going on.

"Okay, great. We'll meet you guys there," Matt flashes a dazzling smile that strongly resembles his handsome brother's. He opens his car doors, and Maggie climbs in the backseat while Suzette gets in the front passenger's side.

"What do you make of all that?" I ask Peter as we walk to his truck.

"I don't know, and I can honestly say I'm not sure I care all that much about it right now," Peter wraps his arms around me. "They're all adults. They can take care of themselves."

"I know, but Suzette is so…and where's his wife, anyway?" I ask before Peter plants a fiery kiss on my lips. All my thoughts and worries about my friends drift away. Then he opens the car door for me and helps me up.

I stare at Peter as he drives us from the hotel to our rehearsal dinner at the Palos Verdes Country Club in Palos Verdes Estates, California. I can't seem to take my eyes off him since he's been home. He looks at me and smiles.

"What?"

"You," I say. He reaches over, rests his hand on mine, and I squeeze it. "I missed you so much when you were gone."

"I missed you, too, but I'm here now. And you won't be able to get rid of me—not ever."

"Good." I clasp both my hands around his hand and hold it tightly.

He is silent for a while. "To answer your question," he finally says.

"Which question?"

Peter exhales deeply. "About Matt's wife."

Chapter Thirty-three

hat about Matt's wife? Is she coming?" I ask Peter while he drives us to our rehearsal dinner, almost thirty minutes from the hotel.

'That's what I asked him."

"And?"

"She most definitely will not be coming to the rehearsal dinner tonight or to our wedding tomorrow."

"Why not? Where is she?" I get the feeling Peter knows what is going on with Matt and his wife, but he is hesitant to tell me. And I'm a little agitated that Matt is coming onto my friend.

"She's in South America."

"Um, why is she there and not here with Matt?"

"She's working."

I'm trying not to get impatient. I wish he would tell me what is going on, so I decide to just ask him. "What's going on?"

Peter exhales, and looks disheartened. "They're getting a divorce."

"What?! Already? What happened?"

"She's a clinical research associate, and she's been working in Peru on some kind of medical research project. She told Matt she is not coming back for a long while, but when she does come back to the States, it won't be to him."

"That must be some kind of project to make her not want to come back. But to make her want a divorce, that's a little odd, don't you think?"

"It's not about the project. She told Matt she is in love with the doctor in charge of their research team and that he's in love with her too, and apparently, they have been involved with each other for some time."

"*Whoa!* But she and Matt have only been married for, like, six months, right?"

"Apparently, she knew him pretty well before she married Matt. So when this guy offered her the job in Peru only two months after she and Matt got married, it seems that she took it immediately, without talking to Matt about it or anything."

"Oh man…" is all I can say. I can't wrap my head around this. "How long have you known about this?"

"Matt told me everything this morning. He got a letter from her two days ago explaining the whole situation, and she also asked Matt to file for a divorce since she is out of the country and cannot do it."

"She asked him for a divorce in a letter? Omigosh, poor Matt. He must be devastated."

"It's a mess. Matt was upset, but he says now he feels relieved."

"Really?"

"Yeah, he said he had a gut feeling she didn't love him. That she never did. I guess that explains why he was nervous that morning of his wedding."

"Oh man, poor Matt," I say. "Divorce is so awful. I totally understand why it's not part of God's plan for us."

"Yeah, I feel terrible for him. He asked me not to tell anyone. He said he's not ready to answer questions about it yet, which I completely understand. He told me it was okay to tell you, though. He knows we don't have any secrets."

"What a bummer. I didn't much care for his wife, but not to the point where I wanted them to get a divorce."

"Yeah, that's how I feel," Peter glances at me. "But one positive thing that has come from all this is that it's causing Matt to take a closer look at himself and his life. When I asked him if we could pray for him, he said he hoped we would. He told me he sees what you and I have, and he wants that in his life."

"In a relationship?"

"That and with life in general. He said he figures there's got to be more to life than work, work, and more work. And he said he wants to find a woman who really loves him."

"Hmm, sounds like he's searching for some truth."

"Yeah, he is. I've been praying for him all day."

"I will, too."

"I was hoping you would," he smiles at me. "I figure, with your prayers covering him, he's bound to see the light soon."

"And your prayers, too." I squeeze his hand and smile back at him.

We pull into a parking space near the entrance to the Palos Verdes Country Club. The red tile roof glistens in the setting sun. The palm tree branches rubbing against the tiles in the ocean breeze make a loud swishing sound. Peter grabs his velvet sports coat off the back seat and comes around the front of his truck to open my door for me.

"I swore I would never set foot in this place again," he slides his jacket on.

"So not only have you been here before, but it holds a bad memory for you," I adjust my shawl around my shoulders.

"It's one of my father's hangouts. And the scene of one of the worst fights he and I have had."

"Ohmigosh, I'm sorry, Peter. If I had known, I would have asked my mother to hold the rehearsal dinner somewhere else."

"It's okay, it's not a big deal," he grabs my hand. "I think it's God's way of helping me get over past junk."

"Could be," I squeeze his hand. "What happened with your father, if you don't mind talking about it?"

"He threw a big fiftieth birthday party for my mother and invited all his business colleagues, and everyone in his and my mother's social circle. Everyone except for my aunt and uncle. When my mother asked him if my Aunt Mureille and Uncle Gabriel had RSVP'd because she didn't see them at the party, my father told her point blank that they were not invited. And not welcomed."

"Yikes! To *her* birthday party? That's so mean."

"Yeah, super mean. My mother got this really heartbroken look on her face, and she started to cry. Something I have never seen her do in public. It made something in me just snap, so I ripped into my father. In front of everyone. I told him he was nothing but a selfish bastard and a few other choice words I'll spare you from," he shakes his head.

"Whoa." I can't picture my gentle, sweet-spirited man yelling at his father in a fit of rage in front of a room full of people.

"And this only made my mother cry even harder. It was not a pretty scene. Looking back on it, I should've confronted him in private or maybe not have said anything at all. I don't know. I apologized to my mother for ruining her party before I stormed out of the room and swore to myself I would never set foot on this property again. But here I am."

"But on a happier occasion," I wrap my arm around his waist as walk to the entrance, snuggling close to him. The tormented look on his face melts away, and a smile takes its place.

"Mmhmm...a much happier occasion," he wraps his arms around my shoulder. "Time to forget what lies in the past, and press on."

He stops walking. He softly kisses my cheek, then my neck, which sends a sensuous shockwave through my entire being.

"Hey, you two! Get a room!" Matt teases as he walks up with Suzette at his side and Maggie walking behind them and fussing with her compact. We all laugh.

Matt gives his brother a couple of firm pats on the back as we walk up to the front entrance of the country club. The two men exchange a silent expression of encouragement as Peter holds the door open for all of us.

I grab Peter's arm as we walk down the softly lit hallway of the country club to the room where our dinner is to take place. He seems relaxed as he smiles down at me and then looks away quickly.

"What?" I hope a bad memory hasn't popped into his mind.

"I don't think you should give that dress back to your mother for a while," his eyes are hooded. I want to admire you wearing it when I can allow my thoughts about you and your lovely body to flow freely."

I grip his arm tighter and blush.

The Monte Malaga Room has the same soft lighting and plush pastel muted patterned carpeting as the hallway. One long table covered in white linens is set up in the middle of the room, and matching white linens cover the chairs lining both sides of the table. The windows and terrace just outside the room offer views of the Pacific Ocean and an immaculate golf course.

As we walk into the room, almost immediately, I begin to feel nauseous, my throat tightens, and my mouth begins to water profusely. I stifle the deep gag that is forming in my throat and head straight for the terrace.

"Mad, what's wrong?" Peter walks quickly after me, his face full of concern. "Your face is almost as green as the carpet."

"Oh Peter, oh my Lord, that smell," I say between loud gags and deep breaths.

"The seafood?"

"Yes! I hate it! It's the worst smell ever!" I grip the terrace railing. "I hate seafood, and *she* knows it. The smell of it makes me sick to my stomach!" I wipe my eyes, part tears from waves of nausea and part tears of frustration. Peter hands me his handkerchief from his pocket and rubs my back. I lean my head on his chest.

From the terrace, inside the room, I can see my mother ostentatiously greeting and talking with the guests. She is dressed in a bright red skin-tight sleeveless Oriental gown, with a cutout in the front below the mandarin collar revealing to everyone that she is sans brazier this evening. The decorations on her Geisha hair stick in her up-do swing wildly as she wags her head and talks.

Peter thinks for a minute. "I'll be right back," he stalks back inside the room.

I watch my mother watch him cross the room. *Yuk!* I hate the way she looks at him, the way she always looks at him. I silently pray for patience, for God to help me get used to the fishy smell, and for strength to forgive my mother.

After a few moments, I see a small crew of wait staff emerge from the kitchen. They quickly remove trays of round black-and-white sliced rolls of fish and rice and bring them back to the kitchen. A couple of the staff members place several pots of steaming water on the warming trays. And then I hear the roar of air conditioners on the roof cranking up.

As Peter makes his way across the room toward the terrace, I see my mother stop him and talk to him. He smiles coolly at her as he listens to her animatedly speak at him. He shifts his stance ever so slightly so the hand she had placed on his arm falls down. He says a few words to her, smiles, lightly pats her shoulder, and turns toward the terrace.

"The smell should air out in a few minutes. How are you feeling?"

"Better, thanks. What did you do?"

"I asked the catering manager if there was anything we could do to get rid of the fish smell in the room because it was making the bride extremely sick. She said they could bring some of the trays with the more 'aromatic' sushi back to the kitchen, and they would bring out pots of boiling water with a little vinegar mixed in to neutralize the fishy smell. And they cranked up the air conditioning so the air will circulate more."

"Thank you! You're so awesome," I hug him.

"You know it. But Mad, I'm afraid we won't be able to get rid of the smell completely, and I can't have you spending the evening out here on the terrace."

"It's okay. I'll make it. I'll slip out here if it gets too much for me."

"This sucks!" he is more than a little agitated.

"I know," I rub his arms. "But it's the last time she can do this to me. From now on, we can just leave, right?"

"Yeah, I guess."

"Sweetheart, are you okay?" Dr. Bill walks up to us, looking at me in a half-concerned parent, half-examining doctor sort of way. "You look a little green? Are you sick?"

"No, not anymore," I glance at my mother inside the room.

"It's the sushi, isn't it? I told your mother it was a bad idea. But she insisted on dragging her favorite sushi chef out here to cater this dinner," he matches Peter's look of frustration. "The smell of seafood has always made Maddy feel sick, even when she was a little girl," he tells Peter.

"Yeah, I can see that. Poor girl," he hugs me close.

"I'll be okay," I smile up to Peter and Dr. Bill. I take one last lung full of clean air, and we head back inside the room.

The wait staff begins to distribute plates of food for everyone. A large salad of greens is placed in front of me and Peter, not that I'm going to be able to eat anything.

Peter goes to the microphone. He greets everyone, thanks them for coming, and asks them to begin enjoying their dinner as soon as Josiah asks for the blessing over the food.

My mother looks noticeably irritated since I think she thought she would be the master of ceremonies for the evening.

"I figure we should get the show on the road as quick as possible and get this smelly food out of here," he sits down next to me. "How are you feeling?"

"I'm doing great," I grin at him. "I love you, you know."

"And I love you, too," he takes my hand, kissing it gently.

I sit back and watch some people eat, and others just nibble their salads and bread as the sound level of voices in the room increases as people converse more. It's so odd to watch all the different little scenes take place. My mother speaks flamboyantly at Chloe, who sits quietly, listening and looking slightly amused.

Josiah, Leah, Philip, Sarah, and Maggie seem to be sharing funny stories since the sound of their laughter fills the room.

Suzette is telling Matt something that makes him give her his full and undivided attention.

The strangest pairing of all is Dr. Bill and Peter's father, who are deep in a seemingly very amicable conversation. Every so often during their conversation, Mr. McManus glances over at Peter with what seems like a softer look on his stern face. I watch as Peter engages one of his father's glances, only for a moment, and then both men look away.

"How are you feeling?" Peter asks me for about the twentieth time tonight, but I don't mind. I take much comfort in his love and concern for me.

"I'm doing fine, really well," I look into his eyes as they reflect the candlelight in the room making them like pools of gentle green water. My heart swells with love for this man.

"How are you?" I interlace my fingers with his.

"Okay, I guess. This type of stuff is not my idea of a good time."

"Me neither," I squeeze his hand. "But I mean, with your father and all the past stuff."

"Oh, fine. I haven't spoken to him all evening, and not on purpose. Our paths just haven't crossed tonight. I'm guessing that's a good thing."

"I wonder what he and Dr. Bill are talking about. They've been engrossed in their conversation for a while."

"I can only imagine," he turns his eyes toward the men. "I hope my father isn't being a jerk. Dr. Bill is cool."

"It doesn't look like it. But even if he is, Dr. Bill can diffuse people pretty easily. Remember, he lives with my mother."

"True," he laughs. "She's had a few cocktails this evening, I'm guessing?"

"Probably, why do you ask?"

"I saw her corner my father near the kitchen earlier."

"Oh NO! What did she do?" *Oh, Lord, please help! Please don't let my mother do anything horrible to my future in-laws, especially my father in-law.*

"Nothing really. She was just flirting with him, you know, laughing loudly and putting her hand on his arm a lot."

"What did he do?"

"He looked like he was enjoying the attention of a bleach-blonde geisha girl, but that was about it. His phone rang, and he left the room."

"*Phew!* Good." I am relieved. "Did your mother notice?"

"No, probably not. But she's used to women flirting with my father."

"I don't know how she handles it. I think I would go all psycho-chick if I saw a girl flirting with you."

"She knows he's not going to pursue the flirtation and cheat on her again. He almost lost everything the last time he did that. I bet you would be just fine if we were put in that same situation. Mad, you gotta know I will *never* cheat on you. You can be sure of that."

"I know, but it's not you that I worry about."

"No, Mad. No other woman could tempt me away from you. You are my gift directly from the Creator; I am so thankful for that every day. I wouldn't do anything to tarnish that, or hurt you, or hurt my Lord. No moment or thought of infidelity is worth that." He speaks with such conviction I am deeply comforted by his words. "Now, if some dude made a move on you, well, now that's a different story," he adds, with a tough guy look on his face, which is actually very cute and makes me giggle.

"How is that different?" I tease. "You have to know I would never cheat on you. I've been cheated on a number of times, and I know how much it hurts, and I would never ever, ever do that to you."

"It's a physical thing, though," he explains. "There's no danger of some chick overpowering me. But, you, you have no idea how beautiful you are," he pauses. "And you don't know how powerfully attractive that is to guys."

All I can do is stare into his eyes and let his words wash over me, filling me with a sense of protection and adoration. He puts his hand on the side of my face and kisses me tenderly on the lips.

"Do you want to go get some air?" he asks softly. He clears his throat and slides his chair back.

"That sounds good." I am still mesmerized by his kiss. I take his hand so he can help me up.

"So tomorrow should be fun," he stands behind me rubbing my shoulders, as we gaze up at the stars and the faraway lights on the ocean.

"Which part, the wedding or after the wedding?"

"I was thinking about the ceremony and reception, but now that you mention it," he nuzzles my neck, then tickles my side making me jump and laugh.

The sound of a lighter flicking makes us both turn around. Peter's father slowly walks to the railing next to us, puffing a cigar until it lights. I feel Peter's body tense, and his arms tighten around my waist. *Oh Lord, please help…*

"So tomorrow's the big day," he exhales a cloud of blue smoke. Thankfully, the ocean breeze blows it away from us. I hate the smell of cigars. "You two must be excited."

"Yes," Peter answers cooly. "We are."

"Well, good." Mr. McManus stares out at the view. "Have you talked to your brother?"

"Yes."

"Then you know about him."

"He told me everything."

"He seems to be handling it well. He's already moving on, it seems. He's been talking to the same pretty gal all evening."

"Suzette," I say. *Oh Lord, please protect her. She's so innocent.*

"She seems like a nice enough young lady," Mr. McManus says.

"Yes, she is," I state.

"Well, good," he exhales another big cloud of smoke. He is silent for a few minutes, which thickens the tension in the air. "Peter," he finally speaks. "Your mother and I want you to know, if you ever need help with anything, financially speaking, to let us know."

"Thanks, I appreciate that," Peter answers. I can feel him relax a bit. "But we're good. I just signed another contract with the band's management company and the record label. They want to use me in the studio on some other projects, as well as the new album, when we finish the tour."

"That's excellent news," he says with another plume of smoke.

As the tension decreases, I notice two young guys, probably high school age, looking at Peter and whispering to each other as they stack empty glasses on a large tray and clean ashtrays. They notice me noticing them, so I smile. One of the boys smiles back shyly and walks over.

"S'cuse me, I hate to interrupt, but you're Peter McManus, right?" the boy smooths his long brown hair, which is tightly pulled back into a ponytail at the nape of his neck.

"Yeah, hey, how's it goin'? It's good to meet you," Peter holds out his hand. It seems like he has done this before when he has been recognized by a fan.

"I'm Rich," the boy shakes Peter's hand. "Dude! This is radical! I'm the biggest Faith Not Fear fan ever! Dude, you rock! My buddy and I just saw you guys play when we were visiting my brother in Phoenix. You guys rocked the house!"

"Yeah, dude, you're like the best guitar player ever! You rip! Like God is playing through your fingers!" the other young guy mimes playing air guitar. "Way better than that other dude that was in the band!" Tiny fuzzy blond hairs have escaped his tight ponytail, creating a soft halo around his head and around the long blond braid down his back.

"Thanks," Peter shakes his hand, too. "I'm glad you enjoyed the show."

"Bro, do you mind?" Rich holds out a clean napkin and a pen.

"Not at all," Peter takes the pen and napkin. Rich turns around so Peter can use his back to write on.

"Aww dude, me too?" the other boy hands Peter another napkin. "Make it out to 'John Mark,' that's me."

"Sure," Peter hands the autographed napkin back to Rich and takes John Mark's napkin who also turns around and offers his back as a writing surface.

"Thanks, bro. You're cool," Rich grins widely. "Hey bro, is this your wife? She's really pretty."

"Yeah, thanks," Peter smiles at me. "Guys, this is my wife, Madeleine. Well, she'll officially be my wife tomorrow."

"Oh hey, nice to meet you," Rich and John Mark guy wave timidly.

'It's nice to meet you guys," I wave back.

"So you're getting married tomorrow! Totally awesome! Hey, congrats!" Rich raises his hand for a high five.

"Thanks!" Peter responds with a high five.

"And, this is my father, Marcus McManus," Peter says stiffly.

"Nice to meet you, sir," the guys mumble in unison.

"Boys," Mr. McManus regards them regally.

"Well, um, we better get back to work. Thanks for the autograph. Keep on rockin', bro!" Rich folds the napkin carefully and puts it in his shirt pocket.

"Bless you guys," Peter tells them as they pick up their trays.

"Hey, bless you guys, too!" the guys shout as they head back into the room.

Peter's father, usually stoic or disapproving, looks surprised. "You have fans."

"Yeah," Peter wraps his arms around me, smiling brightly.

"So I take it that has happened before?" I ask him.

"A couple of times when we were out on tour."

Peter's father's cell phone rings, and he promptly turns and walks away to answer it.

"That went pretty well, don't you think?"

"Yeah. It was kinda weird, though."

"What was?"

"I've never seen him try to be so...so civilized before," Peter frowns. "I still can't let my guard down around him."

"Maybe in time, you will. But I think this is a good start."

"Maybe," Peter murmurs. "So what are we gonna do with your mom and the whole stinking seafood rehearsal dinner incident?"

"I'm going to try very hard to forget about it. Other people seemed to enjoy the food, so that's cool. It's not just about me, right?"

"I think it is. This is your wedding rehearsal dinner, your one and only."

"True. But it really doesn't matter that much to me in the grand eternal scheme of things."

"I was thinking," he turns me around to face him. "Since you didn't have dinner yet, and you need to eat to keep your strength up for tomorrow night," he waggles his eyebrows. "We could round up just the bridesmaids and groomsmen and have our own little post-rehearsal, pre-wedding celebration at In-N-Out tonight, on the way back to the hotel. What do you think?"

"I love it! Let's go!"

We head back into the room, where everything is winding down. Some guests come over to us to say their goodbyes. Peter secretly tells Matt and Josiah to follow us to the In-N-Out near the hotel, and I tell Maggie, Leah, and Suzette what the plan is. We thank Dr. Bill and my mother for a lovely evening (Dr. Bill gives me a little wry smile), and we tell them we'll meet them back at the hotel a little later.

"So Matt and Suzette are riding alone?" I ask Peter as he drives us back to Long Beach.

"Yeah, I think so. I think Maggie said she was going to ride with Josiah and Leah. Are you okay with that?"

"Honestly, I don't know how I feel or if I have a right to feel anything. Suzette is a grown woman who can make her own choices. She teaches English halfway around the world, for heaven's sake. I think she can handle making the right choices when it comes to relationships, right?"

"I think so. I'm still getting to know Matt more and more, but I've never seen him like this. Not ever. He's so quiet, almost pensive. And he's got almost a lovesick look on his face, like a puppy. He was never like this with his wife, or soon-to-be ex-wife, I should say."

"Yeah, but he's not even divorced yet. I hope Suzette knows what she's getting herself into. I'd hate to see her or him get hurt."

"Yeah, it's a technicality though. Matt's wife is gone. She deserted him, and now she's having a full-on affair. Really, I think she was gone before she and Matt got married."

"It sure sounds like it. Poor Matt."

"I plan to stay close to him through all this. And I'm going to ask him if he would please take it easy with Suzette."

"That's a good idea. He's going to need you. I'll continue to pray for him, for both of them."

"I keep getting the sense that God is moving in this situation. That's why I'm not too concerned, ya know, about him and Suzette. I think it's going to work out for the best. Maybe they are just going to become friends. Maybe not. In any case, I'll make sure I warn him about you Biola girls," he grins as he drives.

"What about us 'Biola girls'?"

"Oh, you know."

"Know what?" I poke his side.

"That you tend to be sweet, pure, beautiful, encouraging, loving women of God, and he would be extremely blessed beyond belief to end up with someone like Suzette or someone like my Mad." He kisses my hand until the traffic signal we are stopped at turns green.

"I love you, my man. So much."

"I love you, my bride, my beloved."

I close my eyes and speak a silent prayer.

Oh Lord, thank You for bringing me such an awesome man. And for the work, You are doing in both of us. I'm so very grateful. I thank You, and I love You.

Chapter Thirty-four

"Miss Winger, are you aware that your handsome husband-to-be and his darlin' brother are both walkin' around the hotel wearin' skirts?" Maggie waltzes back into the ground floor bridal suite of the West Coast Long Beach Hotel, carrying an ice bucket. Her long, buttery gold bridesmaid gown, which my mother picked out, swooshes around her.

"Oh no! I thought Peter had achieved victory over his cross-dressing issues. Oh well. For better or for worse, right?" I laugh out loud, mostly, because I'm hopelessly giddy.

"You are so funny." Maggie gives me a sarcastic smile and then a real smile. Her new dark honey-blonde hair color softens her features and complements the glistening new life in her eyes.

"I think they look so handsome!" Suzette giggles as she touches up the ends of my curled hair with hairspray. "Cute guys in skirts." She giggles again.

The wreath of flowers looks so pretty on Suzette's soft shoulder-length curls. When I picked her up at the airport a couple of days ago, I was shocked to see her usually waist-length hair cut up to her shoulders, making her look more sophisticated. She told me she hacked her hair off herself because it was too much work to take care of while she was working at a school in Gansu, a province in northwest China.

"They're called kilts, ladies," I use my best infomercial voice. "Men of Scottish heritage are known to wear them on special occasions." I have no check on my level of sarcasm today. It's my wedding day, right?

"So, tell us...is it true?" Maggie gives me a devious grin.

"Is what true?" I'm almost afraid to ask.

"You know, about Scotsmen and their kilts!"

"What about Scotsmen and their kilts?" Suzette asks innocently.

"I suppose I'll find out tonight!" I return a playful smile.

"Find out what?" Suzette looks puzzled.

"The legend is," Maggie speaks ominously, "they go au naturel."

"Totally commando," I add.

"You mean nothing at all?" Suzette looks a little shocked.

"Too bad it's not windy today. Ya'll could get a little sneak peek." Maggie laughs.

"You are so bad!" I tease.

"Seriously though, I'm so proud of you two, keepin' your hands off each other until your weddin' night," she smiles at me in the mirror.

"Thanks, Mag. It wasn't easy, believe me. We came really close to messing up a couple of times, but we didn't. Thank God. It was really tough, though."

"You know I prayed for ya'll. That crazy little key necklace you gave me would remind me to."

"That's awesome! Thank you."

She has no idea about the key and how it was instrumental in saving Peter and me from giving in to temptation. I will tell her someday. Someday soon.

"I prayed for you guys, too." I hug Suzette.

"Thank you, Suz. I really appreciate it."

Maggie goes to the ice bucket and begins filling a couple of glasses with ice and water. I turn to Suzette.

"So, Suz," I say softly. "You seem to be hitting it off with Matt really well."

"Yeah, he's really great. But don't worry, we're just friends. I told him I will be working at the school in Gansu for at least another year, maybe more. He asked if he could write to me, and I told him I would like that."

"Really?"

"Yeah, then he asked if he could visit me there because he said it sounded really interesting and he would love to see the school and the city. And I said as long as he understands, he will be staying in the men's dormitory while he's there."

"Good girl."

"And Maddy, he said he wouldn't expect any other arrangement."

"Do you believe him?"

"Yes. Yes, I do."

"Wow, that's so cool." I make a note to share this good news with Peter later—much later.

"Yeah. I like him, but I know he's a work in progress. Still, it will be nice to have a new pen pal." Her sweetness amazes me.

There is a loud knock on the hotel room door. Maggie goes to answer it.

"Oh, Maggie, you look lovely!" My mother's boisterous voice cuts through the room. She is squeezed into a low-cut, skin-tight gold sequin designer cocktail dress.

My mind quickly flashes to the exquisite soft celadon green Carolina Herrera gown Chloe showed me she is wearing to the wedding today. It's so stunning and fitting of her impeccable taste. I guess my mother has her own style, as do I, so I should learn to accept it.

My mother gives Maggie a quick air kiss. "I love your new hair color. It really suits you." Translation: *Good, now I'm the only platinum blonde at the party.* "I came to see how my little girl is doing." She turns and looks at me. Despite all our differences, her eyes well up with tears.

"Oh, Mimi…" she whispers. She hasn't called me that since I was about seven years old. It was her nickname for me, she said, until I grew into my real name. "You look gorgeous, just like a princess. My beautiful little girl."

She comes over, and we hug, and then I quickly hand her a tissue so her very costly makeup job doesn't get ruined. I grab another tissue and dab at my own expensive makeup job, too.

My mother hired her favorite hair and makeup stylists, Sean and Toby, to come do her up and me while they were here. I have to admit it was pretty nice to just sit there on my wedding day and let the professionals do what they do best. I'm rather pleased with the outcome.

Toby pulled up small sections of my hair in the front and sides, pinned them, and then curled them so they fell just behind my headpiece of simple, small ivory silk flowers that my waist-length veil will hook into. He curled the rest and let it fall down my back in big, soft curls, and then used what seemed like an entire canister of hairspray on me.

My mother insisted on an updo for me, but I was dead-set against it. How unromantic for me to be standing in the bathroom on my wedding night, pulling dozens and dozens of hairpins out of my head while Peter waits for me in bed.

No, I want something I can take out quickly and easily. There are only twelve pins in my hair. I counted. Also, I know Peter likes my long, thick hair down. Pleasing him is very important to me.

Sean did an excellent job on my make-up. He did basically the same thing on me that he did for Matt's rehearsal dinner, but a little softer and less dramatic. But more than my hair and make-up, I love my dress.

My wedding dress was the last wedding task I accomplished. When I went back to school for the second semester, Maggie was one step ahead of me and had bought every wedding magazine for sale. She put them all over my bed and dresser and a few books on weddings on my desk.

It initially started out as just a joke, but it provided hours of entertainment for us, laughing at all the super-lacy, mega-beaded, and over-the-top crazy dresses in the magazines. It was great to have Maggie back. Actually, she is better than she was before.

One dress in an advertisement caught my eye. It was simple but not too plain. Ivory, not white, which is what I wanted. It had flowers made out of the same fabric as the dress on the off-the-shoulder straps and just below the waist in the back.

The bodice was simple, with boning like a corset, a princess waistline, and a full skirt. Honestly, it looked like a stylish Disney princess gown. I have to admit, the princess-ness of it appealed to me. Maggie said she liked it, and it was perfect for me. So I ripped the page out and taped it to the mirror on my bureau. I wanted to see if this was truly the dress I wanted and if I would get sick of looking at it or not.

In May, when Dr. Bill and my mother came to Biola for my graduation, they saw the picture, and they both agreed that was the dress for me. I think my mother was more pleased that I had finally picked out a wedding dress, than what the dress actually looked like.

My mother made an appointment at the nearest bridal salon listed on the ad that carried this dress, which was in Brea. So when the dust settled after graduation, and I got all my stuff moved out of the dorm room and back into Mom's house (Peter and his truck were such a big help with this, one of the many, many reasons I was so glad he was home), I was ready to focus on my wedding dress.

The salon only had one of this style of dress in stock, and it was in my size. Not only was it in my size, but it fit me perfectly, which is a miracle in itself, with my ultra-curvy shape. The only alteration that had to be made, of course, was the foot and half-length of fabric that had to be hemmed off the bottom.

But it's beautiful. I can't believe it. As I stand here and gaze at this bride in the mirror in an absolutely gorgeous wedding dress, with elegant hair and make-up, I can't believe it's me. And that this day is finally here. July tenth. My wedding day.

Another knock at the door pulls me out of my reverie. Maggie gets up off the bed to answer it.

"Leah! Hey, yawl, Leah's here. So how was your evening, you newly-wed?" Maggie gives her a hug, both women trying not to wrinkle their bridesmaid gowns.

"Wonderfully fantastic. Thanks for asking." Leah is positively glowing.

"Leah, that color looks awesome on you," I tell her.

"You see, I told you," my mother chimes in. "It's a color that compliments all your bridesmaids and goes well with those kilt-things."

I decide not to roll my eyes at her but force a smile and nod my head in agreement, like a bridal bauble-head doll.

"Josiah looks very handsome in his kilt, very nice indeed, thank you very much. Which reminds me…sorry I'm late. Josiah needed something taken care of." She starts giggling like a teenage girl. We all laugh.

Another knock at the door. This time, Leah goes to answer it.

"Is this the Winger-McManus wedding party?" It's the photographer.

"Thank goodness! You're right on time. Girls, are you ready? I want plenty of time for photos before the wedding," my mother says, asserting her leadership role in this event.

She rounds us up to go take pictures. I figured I would not stress and let her have this, since it will be the last time in my life she will have any control. I will belong to someone else in a few hours. Besides, she's really into all this wedding stuff. I mean, yeah, I am having fun with it, too, but it's not really my thing. I'm more focused on the *after-wedding* part, in which my mother has absolutely no say whatsoever.

And now I'm starting to really miss Peter. Isn't that nuts? I just talked to him like an hour ago. I am *so* looking forward to tonight. I can't even begin to tell you how much. We will be spending our first night together in the same bay view room we stayed in for Matt's wedding, but there will be no extra cot next to the bed this time. You can be sure of that.

We finish a seemingly endless series of bride and bridesmaids photos, and head back to the room to freshen up before the wedding. Just over thirty minutes to go.

As we enter the room, we are hit with the most luscious, heady scent of roses. Sitting on the dressing table is the biggest bouquet of roses I have ever seen—not just any roses, but the Black Beauty roses from Ecuador, just like the one Peter gave me early on in our relationship.

I feel my eyes start to get hot with tears. I go to them and deeply inhale their velvety, sweet scent.

"What does the card say?" Maggie hands me a tissue.

I take the card from the plastic forked holder and open it with trembling fingers. "To my precious Madeleine, my beloved, my best friend, on the day we become one. I love you so very much and thank and praise God for you, my gift. With much love, Peter. P.S. Don't forget your key."

I have to fight the tears from running down my face. Maggie is right there handing me another tissue and fanning at my eyes furiously.

"Hon, bend over at the waist and dab your eyes; that way, your tears won't run down and ruin your makeup." I do what Maggie suggests, and it seems to work.

"Just remember, Madeleine, it's not always going to be roses and romance, you know," my mother announces loudly. "Real marriage isn't like that. Someday, the most romantic thing he'll do for you is say 'please' when he yells for you to bring him another beer."

Ugh! It may be like that if God is not at the center of your marriage, I want to snap back, but I decided against it. Everyone turns to look at my mother like, "Who let this alien in the room?" But I'm used to her bubble-bursting comments. I shake-off her comments and try to find my cell phone to call Peter to thank him for my beautiful roses.

"Twenty minutes," he answers my call.

"Thank you so much for the roses. They are so beautiful. And the card is awesome. And yes, I won't forget my key." I hear him laugh softly. And now I'm starting to giggle a little.

I took my little garden key off the silk cord, wrapped it in a bit of tissue, and tucked it into my bustier. I was going to sew it onto my garter, but I remembered that Peter is supposed to toss that to all the unmarried men, and I want him to be able to keep the key.

"You're so welcome," Peter says softly. "I meant what I wrote. I feel like the most fortunate man alive."

"I love you so much, Peter." My heart is bursting at the seams.

"Mmmm, I love you, too." I hear voices behind Peter. "Mad, I gotta go. They are asking us guys to go downstairs and take our positions. Hey, I'll meet you in front of the flower-covered arch thing down by the water's edge."

"Okay, meet you there. I'll be the one, you know, walking down the aisle in the big white dress."

"I can't wait. See you in a few," We both laugh and hang up.

I check myself over one more time in the mirror to see that everything is in place. Dr. Bill comes to the room. He gets a little choked up when he sees me in my full bridal regalia. He's so sweet.

I asked Dr. Bill to escort me down the aisle since he's really been more of a father to me than my biological father. When I tried to call my birth father, just to maybe give him a chance to participate in some way in my wedding, all I got was the "this number is no longer in service" message, so that made the decision easy at that point. Honestly, having Dr. Bill escort me down the aisle is really what I wanted.

Dr. Bill and Peter get along so well. You'd think they were old friends if you saw them sitting together by the pool, talking and laughing while my mother and I went out on endless wedding errands. I never would have thought they would have much in common, but I'm so thankful they do.

There is another knock at the door. The hotel wedding coordinator comes in to tell me it's time. *Finally!* My mother hands me my bouquet of ivory roses and gold alstroemerias, and Maggie, Suzette, and Leah take their bouquets, as well. We file out of the room and walk to the place where we wait before we go down the aisle.

I hear acoustic guitar music playing, which Peter wrote and recorded just for this occasion. I also hear the soft voices of many people.

As we turn the corner of the walkway, I can see hundreds of people seated in soft white folding chairs. I peek through a bush and watch as Peter, his best man Matt, Josiah, and Philip walk out into position in front of the flower arch.

Oh. My. Goodness. Peter looks so unbelievably handsome. His hair has grown out to a little past his shoulders again (a subtle request on my part since he's been home), and is gently blowing in the ocean breeze. No slicked-back ponytail that he would have to wash out before bed. Simple, remember. He looks a little hot (literally and figuratively) in his waistcoat and wool kilt. Thankfully, the temperature is only in the low eighties this afternoon.

I hear the music change, and then the wedding coordinator signals for the bridesmaids to start making their way down the aisle. As soon as Maggie, my maid of honor, makes it to her place in the front, the wedding coordinator signals the music to stop. At this point, everyone seated rises to their feet.

A bagpipe player begins playing "Amazing Grace" as he slowly walks down the aisle. I know this song is usually played at funerals on bagpipes, but it has spiritual significance for Peter and me and actually sounds wonderful at our wedding.

When the bagpipe player nearly reaches the front, Dr. Bill and I begin our way down the aisle slowly. It's so moving. I feel everyone's eyes on me, but I can't take my eyes off Peter. My heart feels like it's filling up with more love for him. He reaches up and wipes his eyes quickly.

I can't believe this is for real. The day is finally here, and I'm really marrying this man. This awesome, Godly, wonderful man.

It seems like only a short time ago, he was this anonymous guy I would see at church and at my work, who I had this huge crush on and would have endless daydreams about, and I was too frightened to speak to.

Now I know him and love him, and he is way better than I ever imagined he would be in any of my daydreams. And we are about to become husband and wife. Isn't God great?

I can't really remember saying my vows, but I will never forget looking into Peter's eyes and seeing the deep, encompassing love there, shining with the Spirit of God. I won't forget the rush of passion I let surge through my body for the first time with our first kiss as husband and wife.

I will never forget the strong sensation that God Himself was there with us, blessing us, binding us, and recreating us as one.

I float through the reception, from table to table, meeting and greeting people that I'm not sure I would remember if I met them again on the street. I love looking down at Peter's hand in mine, a new brilliant wide band of white gold shimmering on his left hand, which matches the new ring guard he had specially designed to fit around my engagement ring.

When we are all seated at our tables and glasses of champagne are distributed, Matt rises to his feet and taps his glass with a butter knife. He clears his throat.

"What can I say about my little brother, Peter, and my new gorgeous sister-in-law, Madeleine? Other than I've never seen a couple more made for each other than these two are. Well, except, of course, for our parents, and oh yeah, our grandparents, and our friends who are married. But seriously, Peter has always done things a little differently than family traditions dictate, so when he told me that he and Maddy vowed not to sleep together until their wedding night, I thought he had gone a little overboard in his bucking against the reins, and was, frankly, more than a little nuts. But seeing how happy they are, I think they may be on to something. In any case, if you two mysteriously disappear before the reception is over, we'll all know why!" Everyone laughs. "To Peter and Madeleine." He raises his glass, and we all sip our glasses.

After Matt's toast, Josiah says an excellent blessing over dinner. And I know that this is a tough crowd to pray a blessing over.

During dinner, Peter leans in close to me kisses me lightly on the neck, and whispers in my ear. "I love you, my beautiful bride." It's so awesome that, for the first time, I don't have to suppress the flash flood of heat I feel when he is so close and touching me. "In just a few hours, I will make you mine."

He smiles sweetly and seductively at me, raising my body temperature about twenty degrees, or so it feels like. I married a very passionate man, indeed. Praise God!

"Hours? I don't want to wait that long!" I whisper back to him. "Let's feign exhaustion, or food poisoning, or scurvy, or rickets, anything, and go up to our room right now!" He laughs and kisses me again.

The reception goes on as most receptions do, with cake, dancing, more meeting and greeting of people I don't know, more dancing, more toasts, etc. When it comes time for Peter's father's toast, he manages to toast us without insulting Peter or saying anything negative.

I can't help but glance at Chloe as he speaks, who sits with a very watchful eye on her husband. I suspect she has something to do with the noticeably more positive content of his speech. Though cold and corporate, it's definitely more affirmative than critical or demeaning. I sense the secret of this great businessman's success is the wise counsel of the petite European beauty sitting quietly next to him.

As she dances with Dr. Bill, Chloe also keeps a watchful eye on Peter's father closely as he dances with me. As does Peter, who is oblivious to my mother's groping of him as he dances with her. But my father-in-law only glances down at my breasts once or twice as we make light conversation.

I'm a little apprehensive about dancing with Matt because I know he has had a few too many glasses of champagne, but he is my new brother-in-law, so I guess I can bear a few minutes of inebriated leering.

"Madeleine, you look so beautiful, like a gothic princesz," Matt slurs as we dance together. "My little brother'z a lucky guy."

"Thanks, Matt." I look around the room for Suzette but don't see her.

"Maddy…do you mind if I call you Maddy?"

"Sure, it's fine."

"Maddy, will you do me a huge favor?"

Uh oh. It depends on what it is," I laugh and try to keep things light.

"Will you take good care of my little brother? Will you be real sweet to him? He'z had a real sh–, uh, I mean, crappy upbringing. He'z a great guy, and he deserves to have someone who loves him and treats him good, unlike our parentz did. I mean, not that I think you would, I mean, uh…"

"I know what you mean," I can't help but smile at him. How truly touching his concern for his brother is. "Yes, I promise to love him and be as sweet to him as I can possibly be."

"Oh thankz, Maddy. You're a doll," he slurs. The song finally ends, and he gives me a big bear hug.

I look for Peter so I can tell him how sweet his brother is when I notice he and Andrew are sitting at a table talking. I'm glad Andrew decided to at least come to our wedding. Andrew looks relieved to be talking with his old friend again, and Peter does, too, but they look far from being the best buddies they used to be.

I'm proud of Maggie that she hasn't flirted with Andrew at all, even though she knows he's single. She told me back in the hotel room that the "old Maggie" would have it all planned out how she would get him alone in her room, but she said she wasn't going to go there, even as "delicious-looking" as he is. I think maybe the pregnant ex-girlfriend would have been a deterrent on Andrew's part from receiving any of Maggie's flirtations if she had thrown any his way. But I could be wrong. I'm just glad I won't get a chance to find out.

Maggie and I had some good talks while she was staying with me at my mom's house a week before the wedding. She was a big help with all the wedding stuff and diffused my mother before she got too explosive.

"So, got any plans?" I asked her as we sat at the kitchen table, assembling two hundred tiny baskets of wedding favors for the tables at the reception.

""Bout what?" She asked, but I think she knew what I was talking about.

"You know, PLANS, like what's on the horizon in the adventures of Maggie the Cat."

"Oh nothin' too excitin'." she sighed. "I'm gonna stay home in Plano, and stay away from datin' for a while, too. Tini's not too pleased about me livin' back in her house, but my Daddy thinks it's the best thing for me right now."

"Yikes, good luck with her."

"I think it'll be fine. Besides, I'm gonna be super busy. My daddy is puttin' me on staff at his church to help start up a new single women's ministry. He said he couldn't have asked for a better or more knowledgeable person than me to minister to single women, especially in the celibacy department."

"How cool! You'll be great at that."

"I don't know. I still feel like I should be one of the ones bein' ministered to, not doin' the teachin'."

"Then you know you're perfect for the job. Maggie, God is going to use you in a mighty way. I know it."

"You really think so?"

"Yes, I know so. Our Lord is in the business of reversals and using people that He has done work inside in a great way. Just think of the lives of some of the apostles, like Peter and Paul, and others like Mary Magdalene and the Samaritan woman at the well, and regular people like Peter and me."

She was quiet for a moment, seemingly contemplating what I told her. "Yeah, I guess so. Can I call you if I get stuck on anything?"

"Of course. Mag, you're going to do great. You'll see. Your dad is very wise and wouldn't have appointed you to this position if he didn't think you were ready for it. And remember to pray always, and you'll get the help you need. Trust me on that, I know!"

"I know, hon, I know," she smiled at me, her eyes slightly misty.

As I straighten the little baskets on the table nearest to me, Chloe walks up to me smiling. The diamonds and emeralds in her pieces of jewelry shimmer in the candlelight. "Come, sit with me, and rest a while," Chloe hands me a fresh glass of iced tea, and we sit down at the table. "How lovely the ceremony was, and I am enjoying the reception very much."

'Thank you, thank you so much."

She takes my hand. "Madeleine, I am so very happy to finally have the daughter I have always wanted."

"Oh, Mrs. McManus, thank you…" is all I can say. I'm deeply touched.

"Promise me that you and Peter will join me for dinner often, d'accord? I want to hear all about your trip when you return," she smiles at me. She is referring to our honeymoon in Jamaica, a very generous gift from my new in-laws.

Peter teased me that when we get to our hotel room at the Sandals Resort in Negril, he is going to fill the bathtub with sunscreen with an SPF of at least a thousand and then completely submerge me in it so I don't get sunburned at all while we are there. Most of my pale white flesh hasn't been exposed to sunlight since I was a little kid. Snorkeling, swimming, walking on the beach, and, of course, making love are a few things we plan to do on our honeymoon. Getting a bad sunburn, so I can't be touched, is absolutely *not* part of our honeymoon plans.

With Chloe's dinner invitations, along with those of Peter's aunt and uncle, and more time with Dr. Bill and my mother, I can see my life is going to change and that I will have the big family I've always wanted.

I thank Chloe again, and she gives me a gentle hug. Over her shoulder, I see a sight that makes me gasp out loud. I excuse myself and quickly make my way over to a table in the corner.

Bethany is sitting at a table with her date—a beautiful bald baby boy dressed in a light blue sailor suit. He's the tiniest baby I have ever seen.

"Hey there!" we hug genuinely for the first time ever. "It's great to see you. I'm so glad you came." It's all the truth, really.

"You look so beautiful, Maddy. I love your dress," Bethany sounds sincere.

"What, this old thing?" I joke. "So, who is this young fellow you have with you?"

Bethany looks over at him in his baby carrier and beams. "This is my son, Thomas." He returns her gaze with a big, toothless smile and wiggles his arms and legs.

"Hi Thomas," I smile brightly at him, and he raises his eyebrows at me. "He's so beautiful, Bethany."

"Thanks. He's, um, the reason I—"

"Does he sleep through the night yet?" I quickly inquire as Thomas wraps his tiny hand around my pinky finger.

I purposely interrupt Bethany from trying to give me an explanation, which is not needed, nor do I want it. This is the only question I can think of that people usually ask people who have small babies.

"He's starting to," she exhales. "He was two months premature, so it was a little rough in the beginning. My mom helped me check on him during the night when he first came home from the hospital. But he is healthy and doing very well now. He screams like a banshee when he's hungry." She laughs.

Suzette and Maggie join me as we circle around Thomas, cooing and tickling him until he laughs and gives us a big gummy grin. I glance over at Bethany as she stares at her tiny son with a look of tender love on her face that I have never before seen her wear.

Maggie and Suzette leave us to pack my things in the bridal suite and bring them up to Peter's room, the bay-view suite on the fifth floor. Bethany looks at me with a weak smile.

"Chad cried hard when he saw his son for the first time in the hospital," she confided in me. "Thomas was totally encased in one of those clear plastic incubators in the neonatal intensive care unit. He was such a tiny being, with so many tubes and monitors hooked up to his tiny, dark pink, wrinkled body. Chad pleaded with God right then and there out loud to forgive him and to heal his son."

"Wow…" I'm totally dumbfounded.

"That really changed Chad. We are talking more now. I don't know if we'll get back together. There's a lot of stuff to resolve before that happens. But I know Thomas needs to know his father," she looks at him.

"Yeah, that's got to be rough, though."

"It is, but God helps me. He helps me a lot." I feel I'm supposed to give her a hug, so I do.

Bethany seems so different now—more mature, more loving, and definitely more humble. It's shocking to see her with a baby, but I'm so glad she came.

At the close of the evening, Peter and I stand and raise our glasses. Peter toasts the guests.

"Thank you, everyone, for coming to share this amazing day with us. We feel so blessed to have you all here. We love you all, but it's time for us to go. We've got some private business to attend to." He smiles broadly and looks at me, and everyone laughs. I feel my face burn as I blush, but I don't mind.

"Here, here! Finally!" Matt yells.

I so love that whenever Peter and I were near each other, we had constant physical contact all night. I love the feel of his arm around me, the warmth of his hand on my back, and his kisses. He kissed me so passionately after our first dance I was ready to steal him away to our room right then.

We say our goodbyes to our families and friends. Maggie quickly pulls me aside.

"Do you have it?" she whispers.

"Yes." I whisper back.

"You're not seriously gonna give it to him, are you? I mean, don't ya'll think it's kinda cliché?"

"Yes, I seriously am, and I don't care if it's cliché. That little key saved us from totally going all the way one night." Maggie has a puzzled look on her face. "I'll tell you later!" I turn to go.

"You better. I want to hear everything!" She calls after me.

I smile at her as Peter comes to my side, and we slip out of the room.

What a perfect day. My mother would beg to differ, of course. During the reception, she complained to me that the linens on the tables were a darker gold than she picked out, and few other things, all of which I chose to tune out. I'm so exhausted and exhilarated at the same time. I lean my head on Peter's shoulder as we wait for the elevator to come to take us up to our room, and I whisper a prayer of thanksgiving.

"Thank You, Lord, for such an awesome day. It couldn't have been more perfect."

"Yes." Peter agrees. "And thank You for an even more awesome evening ahead of us."

"Yes," I whisper with a smile. "In Jesus' name, we pray, Amen."

"Amen." Peter hugs me tightly as the elevator doors open to take us to our room—up to our own walk in the garden in the cool of the evening, with God's blessing on us all the way.

Chapter Thirty-five

Even though this isn't my first time, I feel really nervous. My hands are shaking as I remove the twelve pins from my hair, partially from anticipation, partially from excitement.

The time is finally here. I'm about to make love with my husband for the first time. *Yikes!* I'm married. The diamonds on my wedding ring flash in the bathroom lights, as I pull through some of the super hair-sprayed sections of my hair.

Peter comes to the doorway of the bathroom, and leans on the door post. He's still wearing his white shirt and kilt, but the jacket and bow tie are gone. He watches me with a wide grin on his face. Suddenly, I don't feel so nervous. I feel something else, something warm and exciting.

"Will you unzip me?" I turn around and pull my hair to the side, as he steps into the bathroom and unzips my wedding dress. I look over at our reflection in the huge bathroom mirror. This is so surreal, watching this guy I've longed for, for so long, casually unzipping my wedding dress. It's even more surreal to see us together in such a familiar and intimate setting as the bathroom.

"Thanks," I say softly.

"My pleasure," he kisses the back of my neck lightly, as he runs his fingertips down my bare back, making me quiver with excitement.

He gives me a big smile in the mirror, and then steps out of the bathroom. I close the door some, feeling a little silly for doing so. He's my husband, right? As Maggie said, I need to get over my body issues.

I step out of my wedding dress and slip, and remove my bustier and stockings, and carefully place the little tissue-encased key on the bathroom counter. I slip on the short white satin nightgown from Victoria's Secret that Maggie gave me at my bridal shower, which she and my mother threw me at my mother's house. The little nightgown is so flattering on me and feminine with its soft lace inserts at the waist, and bust line, without being too frilly. I'm grateful for Maggie's good taste.

I turn to look at myself in the mirror. My wedding night. My stomach does a summersault. I take a deep breath, unwrap the little key from the tissue, and open the bathroom door.

The room is dark except for the lights coming in through the sliding glass door from the cityscape across the bay. Peter is lighting the last of several little white candles in clear votive glass containers he placed throughout the room. He is wearing just sweatpants and a smile.

"You look so beautiful, like an angel." Peter walks over to me and puts his hands on my waist.

"Thanks. You look pretty great, too." I feel so shaky inside. *Relax.* I take a deep breath.

"Are you nervous?".

"Yeah, isn't that silly?"

"No, I'm a little nervous, too."

"It's not like I've never done this before, but I really wish I hadn't." I slip my arms around him and rest my head on his chest.

"Yeah, me too," he whispers, wraps his arms around me, and holds me tight. "But in a way, it is our first time since we both have been renewed. Out with the old nature, in with the new."

"Very true." I so love him holding me like this.

He pulls away, and leads me by the hand to one of the wooden chairs in the suite, and I sit down. He gets down on his knees in front of me and carefully slides over a small basin of water and some towels that are under the table next to the chair.

"Mad, last night, I asked God to help me be an excellent husband for you, especially since the husband is supposed to be the leader in the household, and that's such a huge responsibility. He told me that an excellent leader is first a willing servant. Then, He showed me where to start."

Peter dips a white linen cloth in the basin and then begins to gently wash my feet with it.

"As Jesus loves the church and washed His apostles' feet in servanthood and love, I wash the beautiful feet of my beautiful bride to serve you and love you always," Peter gently washes my other foot.

My tears flow in torrents down my cheeks. I grip the arms on the chair tightly and take slow, deep breaths so I don't start crying too loudly. I don't want to ruin this beautiful, intimate moment that I will remember for the rest of my life. I love him so much.

Peter pushes the basin back under the table and dries my feet tenderly with the towel.

"I love you," I whisper. "So very much."

He smiles up at me. There are tears on the sides of his face as well. I reach forward to wipe them away and place my hands on his shoulders. He begins to massage my feet until they are completely dry.

Peter stands up and pulls me up with him. The new band of gold on his left hand catches the candlelight, reminding me that he is my husband, at last. He folds me into his arms and holds me tightly. He can hold me like this forever.

He begins kissing me so sweetly and affectionately. After a long moment, I pull back gently, remembering what's in my hand.

"I have something for you." I place the little gold key in his hand. "For you, my beloved, my best friend, my husband."

He closes his hand tightly around the key and holds it to his heart, drops his head, and closes his eyes tight. "I love you so much, Madeleine," he whispers. When he opens his eyes, they are glossy with fresh tears.

"I love you, too," I wipe away my own fresh tears.

He wraps his arms around me again, lowers his head down, and kisses me softly at first, then long and passionately. I feel his gentle hands all over me. My head is spinning, and my body begins to burn with anticipation.

He leads me over to the side of the bed. He puts the key on top of his Bible on the nightstand, which is open to the Song of Solomon. He slides his pants off and then gently slips my nightgown over my head. He runs his fingertips over my shoulders and down my back and kisses me again.

There are no feelings of shame of being naked in front of him or with him, in the presence of God. No hang-ups about body issues or embarrassment. His skin feels so smooth and warm against mine. He reaches down to the bed, pulls back the covers, and we climb inside.

His left hand is under my head, and his right-hand embraces me.

> *You are a fountain springing up in a garden,*
> *A well of living waters, and flowing streams from Lebanon.*
>
> *You have called me a garden, she said*
> *Oh, I pray that the cold north wind and the soft south wind may blow upon my garden,*
> *That its spices may flow out in abundance for you in whom my soul delights.*
> *Let my beloved come into his garden and eat its choicest fruits.*
>
> *I have come into my garden, my sister, my promised bride;*

*I have gathered my myrrh with my balsam and spice from your
sweet words I have gathered the richest perfumes and spices.
I have eaten my honeycomb with my honey;
I have drunk my wine with my milk.*

*Eat, friends;
Drink and imbibe deeply, O lovers.*
                             --Song of Solomon 4:15-5:1

*So sweet, right? Please keep in touch by subscribing to my
newsletter for news and other stories about Maddy and Peter at*
www.angeladolbear.com

*Also, please consider leaving a review on Amazon…reviews are
a HUGE help to authors.
Thank you!
– AD*

Want more adventures of Peter and Maddy?
Check out *The Garden Key Tales* series.

KEEP IN TOUCH:
Connect with Angela Dolbear:
www.AngelaDolbear.com
Facebook: **Angela Dolbear Author**
Instagram: **AuthorAngelaDolbear**
Twitter: **@AngelaDolbear**

ACKNOWLEDGEMENTS

In recognition of their much needed and appreciated guidance and support, I would like to thank Amy Stevens of Go Beyond Marketing, Denise Lansford, Carrie Dolbear-Robinson, and Tim Dolbear, who is my essential "Ideal Reader" as Stephen King states in his book, ON WRITING. And much love to Kyle Dolbear, and Gracie, Caleb and the rest of the "ani-pals" for making our house a home—a warm and loving place in which to receive this novel…night after night, until its completion.

RESOURCES

Scripture reference list from Maddy's study on page 270:
Song of Solomon 2:7, I Peter 1:13-16 and 2:11; Ephesians 5:3 and 6:12; Galatians 5:19, 24 and 6:8; I Corinthians 3:16, 6:18 and 7:1; Romans 7:23, 8:5-9, and 13:14; I Peter 2:11; I Thessalonians 2:12 and 4:1-6.